About the Author

Claire Boston is a contemporary romance author who enjoys exploring real life issues on her way to the happily-ever-after. She writes heart-warming stories, with resilient heroines and heroes you'll love. In 2014 she was nominated for an Australian Romance Readers Award for Favourite New Romance Author.

When Claire's not writing she can be found creating her own handmade journals, swinging on a sidecar, or in the garden attempting to grow something other than weeds.

Claire lives in Western Australia with her husband, who loves even her most annoying quirks, and her grubby, but adorable Australian bulldog.

You can connect with Claire through Facebook (https://www.facebook.com/clairebostonauthor) and Twitter (https://www.twitter.com/clairebauthor), or join her reader group (http://www.claireboston.com/reader-group/).

Also by Claire Boston

Nothing to Fear

A Blackbridge Novel

Claire Boston

First published by Bantilly Publishing in 2017

Nothing to Fear: The Blackbridge Series

EPUB format: 978-1-925696-09-7
Mobi format: 978-1-925696-10-3
Print format: 978-1-925696-11-0

Cover design by Lana Pecherczyk
Edited by Alexandra Nahlous
Proofread by Teena Raffa-Mulligan

DEDICATION

To you, my reader — because you're awesome!

Chapter 1

The numbers in front of Hannah Novak blurred as she stared at them, but they didn't change into the numbers she wanted. She sighed. Not once had she thought building a luxury retreat was going to be easy, but she hadn't expected it to be quite so hard either. She shouldn't have let her grandparents push her into it so soon. She wasn't ready, but she couldn't tell them that – not without them asking why.

Her skin tightened.

That was something they never needed to know.

The phone's ring was shrill and she reached for it in relief. "Blackbridge Holiday Park. How may I help you?"

"Help me, Hannah Banana. You're my only hope."

Hannah grinned at the plaintive tone in Lincoln's voice. "What can I do for you, Sergeant Zanetti?"

"You can tell me you've got an onsite cabin free for the next few weeks."

She laughed. "The summer holidays start next Thursday," she said. "We're booked solid until February."

Lincoln swore. "Everyone is booked solid."

"Glad I was the last one you came to," Hannah joked. "Why do you need accommodation?"

"It's for our new senior constable. Do you remember Ryan Kilpatrick? He lived here for a couple of years during high school."

Hannah's heart fluttered. "Yeah, I remember him." She'd never forgotten her first crush. He'd arrived in town when she was eleven and he was a much older sixteen. She'd been so in love with him that she'd ridden into a ditch one day when she'd seen him unexpectedly. That most mortifying experience had morphed into the best day of her eleven-year-old life, when he'd picked her up and taken her home to her grandparents to have the grazes on her knees tended. She smiled at the memory. He'd been good-looking then, what would he look like now?

"I don't know what I'm going to do," Lincoln said. "The government house he was supposed to stay in has been trashed by the last tenants, and with Christmas coming up, we can't get it repaired in time. The closest accommodation available is in Albany and it's a reasonable drive if he needs to come out in an emergency. Plus, he can't leave his kid at home."

"He's got a child?" She ignored the flash of disappointment. Of course Ryan would be married by now.

"Yeah, an eight-year-old boy."

She hesitated, glancing at the spreadsheet in front of her. "When's he due here?"

"Sunday night. Have you got something in mind?"

It would be tight to get the cabin finished, but it was possible. It would give her a boost of funds, and having a family as her first guests would give her a chance to get used to having someone else on her property. A way to ease herself into the situation.

"Hannah, I'll be forever in your debt if you find me a solution," Lincoln pleaded.

The idea of taking the next step sent her pulse racing, but his plea twisted her arm. "Ah, well it's not ideal ..."

"What have you got?"

"It's kind of small for a family." She winced at her tone. She was supposed to be trying to rent the cabin not trying to make him change his mind.

"It's just Ryan and his boy."

Hannah froze, her chest tight. "What about the boy's mother?"

"Ryan's divorced. Have you got a place for them to stay?"

No Mrs Kilpatrick. That wasn't good. Her breath came in

short pants and she closed her eyes, concentrating on her breathing. She'd be out there on her own with only Ryan and his boy. It was too risky. She couldn't be alone with any man these days. So few could be trusted.

"Hannah? You gotta help me." Lincoln wasn't going to let up.

She opened her eyes. If she was ever going to make the retreat succeed, she *had* to do this.

Ryan had been kind to her when she was a child. She had trusted him then, and now he had a son. Surely, he wouldn't do anything bad with his son around.

Hoping she wasn't making a mistake, she said, "The first cabin at Hideaway Retreat is almost finished. It needs the flooring and curtains installed, and the walls painted. I might be able to get it done by the weekend." She still hoped he would refuse.

"Can I take a look at it?"

She sighed, checking the time. Lynette would be starting soon. "I'll meet you out there in half an hour."

"Perfect, I'll see you then."

Hannah hung up and put her head in her hands, hating the nausea in her stomach. She should have kept her mouth shut.

The back door rattled as Lynette came into the office. "Morning, Hannah," she said. "It's already shaping up to be a scorcher today." She hung her wide-brimmed straw hat on the hook in the hallway and wiped her forehead.

"Morning." Quickly, Hannah went over the work that was required around the park.

"I've got this," Lynette said. "You've got plenty of work on your construction site."

Hannah forced a smile to her face, thinking about Lincoln's request. "I sure do." The summer holidays would cut into the time she had to work at the retreat as the caravan park would be full and there were always guests needing something. She whistled for Joe, her brindle-coloured bull mastiff who was lying on his bed in the corner, and grabbed her keys. "Shirley will be in at ten. I'll see you this afternoon."

The warmth hit her as she stepped outside, holding the door open for Joe to follow her. She breathed deeply. It was still early so there was no one in the pool, and no kids in the playground. Most of the people staying in the park at the moment were grey nomads – retirees who travelled the country in their caravans. Many of the park sites nearby were empty, but there was a red car parked at one of the onsite cabins. By the end of next week, the park would be full of people who wanted to get away before Christmas. The southern coast of Western Australia was a popular tourist destination. Breathing out, some of the tension left her. Having grown up at the park with her grandparents, she knew every bit of this ground. It was her safe zone, the place she'd fled to after both traumatic events in her life.

She wanted her retreat to feel like that for her guests – a safe haven, a place to get away from it all and just *be*.

With that in mind, she headed for her car.

Lincoln was waiting at the entrance to her property when she arrived ten minutes later. She waved at him as she drove in and he followed her in the police car. Her four-wheel drive shuddered as it bounced over the potholes. She'd have to grade the gravel drive if Ryan took the cabin. It had been on the list of things she had to do before she made the cabins available, along with setting up more of the facilities – the nature walks, widening the path to the beach and fencing off the lookout area so no one fell off the steep cliff. She would have to do all of it at once if she rented the cabin. She'd hate for Ryan's son to wander off and hurt himself.

The scent of peppermint trees floated through her open window, reminding her of how much she loved this land. On a quiet night she heard the waves washing up against the shore, and the cows from the next property quietly mooing. It was the perfect location for a retreat, for people to get away and relax.

When the road forked, she took the left branch and pulled up in front of the wooden cabin. It looked good, comforting, quaint. There was a short path up to the front door and she still needed to plant the garden beds under the windows with some hardy Australian natives, but aside from that, the outside was finished.

Getting out of the car, she waited for Joe to jump down before facing Lincoln.

"You've done a great job, Hannah." He stood at a comfortable distance from her with his hands in his pockets, looking at the cabin.

"You haven't seen inside yet." She opened the door. The concrete floors and bare walls needed a good clean to remove the remaining building dust before they could be finished. "The kitchen's small, but equipped with stove, oven and microwave." She led him into the main room, making sure Joe was with her. "There are two bedrooms in this one, both with ensuite."

Lincoln peered into the bathroom and grinned. "Very nice!"

She smiled. "I can get the painting finished by Sunday, but the flooring isn't due to go in until the end of next week." They wandered back out into the main living area.

"What about furniture?"

"Hasn't Ryan got his own?" she asked.

"He left most of it with his ex," Lincoln said.

Damn. She'd been hoping to spend the furniture budget on grading the road. "All right. I've got pieces picked out and on order in Albany. I'll ask if they can deliver it this week."

"This is perfect, Hannah. Ryan said he didn't need a lot of room. How much do you want for rent?"

She hesitated. No, she had to do this. She had to get over her fear of being alone with men. If she was going to run this facility, she needed to be comfortable with people coming and going. Though her target market were couples and groups, there were sure to be times when singles came to stay. Still, she added a little more to the price than she needed, in the hope Lincoln might refuse.

"That's perfect," Lincoln said as they walked back out to the police car. "I finish work at five. I'll come around and help you paint."

"Oh, no, you don't have to."

"You're doing me a huge favour here. I'll rustle up a few more people to help and we'll be done in no time." He got into the car and drove off before Hannah thought of some way to dissuade him.

"You'll be fine," she told herself. "It's Lincoln and if he brings others, it'll get done twice as fast. You're safe here."

Joe nudged her hand and licked it.

She had Joe to protect her as well. Joe was a complete softie, but a great deterrent. Arguments tended to end pretty quickly with him by her side.

Everything would be all right.

She just wished the tightness in her chest would ease.

Ryan Kilpatrick pulled in to the Zanetti property early in the afternoon on Sunday. The driveway was lined with towering eucalyptus trees that shaded the road from the hot summer sun. The cheese factory off to the right was a large silver building that reflected the sun's light, and the little shop next to it was a quaint rammed earth building with outdoor seating and a small playground for children. As he rounded a bend in the road, the farmhouse came into view. It was nestled amongst a lush garden, lovingly tended by Mrs Z and had a huge tin roof that came down to a wooden verandah, which wrapped all the way around it.

"Are we going to live here?" Felix asked, the hope in his voice clear as he peered out the window at the farmhouse and surrounding land.

"No, mate. This is Lincoln's parents' place. He said he'd meet us here and show us where we're going to be staying." After driving for four days, Ryan was exhausted, but for the first time since he'd made the decision to leave Karratha and move his son two thousand kilometres away from his ex-wife, he relaxed. The farmhouse was like coming home. It was the only place where he'd ever felt he belonged. The tension eased out of his shoulders.

"There are so many trees."

"Sure are." It was vastly different from the red dust of the Pilbara, the only landscape Felix had known. It had been an amazing car trip south as Felix had exclaimed over every new thing he saw.

A couple of dogs came racing out from around the side of the house and they were followed by a tall, dark-haired man. Ryan grinned. "There's Lincoln. Let's get out."

Felix scrambled out of the car and ran over to the two dogs, patting them enthusiastically. Perhaps when they were finally settled, he could get Felix a dog. Paula had always hated them.

"You made good time." Lincoln held out a hand.

Ryan shook it and they hugged. "Yeah. Once we got through Perth I just wanted to get here." Felix slipped his hand into Ryan's. "You remember my son, Felix."

"The last time I saw you, you were about this big," Lincoln said, holding his hand to his thigh. "Why don't you both come inside? Mum's putting on the kettle and I heard mention that she's made her famous cassata cake."

Felix perked up.

Ryan grinned. He fondly remembered Mrs Zanetti's cake. "Lead the way."

They followed Lincoln inside the farmhouse. The scent of the trailing honeysuckle on the verandah took Ryan straight back to his teenage years when he and Lincoln would sit out there after a day of surfing and talk about what they were going to do after high school.

"Ryan!" Mrs Zanetti rushed over and embraced him.

His chest swelled as he wrapped his arms around the small woman, inhaling the scent of roses. She'd barely changed in the nine years since he'd seen her last. "It's great to see you, Mrs Z."

"And who is this?" she asked as she stepped back.

"My son, Felix."

Felix looked up at her wide-eyed. "Hello, Mrs Z—"

"Zanetti," Ryan prompted.

"Nonsense. Call me Nonna." Mrs Z cuddled Felix. "I've been waiting for grandchildren for years, but neither of my boys is willing to give me any." She took his hand. "There's a piece of cake in my kitchen with your name on it."

Felix glanced over his shoulder at Ryan, his expression one of excitement as he followed Lincoln's mother down the hallway.

Ryan's eyes watered at her instant acceptance of him and his child, and he blinked rapidly. Mrs Z had been more of a mother to him than his own had been. He shook his head. "She hasn't changed."

"No," Lincoln agreed. "She was thrilled when I told her you were moving back."

He swallowed hard and forced a smile to his face. "We'd better get in there, or Felix might not leave us anything to eat."

Lincoln clapped his hand over Ryan's shoulder. "It's good to have you here."

"It's great to be here." He'd been stupid not to come back sooner. No, he'd been naive, hopeful … delusional more like it.

He shook his head. He didn't want to think about Paula now.

He was going to enjoy his homecoming.

Hannah checked her watch for the third time. Lincoln had promised they would be there by three and it was coming up to half past. She had half a bathroom tiled at the other cabin and wanted to finish the rest before she called it a day.

Finally, she heard tyres on the gravel road and Joe barked. She scanned the room one more time to make sure everything was in place. Aside from helping with the painting, Lincoln had called in a few favours and got the flooring done early, and picked up the furniture she'd ordered. She was pleased with how it had turned out – it was comfortable but with touches of luxury in the bathrooms and bedrooms. The perfect little getaway. With a deep breath to brace herself, she went outside to greet her new neighbours.

The white four-wheel drive that pulled up was covered in a film of red dust. There was a winch on the front that meant business, and a heavy-duty roof rack on the top full of containers. Ryan climbed out of the driver's side and her stomach flipped. He had definitely improved with age. His thin, wiry frame had bulked out into lean muscle, his skin was brown from the summer sun and his short brown hair was trimmed neatly. He smiled at her and it was the same as she remembered – slow and sweet.

Ignoring her rapidly beating heart, she held out a hand. "Welcome, Ryan. I'm Hannah." His hazel eyes had mesmerised her when she was eleven, but there was no recognition now – not that she expected him to remember her. She'd been so much younger than him.

"Nice to meet you." His grip was strong, firm and he held on a little too long.

Nerves flooded her body, swamping the attraction. "Where's Lincoln?"

"He got recalled to duty – a car crash in town." His voice was the same gentle, calm tone. "Thanks for letting me stay."

The tension leapt to Hannah's shoulders and she moved away. Lincoln wasn't here. She was alone with Ryan. Where was Joe?

"Dad, is that a dog or a horse?"

The voice startled her. She hadn't noticed the young boy get out of the car. He was the spitting image of his father and he was staring wide-eyed at Joe, who was sniffing at one of the newly planted kangaroo paws. Hannah whistled and the dog trotted over. "This is Joe. He's a dog – a big one. He likes to be patted, if you want to say hi."

The boy inched forward and then patted Joe's coat. Joe sniffed him and licked his hand.

"You've been given Joe's seal of approval," Hannah told him.

The boy laughed and wiped his hand on his pants.

"This is my son, Felix," Ryan said.

"How's it going, Felix?" Hannah asked.

"Pretty good. Are we staying here?" he asked his dad.

"Yeah, for a while," Ryan told him.

Felix glanced around, and then nodded.

Hannah smiled. "Why don't you come inside?" She was careful to keep Joe with her as she led them into the cabin.

"This is nice," Ryan said.

She warmed at the compliment. "There's a bedroom with a bathroom at each end, and the kitchen has all the essentials." She handed him a card with the key. "There's a lookout near the beach that I haven't fenced off yet. If you go up there, don't go too close to the edge. If you have any problems, you can find me at the Blackbridge Holiday Park."

Their fingers brushed as Ryan took the card and put it in his pocket. He was so very male and awareness hummed along Hannah's skin, startling her. She needed to go.

He could easily overpower her. He was taller than her and

the muscles in his arms were well-defined. All he had to do was grab her and she wouldn't be able to get free. Her breath quickened. There were two exits and she had room to move. She placed a hand on Joe's head, letting the softness of his fur under her palm calm her. She could do this. "Have you got any questions?"

"No."

"All right." Relief flooded her. "I'll leave you to get settled in." Saying goodbye to Felix, she left, hurrying up the path to the next cabin.

She was OK. Nothing had happened. She was safe, and she had Joe with her.

Still, when she entered the isolated cabin, she checked that all the doors were locked before she continued tiling.

Hannah walked out the door and Ryan admired the way her hips swayed in a natural, sensual way. It was the only thing overtly feminine about her. She'd not cleaned up to greet him, wearing a blue T-shirt two sizes too big and baggy black shorts that were covered in smears of cement. The clothes hid any shape of her figure. Her hair was held off her face in a headband that made the short blonde strands poke out in different directions. She obviously didn't care about her appearance, but her face was pretty.

There was something both familiar and odd about her. He would have to ask Lincoln if Hannah had lived in Blackbridge when he had. She seemed nervous around him. She'd checked where her dog was a number of times during their very short conversation. Why would she build a retreat if she wasn't comfortable around people?

"Dad, can I have this room?" Felix called.

Ryan wandered through to the bedroom that had a double bed in it. It was nicely made up with a pastel-green bedspread and mountains of pillows at the head, and a modern steel lamp on each side table. He had an urge to flop onto it and go to sleep. It had been a tiring few days.

"Let me check the other room first." He went across the

living area. Both bedrooms had double beds and his ensuite included a spa bath. Felix would love having such a huge bed to himself. "It's all yours, champ," he called.

"Yes!"

Ryan smiled at his son's enthusiasm. Felix had far more energy than Ryan had at the moment, but he needed to get some of their things unpacked, including the few groceries he'd bought.

"Come and give me a hand," he called and went out to the car. He handed Felix the lightest of the grocery bags, and he carried the rest. On the next trip in, he brought Felix's toy bag and left it in the living area, where Felix dived straight in. Ryan was happy to let him play. The rest of the stuff was too heavy for him to carry. He wandered back out to the four-wheel drive and stared at the boot and roof rack full of containers. Nine years of his life and it all fit into one car.

This was all he needed. He had escaped Paula's barbed tentacles and he had his son. They could easily buy more things, and he would make sure Paula never hurt either of them again.

A couple of hours later, he tucked Felix into his new bed. He picked up the book they were reading together and opened to the chapter they were up to.

"Dad?"

"Yes, mate?"

"Will Mum be able to find us here?"

Ryan put down the book. He couldn't read the expression on Felix's face. "I have to let your mum know where we are." He hoped that she didn't want to contact them. "Are you all right with that?"

Felix shrugged. "She won't be able to take me away, will she?"

His throat tightened. "Not if I can help it." He sighed. He should be honest with his son. "She's still your mum, and that means she has a right to see you."

"But she won't want to, will she? She said she didn't want me."

He hated that Felix had heard one of Paula's rants – this one about Felix ruining their life. He hated that his ex was manipulative and cruel, hated that he'd stayed with her for so long, hoping she would learn to love them both. "I hope not."

"Good. It's better when it's just you and me." Felix snuggled down in bed. "Where did we get up to in the story?"

Ryan was more than happy with the change in subject. He began to read.

Later, after he'd switched off the light in Felix's bedroom, he grabbed a beer from the fridge and went outside to sit on the narrow verandah. The light was beginning to fade and something moved in the bushes. As his eyes adjusted, he spotted a kangaroo grazing. He debated waking Felix, but there were likely to be other days when they would see them. He relished the scent of eucalyptus and dirt.

He was here.

After six months of planning and four days of driving, he was finally back in Blackbridge. The town was as he remembered it and the Zanettis had welcomed both him and Felix the same way as they'd welcomed him a decade earlier. This was a place of family, of community and he'd wanted to return years ago.

But Paula hadn't wanted to leave Karratha.

He scowled. He'd wasted too much of his life on his ex already. Still, he couldn't ignore the ache in his heart. He'd failed at the one thing he wanted desperately to be good at – being a family. He'd wanted Felix to have the security, support and love he'd never had growing up, but it hadn't worked. Paula had only cared for herself.

Ryan sipped his beer as he forced his thoughts elsewhere. He'd be starting work tomorrow, and Mrs Z had agreed to take care of Felix during the school holidays. Felix would adore playing on the small hobby farm and Mrs Z had promised to introduce him to kids his own age so that when he started school next year he'd have some friends.

He'd made the right decision, bringing Felix here – he was almost positive of it. Paula had become increasingly manipulative, making threats and accusations that made Ryan worry about her mental health, but he hadn't been able to convince her to seek help. Now she was too far away to hurt either of them.

Felix needed a more stable influence in his life and Ryan could give him that in Blackbridge. Here, he had the Zanettis for support and a decent work roster so he'd be available when Felix needed him. He would be able to make it work. This would be good for Felix.

He hoped.

As he played with the label on his beer bottle, the gravel crunched in front of the cabin. They were a good ten minutes' drive out of town, so it could only be Hannah. Still, he got to his feet to check. He walked around the cabin as Hannah and her dog passed. "Finished for the night?" he called.

Hannah shrieked and whirled as Joe let out a low growl.

Ryan held up his hands. "Sorry. Didn't mean to startle you."

Hannah put a hand on her dog, but he continued to growl. "Did you need something?"

"No. I heard footsteps and was checking it out."

"Ah, well I've finished at the next cabin over and I'm heading home."

"You walking back to town?"

"No." She hesitated before she added, "I've got a place on the property."

He hadn't noticed any other cabins on the drive in. Though he couldn't see the cabin she'd been working on either. It was as if they were in the middle of nowhere, on their own private property. "Do you need a lift?"

"No!" She took a step back and stuttered. "It's a-a nice n-night for a walk. I'll see you later." Without waiting for a response, she hurried away, almost at a jog, checking over her shoulder before she disappeared from view.

What was wrong with her? She seemed almost scared of him. It made no sense. He had done nothing to threaten her and he was a police officer.

Did she have something to hide?

Chapter 2

Hannah slept poorly. When she'd arrived back at her shed, she'd double-checked the locks, made sure all of her windows were shut and kept the curtains closed. She'd been stupid to agree to let Ryan stay at the cabin. She wasn't ready, she hadn't had time to mentally prepare for her first guest to be a single male – and a gorgeous one at that. Such a bad idea.

She didn't want to be attracted to him, but her mind had refused to cooperate, filling her head with childish romantic fantasies, which then had morphed into real nightmares.

She'd tossed and turned, waking at the slightest noise. Normally, the possums scrambling over the roof and the owls' hunting cries didn't disturb her, but last night every single sound had her waking with her heart racing.

She got ready and drove to the holiday park office. As soon as she unlocked the door, she went straight to the coffee machine. She needed a double shot today. There was still a stack of work to be done around the grounds before the summer holidays began and the park would be inundated with holiday-makers.

Joe settled on his dog bed behind the counter and she gave him a treat. She'd take him with her when she went to check the reticulation on the lawn that had been playing up, and later they'd go to the beach so he could stretch his legs.

Hannah fired up her computer and checked her list of

bookings for the day. There were three people leaving and another two arriving. There should be enough time to clean the ensuite toilet blocks in between. She also had a couple of groups booked into the cabins – getting away down south before the crowds hit.

The door chimed as it opened, and one of the grey nomads who'd been staying with her for the last week walked in.

"Getting off to an early start, Daniel?" she asked.

"Yeah. We promised the kids we'd be home for Christmas and don't want to rush across the Nullarbor."

"Good idea. Make sure you take it easy." She took the ensuite key he handed her. "Did you have any issues while you were here?"

"No. Norma and I had a great time. We loved your Sunday-morning pancakes and will definitely recommend you to our friends."

Hannah beamed. "Thanks so much."

Daniel took a couple of the tourist pamphlets for Esperance. "Have a merry Christmas," he said as he left.

"You too." She waved and then made a note that they had left on her job list. The morning was one of her busiest times as the guests who were leaving had to be out by ten o'clock and then she needed to clean the bathrooms before the new group checked in at two.

She ate breakfast in between her customers, and made notes of what needed to be done. During the week, Hannah took turns with Shirley and Lynette in the office, as well as doing the cleaning and maintenance around the park. She didn't mind the work, had been doing it since she'd left university. It was familiar and routine – safe.

The phone rang and she reached over to answer it. "Blackbridge Holiday Park. Hannah speaking."

Silence.

"Hello?" There was the faint sound of breathing. "Can I help you?"

Nothing.

She hung up. Probably kids messing around, or one of those call centres where the person on the other end hadn't realised she'd picked up.

By the time Lynette arrived at nine, Hannah was ready for some time out. "Why don't you take the desk this morning?" she said. "There's a bit of filing to do and the phone hasn't stopped ringing. People have realised the school holidays start at the end of the week and are trying to find accommodation."

"That'd be right," Lynette said. "But before you go, I want to hear about Ryan Kilpatrick."

Hannah's pulse skipped at his name. She shouldn't be surprised that Lynette remembered he was arriving yesterday. She always knew what was going on in town. "Why?"

"Honey, I might have been a few years older than him, but I remember how gorgeous he was. Tell me, is he still as hot?"

Hannah shrugged. "He's all right."

"All right?" Lynette pouted. "Has he grown bald or got a beer gut?"

"No, he looks fit enough." Her body betrayed her by warming. She *wasn't* interested.

"Oh, come on. Give me something. I'm a happily married woman with three kids living vicariously through you. Would you do him?"

Hannah forced a laugh and shook her head, quickly taking her keys from the bench. "I'm not answering that." She called Joe and hurried out.

Once outside, she took a few deep breaths and rolled her shoulders to release the tension. She did not want to think about Ryan in any sexual context at all. She didn't want to fantasise about any man. She went cold at the very idea. Justin had well and truly stuffed her up.

She squeezed her eyes closed at the pain. How she wished she could be as casual about men as her friends were. But life had taught her otherwise.

She stopped outside the cleaning storeroom and paused as she went to put the key in the lock. The door had been jimmied open. Again.

She sighed and pulled out her phone. What was it about people who thought it was perfectly acceptable to steal from a caravan park? She took a couple of photos before calling the police station. Lincoln answered. "Hannah Banana, what's up?"

"Someone has broken into the storeroom again," she told

him.

"Much taken?"

"I haven't gone in yet. Wanted to check that I could."

"I can send someone around in half an hour, if you can wait," Lincoln said.

"All right. I'll fix the broken sprinkler on the grassed area in the meantime. You can find me there." She hung up and changed directions, walking to the gardening shed. This was the third time the storeroom had been broken into in as many months – since her grandparents had left to do their own grey nomad tour of Australia. Each time the person had stolen toilet paper, bathroom cleaner and drain cleaner. It was getting beyond a joke. At first, she'd believed it was one of the guests at the park who was low on funds, but now … Was someone in town stealing from her? She hated the idea.

Not wanting to think about it, she took what she needed from the shed and went to fix the sprinkler.

Joe growled just before a man's voice said, "Hannah? You reported a break-in?"

Hannah startled and lost her balance, sprawling over the grass. She shaded her eyes. She'd been expecting Lincoln, but it was Ryan standing above her, looking incredibly commanding in his blue police uniform. She stared at him, her pulse racing. He was so close and she was vulnerable. Panic fluttered in her chest and she scooted away as Joe got to his feet, his hackles raised. "Joe, stand down."

Joe sat and Hannah shifted to a sitting position, noticing Adam, the rookie constable standing a couple of metres away.

"Sorry for surprising you." With a wary eye on Joe, Ryan offered her a hand up.

She forced herself to take it. His grip was firm and strong, and after he tugged a little too hard, she found herself pressed up against his firm chest. He smelled delightfully of some musky aftershave that made her want to take a deeper breath. Hastily she pushed herself away, ignoring the pull of attraction and push of fear. "Thanks." She gave the sprinkler one last turn and greeted Adam. "It's this way."

Joe fell in beside her, her ever-present guardian, walking between her and Ryan, and Adam brought up the rear.

"Do you want to tell me what happened?" Ryan asked, pulling out a notepad as they reached the storage area.

"I came out this morning to get some supplies and found it like this." She stepped away from the door so they could get a closer look. "I haven't been inside or touched anything."

"This is the third time it's happened," Adam commented.

"Yes. I've replaced the locks and improved them, but it hasn't helped."

"What do you keep inside?" Ryan asked.

"Cleaning products and supplies for the bathrooms."

"What about fertilisers and such?"

"That's kept in the gardening shed." She pointed to it. Every pore of her skin was tingling, acutely aware of how close Ryan was to her. She checked the time and tried to sound casual. "Any chance I can grab a few things and start my rounds?"

Ryan glanced at her. "Rounds?"

"Cleaning. We've had three check-outs this morning and I've got people arriving at two."

"We'll be as quick as possible," he said. "Is there something else you can do?"

"Always." And wasn't that the truth? It also meant she didn't have to stay near Ryan. His presence was unsettling. She had a warm ache in her belly she didn't like, didn't trust. "When you're done, go to the office. Lynette will be able to contact me." She hurried away.

Half an hour later, Hannah got a call. "Senior Constable Kilpatrick is in the office for you," Lynette said.

Hannah sighed. She didn't want to see him again. Checking the cabin, she made a note to bring out some fresh milk when she returned and then locked it. She went into the office via the back door so she didn't have to stand close to Ryan.

He was telling Lynette about his son, Felix, and Adam was flicking through his notepad.

"Find anything?" she asked.

"Got a couple of fingerprints," he said. "Can you tell me if anything's missing?"

She nodded and picked up her inventory. "I'll just be a second. Lynette, do you want to get the officers a drink?" She didn't wait for the reply as she hurried back outside.

As usual, it was cleaner and a whole heap of toilet paper. Returning to the office, she gave Ryan the list. His fingers brushed hers and a zap went straight up her arm. She took a step back.

"Thanks. I'll add it to my report." He paused. "Have you considered installing a camera?"

"No. I didn't want to alarm my guests, make them think the park wasn't safe, or that I was watching them." She wanted to back further away. It didn't matter that she was behind the counter, which spanned the whole width of the office, and Lynette was with her. Ryan had a presence that was larger than himself. His uniform clung to him in all the right places, and that made her nervous. Attraction led to bad things.

"You could always put it on the inside, pointing towards the door."

She nodded. "I'll check out prices."

"Have you noticed any pattern or particular time of the month?"

"What were the dates of the other break-ins?" she asked Lynette.

Lynette flicked through a file from the desk. "They were all on a Sunday night," she said. "But at different times of the month."

They were coming into the busiest time of the season and she couldn't afford to waste a whole morning waiting for the police to do an investigation. "I'll look into some sort of surveillance."

"I can recommend a couple of different brands," Ryan said.

"Thanks. I'll ask Lincoln if he knows who can install one." She smiled. "Do you need anything else from me?"

He shook his head. "I'll send you a copy of the report."

"Thanks."

He left, with Adam trailing after him, and Lynette twirled on her office chair to stare at Hannah. "Oh my God, he's as sexy as ever. How can you not see that?"

Her eyes pinned Hannah to the spot and Hannah's face grew warm. She couldn't tell Lynette the truth. She shrugged. "Everyone has different tastes." She grabbed her clipboard. "I'd better get back to work, I'm running behind." She made herself scarce.

Ryan frowned as he drove away from the caravan park. It wasn't his imagination. Hannah wasn't comfortable around him. She was the complete opposite of Lynette, who had casually flirted and then promised to call Mrs Z to set up a playdate between Felix and her youngest boy.

Hannah, on the other hand, didn't want to be near him. She'd pushed him away when he'd helped her up and kept her distance, only saying the bare minimum to him. She was twitchy and tense, and he would have thought she was guilty of breaking into her own storeroom if she hadn't been as twitchy the night before. It was odd, but not so strange that he wanted to figure it out.

She was appealing to look at though. The baggy clothes she'd worn yesterday had been replaced by trim cargo shorts and a holiday park polo shirt that nicely showed off her curves. Yet, those green eyes of hers hid a lot of secrets.

"What do you think about the break-in?" he asked Adam to get his mind back on the job.

"Seems straightforward enough. We'll have to take the prints to Albany to be run. There might be a match."

Ryan glanced at him. "We can't run them at the station?"

"Nah, we don't have the equipment."

Ryan frowned. Karratha had been the regional centre for policing in the Pilbara and so they had most of the equipment they needed. He was going to have to get used to the differences of working in a small-town station.

When they arrived back, Ryan wandered straight into Lincoln's office.

"How did it go?" Lincoln asked.

"Got some prints, but they're likely Hannah's or Lynette's."

"Sue's heading over to Albany this afternoon, so get her to take them," Lincoln said. "I don't like Hannah being targeted like this."

There was something kind of possessive in the way he said it and Ryan studied him. "Is she someone special?"

Lincoln's jaw dropped and then he laughed. "Not in a romantic way. She's one of the musketeers, the girls Jamie used to hang around at school. You must remember Kit from the dairy farm next door. On the weekends, you never found one without at least one other; Kit, Fleur, Hannah and Mai. Hannah's lived at the holiday park with her maternal grandparents since she was a kid. She's practically my sister."

He did have vague recollections of Lincoln's brother, Jamie, hanging out with a bunch of girls. They were about eleven when he was there, so he hadn't paid much attention. "What happened to her parents?"

Lincoln hesitated. "It's pretty grim. Her father killed her mother and went to jail. Hannah was about eight."

Ryan sucked in a breath. "Shit." His parents might not have paid any attention to him, but they had never been violent, and they loved each other. An event like that would have ripped the very foundations out of Hannah's world.

"The rumour is Hannah was home at the time, but I've never asked her. She's pretty well adjusted if that's the case."

Ryan hesitated. Lincoln was close to Hannah, but Ryan needed to share his observation. "She seemed kind of skittish of me."

His friend frowned. "Really? Hannah's one tough cookie. All those girls are."

"Every time I've seen her I startle her." Was he reading too much into it?

"Must be your shocking personality." Lincoln grinned.

Ryan rolled his eyes. "Thanks." He reviewed his notes. "The chemicals that were stolen could be used to make meth. Do you think that's what's going on?"

Lincoln pursed his lips. "That had occurred to me as well. I suggested to Hannah that we put up cameras, but she wasn't keen."

"I suggested the same thing – thought we could set them up inside the room. She said she'd talk to you about it."

"That's great. We might be able to catch them coming in. They won't be expecting it. I'll call her this afternoon."

"Mrs Jameson's lost her poodle," Adam called. "And Gladys has crashed into someone's car again."

Lincoln sighed. "Take Ryan," he called back. He glanced at Ryan. "Gladys is one of our resident retirees. She keeps forgetting she no longer has her licence, and won't sell her car. Get all the details and then get Adam to give you a tour of the town to reacquaint yourself. I'm sure you'll find the poodle. Shirley loses her at least once a month." He paused and then grinned. "Adam believes the poor thing escapes to get a break from Shirley's fussing. Let me know what you think."

There was a mischievous expression on Lincoln's face that intrigued Ryan. "All right."

It didn't take long to deal with Gladys and the crash, and then Adam drove him through town.

"So what does the poodle look like?" Ryan asked.

"Pink and groomed to within an inch of its life," Adam said.

Ryan raised an eyebrow. "Seriously?"

Adam nodded. "It's the most pathetic thing I've ever seen, but at least she's hard to miss."

"Name?"

"Fairy Floss."

Ryan chuckled. "This I've got to see."

"You can't unsee it once you do," Adam warned.

They drove through the town, stopping at the park by the river and the football oval, before swinging past the district high school.

"It's lunchtime," Adam said. "Flossy likes to get a share of food sometimes."

Sure enough, as they walked into the school there was a bunch of kids huddled around what could be called a dog. It was a miniature poodle and its fur had been shaved so its snout was bare, but its ears and the top of its head were groomed in a bright, lollypop pink. Its tail was a ball of fluff at the end and each foot had pink balls on it, but the rest of its legs and its back end were shaved.

Adam walked into the group. "All right, Fairy Floss, you've been nabbed. Time for you to go back."

The kids protested as Adam clipped on a lead. The dog sat down, straining against it.

"She doesn't want to go," one of the girls said.

"Yeah, but she can't stay here," Adam answered. "Mrs Jameson is terribly upset." He dug into his pocket and pulled out a dog treat. Fairy Floss was instantly on her feet.

"You've come prepared," Ryan commented as they walked back to the car.

"Yep. There's a box of treats at the station, just for Flossy."

He was curious to meet Mrs Jameson. What kind of person dyed their dog pink?

She lived across from Hannah's caravan park in a lovely old wooden miller's cottage. Ryan stood next to Adam as he knocked on the door.

"You found her!" The delight was clear as a middle-aged woman opened the door. She was in her late forties or early fifties, with jet-black hair styled in an elaborate braid and wore a dress made of patchwork squares. She screamed hippy and wasn't at all what Ryan had envisioned.

"She was at the school getting treats," Adam told her, unclipping the lead.

Mrs Jameson ran her hand down Adam's arm. "Oh, you naughty girl," she purred. Then she noticed Ryan and looked him up and down with appreciation. "Who do we have here?"

Ryan just managed not to smile. "Senior Constable Kilpatrick, ma'am."

"Oh, don't call me ma'am," she said. "You'll make me feel ancient. Call me Shirley." She still had her hand on Adam's arm.

Was he in the way? "We'd better be going."

Shirley pouted. "Are you sure you can't stay for … coffee?"

Ryan did smile then. "No thanks. It's my first day on the job, and I want to make a good impression."

"Well don't be a stranger." She twitched her fingers in a wave as they went back to the car.

"Is she always like that?" Ryan asked.

"Always," Adam muttered.

"Was I disturbing you?"

"God, no!" Adam stared at him with horror. "I'm glad you were there. That woman …"

"Loses her dog on purpose." He was kind of enjoying Adam's discomfort.

"Do you think?" Adam was quiet for a moment and then slouched. "You're probably right. Why do I always get the call?"

"Probably because you're the youngest and Lincoln thinks it's funny."

Adam grimaced. "Probably. I'll have to pay him back somehow."

"I'll tell you if I come up with anything." Ryan remembered fondly the pranks they used to play on each other in high school. It was good to be back in Blackbridge.

It was good to be home.

Hannah headed back to the office when it was time for Lynette to pick up her kids from school. The work around the park was done and now she had to put together a marketing plan to attract customers during the winter months. This was the best part of her job. Event planning had been her dream ever since the circus had come to town when she was a kid. She remembered the excitement that had flowed through Blackbridge and how it was all anyone had talked about for weeks afterwards. She'd decided then and there that she wanted to arrange events that appealed to people and made them happy. It was why she was building her retreat.

The phone rang, and annoyed at the interruption, she picked it up.

"Why do I have to hear about Ryan Kilpatrick staying at your cabin from Lynette?" The droll comment could only come from one person.

"Hi, Fleur." Hannah smiled.

"Seriously, though. Are you really OK with that?"

She couldn't ignore the concern in Fleur's voice. Only Fleur knew the reason why Hannah didn't like to be alone with men. No one else suspected a thing – Hannah had a lot of practice in hiding her fear. "I thought he was married when Lincoln mentioned he needed a place to stay. He said he had a kid."

"Hannah." The exasperation in Fleur's voice was clear.

"I couldn't exactly refuse when I found out the truth," Hannah argued. "Lincoln was desperate and you know what he's like."

"Yeah, like a dog with a bone." Fleur sighed. "Do you want to come and stay with me while he's there?"

The offer was tempting. Too tempting. But who knew how long that would be? Her whole life would be in limbo – if she was too scared to stay at the retreat she wouldn't be able to work on the cabins.

She'd be delaying her dream again.

She was tired of running away.

Hannah sat up straight, the realisation sweeping through her like a summer breeze. She had been running, had been hiding. "I need to move on."

"There's a good psychologist at the hospital," Fleur said immediately.

Hannah frowned. Fleur had been on at her for years to get help, but therapy was a sham. She'd been forced to visit a psychologist for a year after her mother had died and the guy had done nothing except ask her how she was feeling. Her stomach clenched. What the hell could she say to that? Her father, the man she'd loved with all her heart, who had called her his little princess, had killed her mother. Hannah had seen him standing over her mother holding a knife, while she'd bled out on the floor. How was she supposed to feel? "I don't want people asking questions."

"You could go to Albany."

"It's fine," she reassured her friend. "It's a stupid phobia. I can manage."

"Honey, it's not a phobia. You were raped."

Hannah stiffened and her gut clenched. "Where are you?"

"Relax. I'm in my car. No one can hear me."

She didn't want to continue the conversation. Just the mention of the assault made her want to hide. She got up and walked over to Joe, rubbing his belly to soothe herself. The bell above the door rang. "I've got to go. I've got a guest." She turned and her whole body froze.

No.

This couldn't be happening.

It wasn't possible to conjure up a person by thinking about them. Her legs trembled.

"Do you want to have dinner tonight?" Fleur asked.

Hannah couldn't answer. She couldn't make any muscle in her body move as the man who'd walked in smiled at her. "Hannah, it's been ages."

Her stomach lurched and she wanted to vomit.

"Hannah?" Fleur's voice in her ear reassured her.

"Justin," she managed to squeak.

"What did you say?" Fleur asked.

She forced herself to breathe, her eyes not leaving the man who'd raped her five years ago. He frowned and sweat broke out on her skin. She had to speak, had to tell Fleur what was going on. Fleur could get help. "Justin Lodeham just walked in." Her throat hurt saying it and she trembled once again.

Fleur swore. "What the hell? I'll be right there. Don't hang up. Do you need me to call the police?"

"No. Hurry." Joe got to his feet, as if sensing something was wrong, and growled. Hannah didn't quieten him.

"Hannah, are you all right?" Justin asked. "You're as pale as a ghost."

She couldn't answer. Didn't want to speak to the man, didn't want to be in the same room as him, but her feet wouldn't move.

"Do you need a doctor?" he asked. He looked around as if to find a way to get behind the counter to her.

Joe barked a warning.

Hannah had to say something, if only to get him to leave. "We're fully booked." Her hands found the low cupboard behind her and she clutched on to it, needing something solid to touch. In the corner stood the cricket set they hired out to guests. She could use the bat if he tried anything.

"My friend booked a cabin. Should be under the name Smith." He smiled. "I wasn't expecting to see you here, but you're from this area, aren't you?"

Where was Fleur? Surely she had to be here soon. What if she wasn't? Joe stood between her and Justin. Hannah had to get rid of Justin. She nodded.

"Weren't you studying event coordination or something? What are you doing working in a caravan park?"

She didn't answer. To get to the computer and check the booking she had to step closer to him, but that wasn't possible. She was frozen in place, staring at him, her breath fast. He couldn't stay here. No way could she function if she knew he was anywhere in the park. She had to do something. He was waiting for an answer, but she couldn't remember what he'd asked.

"Hannah?"

The back door slammed open and Fleur strode in, still wearing her hospital scrubs, her brown hair tied back in a ponytail and looking as mad as hell.

Relief flooded Hannah and her legs went weak.

Justin grinned. "Fleur! Nice to see you."

"I can't say the same," Fleur said. "Are you finished here? I need to speak with Hannah."

Justin frowned. "What's up with you?"

She looked at him, head tilted and gestured to the door.

Justin glanced between the two of them. "I still haven't checked in yet."

Fleur ran a hand over Hannah's arm. "Hannah, why don't you get a glass of water from the kitchen? You don't look very well. I'll deal with Justin."

Hannah wanted to tell her Justin couldn't stay, that he wasn't welcome, but she couldn't speak, still couldn't move.

Fleur sat at the computer and quickly typed in some details. "There's no booking under your name."

"It's under Smith."

She typed again. "Oh, damn," she said. "I'm sorry, you've been double-booked. We don't have any other cabins available." She didn't sound sorry at all. "There's another park down the road."

"What? Smithy checked the booking last week."

"Sorry, Justin. There's been a software glitch. It's going to take an age to sort through all the bookings and check them. You'd better get going."

"What do you know about it?" Justin's voice rose. "You don't work here. Hannah, aren't you going to check?"

Hannah swallowed. "Fleur knows the system." Why wouldn't he go?

"The other park is out the road and to your left," Fleur said. "You'd better hurry in case they're booked out too." She crossed her arms and stared at him.

Justin sneered. "I'll be going, then. I'll see you later." He turned on his heel and left.

Hannah closed her eyes, desperately trying to control the tears welling up inside.

Joe nudged Hannah's arm and she slid to the floor, putting her arm around him, clinging to him. She'd never, *ever* thought she'd see Justin Lodeham again. Couldn't quite believe he was acting as if everything was fine between them.

Fleur turned to her. "Honey, are you all right?"

Hannah shook her head, the sobs coming now, big racking sobs that shook her whole body.

"Come with me." Fleur pulled her to her feet. "Come into the back room so you don't have to deal with anyone coming in."

Hannah let herself be led into the little kitchen next to the office.

"What is he doing here?" Fleur asked as she pulled out a chair and handed Hannah a box of tissues.

"A holiday, I guess." She choked on the words. "He's here for a week."

"Bloody hell." Fleur sat down next to her. "You should press charges. It's never too late."

"No." They'd had this argument before. "We were dating. No one's going to believe he raped me. It'll be his word against mine."

"So what are you going to do?"

Her chest hurt. "He's not staying here anymore. Thank you for sending him away." Blackbridge was her safe place, the place where she could function, where she knew almost everyone and he'd invaded it. And she'd gone completely to bits. Her reaction terrified her. What if she bumped into him again?

"Let me tell Lincoln," Fleur said. "There's got to be something he can do, if only to keep an eye on him."

"No!" Lincoln would go into protector mode and make things worse. Plus, she didn't want him to find out how badly she'd stuffed up.

"What about Ryan? He's staying near you. He should know so he can keep an eye out for the bastard."

She shook her head. "No one needs to know. It's in the past."

"Yeah, right," Fleur scoffed. "If it was so in the past, you wouldn't be having a breakdown right now."

She let out a shuddery breath, wishing her friend wasn't right.

"Why don't you stay with me while Justin's in town? I'm sure you can arrange the duties around this place so you're not alone. He might come back. I've got the next two days off work, so I'll hang out with you, and I'm sure Mai and Kit can arrange some time to be with you as well."

Hannah was shaking. She wrapped her arms around herself. She had to get a grip. She'd let what happened to her rule her life for far too long. She couldn't ask her friends to interrupt their lives for this, not if she wasn't willing to do something about it. "Let me think about it."

"We're here for you."

"I know." She hugged Fleur. "Thank you." After a few moments, the tears began to slow. She checked the time. She could shut the office now.

"Go wash your face," Fleur ordered. "You look like hell."

Hannah smiled. "Yes, ma'am." She stroked Joe and went into the bathroom to freshen up. She stared at herself. Her eyes were red, her cheeks stained with tears and her usually styled blonde hair was all mussed up. Her concern about Ryan paled in significance against the reality of seeing Justin again. It was almost laughable – except it wasn't the least bit funny.

For five years she'd lived in fear and now her nightmare had come to her door.

She straightened her spine.

She'd had enough. It was time to defeat it.

Chapter 3

After freshening up, Hannah went back into the kitchen. "I can't go on like this," she told Fleur. "I'll take you up on your offer to stay at your place tonight and we can discuss a plan of action."

Fleur hugged her. "Good. I'll invite Mai and Kit as well."

Hannah hesitated. "They don't know about it."

"Don't you think they should? Particularly if Justin is in town. They never met him and he's just Kit's type. What if she runs into him and decides to go on a date?"

She winced. Fleur was right. She'd never forgive herself if something happened to Kit. She nodded. "All right."

Fleur checked her watch. "Have you got any more guests arriving?"

"No. I'll lock up early."

"Great. Why don't you pick up a change of clothes and come to my place? I'll buy some drinks on the way home."

Hannah gave her friend another hug. "Thank you."

"Nothing to thank me for."

Hannah locked the office and then stopped briefly at her place to grab a change of clothes and food for Joe, before heading to Fleur's house in town. It was an old wooden fifties house, and it had a front porch with a bullnose verandah. Flowers bloomed in the garden, a riot of colour contrasting against the dirt driveway. Mai's red Mazda was already there, and as Hannah let Joe out, Kit pulled up in her dirty white ute.

"Hi," Kit said. She must have come straight from the farm as she wore what Hannah considered her work uniform: khaki shorts, white singlet with a red flannel shirt over the top and steel-capped boots. She slung a bag over her shoulder. "Do you know why Fleur's called an emergency meeting of the musketeers?"

Hannah smothered her groan. When they'd been kids, someone in town had given them the nickname. They'd embraced it with enthusiasm and formed their own not-so-secret club. All their most important decisions had to be made at an official meeting. Fleur was enacting the rule again. She hesitated. "Let's go inside and have some wine."

Kit frowned. "All right."

They let themselves in the front door and Hannah called a greeting to Fleur and Mai as she walked through the house to let Joe roam in the large backyard. Mai was sitting at the kitchen table sipping a frozen mango daiquiri, looking gorgeous in a blue summer dress. Mai was the shortest of them, almost petite, and always made Hannah feel large and ungainly. Her straight, dark shoulder-length hair and beautiful brown almond-shaped eyes showed her Vietnamese heritage.

"Who wants a daiquiri?" Fleur asked as she reached into the freezer for more ice.

"Yes, please," Hannah replied.

"Me too," Kit said as she took a seat. "So, what gives? Why are we drinking daiquiris on a Monday night and why the emergency meeting?"

"Let me make the drinks first."

Hannah grabbed the packet of chips from the kitchen bench and poured them into a bowl, needing to keep busy. She wasn't sure what to say, how to say it. How would her friends react? Would they blame her for going back to Justin's place that night, for going into his room? God knows she blamed herself enough. What else had she expected was going to happen, if not sex? She'd as good as given him the green light. Her hands shook and the empty packet rustled. Hurriedly, she placed it in the bin and focused on her breathing.

She was glad the noise of the blender made conversation

impossible as Fleur mixed the drinks. It gave her a bit of space. When Fleur finally put drinks in front of them all, it was Mai who asked, "What's wrong?"

Fleur looked at Hannah.

Of course it had to come from her. She couldn't expect Fleur to tell them. She took a sip of the cold, sweet drink. Would her friends think her stupid? Would they say it was her fault? Could they even comprehend what she'd gone through – what she still went through every day? "I have to tell you about something that happened when I was studying in Perth."

"Has this got something to do with why you did the final semester online?" Kit asked.

She nodded. She couldn't even remember what lame excuse she'd given her friends.

Mai reached out and squeezed Hannah's hand. "We'll still love you, no matter what it is."

Tears pricked her eyes. Mai meant well, but there was that hint of blame, that it was something she'd done wrong. And perhaps it had been. She swallowed hard. Start with the basics. "I was dating this guy, Justin. We'd been dating for a couple of months and I really liked him." More fool her.

"I remember you talking about him," Kit said.

"One night, after we went to the movies, he invited me back to his place." She'd been a little nervous, but excited as well. She and Justin had clicked – they liked the same movies, had the same music tastes, and they could talk for hours.

Her friends were silent, waiting. "I knew he wanted to have sex and I thought I was ready." The nerves that had fluttered around her stomach were nothing compared with the beasts in there now. "Two of his housemates were playing computer games, so we went into his bedroom." She took a big gulp of her drink, but the sweetness and the alcohol clashed with the swirl of her stomach, making her nauseous. She pushed away the glass and clenched her hands together. "We started kissing and he got handsy, kind of aggressive, and I didn't like it. I pushed him away and told him no."

At least Hannah was pretty sure she had. Had she not been loud enough, or forceful enough? Had she only shouted in her head and not aloud? She closed her eyes, her chest tight, and the scene played out behind her eyelids. The warm kisses had stirred her, until his hands began groping her breasts, pinching them hard, his breath smelling like popcorn as he thrust his tongue in her mouth. The way he'd shoved her jeans down her legs, his touch no longer gentle, no longer caring. She squeezed her legs tightly together, wrapped her arms around herself and rocked back and forth.

"Hannah," Kit said.

She flinched and opened her eyes again. They were staring at her. She breathed deeply, once, twice, three times and the panic lessened. She cleared her throat. "Justin didn't listen to my protests. He forced himself on me."

"Son of a bitch," Kit swore, pushing back her chair and getting to her feet. She paced the small kitchen, her eyes wild.

Hannah had never seen her friend so angry. It gave her some comfort. "When he was done, he said how much he liked me." As if he hadn't realised what he'd done.

"What did you do?" Mai asked softly.

"She called me and I picked her up," Fleur said.

"Then what?" Mai said.

"I did my exams and came home."

"He didn't contact you?"

"He rang and Fleur told him I had to leave Perth suddenly. I changed my number." That last week at university had been terrifying. She was sure she was going to bump into him around campus. She almost didn't go to her exams at all. The moment uni was over, she'd packed her things and gone home.

"You didn't go to the police?" Kit was outraged.

The disbelief in her tone stole Hannah's breath away. It took her a second to adjust. "And say what?" she demanded. "I went to his house expecting to have sex. I didn't yell or scream. I struggled, but he was too strong, so in the end I lay there until he finished. None of his housemates would have testified against him." She'd remembered her mother lying bleeding on the floor of the kitchen some twelve years earlier and she'd stopped fighting, stopped speaking. She didn't want to die too.

"Hannah." Mai's voice was insistent as she shook her shoulder.

Hannah blinked, tears flooding her eyes.

"I'm sorry." Kit pulled her to her feet and embraced her, and Mai and Fleur joined in. She sobbed as they murmured words to console her. But it didn't matter. No words could fix what Justin had done to her.

When she pulled back, they let her sit. She was drained.

"Maybe you should tell Lincoln," Kit said as she sat down again. "He'd listen."

She couldn't have at the time. She'd been so confused, so unsure, so damn frightened and hurt – she'd just wanted to hide. The thought of Lincoln or anyone else finding out still filled her with dread. He'd been like a big brother to her, to all of them. He would have been disappointed that she hadn't fought back.

"Why are you telling us now?" Mai asked, her gaze intense.

"Because the bastard is back," Fleur said. "He tried to book in to the holiday park for the next week, but I sent him packing. He checked in at the other caravan park." She glanced at Hannah. "I called and asked."

Mai swore and Hannah stared at her. Mai never swore.

"I've got some castration equipment out at the farm," Kit snarled. "I reckon we could put it to good use."

Mai nodded. "Good idea."

Hannah barked out a laugh. They sounded serious and it was kind of soothing.

"Not that I don't totally agree with you," Fleur said, "but it's best we don't get arrested. We need to make sure someone is with Hannah at all times while he's here. I can do the next two days."

Hannah wanted to be strong, wanted to refuse the offer, but she didn't have it in her. She *was* scared. Having to face Justin alone was terrifying.

"Put me down from midday," Mai said.

"I'll do whenever you need me," Kit said.

"It'll just be for a couple of days, in case he comes around again," Hannah said. "He's with friends and will probably spend the whole time surfing." She fervently hoped that was the case.

"We'll make sure it's not a problem," Kit told her. "You can sleep at my place, but it might be too far out of town for you."

"She's staying here." Fleur gave her a look that brooked no

argument. "It's only for a few nights and Joe will be pleased to have some time out of the shed."

Hannah sighed, the relief flowing out of her. She would feel better if she wasn't alone. Her property was isolated, which was usually comforting, but not now. Not with Justin so close.

"Have you got a picture of him?" Mai asked. "So we know who to look out for?"

Hannah shook her head. "I got rid of them all."

"I might." Fleur took her tablet off the bench. "He came to our Christmas in July celebration that year." She flicked through her photos until she found one. "This is him."

"He looks like a nice guy," Kit said. "I can see how you were deceived."

Her words were a balm to Hannah. She'd always wondered whether she'd missed some kind of sign that he was a rapist. But then appearances were deceiving. She wouldn't have picked her father as a murderer either. She sucked in a breath at the old, sharp pain. Maybe it *was* her fault. Maybe she was attracted to bad men, maybe it was some flaw in her personality and she would forever make the same mistake of trusting the wrong person. Her chest squeezed.

Mai rubbed Hannah's back and Hannah came back to the present.

"Print out a couple of copies for me," Mai said. "I want to show the women who work with me."

The guilt was sharp. Had she done the wrong thing by not reporting Justin? Was she potentially letting another woman go through what she'd gone through? No. It would have been her word against his and that wasn't enough to convict him, was it?

Fleur came back in with the printouts. "You should tell Lynette something, in case he comes in looking for you."

She hadn't considered that. "What do I say?"

"Tell her the truth," Kit said. "Say he's an ex and you don't want to be left alone with him."

She could do that. It was going to be all right. She had friends around her. "I don't want to talk about this anymore," she said. "Let's order pizza and talk about something else."

Fleur got to her feet. "Everyone happy with the usual?"

Mai and Kit nodded and Hannah changed the subject.

"What's happening at the farm?"

Kit rolled her shoulders. "Paul hasn't been pulling his weight lately. I'll send him to check fences and he'll take all morning doing what should take an hour or two. I'm going to have to have a word with him."

"That sucks," Mai said. "I've got some great employees at the moment."

Hannah relaxed as they spoke about work and life. When the pizza arrived, Kit cleared her throat.

"Can I ask you about something?" She looked a little unsure, but there was a slight smile on her face.

Hannah braced herself. "Sure."

"Tell me about Ryan Kilpatrick."

Hannah laughed, surprised that she could. "Why is everyone so obsessed with Ryan?"

"Because he's single, gorgeous and staying at your place," Fleur said.

Kit nodded. "Is he divorced, widowed, what?"

"Divorced." Hannah drained her glass, hoping they would drop the topic.

"How old is his son?" Mai asked.

"Eight."

Fleur got up and poured more drinks for everyone. "What's he like?"

"I've only seen him once. He's cute. He looks like his father."

"So you reckon Ryan's cute?" Kit's tone was triumphant.

"No!" Hannah groaned. She'd walked into that one. "The boy is cute."

"And so is Ryan." Kit wasn't going to give up.

Hannah sighed as she gave them what they wanted, forcing some enthusiasm into her tone. "I wouldn't call Ryan cute. I'd call him hot – like scorching."

The girls cackled in glee. "I'm going to have to drop by the police station tomorrow," Mai said. "And check him out."

"It's worth a trip," Kit agreed and turned to Hannah. "Are you going to ask him out?"

She shook her head. "I don't know anything about him."

"That's the point of dating," Fleur said. "You'll get to know him. Besides, you had a massive crush on him in primary school."

Mai perked up. "Did she?" Mai had arrived in Blackbridge after Ryan had moved away.

Kit nodded. "You should have heard the stories she used to make up about him. I swear, sometimes she came to my place hoping to get a glimpse of him on the drive out."

Hannah's face heated. Kit's statement had a smidgen of truth to it.

"Don't you want to see those fantasies realised?" Fleur asked.

Hannah shook her head. "Reality can never live up to fantasy." None of them understood how hard it was for her. There was a tiny part of her that wished she was brave – that wished she could move on from her assault and ask Ryan out – but her taste in men couldn't be trusted. The moment she became emotionally involved with men, things went wrong.

"Go on," Kit urged.

"I don't date." There was a finality about her words.

Kit opened her mouth to say something else and Hannah cut her off. "I can't, Kit. Not after Justin – I just can't."

Kit's eyes widened as she realised what Hannah was saying.

Hannah couldn't stay here, she needed to breathe. She fled the room.

Late Tuesday afternoon as Ryan was packing up at the end of his shift, a woman walked into the station as if she owned the place. She was dressed in a white singlet, khaki shorts and steel-capped boots, and her long brown hair was tied back in a ponytail.

"Hey, Adam, where's Lincoln?"

"In his office," Adam called. "Come on through."

She walked into the back room, her gaze sweeping the area and she spotted Ryan, her smile warm and friendly. "You have to be Ryan. Still as good-looking as ever."

Ryan smiled, a little bemused, not sure who she was.

"I'm Kit Van Ross," she said. "I own the dairy farm next to

the Zanettis."

He had vague recollections of the girl – she'd been a tomboy, always grubby and confident – but she was now all grown up. "Nice to see you again."

"Likewise." She breezed past him into Lincoln's office. "Slinky, we gotta talk."

He chuckled. *Slinky?* He glanced over to ask Adam about the nickname and found him staring after Kit slightly wistfully. "Friend of yours?"

"I wish," Adam sighed. "Kit never dates guys from town."

Before Ryan could ask why, Lincoln called, "Ryan, come in here."

He wandered in. Kit was standing with her hands on her hips, as if looking for a fight.

"Ryan's staying out at Hannah's cabin," Lincoln told Kit. "Tell him what you told me."

She assessed him. "Hannah's ex is in town. It didn't end well and I'm asking Lincoln to keep an eye on the caravan park for a couple of days."

"Is he a threat to her?" Ryan asked.

"To her mental state, definitely. Physically? Possibly."

"Have we got a name or description?"

Kit handed him a photo. "Justin Lodeham, aka scumbag."

His brown hair was slightly longer than normal and coiffed in the front, and he was wearing a hideous knitted Christmas jumper and jeans, holding a bottle of beer. He looked like your typical university student. But appearances could be deceiving. Ryan had been thoroughly fooled by Paula. "What did he do?"

Kit frowned.

"What did he do to make Hannah scared of him?" he clarified.

Kit pursed her lips. "That's classified."

Ryan raised an eyebrow and looked at Lincoln.

Lincoln sighed. "I can't make it official unless you give me something, Kit."

"I can't tell you. I promised."

"Then get Hannah to come in."

Kit shook her head. "I can't do that. She doesn't know I'm here."

"She hasn't asked for police help?" Ryan asked.

"No. She wouldn't. She's too damn stubborn."

"Like her friends," Lincoln muttered.

Kit whirled around to face him. "Lincoln, you know I'd never ask you for anything unless it was serious."

He nodded.

"All I'm asking is for one of your officers to drop around the caravan park once or twice a day. Show your face so that if the scumbag is around, he doesn't get any ideas."

Lincoln ran a hand through his hair. "All right." He turned to Ryan. "This next bit is unofficial. You're staying on Hannah's property. If you hear any cars at night, call me. I'll come and check it out."

"I can keep an eye on things." Ryan hated the idea that Hannah was feeling threatened. Was that the reason she was so scared when she was alone with him? "How far away does she live from me?"

"About five hundred metres," Kit answered. "Her shed is where the office will eventually be."

"Shed?"

"She's living in a converted storage shed, but for the next couple of nights she's staying with Fleur."

"Good," Lincoln said. "Keep us posted if anything changes."

"Will do." She smiled then and her face lit up. "Thanks. I appreciate it." And with that she walked out.

Lincoln watched her go, fondness and exasperation on his face. "I can never say no to that girl."

"She didn't ask for much," Ryan said. "It won't be hard for any of us to swing by the caravan park on our way back from something else. I'll drop by now on my way to pick Felix up from your mum's."

"Thanks, mate."

He'd like to check how Hannah was holding up. And find out exactly what her secret was.

Hannah hated the nerves that clung to her skin when she

arrived at work on Tuesday morning. She hated that her safe haven was now under siege. She shook her head. She was being melodramatic. Justin was only going to be in Blackbridge for a week and things would go back to normal.

"Let's get inside and eat these croissants." Fleur opened the car door.

They'd stopped by Mai's bakery and picked up coffee and croissants, as well as a treat for morning tea. The smells made Hannah's mouth water. She never understood how Mai was so slim when she spent her day surrounded by such amazing food.

Hannah followed Fleur to the front door.

"What's this?" Fleur asked, bending down to pick up a small parcel wrapped in red-and-green Christmas paper.

"No idea." She unlocked the door, turned the sign to "open" and then took the box from Fleur. There was a little card with her name on it. She read out the words on the inside. "Merry Christmas, Hannah." Unease skittered over her skin as she walked around the back of the building to let them in to the office. She couldn't see anyone who could have left it.

"Think you've got a secret admirer?" Fleur asked.

"No." She couldn't imagine anyone being interested in her. Once inside, she put the box on her desk and switched on her computer. It was unsettling coming so close after Justin's arrival. Who would be leaving her a gift? And why wouldn't they sign it? She didn't want an admirer, particularly a creepy anonymous one.

"What is it?" Fleur called from the kitchen. She walked in carrying plates with the croissants on them. She handed one to Hannah.

"I don't know." She bit into her croissant as she examined the package. It was only ten centimetres square and tied with a silver bow. With a sigh, she pulled the bow apart and carefully unwrapped the paper. Inside was a plain brown box. She lifted the lid to reveal a gorgeous silver necklace with a charm of a bird in a tree.

"That's really pretty," Fleur said.

It was, but she couldn't shake the discomfort.

"Are you going to wear it?"

Hannah shrugged. "What if it's from Justin?"

Fleur scowled. "Don't let him ruin this for you. He only arrived yesterday and he didn't know you were going to be here."

"But who else could it be from?"

"Who cares? You've got a nice necklace. Want me to help you put it on?"

She hesitated. "Not right now." She put the lid back on and shoved it in her top drawer.

Fleur sighed and sipped her coffee. "All right, then. What can I do to help?"

They worked together in the office all day. It was Lynette's turn to do the cleaning and so Hannah did paperwork, with Fleur helping her with a bit of filing. By mid-afternoon, Fleur was reading a book in the kitchen and Hannah was beginning to think she was being paranoid. Justin wasn't here to see her – he was having a holiday with friends. It wasn't fair of her to have Fleur cooped up in the office on her day off. Hannah needed to put on her big-girl knickers and she'd be fine. She stood to tell Fleur to go, when the doorbell chimed. She glanced up and the smile froze on her face.

Justin.

Her mind went completely blank, and she clutched her throat as bile rose in it. She wanted to close her eyes, pretend he wasn't there, but it was too dangerous.

"Hi, Hannah." He smiled, large and open, but to her it was like a shark showing its teeth. "I wanted to check how you were feeling. I was worried about you yesterday."

She'd been fine until he'd arrived. Swallowing hard, she said, "I'm fine."

He studied her. "You're a little pale still," he said. "Are you feeling up for dinner tonight? It'd be great to catch up."

Hell no. She clutched the back of the chair. "I'm working."

"That's a shame. What about tomorrow night?"

She shook her head.

"How about lunch?"

Fleur walked in. "Justin. I thought I smelled something off."

"What's your problem?" He seemed genuinely upset, but Hannah knew it was a game.

"You are. Why don't you go? We're busy."

"I'm not leaving until Hannah asks me to."

The door opened, and Ryan walked in. Hannah's legs went weak and she sighed in relief. "Ryan," she greeted him. "Can I help you with something?"

Ryan glanced at Justin and then back at Hannah. "Yeah. I wanted to discuss the break-in yesterday if you've got a couple of minutes."

"Of course." Anything to get rid of Justin.

Justin glowered. "I'll catch you later, Hannah." He walked out.

She gasped. Was that a threat? She wrapped her hands around her waist as if she could protect herself. Before she let the fear truly take hold she took a few breaths. It was just a saying. He wouldn't be back.

"Was he bothering you?" Ryan asked.

Hannah looked at Fleur. What should she say?

"He's her ex," she said. "It's nice to see you back in town, Ryan. You probably don't remember me, I'm Fleur." She shook his hand.

Hannah loosened her hold. "Sorry, I should have introduced you." She turned to Ryan. "Did you want to come around the back?"

He hesitated. "No, it's fine. I don't actually have anything to report."

She frowned. "Then why did you say that you did?"

He ran a hand through his hair. "Well, Kit asked us to keep an eye on the park for a couple of days, said your ex was in town."

Hannah stilled. She didn't want Lincoln knowing. He wouldn't understand.

"What exactly did she say?" Fleur asked.

"That Justin wasn't very nice and it would be reassuring to have a police presence around while he was here. She gave us a picture of him."

It might be enough for Ryan, but Lincoln was going to want to know more. He would keep at her until she told him everything, until she confessed her shame. She squeezed her eyes shut. Damn Kit. Hannah knew her friend was doing what she thought was best, but Hannah didn't need Lincoln's questions. She opened her eyes and forced a smile for Ryan. "Thanks for dropping by."

Lynette walked into the office from the back door. "Hi, Ryan. I was going to call you. Jacob's third-grade class is having a Christmas wind-up Thursday afternoon and I thought you could bring Felix and introduce him to his classmates."

Ryan's smile was big and genuine and Hannah's breath caught in her throat. "That would be great, Lynette. What time?"

"From midday at the park by the river. They're having a barbecue, games, and make sure he brings his bathers because they'll probably swim too."

"I'll let Mrs Z know. It'll be good for him to meet some kids his age."

"No problem. If you tell her to bring him around here tomorrow after three, he can meet Jacob."

"Thanks, I'll do that."

Lynette turned to Hannah. "The cleaning is done and the plants have been watered. Anything else you need me to do?"

"No. Why don't you head off? I know you had some Christmas shopping you wanted to do."

"That would be wonderful. Thanks." She waved at the others. "I'll see you later."

"I'd better get going as well," Ryan said. "I've got to pick up Felix."

When the door was shut Fleur fanned herself. "*That* was Ryan Kilpatrick? He just got better with age, and he was fine to begin with."

Hannah busied herself with tidying up the desk.

"Hannah?"

She cleared her throat. "Yeah, I mentioned last night that he's good-looking."

Fleur put a hand on her arm and raised both eyebrows. "Honey, what happened to you was horrible, but you can't let it stop you from moving on with your life. Not all guys are like Justin and your dad. There are good men out there: my dad,

Lincoln, Jamie, your granddad."

The idea of going on a date, being alone with a man in that way, made her feel ill. She wished things were different, wished she could be like other women and date. She shook her head. "Rationally I know that, Fleur, but emotionally …" She held up a hand. "I can't go there."

Fleur sighed. "There are some good counsellors up at the hospital. Think about it." She smiled. "In the meantime, it's not going to hurt to look at some eye candy like that."

Hannah grinned, relieved she'd dropped the subject. "You're right."

Ryan was very easy on the eye and perhaps she could let her imagination run away with her.

It didn't mean she was going to act on it.

Chapter 4

Ryan drove out to the Zanetti farm, his thoughts on Hannah and what he'd interrupted. Seeing Hannah's fear of Justin had Ryan's protective instinct kicking into gear, and he'd lied about needing to speak to her, something that definitely wasn't appropriate while he was in uniform.

Perhaps, his empathy was too strong because he'd seen his fair share of domestic abuse cases while working up north. Been on the receiving end more than a few times as well, and the feelings of helplessness, confusion and fear weren't ones he was going to forget anytime soon. He wanted to hear Hannah's story, wanted to help her.

Ryan sighed. Only two days in town and he was already involved in the community. He'd forgotten that was what being in a small town was like.

Turning off the main highway, he drove along the dirt road that led to the farmhouse. He slowed the car as he came to a junction lined with half a dozen letterboxes, then turned and headed along the road to where he used to live. The properties out here were all five to ten acres in size, and a mixture of hobby farms and single residences. Peppermint trees grew close to the road, hiding the buildings from view, making them even more secluded and secret.

He pulled up in front of a driveway. Through the trees was a large stone house with gardens, both functional vegetable patches and beautiful clumps of roses in bloom. There was no remnant of the composting toilet, or the rusted urn they'd used to heat the water for their outdoor shower.

When he'd lived here, there'd been no house, and all the garden beds had been functional. It was here he'd realised that his parents hadn't owned the property. They weren't even renting, they were squatting, living in their caravan until someone realised and came to kick them off the land. It was why they'd moved so regularly at a moment's notice all through his childhood.

Sadness squeezed his chest. It was here – with Lincoln's help – he'd realised life didn't have to be the way his parents lived, that parents were supposed to care for their children instead of leaving them to their own devices, that having a little bit of money didn't mean you'd sold your soul to the devil.

It was here he'd decided he wanted more out of life.

And being so clueless as to what normal life was like had led him straight into the problems with Paula.

He sighed and did a U-turn. He was starting over – again – but this time he was going to do it right.

As he took the driveway into the Zanettis' property, he waved to Mr Z, who was walking from the cheese factory to the shop. The house came into view and Felix was playing on the swing set up under a peppermint tree. Felix waved at him and leapt off the swing. By the time Ryan had come to a complete stop, Felix was by the car.

"Hi, Dad!"

Felix's enthusiasm always cheered him up, always made him feel as if he was important. "Hey. How was your day?"

"Awesome! Mr Z showed me how to make cream and then Mrs Z taught me how to bake a cake and we topped it with fresh cream that came from the cows next door." His eyes were wide as if he could hardly believe it.

Ryan grinned and forgot his concerns. "Any of that cake left over?"

"Yeah. We saved you a piece. Come inside."

He let his son drag him inside the farmhouse and into the kitchen, where Mrs Z was pouring boiling water into a teapot.

"I thought it would be you." She smiled. "Would you like a

cuppa?"

"If you're having one." The Zanettis were doing so much for him and he didn't want to take advantage of them. Mrs Z had refused any payment for taking care of Felix.

"Always. Felix, why don't you get out the mugs?"

The boy hurried to the cupboard and fetched three mugs.

"Better get four," Mrs Z said to Felix. "I'm sure Nonno will be along shortly." She turned to Ryan. "How was your day?"

"Good." He told her about Lynette's offer. "I met Kit and Fleur today as well. Lincoln tells me they used to play with Jamie."

Mrs Z smiled. "Yeah. Where there's one musketeer, there's usually another not far behind. Those girls are the best of friends. You should stop by On the Way bakery and meet Mai. She makes the best vanilla slice in the world."

"I might do that."

There was a scuffle at the back door as Mr Z took off his boots and walked in. "G'day."

"Nonno, we're having cake and tea," Felix called.

"Sounds great." Mr Z shook Ryan's hand.

Ryan loved how comfortable Felix was in the Zanettis' house. This is what he wanted for his son – warmth, love, comfort and people who wanted to be with him. Felix deserved to be spoilt a little. He barely saw either of his grandparents – Paula's parents lived in Perth and he wasn't exactly sure which state his parents were in at the moment, but they had never paid their grandchild much attention. The last time he'd heard from his sister, over six months ago, she was in Tasmania and going off grid, whatever that meant.

"How's work?" Mr Z asked.

"Good. Adam and Sue are nice and the boss isn't too much of an ogre," he joked. "I've already met Fairy Floss and Shirley Jameson."

Mr Z smirked and Mrs Z lightly smacked his arm. "Shirley's a lovely woman. She's just lonely. Has she got her eye on you?"

"She seemed keen on Adam when we took the dog back."

"Poor dear. That boy is so green. I don't know why he became a cop. He's far too nice."

"Hey!" Ryan protested.

Mrs Z smiled. "You know what I mean. He's naive and optimistic. You, on the other hand, left your naivety behind a long time ago."

That was true, though he'd been far too optimistic in his life, always hoping for the best in people and being constantly let down. "So, is there anyone in town I need to keep an eye on?"

"You'll find out soon enough," Mrs Z said. "I don't want to put ideas in your head."

"What's Hannah's place like?" Mr Z asked. "She's only shown a few people what she's up to in there."

"Really nice. The cabin is small, but for a short getaway it's perfect. She's working on another place, but that's all I know."

"She told Lincoln there were going to be conference facilities there eventually. Kind of like a corporate getaway or something," Mrs Z said.

Sounded expensive. "Has she got any investors?"

"She's doing a lot herself. She inherited the land from her mother, but I don't know where she got the money for the buildings."

Running a caravan park wouldn't bring in much money.

"Dad, can we go to the beach later?" Felix asked. "I want to see the ocean."

"Sure. We'll drive by on the way home."

Ryan smiled as Felix did a happy dance. He pushed work and Hannah aside. This was Felix's time. He deserved Ryan's absolute attention.

He glanced at Mrs Z. "Which is the best beach from here?"

There was another gift waiting at the office door on Wednesday morning. The card with it read, *On the second day of Christmas ...*

Hannah's lungs squeezed, making it hard to breathe. Images of her mother flashed through her mind, slightly faded by time. She'd loved the "Twelve Days of Christmas" song, and each day in the lead-up to Christmas she had given her husband and Hannah some small token. Hannah had forgotten about it until now.

Slowly, her hands trembling, she unwrapped two china

turtledove ornaments.

She closed her eyes as the pain of the past washed over her, leaving goosebumps on her skin. Whoever was sending her the gifts couldn't possibly know about her personal connection to the song. Her father was still in jail, still had two more years of his sentence to serve. So who the hell was it? No one had shown the slightest bit of interest in her lately; she'd had no invitations to coffee or the outdoor cinema, no one interested at all – except Justin. She shivered.

Fleur took the card from her. "Do you recognise the writing?"

"No." She placed the box on the desk. One gift was OK, but two was definitely unsettling. The rest of the line of the song went *my true love sent to me* and the words *true love* sounded kind of obsessive to her. How could someone be her true love if she didn't know who they were? They couldn't know her. Or was she reading far too much into this?

"Shall I put them on the filing cabinet?" Fleur said.

Hannah nodded. It would do for now. She didn't want to fixate on it and Lincoln would question why she was making such a fuss if she mentioned it to him. For all she knew, it was one of her guests doing something nice for her. Though she doubted it.

Unease clung to her skin as she got to work. When Lynette arrived, Hannah was relieved to get out of the office. She needed space to breathe and the office had lost its sense of security.

Together with Fleur, she did the necessary rounds of the park. They worked in a nice rhythm and it reminded her of when they'd shared a house in Perth. They'd dedicated Saturday afternoon to cleaning and spent the time talking about classes or friends. Today the topic of conversation was unfortunately Ryan. Fleur was scrubbing shower tiles while Hannah cleaned the toilets.

Fleur broke the silence. "Why do you think he left his wife?"

Hannah frowned. "Who?"

"Ryan. He must have left her. No sane woman would let someone that gorgeous go."

"Just because he's attractive, doesn't mean he's a nice

person." Justin had showed her that.

"He's gotta be nice," Fleur said. "He's Lincoln's best friend. Slinky doesn't put up with dickheads."

She was right. Lincoln didn't suffer fools. So, it was likely that Ryan was a decent guy. He'd probably be a real gentleman on a date. *You should ask Ryan out.* Hannah blocked the voice. It was ridiculous to even contemplate. Not only would it be impossible for Ryan to live up to her teenage fantasies, but she struggled to be alone with any man. She could hardly take Joe on a date with her. Besides, the idea of going on a date again made all her warning signals flash and scream. It wasn't safe.

So what if when Ryan had interrupted Justin yesterday, she'd been so relieved she'd wanted to hug him. That was instinctive. It didn't mean she liked or trusted him.

She changed the subject and scrubbed harder.

Later that afternoon, Hannah worked in the office with Lynette, reviewing the marketing plan and serving customers. Lynette was chatting to a couple when a delivery woman arrived. Hannah hesitated. She could hardly interrupt Lynette and make her go outside. It wouldn't be good customer service. Plus, there was nothing to be afraid of. Justin wasn't here and she could sign for the goods.

She called Joe and went outside. The delivery driver had already started unloading the large boxes. When she was done, Hannah got the electric cart to move the goods into the storeroom. It took her three trips and Joe moved over to the lawn, where Jacob and Felix were playing. She kept an eye on him for a minute to make sure he wasn't being rough, and then scanned the park.

She would be fine in the storeroom. Joe was close by. Still, her heart beat a little faster as she unpacked the first box full of toilet paper. She started on the next box when a voice behind her said, "Don't you have someone to do the grunt work for you?"

Her skin crawled and she whipped around fast. Justin leaned against the doorframe, the only exit to the room. Her heart thumped hard in her chest and her mouth went dry. She had to get out of here, had to move, to speak, to do something. She swallowed. *Don't show him your fear.* She had a plan. She had to work through it.

But that had involved having a counter between them.

"What are you doing here?" she croaked.

"I wanted to see you." He stepped forward.

She stepped back, bumping into the box on the ground. "What about?"

He smiled. "I've missed you, Hannah. You disappeared without a trace and I've always wondered where you went." He wrapped his hand around one of the struts holding up the shelves.

Her attention was captured by his hand. She knew the strength of it, knew how rough and hard it was, knew what it could do to her. Her heart rate increased. *Focus.* "Shouldn't you be surfing?"

"Nah." He took another step forward. "The surf's been crap."

He was close, way too close. All he had to do was reach out and he would touch her. He could trap her against the wall and do whatever he wanted with her. Her breath came in short pants. She needed Joe. She glanced over Justin's shoulder, where her dog was still playing with the kids. "I-I have work to do," she stuttered.

"Looks like you're about finished to me." He brushed his hand along her arm.

She froze, watching him like a mouse face to face with a snake.

"I always had a fantasy about doing the maid in the storeroom," he murmured.

Her stomach heaved. No. She wouldn't go through this again. She tried to whistle, but her mouth was too dry. She licked her lips and his gaze dropped to her mouth. Sweat broke out on her skin. Losing all pretence of not being scared, she yelled as loudly as she could.

Ryan walked around the corner of the holiday park office and spotted Felix playing with a young boy and Hannah's dog. Where was Hannah?

"Joe!" Hannah's yell was high-pitched and terrified. Joe whirled around, hackles raised, and ran towards the storeroom. Ryan raced after him, heart pounding.

Hannah was cowered in a corner, her eyes wide, skin pale and Justin standing over her.

Son of a bitch.

Justin spun around as Joe barrelled past him to Hannah, barking wildly. Her hand shook as she placed it on Joe's head.

Ryan stepped into the room. "Is everything all right in here?"

Hannah scrambled to her feet and put a hand on her chest as her eyes met his. "Ryan." Her relief was evident.

"Absolutely," Justin said. "We were catching up." He took a step towards Hannah, but Joe's growl had him moving back.

"Hannah?" Ryan asked. Some of the colour was seeping back into her face.

"I was just finishing." She closed the box. Her eyes darted between Justin and Ryan, as if measuring the distance between each one.

Justin smiled. "If you're finished, why don't we go for a drink? My shout."

"No!" Hannah cleared her throat. "I already have plans."

"Change them," Justin said.

Ryan didn't like Justin's tone, or his arrogance. Hannah's gaze flittered towards the doorway, and he moved further into the room, clearing the way so she could exit. She met his gaze and her smile was tremulous. It ripped right into his heart. He wanted to offer her words of comfort, but she was already responding to Justin.

"I can't."

"Why not?" Justin asked.

Her eyes widened and she glanced around the room, as if looking for an excuse. "Because I'm having dinner with Ryan." Her expression begged him to play along.

He fought to hide his surprise and slowly moved forward, placing himself between Justin and Hannah. He smiled at Justin.

"That's right."

Justin frowned. "Didn't you just arrive in town?"

How did he know that? It made Ryan distinctly uneasy. "Yeah, but Hannah and I go way back." He gently drew her to his side, closer to the door. "Why don't you lock up and we can discuss where we're going?" He nudged her out of the room.

Her breath whooshed out as she stepped into the open area.

Justin still stood inside.

"Coming?" Ryan asked.

"Yeah." Justin ran a hand through his hair, a scowl on his face. "I was looking forward to catching up with you. I might see you out tonight."

As he walked off, Hannah sagged against Ryan.

"It's all right," Ryan murmured. "I've got you." He put an arm around her shaking body.

"Dad?" Felix called, his face concerned.

"Everything's fine." He waved at the boys. "Keep playing and I'll be back in a minute." He took her keys and locked the door, then with Joe by Hannah's side, he walked her back into the office, where she collapsed onto a chair in the kitchen, buried her head in her hands and started crying. Joe shoved his head into her lap.

Ryan's throat tightened. Whatever Justin had done to her, it had been bad – not a simple breakup. He wanted to wrap his arms around her and comfort her, but he didn't want to scare her further.

"Hannah, is that you?" Lynette called. She came into the room and her mouth dropped open. "What's wrong? What happened?" She glared at Ryan as she hurried over and put her arms around Hannah.

"A run-in with her ex," Ryan said.

"That bastard. What did he do?"

"I'm not sure," he said, but he wanted to know. Hannah was a complete mess. "Where's Fleur?"

"She had to pick up her dad from the hospital. He had a fall." Lynette rubbed Hannah's back. Slowly Hannah's sobs lessened.

The bell in the front office rang. Lynette looked towards the door and then at Ryan.

"Why don't you get that?" Ryan said. "I'll stay with her." He pulled out a chair and sat down, careful to keep his distance and his body language open and non-threatening.

"You going to be OK, Hannah?" Lynette asked.

Hannah lifted her head and nodded, wiping the tears from her face.

Ryan waited until Lynette was gone before saying, "Want to tell me what happened?"

She glanced at him and then away. "He didn't do anything."

"Not this time, maybe," Ryan agreed. "But at some stage he did."

Hannah stared at him and then gave a tiny nod.

"I can't help if I don't know what I'm up against," he said.

"It's not your problem."

The words annoyed him, but he didn't let it show. "Sure it is." He smiled. "You're my date tonight, aren't you?"

"Oh, no. Of course not." She looked horrified. "I said that to get rid of him."

"Yes, but if he doesn't see us tonight, he might get suspicious." It was a small town and there weren't too many places to go. "If I were Justin and didn't see you on a date, I'd ask you out again tomorrow." He hated the scared expression on her face. Perhaps it was wrong of him to push, but he wanted to help her.

"You have Felix to worry about."

He'd have a couple of hours to spend with Felix before he went out and Lincoln would babysit, especially when Ryan told him what had happened. "I'll find someone to look after him."

Hannah appeared almost as panicked about the idea of a date with him as she had in the storeroom. At least he didn't have to worry about her reading more into the offer. He wasn't looking for a woman in his life.

"It's just for show," Ryan promised her. "We'll have a nice meal, you can tell me about your retreat and fill me in on the Blackbridge gossip and then I'll drop you at home."

"I'm staying with Fleur."

"Even better," Ryan said. "How about I pick you up at six-thirty?"

"What's this?" Lynette asked as she walked in.

"Hannah told her ex we were going on a date tonight to get rid of him. I think it's worth going out in case he's looking for us."

"Great idea," Lynette said. "Going out with a sexy man on your arm will cheer you up." She winked at Ryan.

Ryan chuckled.

Hannah took a deep, shuddery breath. "All right." She gave him a small smile. "Thank you."

Her quiet thanks hit him right in the chest. She looked thoroughly defenceless and exhausted. This was his good deed for the day – he wasn't getting more involved than this. He got to his feet. "I'd better go and get Felix. Should I pick you up from here?"

"No. I'll get ready at Fleur's." She gave him the address.

He smiled. "I'll see you in a couple of hours."

Excitement at the idea of going out with Hannah shimmered over him as he walked out. That wasn't good. He was just doing something nice.

He wasn't interested in Hannah Novak in that way.

Not at all.

Chapter 5

"Justin did what?" Fleur shrieked.

Fleur's father glanced at them through the kitchen door, so Hannah dragged Fleur further into the living room.

"He caught me in the storeroom." Hannah was able to speak calmly now that it was over. After Ryan had left, Lynette had insisted she'd close the office, and Hannah had been more than happy to agree. She'd dashed back to her shed to get something suitable to wear on tonight's date and was now at Fleur's place, trying to ignore the nerves storming her stomach.

"Are you all right? Where was Joe?"

"Joe was playing with Lynette's kids." She should have kept him by her side, shouldn't have been so trusting. "He came as soon as I called."

"You're not hurt?"

"No." Not physically. She sighed. "I froze, Fleur. There was no fight-or-flight response from me, it was like I was solid ice." That was probably the scariest thing. Why couldn't she fight back, or at least run? She'd had a plan and it had vanished the moment Justin had appeared.

An image of her mother lying dead on the floor stabbed into her mind and she clutched her stomach in pain. OK, so she knew why she couldn't fight.

"Maybe we should do some self-defence classes. I'm sure Lincoln can teach us a few things."

It was a good idea, and she trusted Lincoln. Perhaps if she knew what to do, she wouldn't freeze. "I'll ask him about it tomorrow."

"So what do you want to do tonight?" Fleur asked as she walked back towards the kitchen.

Hannah cringed. "I'm, uh, actually going on a date."

"What?" Fleur whirled around and stared at her.

Hannah winced. "Ryan arrived when Justin had me trapped. I needed an excuse when Justin asked me out, so I said I was going out with Ryan." She should have said no and not given him a reason – he didn't deserve one. "Now, Ryan believes it's a good idea that we have dinner in case Justin is around town."

"I'm *sure* he does." Fleur's smile was quick, but then she sobered. "Are you going to be OK? Do you want me to be nearby just in case?"

When had she become this timid, useless woman whose friends thought needed help? She didn't want to be helpless or useless or so damned scared all the time. Hannah shook her head. "No. I'm sure it'll be fine. It's not a real date." Maybe if she said it enough times she'd believe it.

"I'm only a phone call away if you need me."

"Thanks." It did make her feel better. Going out in Blackbridge felt safer because she knew so many people. They'd all be keeping an eye on her.

"So what are you going to wear?" Fleur asked, her eyes shining.

Hannah smiled at Fleur's enthusiasm. "I brought options. I haven't been on a date since ..." Her optimism deflated. "Justin."

"Then it's past time you went out again."

Fleur was right. She was taking the first step towards a normal life, even if tonight wasn't real.

"You can help me decide." She headed towards the guest bedroom.

A couple of hours later, Hannah smoothed down the front of the green summer dress she was wearing. The low, strappy white heels were already making her feet ache a little as she paced across Fleur's living room waiting for Ryan. She fiddled with her hair, not sure whether the gel she'd put in was going to last the night.

"Stop that." Fleur lightly slapped her hand away. "You'll mess it up. You look gorgeous."

"It's not too much is it?" They weren't going on a proper date. She didn't want Ryan to think she was interested in him. Even if she kind of was. Which was stupid. He was doing her a favour – he barely knew her.

"It's perfect," Fleur assured her as there was a knock on the door. "That'll be him now. Right on time." She hurried to answer the door and Hannah followed, her chest tight. Slowly, she let out the breath she was holding.

Her footsteps faltered as Ryan filled the doorway. His blue jeans were snug and the black V-neck shirt clung to his broad chest, showing off his muscle definition. She itched to run her hands over his chest, and the depth of her desire startled her. She shook her head. That way led to danger.

"You take care of my girl tonight," Fleur said.

Hannah winced. She wanted to be able to take care of herself. "We'll be fine."

Ryan looked over and his eyes widened. His smile was warm and genuine, and it sent a thrill through her. "Hannah. You look lovely."

She brushed a hand over her dress, avoiding his gaze as her cheeks heated. "Thanks. So do you." She groaned inwardly. This was awkward. "Shall we go?"

He nodded. She told Joe to stay, fighting the unease of going out without him. Nothing bad was going to happen.

As they walked out to his four-wheel drive Fleur yelled, "Have fun!"

Ryan opened the door for her. "It's a bit of a step up," he said. "Do you need a hand?"

The thought of Ryan's hands on her heated her body. "I'll be fine," she said quickly. "Thank you." What was wrong with her? Her body was behaving completely inappropriately. She climbed into the car and adjusted her skirt as he went around to the driver's side.

Backing out of the driveway, he said, "I've booked us into Little Italy."

Hannah grinned. "That's my favourite restaurant."

"Lincoln recommended it." He cleared his throat. "If we do see Justin, we should probably hold hands or something." His expression was apologetic. "To make it appear like we're serious and hopefully he'll leave you alone. Are you OK with that?"

For the first time in a very long time, the idea of a man touching her wasn't so scary. But she couldn't get carried away – this was pretend. "Sure."

"Good. Lincoln and I want this guy to get the hint that you're not interested."

"Me too."

He pulled up to the restaurant. "Wait there." He got out and hurried around to open the door for her.

Heat rushed to her cheeks. It was such an old-fashioned gesture and it made her feel special. "Thank you."

He took her hand, his grip warm and gentle. Her pulse raced in response, more attraction than fear. She would enjoy it while it lasted.

Inside the restaurant, the maître d' grinned. "Hi, Hannah, how's it going?"

"Fine thanks, Torben. This is Ryan. He's our new senior constable."

"I've got a table booked under Kilpatrick," Ryan told him.

"Of course." Torben checked his book. "This way."

There were questions on Torben's face. Hannah hadn't considered this aspect of the date. The whole town was going to be buzzing that she had been out with the new cop. She hated gossip, but it couldn't be helped.

After he had given them menus and left, Hannah glanced around. She knew quite a few of the people there and they were watching them with interest.

"Is everything OK?" Ryan asked.

"Do you realise we're going to be the talk of the town tomorrow?"

"Really?"

She nodded and scanned the restaurant as Justin walked in with two other guys. She stared, her chest tight. He'd said he was going out tonight, and there weren't that many restaurants in town for him to choose from. It had to be a coincidence that he'd chosen the same one she was in.

"It's all right, Hannah. He can't hurt you here." Ryan's words were soothing and he brushed her hand, the warmth sending tingles up her arm.

"I can't help it." She sighed in frustration. "I want him to leave me alone." She wanted to keep an eye on Justin, know exactly where he was. Having him behind her somewhere made her skin crawl.

"He's looking right now." Ryan's smile was slow and wicked. "Laugh as if I'm the funniest guy in the world."

His words made her genuinely laugh and she resisted checking Justin's reaction.

"We should give him a little bit of a show," Ryan continued. His fingertips caressed the back of her hand and a burn started in the bottom of her stomach. It was such a foreign sensation, but it was pleasant. A tiny part of her wished the display wasn't a game.

"Can you pretend I've captured your heart?" he asked.

It was easier than she'd like it to be. She was attracted to Ryan. It made her more confident. She could do this. She linked her fingers with his.

"Absolutely." She winked.

He brought her hand to his mouth and kissed it, his lips warm and soft against her skin. His breath tickled her. "Shall we order?"

She was caught in his gaze, his hazel eyes watching her, waiting for her reaction. She nodded, unable to speak, and drew back her hand. His gaze was intense, but she wasn't afraid.

"Hannah, what a coincidence."

Justin's voice shocked her out of her trance. He was within touching distance and Hannah pushed back her chair, her heart racing. For a second she'd forgotten all about him.

"Can we join you?" Justin asked, picking up a chair from a nearby table.

Hannah couldn't speak, couldn't even process his words. He still wore the same overpowering aftershave, and the stench took her right back to that night.

"No." Ryan's voice was firm.

Justin halted halfway through sitting and stood up again. "Oh. Right. Sorry."

One of Justin's friends laughed. "They're on a date, idiot." He followed Torben to a table behind Ryan.

Justin's face flushed and he put the chair back. Without another word he left.

Hannah flinched as Ryan took her hand. "You're safe, Hannah."

She blinked and tore her eyes from where Justin was sitting facing her. "What?"

"You're safe," he repeated. "I won't let anything happen to you." He was watching her like she was a skittish horse.

Hannah let out a deep breath. She could do this. She could enjoy dinner with this kind, gorgeous man. And she had Justin in her sights, so he couldn't sneak up on her. She would be fine. She opened the menu again. "I have so many favourite dishes," she said, trying to get her equilibrium back, trying for normal, casual.

"Great, maybe you can recommend something."

She couldn't focus on the words in front of her. Her eyes kept flicking to where Justin was sitting. She cursed inwardly. This was ridiculous. To regain her composure she asked, "Are you enjoying Blackbridge?"

"So far." Ryan smiled. "Felix has been talking non-stop about the Zanettis' cheese factory and today he had a great time playing with Jacob. They're going to be good friends."

Hannah liked the way Ryan's face lit up when he spoke about his son. "Where is he tonight?"

"Lincoln is babysitting. When I left they were talking about movies, popcorn and chocolate." He laughed. "I should leave Felix there overnight and then Lincoln will discover what a sugared-up eight-year-old is capable of."

"He'd definitely deserve it," Hannah agreed. "So, you two kept in touch after you left Blackbridge?"

He nodded. "It was Lincoln who convinced me to become a cop. We went through the academy together and then I got posted to Karratha and he jagged a posting here."

"What was Karratha like?"

"It was an experience."

Torben came to take their order.

"Do you want to share a bottle of wine?" Ryan asked.

"No." She shook her head. Alcohol and dating weren't a good mix. "I, uh, don't drink much. I'll have a lemon, lime and bitters." She didn't want anything to skew her judgement tonight.

"All right." He ordered a beer and after Torben left he said, "Tell me about the retreat you're building."

Hannah sat back. "Are you sure? I need to warn you, once I start I'll probably bore you to tears."

His laidback grin had her smiling in return. "I don't bore easily."

"I'm beginning with the cabins," she said. "Ten in all, spread out over the property, so they can't be seen. Each one is going to be like its own private hideaway."

"If they're all like my cabin, they'll be wonderful."

"Thank you." She beamed at him, pleasure rushing through her at his compliment. "I'm going to set up a couple of walking trails through the bush as well as a path down to the beach, and offer a booking service for those who want to do things outside of the property." Torben delivered the drinks and she took a sip. "When that's finished, I'm building a conference facility in the middle of the property. I want to put on different kinds of events there: writers' and artists' retreats – get a high-profile teacher in and have a week or weekend of intense creativity."

She wanted to provide experiences for people, things they would remember and enjoy. She wanted to bring joy to people's lives.

"Sounds ambitious," Ryan commented.

She nodded, the nerves always there when she thought about it. She couldn't afford to fail. "It's a five-year plan," she said. "After the cabins start bringing in money, I'll work on the conference facility."

"That's great." He held up his beer bottle. "Here's wishing you every success."

Hannah gently tapped her glass against his. "Thank you." She took a sip. "So, tell me about Karratha. I've never been that far north."

"It's red, dry and dusty," Ryan said. "But the people are nice, and the landscape is incredible. I used to take Felix camping when I had a few days off, and at night the stars were so bright and it was so quiet you could hear yourself think."

His enthusiasm captured her, but he didn't mention his ex. Dare she ask? "Sounds lovely. Why did you move?"

He pursed his lips and his eyes lost their passion.

She wished she hadn't asked. "It doesn't matter."

"No, it's fine. I should get used to talking about it." He waited until their food was delivered and then continued. "It was never really home to me," he said. "When I split up with Felix's mum, I decided to come back here."

She wanted to ask more about his ex, but it wasn't any of her business. She tasted her pasta, the creamy sauce dancing lightly over her tongue. It was delicious. "Have you been surfing yet?"

"How did you know I surfed?"

She blushed. She shouldn't have mentioned it, now she had to explain. "You and Lincoln used to go surfing all the time," she said. "You'd park near the holiday park and I'd see you walk down." No way was she admitting that she used to wait nearby, hoping to catch a glimpse of him. "One day when you were driving home, you stopped to help me when I fell off my bicycle."

His eyes widened and he grinned. "I remember that now. No wonder you looked familiar to me. Your knees were so full of gravel and you were trying not to cry."

"I didn't want to seem like a baby in front of you," she admitted.

"I thought you were very brave." He brushed her hand again.

She smiled, more comfortable now. "And you were my hero. The way you picked me up and carried me to your car was like straight out of a fairy tale."

He laughed. "I wouldn't go that far."

She tried for a playful tone. "I would. I was twelve and this dashingly handsome seventeen-year-old was rescuing me." It was a fantasy she'd played out many times.

His cheeks went red and he reached for his beer bottle. "You were a kid."

Delighted that he was embarrassed, she said, "Yeah. How I wished I was five years older."

He choked, almost spitting out his beer. "I didn't even notice you like that."

She heaved a sigh. "I know. The girls and I had fun making up stories about you though." It was quite amazing the shade of red he was turning. She hadn't had this much fun with a guy in a very long time.

He swallowed. "Well, you're all grown up now."

Hannah's smile fled. His expression almost seemed like he was interested. But he couldn't be. This wasn't a real date. She didn't want him to be interested in her.

Liar.

She cleared her throat, not letting her agitation show. "So, who did you crush on as a kid?"

He examined her while he thought about it. "We never hung around in one place long enough for me to really crush on anyone," he said. "Blackbridge was the longest I stayed anywhere. There was one girl though." He closed his eyes for a moment. "Sherry?"

"Sherry Laverie?" Hannah asked. "Blonde hair, big boobs."

He nodded. "That sounds like her."

Hannah smirked. "Figures. All the guys crushed on Sherry's boobs."

"Hey, don't go judging me," he protested. "I was seventeen. All I thought about was surfing and sex."

A memory surfaced of her Year Twelve ball. Lincoln had gathered the musketeers into a room and told them to be careful. Told them boys were only after one thing. They had laughed at his big-brother antics and Fleur and Kit had shocked him by telling him they hoped that was what their dates were after. It had all seemed like a laugh. But only a couple of years later, Justin had proven Lincoln right.

Her appetite left her and she placed her cutlery together in her bowl.

Ryan brushed her hand, his eyes concerned.

She withdrew her hand and forced a smile to her face. "Have you seen any good movies lately?"

Hannah was disappointed when Ryan said, "We should make a move. I need to make sure Felix gets to bed."

Two hours had flown by. Aside from Justin coming over to the table, the rest of the evening had been lovely. Ryan was easy to talk to. "Of course." She stood, and together they walked over to the counter to pay, Ryan's hand brushing her lower back. Lovely tingles spread through her.

As the waiter gave the total, she reached into her bag.

"I'll pay," Ryan said.

"Oh no, I—"

He leaned closer and murmured in her ear, "We're on a date, remember?" His lips brushed her cheek in a light kiss.

Hannah's brain short-circuited. By the time it had rebooted, Ryan had paid and taken her hand, leading her out of the restaurant. As she walked to the car, Justin watched them through the window. Adrenaline surged through her. She'd forgotten he was still there, forgotten this was all pretend. Fear pushed away the temporary attraction. As Ryan held open the car door for her, she said, "I'll pay you back tomorrow."

He smiled.

What did that smile mean? Had he forgotten this was pretend? Was he expecting more? Goosebumps rose to her skin.

She squeezed her eyes shut. Not now. Don't get freaked out now when things were going well. Just be alert.

Ryan turned down the wrong street and Hannah sat up straight, blood pounding in her head. "This isn't the way to Fleur's house." Had she been so wrong about him? Was he going to take her somewhere isolated where no one could hear her scream? She reached for the door handle, not sure what to do.

"It's OK, Hannah," Ryan said, his tone calm. "Don't panic. I think we're being followed."

"What?" The idea was so ridiculous it took a moment for it to sink in. She shifted in her seat to look at the headlights at the far end of the street.

"Tell me which way to go," Ryan said. "Make it random and double-back so I can check. It might be someone heading home for the night."

Hannah did as he asked, directing him around the block and up and down a couple of streets, tension seeping into her bones.

"Yep, we're being followed." Ryan swore.

"Who would follow us?" Was he lying, trying to trick her so she let down her guard?

"My guess is Justin," he said. "Unless you've got another admirer I don't know about."

She gasped. Those gifts left at the office. What if they weren't from Justin?

He glanced at her. "What?"

"Someone has been leaving me gifts." She told him about them.

"I want to see them tomorrow," he said. "But right now, we have two options. I can try to lose whoever is following us – which might be hard since the town is small and this car is easily identifiable – or I can take you back to Fleur's. I should be able to get a look at the car when I walk you to the door."

She squeezed her hands together. Why the hell would Justin – would anyone – want to follow her, especially when she was with a police officer? "Take me to Fleur's." She wanted to be locked inside where she was safe.

"All right." He was quiet as they drove back to Fleur's. As she was about to get out of the car he stopped her, a hand on her arm. "Wait here for a moment. The car pulled into a driveway a few doors down. It's too far away to get a number plate." He swore. "OK, here's what we're going to do. I'm going to come around and open your door. Then we're heading straight inside. Call Fleur and make sure the door is open."

Hannah nodded as fear took hold of her chest. She phoned Fleur and explained. The light came on out front and she said, "It's unlocked."

"Great." He got out and came around to open her door.

Hannah slipped out and with Ryan behind her, holding her hand, she hurried to the door, her shoulderblades itching. Fleur opened the door as she reached the porch and she raced inside.

Ryan dropped her hand. "I'll be back in a sec."

Before Hannah could react, he sprinted back outside, heading for the parked car. Hannah gasped as he crossed the road. The car roared to life and backed out, heading straight for Ryan.

"Look out!"

Ryan dived to the side, over a small picket fence in the neighbour's yard, as the car sped off.

Hannah ran towards him, her vision locked on where he'd disappeared, wanting to hear him, see him. Had he been hit? Was he hurt? She reached the fence as Ryan stood up and brushed himself off. "Are you all right?"

"Get back inside," he ordered. He jumped the fence and took her by the arm, his grip firm. Fear coursed through Hannah as she glanced down the road, but the car was long gone.

Fleur was on the porch waiting for them. "What the hell was that about?"

"We were followed," Ryan said.

"Did you get the plates?" Hannah asked.

He shook his head. "It was covered in mud." Up on the porch, he brushed the dirt off his arms. "I don't like this, Hannah. Tomorrow I want to look at those gifts you've been receiving."

Fleur gasped. "Are they related?"

"Could be."

Ryan had a couple of leaves in his hair and despite his agitation, Hannah felt safe with him. She reached up and brushed out the leaves and then froze. She was only centimetres from him.

"I'll see you inside." Fleur closed the door.

Hannah didn't move and neither did Ryan. They stood only inches apart.

She wanted to kiss him. Would it be wrong to kiss him? He was here as a favour, and yet she couldn't bring herself to step back. She licked her lips and Ryan's gaze dropped. Her heart fluttered.

He brushed her hair back from her face with the gentlest of touches. "I should be going."

She nodded, but neither of them moved.

Slowly, ever so slowly, Ryan bent down and then his lips met hers. He tasted like coffee, his lips firm but gentle. She pressed into him, kissing him back, wanting more. She hadn't been kissed like this in … ever. His tongue tangled with hers and every nerve in her body warmed and danced in joy.

Suddenly Ryan stepped back, his breath fast. "Shit. I shouldn't have done that. I'm so sorry." He ran a hand through his hair as if undecided, and then headed for his car.

Hannah's cheeks flushed in embarrassment. What was he talking about? Why was he sorry?

This wasn't a real date.

It was like being doused with a bucket of cold water. Ryan wasn't really interested in her. He'd probably only meant to kiss her cheek and she'd launched herself at him like a love-starved fool, forcing him to kiss her.

She was an idiot.

Mortified, she hurried inside. There was no way she was sleeping tonight.

Hannah closed the front door as he backed out of the driveway. What the hell had he just done?

There was no way he should have kissed Hannah. They weren't dating, this had all been a way to help Hannah with Justin, and instead he'd forced himself on her.

He was such a douche.

But when Hannah had brushed the leaves out of his hair and captured his eyes, he'd forgotten himself for a minute. He'd forgotten everything except her. And her kisses were so sweet.

He focused on the road. The streets were quiet and there was no sign of the dark-blue sedan that had followed them.

He'd had a genuinely good time with Hannah tonight and that had surprised him. When she'd laughed, her whole face had lit up and he'd forgotten they were supposed to be pretending. He'd felt a stab of attraction.

That's why he kissed her. He actually liked Hannah.

Which was just stupid.

His taste in women couldn't be trusted – Paula was exhibit A. He wasn't ready to be involved with someone else either, not when he had Felix to consider. And especially not with one that he had a duty to protect. That would make things all kinds of messy.

He wanted simple.

But Hannah was beguiling in her own way.

He knocked on Lincoln's door and heard shrieks and laughter – both child and man – from inside. So much for getting Felix into bed. He knocked again, louder this time, and Lincoln shushed Felix, but his son giggled.

Lincoln opened the door. "Ryan, you're earlier than I expected."

Ryan raised an eyebrow. Over on the couch, Felix was lying down, a blanket over him, pretending to be asleep. "I wanted to make sure Felix got to bed at a decent time, since he's going to his class's end-of-school party tomorrow," he said. "Looks like I needn't have worried."

Lincoln winced and mouthed, "Sorry."

"How much junk did you give him?" Ryan asked quietly. Empty popcorn and chocolate packets were scattered over the coffee table.

"A bit." Lincoln had the grace to look bashful.

Ryan walked over and crouched by the couch. "Time to go, champ."

Felix opened his eyes and faked a yawn. "Dad, are you here already?"

Ryan swallowed his grin. "Yep. Have you brushed your teeth yet?"

"No."

Ryan opened Felix's backpack and took out his toothbrush and toothpaste. "Why don't you clean them before we go?" With any luck, Felix would fall asleep on the ride home.

"'K." Felix thundered down the corridor.

"Go to the toilet too," Ryan called after him. He sat on the couch and Lincoln sat next to him.

"That's a great kid you've got there," Lincoln said.

Heat radiated through Ryan's chest. "Thanks."

"So how was the date?"

Ryan scowled. "Justin tried to join us at the restaurant. Then we were followed back to Fleur's house."

"What?"

"A dark-blue sedan followed us from the restaurant. I went around the block a couple of times to check."

"This is getting serious," Lincoln said.

"Yeah, it almost hit me when I tried to get the plates."

Lincoln swore as Felix ran back out. "Finished!"

"I'll call you when I get Felix to bed." Ryan turned to his son. "What do you say?"

"Thanks for having me, Lincoln. Next time we'll have to build forts."

"Absolutely," Lincoln agreed, giving Felix a hug. "I'll see you later."

They said their goodbyes and Ryan drove them home, keeping one eye on the rear-view mirror.

No one followed them.

Chapter 6

Felix kept up an excited chatter about what he and Lincoln had done for the whole ride home. It was a relief that he'd had such a good time. Ryan had worried that Felix would be upset about Ryan going out without him.

By the time Ryan pulled up to the cabin, it was way past Felix's bedtime.

"Bed," Ryan ordered as they walked in. He gestured towards the bedroom.

"Aw, Dad, can't I stay up a bit later?"

Ryan suppressed a smile. "Not if you want to meet more of your classmates tomorrow."

Felix shrugged. "I don't mind."

"Don't you want to make friends?" He steered his son to the bedroom.

"I guess." He glanced up at Ryan. "But what if they don't like me?"

A lump lodged in Ryan's throat at the worry in his son's eyes. "What's not to like?" He smiled.

"Mum doesn't like me."

Guilt flooded him. He shouldn't have stayed with Paula so long, shouldn't have let Felix feel he was anything but loved. "Your mum has a few issues." He could hardly tell Felix she was a manipulative narcissist. He didn't want to be the one turning Felix against his mother – Paula was doing a good enough job of it herself. "I love you, and Mr and Mrs Z love you, and Lincoln loves you," he said. "And I'm pretty sure Jacob likes you too."

Felix clutched his hands together. "Was I a mistake?"

"No!" Ryan crouched down and hugged Felix fiercely. If only he could go back in time and leave Paula when Felix was first born. "You were *never* a mistake. You are the best thing in my life and I love you so much."

Felix burst into tears.

Ryan's heart broke as he picked up Felix and sat on the bed, with Felix on his lap. "I'll always be here for you, mate. No matter what happens. We're a team."

Felix looked up at him. "Promise?"

"I promise."

Felix sniffed.

"Come on, let's get you into bed." Ryan moved back the sheets. Felix crawled out of his arms and under the covers. Ryan switched off the light and lay next to him, not ready to leave, wanting to show Felix he was there. "Close your eyes."

"Will you sing me a song?"

Ryan smiled. "Sure. Got any requests?"

Felix shook his head and closed his eyes.

Ryan sang one of his favourite songs, the one he used to sing when Felix was a baby and wouldn't go to sleep. By the time he'd finished, Felix was snoring softly. Ryan lay there watching his son. He shouldn't have exposed Felix to such an unstable home life. By trying to make it work, by refusing to acknowledge that Paula was never going to change, he'd given Felix the instability that Ryan had suffered as a child. They might not have moved every year like his parents had, but Paula had been the same absentee mother that his own had been, always too caught up in her own life to care about her child.

He'd been so stupid, so stubborn and afraid to admit he'd made a mistake. He'd wanted to succeed at being a family so much that he couldn't see he had already failed.

He walked into the living room, scrubbing a hand over his face, his eyes heavy. All he wanted to do was climb into bed and forget about his past for a while, but he had to call Lincoln.

"You got Felix to sleep, then?" Lincoln said as he answered.

"Yeah." He sighed.

"What's up?"

Ryan told him about his conversation with Felix.

"Mate, I'm sorry. That's got to be hard to hear."

Hard wasn't the right word. It was devastating. "I thought I was doing the right thing. I thought it was better he have a mother and a father, a proper family. I thought I could do better than my parents did."

"You are doing better," Lincoln insisted. "Felix knows you love him. That's more than you had."

Ryan closed his eyes. He didn't want to think about his parents now.

"And having one parent who loves him, is better than having two parents who argue all the time or a mother who's a manipulative bitch."

Ryan was surprised at the anger in Lincoln's tone. "You're right. Thanks, mate."

"Hey, anytime you need me to tell you you're being an idiot, I'm here."

Ryan chuckled. "I'll keep that in mind."

"Tell me about being followed," Lincoln said.

He told Lincoln what had happened and then said, "There's more. Hannah told me she's been getting gifts from a secret admirer." He gave Lincoln the details. "So, the person who followed us might not have been Justin." He wasn't going to assume the incidents were all connected.

"Or he could be giving her the gifts as well."

"Yeah. I'll stop at the park on my way in tomorrow and check out what she's received."

"Thanks. I really don't like the sound of this." Lincoln sighed. "So how was the date?"

That was another issue Ryan didn't know how to solve.

"Ryan? It can't have been that bad, Hannah's a great person."

"No, it was fine. Fun, I guess." It wasn't the right word to use, but he couldn't tell Lincoln.

"You guess?"

"I'm not getting involved with anyone." His tone was tetchy, but he couldn't help it.

"No one's asking you to," Lincoln said. "It was for show — wasn't it?"

"Yes." He breathed deeply and closed his eyes. "I kissed her."

Lincoln was silent for a moment. "Is this where I'm supposed to congratulate you?"

"No! I shouldn't have. It was unprofessional." He paced the room. "It just kind of happened." The excuse was lame. He'd taken advantage of the situation.

"As long as Hannah was all right with it, I don't see the problem."

"She seemed OK." He grimaced. The way she'd kissed him had made him forget the date was fake.

"So don't worry about it. Hannah's a big girl. I'm sure she's been kissed plenty of times before."

Ryan hesitated. "I'm not so sure."

Lincoln laughed. "Mate, I hate to burst your bubble, but she's twenty-six. You're not the first guy who's kissed her."

Should he tell Lincoln his suspicions or was Lincoln too close to the musketeers? "Do you know what happened between her and Justin?" Her reaction to Justin and to himself had all his thoughts leading to one nasty place.

"No, the girls have withdrawn behind the barricades. Why, did she tell you?"

"Not yet." He hesitated. "I think he might have assaulted her."

"What makes you think that?" Lincoln's tone switched immediately into cop mode.

"When I found them in the storeroom she was cowering away from him. She was terrified."

"Hannah?" He sounded confused.

"Yeah. It reminded me of some of the domestic abuse cases I worked in Karratha."

"I'm not saying I don't believe you, but Hannah's always been so sure of herself," Lincoln said. "I can't imagine her putting up with some guy hitting her."

"Maybe he didn't hit her."

Lincoln swore. "Surely she would have pressed charges ..."

"Not everyone does." He gave Lincoln a minute to process

it. "I'm going to bed. I'll see you tomorrow."

"Yeah. I'm glad you're here."

"Me too." He hung up.

He had to be careful around Hannah. His concern for her wasn't to do with the job. He liked her.

Right now that was dangerous. Felix needed Ryan's full focus – he was fragile and needed to know he was loved. Ryan didn't have time for any other kind of relationship. He had to get used to his new job, get settled. He didn't need this extra complication.

And yet, part of him wanted it.

Hannah was relieved to leave Fleur's place the next morning and head to work. Fleur had wanted all the details of the date and Hannah wanted time to analyse it herself.

Tears pricked her eyes. The kiss had been *amazing*. She'd thought that part of her was broken, she'd thought she'd never be able to be intimate with a guy again. That one kiss had given her hope. Perhaps she could heal. Perhaps she could have a sexual relationship.

But wasn't it just her luck that those feelings, that attraction, were with a guy who wasn't interested in her?

She sighed as she pulled into her parking spot at the caravan park. It didn't matter that Ryan wasn't interested, what mattered was she was making progress.

She let Joe out of the car and wandered up to the office door. Joe ran ahead and was sniffing something in the doorway. As Hannah got closer she wrinkled her nose. Something smelled off, like raw meat on the turn. She glanced down, her eyes adjusting to the dimmer light. She gasped, feeling like she'd been punched in the stomach.

Three dead hens.

Their necks were broken and they were arranged so they were fanned out, their heads in the middle. A card lay on top, tied to the neck of the middle hen with red curling ribbon.

Her heart pounded and she whipped around to check if there was anyone nearby, anyone watching her. The park was quiet.

She grabbed Joe's collar and pulled him off, backing away from the doorway, as she took her phone from her pocket and hit Lincoln's number.

"What's wrong?" Lincoln asked, his voice full of sleep.

She swallowed. "There are three dead hens on my office step. I've been getting these gifts—"

"Ryan told me," Lincoln interrupted, now wide awake. "I'll be right there. Is there someone with you?"

"No. Fleur had a morning shift." She scanned her surroundings, but no one was about. Instead of being relieved, she was creeped out, expecting someone to step out from behind a tree, or the office.

"Can you call someone?"

She shook her head. "I'm fine. I'll stay out here with Joe, stop any customers from seeing it." There was no way anyone could sneak up on her, but her gaze roamed the surroundings anyway. Her shoulderblades itched as if she was being watched.

"I'm on my way now," Lincoln said. "Keep talking to me, I'm just around the corner."

Relief flooded her as Lincoln drove into the car park. She hung up and waited where she was as he strode over. His dark hair was dishevelled and his shirt was buttoned up incorrectly. He scanned the area and then asked, "Where are they?"

"On the front step."

"Stay here."

He took his phone out of his pocket and took some photos before making a call.

Hannah walked closer.

"Have you touched anything?"

"Joe was sniffing them, but I don't think he moved anything." She wrapped her arms around herself.

"You didn't touch the card?"

"No." She shuddered. As if she'd want to go near any of it. "What does it say?"

"I'll show you later. It's going to take me some time to process this, Hannah," Lincoln said. "Have you got any guests checking in or out this morning?"

"A couple."

"Can you move the office somewhere else for an hour or so?"

She could move her computer easily enough, but where to? The cabins were too far away. "I'll let people through the back door and set up a sign directing guests around the back." She wouldn't have the comforting counter partition between her and the guests, but it was the best she could do.

"Good. Wait until Ryan arrives and then he can go with you."

"Ryan?" She blushed as she remembered their kiss.

"I called him, he's on his way. He'll have Felix with him."

She didn't want a child involved in this. "You didn't need to do that. I'll be fine."

"It's police procedure." Lincoln smiled, but there was worry in his eyes.

She didn't like this at all. Worry spoke of danger and she didn't want to be frightened. She'd known the secret admirer wasn't a good thing.

Fifteen minutes later, Ryan arrived with a very grumpy-looking Felix. The pout on the boy's face made her smile. She glanced at Ryan, her cheeks heating as she remembered the fool she'd made of herself last night. She turned her attention to Felix. "Sorry you had to get out of bed so early because of me."

Felix said nothing.

"He would have been up already if he hadn't stayed up so late last night." Ryan turned to his son. "Stay here with Hannah and Joe while I have a quick word with Lincoln."

Felix nodded.

Ryan walked away. The police uniform looked good on him, the pants moulded to his butt, outlining it clearly. She'd never been someone to swoon over a uniform, but Ryan was another story. She cleared her throat and focused on Felix. "I've got a futon in the office if you want to sleep."

"What's a futon?"

"It's a couch that folds out into a bed."

He perked up. "Neat." He walked over to Joe and stroked his head. "Does Joe like to run?"

"He sure does. I take him down to the beach each day so he can chase the gulls."

Felix's eyes widened. "Does he catch them?"

"No, he's too slow. He does it for fun."

Ryan was frowning when he returned. "Have you got your keys for the office?"

She took them from her pocket. "Yes. Can I go inside now?"

"I'll check it out first." He held out his hand.

Aware that Felix was listening, she didn't want to say anything to alarm him. "Do you think there'll be an issue?" She showed him the correct key.

"No." He smiled. "Be right back."

"So what's wrong?" Felix asked, waking up a little more.

"Nothing serious," Hannah said. "Someone left something icky at the door as a prank. Your dad and Lincoln are recording the details to find out who it was."

"What was it?"

"Nothing special," she said. "Did you have fun playing with Jacob yesterday?"

"Yeah. I'm going to see him again today." He frowned. "There's some class thing."

"The end-of-year wind-up," Hannah said. "That was my favourite event when I was in primary school."

He looked at her with interest. "Did you go to school here?"

"Yeah, I moved here when I was your age," she said. "It's tough being the only person who doesn't know anyone."

He sighed. "It is. What did you do?"

"Well I was lucky. I met Fleur and Kit on the first day of school and they were nice to me. Kind of like how you've met Jacob. We've been friends ever since."

"Did your parents get a job here too?"

She took a step back. "No. My mum died and my dad went away, so I came to live with my grandparents."

"My mum isn't very nice," he said. "But Dad loves me." He paused and then asked, "The kids didn't think you were weird?"

"No." She'd be forever grateful that they didn't. She spotted Ryan walking around the side of the office. He waved them over. "Come on, I'll show you my futon."

She raised her eyebrows in question at Ryan when she reached him.

"There's nothing out of place."

In the office, she switched on the computer and then showed Felix how the couch pulled out into a bed. "Do you want to lie down?"

"Nah, I'm good."

"Hannah's got a few things to set up, mate," Ryan said. "Why don't you lie down for a bit while she gets it all sorted?"

"Aw, Dad."

"You've got the wind-up later. You don't want to be tired."

"All right." Shoulders slumped, he climbed on to the bed.

Hannah took out the pillow and blanket she kept for the nights when she had customers arriving late and she needed to sleep there.

Joe hopped up on the bed next to Felix and lay down. The boy giggled.

"*Joe*," Hannah said.

"He can stay." Felix wrapped his arm around the big dog.

Hannah was torn. She hated to disappoint Felix, but she didn't want to go anywhere alone.

"What do you need to do?" Ryan asked.

"I'll print a couple of signs and then I need to get the gazebo out of the storage shed."

"I'll get it if you tell me where it is."

She breathed a sigh of relief. She grabbed the keys from the table and showed him the right one. "It's in the garden shed." She pointed it out on the caravan-park map. "In the corner."

He nodded. "Be right back."

Hannah typed up a sign and printed it out, before bringing up the list of bookings for the day. When Ryan arrived back she was ready, and Felix was fast asleep.

Ryan smiled at the child and dog curled up together on the bed. "I'm going to have to get him a dog when we're settled."

"I'm sure he'll love it." Conscious of his presence now that they were effectively alone, Hannah's thoughts darted back to their kiss the night before. She licked her lips.

"Where do you want the gazebo set up?"

She blinked and blushed. "Out the front." She picked up her signs and the sticky tape, and hurried out of the office.

Together she and Ryan set up the gazebo to block the view of Lincoln's investigation from the public and she stuck the signs to the canvas walls. "Would you like a coffee?" she asked when they were done.

"That'd be great."

"Coffee, Lincoln?" she called.

"Love one, but I'll get it later," Lincoln answered.

She headed back to the kitchen and made the coffees. "Shame it's not a bit later," she said as they walked into the office to avoid disturbing Felix further. "Mai's coming around and she always brings freshly baked treats from the bakery."

"I've heard she's good," Ryan said. "Haven't had a chance to stop by there yet." He took a sip of his coffee. "While I'm here, do you want to show me the other two gifts you've received?"

She reached for the top drawer. "This is the necklace." She pulled it out and handed it to him. "The bird ornaments are on the filing cabinet over there."

"Do you still have the packaging?"

"Maybe." She dug through the rubbish bin and shook her head.

"All right. We might be able to get something useful from the necklace or doves. I'll get some evidence bags from Lincoln's car."

Hannah waited until he'd left and then peered over the desk, out of the door at where Lincoln was documenting her latest gift. She couldn't understand why anyone would be interested in her. She'd never led anyone on, and rarely wore figure-hugging clothes. She did her best not to look desirable. Plus, she carried more weight than any of her friends. But it made no sense that it was Justin either. He'd never kept in touch with her. Why would he send gifts now?

And why the dead chickens?

Had she and Ryan been so convincing on their pretend date that whoever was sending her the gifts was heartbroken? But killing chickens wasn't a normal reaction for heartbreak. It wasn't a normal reaction for anything. Her skin tightened.

Ryan came back in and bagged up the evidence as one of her guests knocked on the back door.

"Come in," she said to the older gentleman. "I'm sorry about the inconvenience." She led him through to the office.

"Did you have a spot of trouble?"

She gestured to the spare chair in the corner. "It's kids pranking." She wished she believed it. "Having the police here will spread around town and scare them from anything further."

"Kids in my day respected people's property." The man handed over his credit card.

Hannah murmured in agreement. "You're staying a week, aren't you?"

"Yes, and we've got one of those ensuite bathroom sites, haven't we? I wish more parks had them."

She smiled. "It's nice to have your own space, isn't it?" She printed off his receipt and walked him back out. "I hope you enjoy your stay."

"Thanks." The man waved and was gone.

Hannah popped her head into the kitchen and found Felix still sound asleep. Lincoln must have worn him out last night.

"I need to get this stuff to the station," Ryan said from behind her. She jumped and spun around. He was looking at Felix curled up next to Joe, but Hannah was very aware of his presence, the strength of his body and the heat coming off him.

"I hate to wake him," Ryan said.

Hannah wanted to do something to help. It was her fault that Felix was here. "He can stay here if you want," she offered. "When Lynette arrives I'll take him out to the Zanettis' property. It's not far past my place."

He frowned. "You're going to the retreat?"

"Yeah. I've got some work to do on the other cabin." With school finishing today, she wasn't going to get as much chance to go out there during the holidays. "Mai's going to join me."

"What time?"

Annoyed she said, "When she finishes work." At his look, she added, "About midday."

"You shouldn't be out there alone."

She paused. Was he suggesting she wasn't safe? "Justin doesn't know where I live."

He looked at her for a long moment. "This might not be Justin. If he followed us, he would have left the restaurant almost immediately after we did, and they were still eating dessert."

"So you think whoever did that," she waved towards the

front of the office, "might be someone who knows where I live? Am I in danger?" Her heart raced in her chest.

"We don't know yet, but it would be wise to take precautions."

She couldn't breathe. She sucked in air fast, but it wasn't helping. She was supposed to be safe here.

"Sit down." Ryan propelled her forward into the office and on to one of the chairs. "Cup your hands over your mouth, you're hyperventilating."

She did as he said and he rubbed her back.

"Hold your breath for a moment … and breathe out."

She followed Ryan's instructions and slowly got her breathing under control.

"It's going to be all right," Ryan said. "We'll find whoever is doing this." He continued the slow circular motion on her back and awareness sprang to Hannah's body. Ryan was touching her … and it felt good, comforting and sensual. She closed her eyes, enjoying the sensation.

The back screen door banged shut and Hannah jerked up. Lincoln wandered in. "Are you all right?"

She nodded.

"She had a bit of a panic attack," Ryan told him.

Lincoln pulled her up and into his arms. "Don't worry, Hannah Banana. We'll sort it out for you."

His words were soothing, and his arms were reassuring, so she allowed herself the comfort of them. "I don't like this."

"Neither do I." He pulled away. "I want you to come down to the station after Lynette gets here. I need to ask you some questions, and it's best if we're not interrupted."

Nerves swirled in her stomach. He'd want to ask her about Justin. She had to decide if she was going to tell him the truth, if she was brave enough to face his disappointment. "OK."

"I'm finished out the front, so you can unlock the door and take away the signs."

"I'll do it." Ryan headed outside with her keys.

"For the next few days I don't want you going anywhere without Joe and someone else with you," Lincoln said. "You need to be super vigilant."

"Why?"

"Because you have a stalker and their behaviour can be unpredictable."

Fear clutched her skin. "But I've not done anything."

"It doesn't matter. Whoever it is has perceived you've done something."

It wasn't fair. She'd been so careful not to give off the wrong kind of signals. "So what do I do?"

"Stay vigilant, keep someone with you and tell me if anything odd happens."

"Lincoln, I can't ask people to give up their lives for me."

"All of the musketeers would offer in a heartbeat and you know it," he told her. "Are you still staying at Fleur's?"

She nodded. "She's got some night shifts next week though."

"Then stay at Mai's."

She scowled. "You can't arrange my life." She might have been cautious since her assault, but she was still independent.

"Sure I can. I'm your honorary protector, remember?" He grinned at her.

Her anger left her. At some stage in primary school, she and her friends had decided they wanted a knight protector to look out for them, and Lincoln had been the logical choice. They'd made him go through a ceremony and he'd gone along with it with great patience. "How long is this going to last?"

He sobered. "I don't know. This could be the end of it. We'll wait and see if he leaves any more gifts tomorrow."

At that moment, Felix called out, "Dad?"

Lincoln went to check him and Hannah's stomach swirled.

This might just be the beginning of her nightmare.

Chapter 7

Mrs Z came to pick up Felix and stayed to chat until Lynette arrived. Hannah suspected Lincoln had asked her to stick around, but she was glad for the company, glad she didn't have to be alone yet.

After Mrs Z left, Hannah told Lynette about the dead chickens.

Lynette frowned. "That's sick."

"Yeah. Lincoln wants me to go down to the station to talk about it. Will you feel safe here on your own? I can call Shirley in to work."

Lynette nodded. "I'll call her."

After saying goodbye, Hannah drove into town. It was a gorgeous day, promising blue skies and pleasant temperatures, but Hannah was unable to take joy in it. She scanned the people on the footpaths. Could one of them be her stalker? She checked her rear-view mirror to make sure no one was following her, her grip on the steering wheel tight, her shoulders tense. She hated this. Hated that she was no longer able to enjoy driving through town. Hated that she was now viewing everyone as a potential threat.

Needing a pick-me-up, she stopped by Mai's bakery.

"Wasn't I meeting you at the holiday park?" Mai asked, as she made Hannah a coffee.

"Change of plans." Hannah told her what had happened.

"That's not good." Mai frowned. "It sounds as if Lincoln is worried."

It did. Having Justin in town was bad, but having an unknown stalker who was cross with her was far worse. "I'm heading to the station now to talk to him."

"Do you want me to come with you?"

Hannah wanted to say yes. She had to tell him about Justin and she didn't want to be alone when she told Lincoln about how stupid she'd been. But Mai had already heard her story and didn't need to sit through it twice. "I'll be fine. I'll drop by when I'm done."

Mai handed her the coffee and gave her a hug. "We're all here for you."

"Thanks. Can I buy some pastries for the police station?"

"Sure, I'll box up their favourites." Mai paused. "What do you think Ryan will like?"

Hannah shrugged. "You choose. They're all good."

Mai blew her a kiss. "Thanks, sweetie."

Hannah pulled out her purse and Mai shook her head. "It's on the house. Thank Lincoln from me."

Hannah smiled. "Will do."

She continued to the station and carefully got out of the car, balancing the box of pastries and her coffee while Joe jumped out. She hesitated outside the station door, not sure how she was going to manage, but it opened of its own accord. Ryan smiled. "Need a hand?"

Her face warmed. "Thanks." She slipped by him, inhaling his rich musky scent. Giving herself a bit of space she said, "I brought a little thankyou gift courtesy of Mai." She walked through the side door to the back of the station where the offices were.

"Is there a bee sting in there?" Lincoln called from his office.

"Of course." Hannah grinned. "Mai chose it herself." She distributed the goods before asking Ryan, "Which would you like?"

"You didn't need to do this," Ryan said.

"Mate, don't refuse," Lincoln said. "Mai is the best baker in Australia."

Ryan grinned and Hannah's stomach fluttered. His face lit

up like the sun coming out from behind a cloud. He was gorgeous.

"Do you have a preference?" he asked Hannah.

She shook her head, unable to form words as Lincoln called, "She has the lamington."

Ryan raised his eyebrow and chose the eclair.

Heat rushed to her cheeks and she stepped away. She was being foolish. She wasn't sure what to do about her attraction to Ryan. She didn't like it, didn't trust it. She needed some distance. "What did you want to speak to me about?" She moved towards Lincoln's office.

He gestured her to the spare chair. "Take a seat."

Her skin tightened as she entered the room. It wasn't large and the furniture was like most government buildings – grey and functional. She sat on the chair that was closest to the door.

"Ryan, you come in too and shut the door."

Hannah tensed as the door closed behind her. She was trapped in here with two men – without Joe. He was begging for dog treats from Adam. There was no way she would be able to escape on her own. Ryan and Lincoln were too strong, too fast. Her breath rushed in and out quickly, painfully. It was all right. This was Lincoln. Lincoln was her friend, he wouldn't hurt her.

"Hannah, are you OK?" Lincoln asked.

She nodded, not daring to look at him, her hands clenched as she tried to relax.

"Do you want me to open the door?" Ryan asked.

Yes. She desperately wanted to say yes. But damn it, she was sick of being scared like this. She shook her head. "Give me a second." She shuffled her chair so she was a bit further away from Ryan and took a moment to compose herself. Finally, the tightness in her chest eased and her hands unclenched. Her cheeks hot, she met Lincoln's concerned gaze.

"What was that about, Hannah?" His voice was soft, calm.

She considered lying for a moment, but she couldn't. Not any longer. Not to Lincoln. It was time she told the truth. Maybe it would help her heal. "I, uh, don't like being alone in a room with men." It was a relief, as if a weight had been lifted from her.

Lincoln frowned. "We've been alone plenty of times."

She shook her head. "Not with the door closed, not without Joe with me."

Hurt crossed Lincoln's face and she felt like a bug. "Don't you trust me?"

"I do! It's not you, it's me," she assured him. "I haven't felt safe with any man since …" The words stuck in her throat.

"Since when?" Lincoln asked.

She squeezed her eyes shut. What would he think of her after she told him? Would he find her pathetic, disgusting, a fool?

"Would it be easier telling someone you don't know so well?" Ryan asked.

She opened her eyes. "No." She didn't want Ryan to know either. He wouldn't want to be involved with someone as damaged as she was. She swallowed. She had to say it – fast, like ripping off a band-aid. "Since Justin raped me."

Lincoln swore. "What? When? Did you report him?"

She shook her head.

"Why not, Hannah?" He'd tensed, his face red.

She knew he'd be upset, knew he'd think her weak.

"Do you want to tell us what happened?" Ryan asked.

She was grateful he was staying calm. "There's not much to tell." She hesitated, the tension back in her chest. Where did she start? How much should she say? "I was dating Justin and went back to his place one night." Heat rushed to her cheeks and she cleared her throat. She couldn't think about it, she had to pretend she was recounting someone else's story. "We started, uh, fooling around, but it didn't feel right. I asked him to stop and he didn't."

A slight twitch over Ryan's eye suggested maybe he wasn't as unaffected as she'd thought.

"I hope you made him hurt," Lincoln said.

"No," she whispered. She stared at the ground. Did that make it her fault? Did she have to fight until it was over for it to be really rape?

"Why—"

"Shut up, Lincoln," Ryan ordered. "Saying no should have been enough."

Relief filled her. Maybe she had done the right thing. Maybe it wasn't her fault.

Ryan gave her an encouraging nod. "What happened next?"

"I called Fleur. She came and picked me up."

"And Justin?" Ryan prompted.

"I didn't speak to him again." She'd never been so grateful for caller ID.

"Did he contact you again or drop around?" Ryan asked.

"He left a couple of messages, but I didn't answer them," she said. "It was the end of semester and we were doing final exams, so we were both busy. As soon as the exams were over I came home."

Ryan made a note. "You haven't seen or heard from him since?"

"Not until Monday."

"I don't understand why you didn't press charges, Hannah," Lincoln said softly.

"What would be the point?" she snapped, the guilt sharp. "It was my word against his as to whether it was consensual. His roommates would testify that I didn't scream or yell." Her hands shook and she clasped them together, hating that she was yelling at Lincoln, hating that she was being so defensive, hating that some part of her still thought she was to blame.

He shook his head, and glanced at Ryan as if not sure what to say.

She pressed her lips together, a heavy weight in her gut. She didn't want to tell them the reason she'd frozen, but it might show Lincoln that she wasn't a complete fool. She sipped her coffee, which had gone cold, aware that they were waiting for her to speak. She needed to give Ryan some background, and wasn't entirely sure how much Lincoln knew of her past.

"My parents had a passionate relationship," she began. That was the word her mother had always used. "Fiery, you could say. When everything was going well the house was full of music and laughter and my parents would be so affectionate – kissing, hugging and it was a joy to be with them." Those were the times she missed the most, the memories she tried to hold on to.

"And when things weren't going well?" Ryan asked.

"Loud   arguments,   accusations,   often   tears.   I   never understood what they were arguing about, but it was usually when my half-brothers were there." It was one of the reasons she had hated when they came to visit.

Lincoln frowned. "You never mentioned you had brothers."

"I haven't seen them since I was eight. They were from Dad's previous marriage." She hadn't trusted them – one day they were nice and the next they would be horrible. They'd gang up on her when her father wasn't around – pinch her and push her around.

Lincoln shifted in his seat. "Did your dad hit your mum?"

"No." She shook her head. "It was never more than words until that last night." She still saw it so clearly in her head, like a movie playing in front of her.

They were both waiting for her to continue.

"I was asleep and something woke me up," she said. "I heard yelling and got up to check what was wrong." She remembered peering down the corridor, a little afraid of being told off for being out of bed.

"What happened?" Ryan asked.

"Mum was lying on the ground, blood on her chest, her eyes open." The way she'd lain was unnatural, her eyes wide but unseeing, and the sight had halted Hannah in her tracks. Her heartbeat slowed as she remembered the fear, the shock, the confusion. She swallowed. "I was going to go to her, but Dad walked into view. He was holding a knife and crying, yelling something in Croatian as he knelt down next to her. I was so scared I ran back to my room and hid under my bed. I didn't move until a police officer found me there hours later." For years she'd regretted her decision. What if there was something she could have done to help? What if her mother hadn't been dead?

"Jesus, Hannah." Lincoln looked horrified. "I'm so sorry you had to witness that."

Her breath hitched and she blinked rapidly, trying to stop the tears. She had to get the rest out. "Mum must have made Dad so angry. I didn't want to make Justin angry." Could he understand that?

"Of course not." Lincoln came around the desk and gently pulled her into his arms. "I've got your back now. Always," he promised.

The relief that he didn't blame her, that he understood, was too much. She began to sob.

Ryan moved back to give Hannah and Lincoln some space. He ached for the woman sobbing in his best friend's arms. She'd been through a lot in her life, seen too much. It was no wonder she hadn't fought back when Justin had assaulted her. He rubbed his chest. He couldn't watch this. It hurt too much.

He walked out of the room, softly closing the door behind him, and went into the kitchen to get a glass of water. When he came back, Adam asked, "Everything all right in there?"

Ryan nodded. "I'll fill you in on the necessary details afterwards." Adam didn't need to know everything. "Any issues out here?"

"No," Adam said. "Though Shirley Jameson reported that three of her chickens are missing."

"She's right across from the caravan park," Ryan said. It couldn't be a coincidence.

Adam nodded.

"We'll go and check it out after we've finished talking to Hannah." He went back into Lincoln's office and Hannah was blowing her nose. He handed her the glass.

"Thank you." Hannah took a long sip of the water and sat back down. She squared her shoulders. "Is there anything else you need to know?"

"We don't need to go through it now." Ryan didn't want to add to her pain.

"No, I'd prefer to get it all done at once." Hannah braced herself. "What did the note say?"

Lincoln scowled. "*Stay away from him.*"

Hannah's face paled. She glanced at Ryan. "Do you think it's Justin?"

It was unlikely Justin had followed them, but he could be leaving the gifts. "We don't know. We'll interview him and his friends later today," Ryan said. The other concern was that today's note was different – it was typed not handwritten, and the ribbon was red not silver.

"But if it's not him, then who?"

"We were hoping you might be able to help us with that," Lincoln said.

She shook her head.

"Any guests at the park who have been overly interested?" Ryan prompted. "Any people around town you've run into regularly, anyone who has asked you on a date recently?"

"You and Lincoln are the only men I've seen regularly over the past few days," she said.

Ryan didn't want his friend on the suspect list, but Lincoln did have a strong bond with Hannah. No, Lincoln knew their date had been fake.

"What about over the last month or so?" Lincoln asked. "Anyone stay at the park for that length of time?"

"No. The most anyone stayed was three weeks, and they've all left to get back home for Christmas."

"Might be worth checking them out in any case." They could have changed their plans, could still be in the area.

"I'll get you a list."

"And write down everyone who has asked you on a date in the last six months," Lincoln added.

Hannah laughed, the sound brittle and disbelieving. "I don't need to. No one has asked me out."

Lincoln raised his eyebrows. "Not even someone from the motocross club?"

"No. Fleur and Kit get all the offers."

What was wrong with the single guys in Blackbridge? Why wasn't anyone asking her out? Ryan would if he wasn't working on her case and was interested in dating again. Which he wasn't. The thought of making another mistake as bad as Paula had him grimacing.

"Anything else out of the ordinary?" Lincoln continued. "Things going missing or being moved, odd phone calls, that kind of thing?"

"Aside from the break-ins?" Hannah asked. "I did get a call the other day where no one spoke, but it was probably someone dropping out of mobile range, or one of those call centres."

"What day?" Ryan asked.

She frowned. "I'm not sure … Monday maybe."

He made a note.

"Is this stalker dangerous?" She clenched the arms of her chair.

"Killing chickens isn't a great start," Lincoln said. "We got some fingerprints from the card, so hopefully we'll find a match and get this resolved fast."

Ryan hated the fear on her face. Hadn't she been through enough? "Keep Joe with you," he said. "He's a good deterrent."

"I always do. Is there anything else?"

"No. You're staying at Fleur's, aren't you?" Lincoln said.

She nodded.

"If you think of anything else, let us know." Ryan handed her one of his cards, even though he knew she would call Lincoln before she called him.

"Will do." Her smile was forced. Ryan resisted the urge to hug her and tell her everything would be all right. He couldn't get involved in that way.

"Holy shit," Lincoln said after she left. He ran a hand through his hair. "I never realised what Hannah had been through."

"Do you want me to take lead on this?" Ryan asked. "You might be too close to it."

Lincoln hesitated and then nodded. "As much as I hate to admit it, you're right. Plus, I've got a whole heap of administrative bullshit to deal with."

"I'll keep an eye on her," he promised. "We should make sure her father is still in jail and I'll take a look around her shed when I head home tonight. Check whether there are any signs of anyone being around." First Justin and now this. Hannah it was having a rough time.

"Good idea. Then take Adam and go interview Justin and his friends."

Ryan nodded. "We'll stop by Shirley's as well. Apparently, she's missing three chickens."

Lincoln raised his eyebrows. "All right. I really hope it's that bastard."

So did Ryan. Because if it wasn't Justin, then there was another psycho in town.

Ryan and Adam pulled up at the cabin where Justin and his friends were staying just as they were returning from the beach, surfboards tucked under their arms. There were four of them, all in their mid-twenties, wetsuits pulled down around their waists. Ryan frowned. There had only been three guys at the restaurant last night. Two sedans were parked in the driveway, one black and one grey.

Ryan examined Justin, taking a moment to control the anger coursing through him, before he got out of the car. Part of him wanted to punch the guy in the face for what he'd done to Hannah.

The dislike was mutual as Justin glowered when he saw Ryan. "What do you want, Officer?"

Ryan kept his voice steady and professional with some difficulty. "We'd like a few words with you all, if we can."

"Give us a second to wash up," the blond guy said.

Ryan nodded, and he and Adam waited on the porch while the guys stacked their surfboards and stripped off their wetsuits, taking turns under the outdoor shower next to the cabin.

"What's the problem?" Justin asked as he came up the steps with his mates, towel drying his hair.

"There was a bit of trouble over at Blackbridge Holiday Park last night," Ryan said.

"Is Hannah all right?" Justin asked. His immediate concern seemed genuine, but Ryan wasn't buying it.

"She's fine," Adam replied. "You must have driven past the park on your way back from dinner. Did you see anyone hanging around?"

"No," Justin replied, looking at his friends. They shook their heads.

Adam made a note. "What time did you get back?"

"About ten," Justin said.

"There were only three of you at the restaurant," Ryan commented.

"Smithy got the trots." Justin nudged the blond guy.

"Did you stay here?" Adam asked.

Smithy nodded. "Barely left the bathroom. Must have eaten

a dodgy chicko roll."

"What time did you leave the restaurant?" Ryan asked.

Justin scowled. "Not long after you and Hannah did."

That was around eight-thirty. "Where did you go from there?"

"The pub," Justin said.

The pub was a big, old, traditional country place on the corner of the main highway and the road that ran alongside the river. It was walking distance from the restaurant. "Do you all know Hannah?" Ryan asked.

"I don't think so." Justin glanced at Smithy. "Were we roommates when I was dating Hannah?"

"I met her a couple of times before you broke up."

That was interesting. "Did you get on well?"

Smithy shrugged. "Didn't really see much of her. She seemed nice though."

"So, what happened last night?" Justin asked.

"Hannah's been receiving gifts from a secret admirer. Do you know anything about it?"

Justin shook his head. "It wasn't me."

The other men shook their heads. Ryan handed Justin his card. "If you think of anything else, give me a call."

Justin reluctantly took it. "Will do."

Ryan walked down the steps next to Adam. His gut told him Justin was telling the truth, which was a shame – he wanted to pin something on the son of a bitch. But there was also Smithy to consider.

"Should we drop by the pub?" Adam asked.

"Yeah, and we need to ask Shirley about her chickens."

Adam grimaced and it made Ryan smile. "I'll protect you."

It was a short drive to Shirley's place. She had a pretty good view of the park office from her porch.

"Ryan! Adam!" The yell came from over at the caravan park. Shirley was waving at them as she strode across the lawn.

They changed direction and walked over. There was none of the flirtatiousness about her today. "Are you here about my chickens?"

Ryan nodded.

"Were they the ones left for Hannah?" she asked, her

expression concerned as she led them up to her house.

"Possibly. Can you describe them for me?" Ryan said as he got out his notebook.

"They were ISA Browns," she said, as if that was all the information he needed.

Adam appeared as clueless at him. "So they were brown?"

Shirley sighed with exasperation. "Of course they were brown, with a red comb on top. Come in and I'll show you the other girls and you can see where they were taken from."

They followed her through the house full of knick-knacks, and out into the large backyard. Fairy Floss trotted up to greet them and Ryan patted her head. The chicken coop took up the back corner of the yard and there was the quiet cluck of chickens as he approached. "Was anything damaged?"

"No. I don't lock the coop. Anyone could have waltzed in and taken them."

"You didn't hear anything last night?" Adam asked.

She shook her head. "I went to the pantomime. They must have been taken while I was out, otherwise I would have heard my girls making a fuss."

"What time did you get back?" Ryan asked.

"About eleven."

Ryan took notes and listened as Shirley talked about her chickens. It was obvious they were dear to her.

"Were they my girls?" Shirley finally asked.

"I'd suggest so," Ryan said. "They fit the description."

Tears welled in her eyes. "Why would anyone do such a thing?"

"We're still figuring it out." This was the part of the job he disliked. Not being able to assure people that they would catch the culprit.

"Well thank you, gentlemen. You can go now." She walked briskly towards the house.

Ryan hurried after her. "We'd like to check for fingerprints."

She stopped, tears glistening in her eyes. "All right. I'll be over at the park office if you need me."

Before she could leave, Ryan asked, "Did you see anything at the caravan park last night when you got home – any lights or noises?"

"No." She frowned. "Do I need to be careful? Is someone likely to break in here?"

"We believe Hannah is the target, but you'd be wise to lock your doors until we catch the person," Ryan told her.

"All right." Shirley hesitated. "Can I have my girls back? I'd like to give them a proper burial."

"I'll see what I can do," Ryan promised.

After they'd dusted for prints and got nothing of note, they drove to the pub. "Do you think it was Justin?" Adam asked.

"He couldn't have been the person who followed us last night," Ryan said. "But the two events might be unrelated."

"What about Smithy? Maybe he didn't have gastro," Adam said.

"Yeah." It was possible. Perhaps he'd liked Hannah more than he made out. He definitely had the opportunity.

At the pub, Ryan showed the barman a photo of Justin. "Did you serve this guy last night?"

He squinted at the photo. "Yeah. Him and two other guys."

"What time did they arrive?" Adam asked.

"About eight-thirty," he said. "They had a couple of beers."

"When did they leave?"

"Near closing time – about ten. They were my last customers to leave."

"No one left during that time?" Ryan asked.

"Not that I noticed."

Damn. "Thanks." Ryan headed outside. Justin's story checked out.

They drove back to the station and updated Lincoln and Sue.

"What do we do now?" Adam asked.

Ryan and Lincoln exchanged a look. "We wait for forensics," Ryan said.

But he'd keep a close eye on Hannah.

Chapter 8

After leaving the police station, Hannah's head was foggy and the last thing she felt like doing was going out to her retreat and working on the cabin. And that annoyed her. She loved working out there and now this *admirer* had taken it from her. Bastard.

Holding on to the glimmer of outrage, she drove to Mai's place.

"Hannah, you look like crap," Mai said as she opened the door to her apartment above the bakery.

Hannah chuckled. "That's what I needed to hear."

Mai tutted and led her into the kitchen. "Take a seat. I'll make you a Vietnamese coffee and you can tell me what Lincoln said." She put the kettle on and then placed a plate of dumplings on the table. "I whipped up these for you." She gave Joe a homemade dog treat and he went into the small living room to eat it.

Hannah smiled and took one of the dumplings. They were her favourite, but Mai only cooked them on special occasions. "Thanks."

"Tell me, what did Lincoln say?"

As she told Mai the details of her stalker, Mai's ragdoll cat, Calypso, jumped onto her lap and demanded attention. Happy to oblige, she stroked his soft fur as he draped himself across her.

"So either Justin is your stalker, or there's someone

completely unrelated who is crushing on you?" Mai summarised.

Hannah nodded. "Pretty much."

"I hope it's Justin. I'm sure they could charge him with something."

"I kind of hope so too." The idea that there was someone else out there she needed to be scared of was even more frightening.

"We need to get your mind off this," Mai said. "Do you want to go to the beach?"

Hannah hesitated. She'd love to go to the beach, but she didn't want this guy interrupting her plans. "I wanted to get the first coat of paint on the new cabin."

"I can help with that."

Hannah bit back a laugh. "Really?" The first and last time she'd seen Mai with a paintbrush was when she'd repainted her bakery. It had not been pretty. In the end, she had been given the task of making refreshments and the rest of the musketeers had finished the job.

"I'm not *that* bad," Mai protested, placing the coffee in front of Hannah.

"Yes you are." Hannah stirred the condensed milk so it mixed with the strong black brew.

Mai laughed. "OK, you're right. There must be something I can do to help."

Hannah thought about it. "I need to create a website. You manage your own, don't you?"

"Yeah, I can set you up something basic."

They spent an hour discussing options before heading out to Hannah's place. On the drive out, Hannah kept checking her rear-view mirror, but it was pointless. She wouldn't be able to tell if anyone was following her. This was one of the main roads out of town – everyone used it.

When they arrived, Hannah set up her laptop on the card table she had in the cabin, and pulled over a deck chair. When Mai was settled, Hannah gazed around the cabin. It was well built and she was proud of her work. She'd designed the kitchen so she could use flatpack cupboards for it and had only got an electrician and plumber in for installation. She'd stuck with a crisp, clean white and accessorised with colour. The splashback was a soft green that picked up colours from the trees outside.

She'd start painting in here.

Normally she liked the task, enjoyed the mindless way she could paint and plan at the same time. But today, instead of planning the next steps in her project, her mind went back to the gifts. Why would someone get so angry about her going on a date with Ryan? It made no sense. No one had asked her out in months, not since the motocross two-day event when an out-of-town visitor had taken a liking to her, and she'd knocked him back firmly. Surely, asking someone out was the first step of showing you were interested, not leaving anonymous gifts.

And the escalation was crazy – from pretty trinkets to dead birds overnight. She shuddered, pushing away the image. There were better, more useful things she should be thinking about, like what equipment she needed to hire to put in the paths, and what was the best way to fence off the lookout while still making it a nice place to hang out. She wanted multiple places around the property where guests could be alone, some garden benches where they could sit and enjoy the bush, or perhaps a gazebo with a picnic table where they could enjoy lunch.

Places where her stalker could leave nasty gifts without anyone seeing.

Hannah scowled. She wasn't going to think about him, wasn't going to let him ruin this for her. She loved her retreat, loved that she was finally working on it after years of planning. Turning to Mai, she asked, "Anything new in your world?"

Mai glanced up from the laptop. "Not really." She pursed her lips. "Well sort of."

"What's happening?"

Mai squeezed her eyes closed and then opened them again. "You know how I was considering buying the bakery building?"

Hannah nodded. The owner had died and the heirs wanted to sell it.

"Well, I got my loan pre-approval yesterday." She laughed, her delight clear. "Now, I just need to wait until they finalise probate and put it on the market."

"That's incredible! Congratulations." Hannah put down her paintbrush and threw her arms around her friend. Mai had worked damned hard over the last three years to make her bakery a success.

"Thanks. I'm terrified," she confessed. "It's a lot of money."

"But you're doing well, and the business is growing. You can expand and you won't have to worry about your lease expiring." Mai had inspired Hannah with her business savvy and her determination to make her business work.

Mai nodded. "I can't wait. I'm going to call Aaron if I haven't heard from him by Christmas. I thought probate would have gone through by now."

"Those things always take time."

"While we're talking about nice things, tell me about your date with Ryan."

"It wasn't really a date." She was like a broken record on repeat. Maybe if she said it enough times she'd convince herself and her friends.

"He kissed you, didn't he?" Mai asked.

"You've been talking to Fleur."

"Kit actually, but she heard it from Fleur." Mai grinned.

Hannah rolled her eyes. "He didn't mean it. It was an instinctual reaction from almost dying."

Mai laughed and shook her head. "I don't think so. Was it a good kiss?"

She didn't have a lot to compare it with. Perhaps it was her lack of experience that had made it so good.

"Hannah?"

She sighed. "Yes. It was a very good kiss."

Mai clapped her hands together. "Tell me more."

"No." Hannah chuckled. It was kind of nice to finally be the one who had a story to tell, but she didn't want to dwell on it. It wasn't real. "It hardly matters because he's not going to kiss me again."

"Do you want him to?"

Yes. There was a part of her that definitely wanted to kiss him again, but she hesitated. "Maybe ... I find it hard to be close to guys since Justin."

Mai was immediately contrite. "I'm sorry. I shouldn't tease. I don't know what it must be like for you."

Hannah was quiet for a long moment, surprised by her desire to confide in Mai. She'd kept it a secret for so long, but there was a sense of relief from having people know what she'd been through.

"I hate being alone with men," she admitted. "Anyone between eighteen and sixty-five freaks me out." She took a deep breath. "Today I was in Lincoln's office with him and Ryan. Joe was getting treats from Adam and they shut the door to give me privacy. I panicked." She shook her head. "It was *Lincoln* for God's sake. Rationally I know he would never hurt me, but there's another part of my brain that refuses to listen."

"Sweetie, it's OK to be scared," Mai reassured her. "Someone you trusted assaulted you. It's normal that you would have issues trusting again."

Hannah sighed. "What should I do?"

Mai pursed her lips. "Trust isn't an issue when it comes to Lincoln, is it?"

Hannah shook her head. Logically, she knew he wouldn't hurt her.

"So maybe you need to work on the instinctual part of your brain. Would you be less likely to panic if you knew how to defend yourself?"

She'd forgotten she'd agreed to ask Lincoln about lessons.

"I did some self-defence classes when I began my apprenticeship," Mai said. "Starting work in the middle of the night was scary sometimes. I knew at my size, I'd never overpower anyone, but I wanted to learn some techniques to help me escape a hold so I could run."

Hannah's stomach clenched. "But I don't fight and I don't run, I freeze."

"Maybe it's because you haven't had any practice," Mai said. "Why don't you ask Lincoln to teach you some moves, and when we're finished here, you can come for a run with me and Fleur – get your body used to the activity?"

Hannah laughed. If only it was that simple. "All right." Maybe it would help. She was determined to get her life back on track.

But right now, she needed to get back to the painting before her brush dried out.

When Hannah woke the next morning, every muscle in her body screamed at her. With a groan she got out of bed and shuffled into the kitchen, where Fleur was making breakfast, already dressed in her work scrubs.

"What's wrong with you?" Fleur asked.

"You never mentioned jogging was a torture sport." Hannah slowly stretched out her muscles.

"Bit stiff this morning, huh?" Fleur grinned.

"A lot stiff," Hannah corrected.

"You did well. I'm surprised you kept up with us for as long as you did."

"Stubborn." Now she was cursing her stubbornness. It had seemed like a good idea to exercise, to get used to running, but perhaps a five-kilometre jog up the beach wasn't the wisest move. Not that she'd done the full distance. She'd fallen behind and turned around when Mai and Fleur had reached the halfway mark and come back towards her – so maybe she'd done two.

"Have a hot shower and do some stretching. It'll help."

She'd give anything a shot. Hannah got Joe some breakfast before pouring herself a bowl of cereal and gingerly sitting down. She should have started off easy.

"You going to come with us again today?" Fleur asked.

"It depends on whether I can move," Hannah said. The exercise had felt good for the first few minutes until her lungs had begun to burn and she'd had trouble focusing on anything other than putting one foot in front of the other. At least it had made her forget about Justin and her stalker for a while. As soon as she thought of him, dread filled her stomach. She pushed away her bowl.

"What's wrong?"

"I'm wondering what I'll find on the office doorstep this morning."

Fleur put her hand over Hannah's. "Do you want me to come with you? We could go now."

Was she being a complete wuss? There might not be anything at all. Whoever it was might have got his anger out and would leave her alone now.

But if he hadn't …

"Yes, please." She got to her feet. "Let me have a quick

shower."

It took her only a few minutes to get ready and the hot water did ease some of her aching muscles. As she came back into the living room and picked up her bag, Fleur opened the door.

"What's this?" Fleur asked.

There was a white envelope tied with the same red ribbon that had been around the chickens' necks on the doorstep. It had Hannah's name typed on it in big bold letters.

Fleur bent down to pick it up.

"Don't touch it!" Hannah's heart pounded as she stepped in front of Fleur. He'd been here, he'd been to her best friend's place. He'd been watching them.

"Shit, sorry – reflex. I'll call Lincoln." Fleur pulled out her phone.

Hannah stared at the envelope. What was inside? Could it simply be a letter of apology – an I-won't-bother-you-again?

She couldn't get her hopes up. She scanned the street, but there was only Mr Corson walking his dog. She returned his greeting, trying to work past the tightness in her chest.

Lincoln arrived shortly after and documented the scene. Hannah checked the time. "You should go to work," she said to Fleur. "You're going to be late."

"I'll call them," Fleur said. "I'm not leaving you here by yourself."

Hannah frowned. "Lincoln's here – and I should be getting to work anyway."

Fleur ignored her. "Lincoln, should Hannah go to work alone?"

Hannah rolled her eyes at her friend as Lincoln looked up. "Will anyone else be there?"

"All of my guests," Hannah said, trying to keep things light. She didn't like the idea of being alone, but she wasn't going to be a victim any longer. She wasn't going to let this interrupt her life.

"When will Lynette arrive?" Lincoln asked.

"Nine."

"Let me call Ryan." He pulled out his phone. "He can drop by the caravan park on his way in."

The thought of seeing Ryan again made her body warm, but her chest tightened at the thought of being alone with him. "Don't be silly, Lincoln. He's got Felix to take care of."

"He's the closest," Lincoln said. "Adam lives in Albany, it'll take him forty minutes to get here, and Sue isn't rostered on until this afternoon." He watched her for a moment, clearly reading her thoughts. "I'd trust him with my life."

Hannah swallowed, and then nodded. She would be fine. She had Joe.

Lincoln made the call and then gave the go-ahead for them both to leave. Hannah drove slowly to the caravan park, hating the fact that it had become a place she didn't feel entirely safe in. Her mobile rang when she was almost there. "Blackbridge Holiday Park, Hannah speaking."

"It's the Hutchinsons from site twenty. We want to check out."

Hannah relaxed. "I'm just around the corner. Or you can leave your key in the drop box outside the door."

"We wanted to get some brochures."

"I'll be right there." Someone would be with her until Ryan arrived. She parked and rushed to unlock the office, apologising to her guests for the inconvenience, and offering some suggestions on where they could go next. The normality of the process soothed her, and by the time Ryan walked in the front door with Felix she was almost calm again. One look at Ryan changed that. The way his blue shirt stretched across his chest made her heart beat faster. She wasn't sure what to do about these strange emotions.

"Hi, Hannah," Felix called. "Is Joe here?"

At his name, Joe's ears perked up and he got to his feet. Felix was here, Joe was here, Lincoln trusted Ryan. "He sure is. Why don't you both come around the back?"

Ryan raised his eyebrows. "You OK with that?"

She nodded. She'd survived – and enjoyed – a date with Ryan, she could do this. She went to the back door to let them in. Felix greeted Joe like a long-lost friend. "Can I take him outside and play?"

Hannah's breath caught in her throat. In the hallway everyone was much too close. She squeezed her eyes shut, trying to ignore the panic. Why was she fine one minute and terrified the next?

"Maybe a little later, mate," Ryan said. "Why don't you do some drawing in the kitchen, while I talk to Hannah?" He moved into the kitchen and put the small backpack he was carrying on the table.

Felix pouted. "All right. Can Joe stay with me?"

"Joe will go where he wants to go," Hannah said, breathing a little easier now. Ryan wasn't going to attack her. She was fine. The front door chimed. "Excuse me for a minute. Help yourself to a drink." She hurried out.

She had two people check out in rapid succession, and Ryan stayed in the kitchen with Felix. Their back-and-forth conversation was sweet.

She wrote out her plan for the day. The school term had ended yesterday so she was expecting a number of people today, before the influx of people tomorrow who were getting away for the week before Christmas. It was going to be busy, but she had both Shirley and Lynette coming in this morning to make sure everything was clean and ready.

"Are you all right in here?" Ryan's voice made her jump. He was leaning on the low cupboard across the room, his feet crossed, his hands either side of his body, keeping his distance, though his gaze on hers made her aware of how male he was. Her body wanted one thing, but her brain wouldn't concur.

"Yes. Just preparing for the day."

"What do you need to do?" he asked, seemingly interested.

"We'll be full by Sunday afternoon, so I need to make sure all the bathrooms are cleaned and mow the grass around the sites. I'll also check the pool area, the pH and such."

"Is it a lot of work?"

"It can be, but I've lived here for so long it's just part of life."

"Your grandparents own the park, don't they?"

She nodded. "They've owned it for thirty years," she said. "They're thinking of selling though. It's one of the reasons they're on their own caravan trip around Australia. They want to experience what it's like on the other side, decide whether to take off permanently." She was glad they were out enjoying life, glad they realised she was a grown woman and didn't need them around all the time. Even glad they'd pushed her into taking the first step on her retreat. She'd been hiding for too long.

"Do you miss them?"

"Yes, but I'm happy they've taken the time for themselves." They'd put their lives on hold to raise her and given her a job when she'd left university, not questioned her desire to stay here too much. Perhaps they'd suspected she needed somewhere she felt safe.

"Where do they live when they're here?"

"The cabin across there." Hannah pointed.

He frowned. "So why are you living out on your property?"

"I like my space," she said. "If I stay here, I'm constantly alert, constantly working, but if I go out there, I can work on my own project and enjoy the solitude." She'd been surprised at how safe she'd felt out there by herself. She'd always thought no one would find her there.

"Until some guy and his son ruined it for you," Ryan said with a smile.

"You didn't ruin it – the guy sending me presents did that." Now that she knew Ryan a little better, she felt safer having him close by.

Ryan scowled.

"Any news from Lincoln?" she asked.

"Not yet."

Before she could ask more, Mrs Zanetti walked in. "Good morning, all." Her smile was large and friendly.

"Morning, Mrs Z." Hannah grinned.

"Thanks for coming in," Ryan said.

Hannah glanced between them and then remembered that Mrs Z was looking after Felix while Ryan was at work. "Oh, I'm sorry. I'm messing with your routine."

"You're not messing with anything," Mrs Z said. "It's far better that Ryan is here with you and you're safe."

Hannah smiled. "Would you like a coffee?"

"No, thank you. I need to pick up Felix and get back to the farm. Harold promised to show him how to make cheese today."

"I'll go and get him." Ryan headed out back.

Hannah clenched her hands together. With Felix gone, it would be just her and Ryan, and there was still half an hour before any of her staff would arrive. But she had Joe as well.

"It's so nice to have Ryan back in town, don't you think?" Mrs Z asked.

Hannah nodded.

"You had a crush on him when you were little if I recall correctly."

Heat flooded Hannah's cheeks. "How did you know that?"

Mrs Z laughed. "You girls always appeared when Ryan was at our place. If he wasn't there, Jamie would go over to Kit's instead."

She glanced towards the back, but Ryan was outside with Felix. She let out a sigh of relief. "That was a long time ago."

"Indeed," Mrs Z agreed.

Felix came back inside. "Hi, Nonna. Are we really going to do cheese making today?"

"We really are. Are you ready to go?"

"Yep."

"Great."

"I'll pick him up after five." Ryan turned to Felix. "You be good, and listen to what Mr and Mrs Z say."

"Yes, Dad."

Hannah and Ryan watched them go.

"Did the Zanettis visit you in Karratha?" Hannah asked.

"Lincoln did. Felix met Lincoln's parents when we arrived here."

Hannah smiled. "They've taken a liking to each other."

"Yeah." He faced her. "It's a relief. I wasn't sure what I was going to do with him while I worked. Lincoln asked his mum if she knew of a child minder and she said she'd do it – wouldn't take no for an answer."

"That's Mrs Z."

He nodded. "She welcomes everyone." He cleared his throat. "Do you want to pass me a chair, and I'll sit on this side?"

The impulse to agree was strong, as was the rush of warmth

that he understood how she was feeling. But she wouldn't improve if she kept avoiding the situation. "You can come back around."

"Are you sure?"

No. "Yes. I want to get better at this."

"All right."

She busied herself filling up the printer paper tray, but was aware the moment he walked into the room. Joe trotted in behind him and went to his bed. She gestured to a chair. "I, uh, was thinking about taking some self-defence classes. Do the police offer any community-training sessions?"

"We did in Karratha, but I'm not sure about here. If not, I can teach you. I used to give the classes up there."

The thought of getting up close and personal with Ryan set her heart racing, but it wasn't fear she was feeling. "Thank you."

Ryan's phone rang and Hannah focused on her work while he answered it. It sounded like it was Lincoln. By the time he hung up, her skin was tight.

"What is it?"

"He got a good print from the envelope and he'll send Adam to the Albany station to run it. He's going to drop around and talk to you."

"What was in the envelope?"

He was silent.

"*Ryan.*"

He sighed. "Four business cards."

"Huh?" That wasn't as bad as dead chickens and nowhere near as bad as the poisonous substances she'd been imagining.

She ran through the song in her head, but couldn't remember what was supposed to be on the fourth day of Christmas. She searched the internet. "It should be four calling birds." She turned and Ryan was right behind her, peering over her shoulder. She stilled, willing herself not to panic. He wasn't touching her, wasn't even looking at her. She was safe.

There was a knock on the back door and Ryan went to let Lincoln in. When they reached the office, Lincoln handed her four clear plastic bags with the cards in them. She flicked through them: the Blackbridge Holiday Park, Mai's bakery, the Blackbridge Hospital and Kit's dairy farm. She glanced up at

Lincoln, her eyes wide. "Calling cards. He's using our business cards as calling cards."

Lincoln frowned at her. "What?"

"Back in Victorian times, you used to leave a calling card when you went to visit a friend." She paused. "But theoretically, he should be leaving his card, not the other way around."

"This means he's been visiting all of you," Ryan said.

Hannah's blood chilled. "But why? It makes no sense. Did he leave a note?"

Lincoln nodded. He handed her another plastic bag.

The note was typed in red ink.

I know who you care for.

The impact of the words was like being stabbed. Someone wanted to hurt her friends. She gasped and sank into her seat. "It's got to be a local. No one else would know we're such close friends."

Ryan shook his head. "You've been staying with Fleur, and spent the day with Mai yesterday. Could be he's following you."

"But what about Kit? I only saw her Monday and that was before this got nasty."

"It wouldn't be hard to find out," Lincoln said. "We'll ask around, see if anyone's been asking about you or the other girls."

"It's probably some stupid prank," she said. "Someone I've annoyed who is getting back at me."

"Who have you annoyed lately?" Lincoln asked.

She shrugged. "No one that I can think of."

"What about your business card? Who have you given it to this week?" Ryan asked.

"They're here for the taking and there's a stack over at the tourist centre. He could have got it from anywhere."

"You all need to be vigilant over the next week or so," Lincoln said. "Could be you're right and after the twelve days are up, this all goes away."

"And if it doesn't?"

"Fleur's house is big enough for you all to stay in."

Hannah shook her head. "No, damn it. That won't work. We all work different hours and Kit works alone half the time. She doesn't need a twenty-minute commute to start her day. There are always going to be times when we're alone."

"Kit can stay with my parents," Lincoln said.

She looked at him. They both knew how well Kit would take being dictated to.

He swore.

"Let's be rational about this," Ryan said. "It might be nothing. We'll meet all the musketeers this afternoon to discuss options. In the meantime, we'll check if we've received any matching prints."

"OK."

"What time do you finish this afternoon?" Ryan asked.

"Three. Shirley's staying back to check in the late arrivals."

"All right. Come over to the station and I'll teach you a few basic self-defence techniques," he said.

Was she ready for that? Ready to be manhandled by Ryan? She tried to focus on the part of her that was excited, not the one that was freaked out. She nodded. She would be fine. They'd be at the station. She'd be safe.

That was her new mantra.

Chapter 9

Shirley waltzed into the office with Fairy Floss right on her heels. Her steps slowed as she noticed Lincoln and Ryan and her hand came to her mouth. "Not more hens."

"No, Shirley," Hannah reassured her. "He left a couple of business cards today."

She frowned. "Business cards?"

"Yeah, nothing to worry about," Lincoln said with a smile. "Though you may be able to help. Has anyone been asking about Hannah?"

"Asking what?"

"Anything."

"There were a couple of people who asked me what was happening at her retreat. I didn't tell them anything."

Hannah smiled. Probably because she didn't know. Only Hannah's grandparents, the musketeers and now Ryan knew the whole plan. She hadn't wanted to tell too many people in case she failed, and Shirley was a bit of a gossip.

"If you hear someone asking questions, please tell us," Lincoln said. "We'll be going now, Hannah," he continued. "Call us if you need us."

Hannah nodded and walked them to the door.

"I'll see you at three?" Ryan asked.

"Yes." It would be good to learn to defend herself. After letting them out, she wandered back to the office, noting that

Fairy Floss was curled up next to Joe on his bed. Shirley was already glancing through the plan for the day. "Do you want to begin in the office?" Hannah asked.

"Sure," Shirley said. Then she hesitated. "Tonight, when I'm waiting for the late arrivals, is it OK if I have someone with me?"

Surprised, Hannah said, "You mean in the office?"

Shirley nodded.

After what had been going on, she could understand why Shirley was a little nervous. "Sure, as long as they don't use the computer. Who is it?"

Shirley blushed. "I've met a guy," she gushed. "He's down for the week, but we spent the evening together yesterday and talked until late. He completely gets me, even if he's a bit younger."

Hannah grinned, pleased for her. Shirley was lonely. She had no children and her husband had died five years ago. "What's his name?"

"Mark. You'll have to meet him. He's a dish."

"Who's a dish?" Lynette asked as she walked in.

"Shirley's new man." Hannah checked the time. "I'd better start cleaning. Lynette, do you want to do the garden stuff to keep an eye on your boys?"

"That would be great."

Hannah called Joe to her side and left them talking about Mark. As she stepped outside, she took in a deep breath and rolled back her shoulders. Lynette's kids were playing on the big bouncy pillow cushion, and some other kids were playing at the playground. As she walked to the storeroom, a family was discussing hiring the kayaks to take up the river. It was normal, holiday stuff. But her life was anything but normal at the moment.

With a sigh, she grabbed what she needed and headed to one of the two big toilet blocks. She cleaned the women's side first, and then walked around to the men's side. She hated this part. Her shoulders tense, she hammered on the door and yelled, "Cleaner! Everyone decent?"

There was no response. She put up her sign to say the room was being cleaned and opened the door. Cautiously she walked in, listening. There were no showers running and no toilet doors shut. Making sure Joe was with her, she locked the door, keeping the key in it, and then walked down the long aisle to make sure each stall was empty.

Her heart thumped in her chest as she pushed open doors, always alert. It would be so easy to get trapped in here. When she finally got to the end, her shoulders relaxed. She was alone.

Quickly she got to work.

Ryan had been on his feet all day and had achieved next to nothing. He and Adam had spoken with people all over town to check if anyone had been asking questions about Hannah and her friends. No one remembered anything out of the ordinary.

When they'd arrived back at the station, they'd had to go out and deal with a complaint about a farmer and his firearm, and then there had been a report of kids throwing rocks at cars on the highway and he'd had to play bad cop to get them to stop. First day of the school holidays and they were already bored. That didn't bode well.

"You knocking off, now?" Lincoln asked.

Ryan checked the time. "Yeah. I need to get down to the hall to give Hannah her lesson."

Lincoln had made some phone calls and arranged for a room at the community hall to be available. They had floor mats, and in exchange Lincoln had promised to put together a six-week self-defence course that anyone could attend.

"I spoke to the others while you were out," Lincoln said. "They're going to join you there."

"Others?"

"Fleur, Mai and Kit. They could all do with a lesson."

The relief was immediate – he wouldn't be alone with Hannah, and Hannah would be far more comfortable with her friends around. With a nod at Lincoln, he left the station.

He could admit to himself that he admired Hannah. After what she'd been through, she was trying to help herself. When it had been just the two of them in the office this morning, she'd been tense, so he'd kept his distance and slowly she'd relaxed, had even smiled at him. He'd been thrilled.

Yeah, sure he wasn't getting emotionally involved.

As he pulled into the car park, he spotted Hannah and Fleur greeting a small Asian woman. That had to be Mai. He wandered over. "Afternoon."

Hannah smiled at him and it felt like a win. "Hi, Ryan. Have you met Mai?"

He shook his head and held out his hand. "No, but I've had one of your eclairs and it's the best I've ever had."

Mai grinned at him. "Thanks. Nice to meet you."

"Lincoln tells me he's organised a room," Ryan said.

At that moment a dirty white ute pealed into the car park. Kit got out and hurried over. "Sorry I'm late."

He raised his eyebrow. "Were you going that fast the whole way here?"

Kit grinned at him. "Of course not, Senior Constable." She linked her arm through his and said, "How about you show me how to take down a man?"

He grinned at her obvious change of subject and let the matter drop.

Fleur rolled her eyes, but Ryan caught a glimpse of displeasure on Hannah's face. Was she jealous? She needn't be because he wasn't interested in Kit. Or Hannah.

Inside the hall, an older guy walked over to them and grinned. "It's the musketeers."

"All for one." Kit let go of his arm and put her hand out in front.

"And one for all," the others replied, adding their hands to Kit and drawing them upwards.

Ryan chuckled. They weren't the least bit embarrassed. The man stepped forward with his hand outstretched. "You must be the new senior constable. I'm Brenton, the manager here. I've already set up the room for you."

Ryan shook Brenton's hand. "Ryan Kilpatrick."

They followed Brenton into a room about half the size of a basketball court. It had a dozen gym mats already on the floor. "You can have an hour and then I need to pack it up for the yoga class."

"Thanks. I appreciate it." Ryan turned to the women. "Let's

get started."

Briefly, he explained the areas of the body that were the most vulnerable to attack. "Your most effective tools are your feet," he said. "If you can get loose and run, then you run, don't fight back. Of course, if you disable them before you run, that's good too."

"So, kick 'em in the balls and run," Kit said.

"Yep – groin, eyes or throat are the most vulnerable areas." He went through the most common attacks, and getting Fleur to attack him, he demonstrated how to defend against them. As he showed them how to escape if they were grabbed from behind, Kit said, "The Calypso defence."

The women cracked up laughing, Hannah holding her sides as her laugh rang out clear and bright. It tugged at something inside him and it was all he could do not to smile in response. Instead, he raised an eyebrow in question.

Mai cleared her throat. "Calypso is my ragdoll cat," she said. "When you pick him up he goes limp like that."

Ryan chuckled. "Calypso it is, then. Now, I want you to pair off and then I want one person to attack the other. First grab their wrist."

They attempted what he'd shown them and he gave feedback when it was needed, keeping a close eye on Hannah. She was paired with Kit.

"Come on, Novak, show me what you've got," Kit dared as she held her.

Hannah's face was a picture of concentration as she slowly twisted out of Kit's hold.

"Not bad if I was your nanna," Kit teased. "A snail is faster than you."

Hannah's eyebrows rose. "Oh yeah? I'd like to see you do better."

Kit raised a hand at Hannah and beckoned to her. "Come at me."

Kit's taunts were working and Hannah became more and more relaxed as she worked through the movements. When he was sure they had it, he said, "OK, now you need to get away from me."

He gripped Fleur's wrist, pulling her towards him. She

immediately went into action, putting what she'd learned into practice and he was on his butt in seconds. He grinned. "Great." He got back to his feet and attacked Kit and Mai, leaving Hannah to last. "Ready?"

She nodded, though there was concern in her eyes. He grasped her wrist, and all her muscles tensed. She stared at him like a startled rabbit. "Come on, Hannah. Pretend I'm Kit."

"You're not prettier than me," Kit called.

Something in Hannah's eyes flicked and suddenly he was on the ground. He chuckled as Hannah high-fived her friends. Now, they needed to work on her freezing.

He worked them solidly through the hour, making corrections, and ensuring he spent time close to Hannah, wanting her to get used to being near him. The final defensive move was one where the victim was pushed up against a wall. Once again, when they had the technique down, he took his turn attacking. It was probably one of the hardest positions to get out of, because there was little room to manoeuvre. Kit and Fleur both added their voices to their response, screaming at him so loudly that he winced and loosened his hold and then they acted. Both of their knees brushed dangerously closed to his crotch and he was more than happy to let go.

Mai was smaller, but she was strong and fast. Before he'd fully backed her against the wall, she had ducked out from under him and was gone.

"Hey, that's cheating," Kit said.

Ryan shook his head. "No, it's a good idea. Don't let yourself get into a vulnerable situation if you can help it." He faced Hannah. "Your turn."

She swallowed, her eyes wide.

Ryan couldn't let himself feel sorry for her — that wasn't going to help her. He deliberately kept his gaze on hers as he advanced. Her green eyes were unblinking and there was fear in them. She took a step to the side as if uncertain, and he mirrored the step, moving closer. She stepped back, two fast steps and her arms fluttered with nerves. He didn't let himself stop. She had to be able to fight. This was for her own good. She bumped into the wall and gasped, her whole body tensing. He smiled. "I've got you now." He pressed both hands against the wall at her shoulder height, inhaling her floral scent, close enough to feel the heat from her skin.

Behind him, her friends were calling out encouragement. "Gouge his eyes!" Fleur cried.

"Break his nose!" Mai yelled.

Hannah didn't move. She stared at him like a kangaroo caught in headlights. "Hannah, are you going to do anything?" he asked.

No response.

Deliberately taunting her, he said, "You're trapped. If you don't move, I can do what I like to you – I could kiss you." Still nothing.

He didn't want to be a bastard, but he had to get a reaction from her, had to get her to fight back. "Maybe you want this," he whispered.

Her eyes darted to his lips, and when she looked back at him, it wasn't fear in her eyes, but desire.

He couldn't do this. This was all kinds of wrong. Before he could back off, Hannah attacked. Her knee came up sharply right between his legs, and her arms flung out, pushing him down.

All the air left him as pain seared through his abdomen and his eyes rolled back in his head. He went down like a sack of shit, holding his crotch as he gasped for air.

"Oh my God, are you all right?" Hannah was standing over him, her face concerned.

"Give me a minute," he wheezed. It was his own fault. He shouldn't have pushed her so hard, shouldn't have been distracted by what he'd imagined he'd seen in her eyes. So dumb.

The girls all congratulated Hannah as he slowly got to his feet, bending over as the pain receded. "Good work," he said when he was able to talk properly.

"Thanks, Ryan," Fleur said. "That was really useful. We should do it again."

He nodded. "Let me know when." He'd invest in a groin protector.

They packed up the mats and left the hall. Hannah was walking on the far side of him, not looking at him. He hated to push her comfort zone, but he needed to apologise. He moved closer. "You did well in there."

She flashed him a smile that didn't quite reach her eyes. "Thanks. Sorry about hurting you."

"My own fault," he said. "I shouldn't have pushed you so hard. Besides, that's what you were meant to do."

"I panicked."

He glanced at her. "You need to work on the way you freeze."

"I'm trying."

"I know." It didn't help that he'd been an arsehole, pushing all her triggers. It was inexcusable, especially considering what she'd been through.

He needed to get his head read.

Hannah was relieved to get into Kit's ute and leave the others behind. They swung by Fleur's place to pick up Joe, before heading out to Kit's farm, stopping only briefly at Hannah's shed to get some more clothes.

She was such a moron!

She hadn't frozen when Ryan had backed her against the wall – at least not in the way he thought. She'd been mesmerised by his eyes, had hoped he would kiss her.

Was she so messed up that she was aroused by being pushed up against the wall, Ryan's musky scent invading her senses? That idea had scared the bejeezus out of her and she'd hurt him.

Now, there was no way he'd kiss her again.

She groaned.

"What's wrong?" Kit asked, glancing at her.

Hannah's face flushed. "Nothing."

"I thought today went really well," she said. "You managed to get away from Ryan each time."

"I kneed him in the balls."

"Yeah, that was the point."

Hannah shook her head.

"I've got to admit, it was kind of nice being manhandled by him." Kit laughed.

Hannah ignored the flick of jealousy. Kit was just playing around, and besides she was right, which was part of the problem.

"Hannah?" Kit's voice was concerned. "Was it too much for you?"

"It was fine." That was an understatement.

"Then what's wrong?"

She couldn't look at her friend. "It doesn't matter." It would only prove to Kit how damaged she was.

"Sure it does. Tell Kit Kat what's wrong."

Hannah couldn't help smiling at Kit's nickname.

"Did Ryan do something inappropriate?"

"No!" She sighed, giving in. Kit wasn't going to let up. "It was too nice."

Kit frowned at her. "What was?"

"Having Ryan pressed against me." Her face was so hot she might combust.

Kit laughed. "There's no such thing as too nice."

Would Kit even understand? She dated regularly and was always full of tales. But Hannah wanted to talk to someone about all these conflicting emotions inside her. "Kit, the only person I've slept with is Justin."

"Really?" Kit's tone was disbelieving.

"That *one* time," Hannah added to clarify.

"Holy shit." Kit slowed the car. "You were a virgin when he raped you?"

She nodded.

"Honey, it's no wonder you're so scared all the time." She pulled over to the side of the road and faced Hannah. "Have you done other things with men?"

Hannah shook her head. "Not since, and before … not much more than fondling and kissing."

"So Ryan feeling nice is a *really* big deal."

Tears pricked at her eyes as relief swept through her. Kit understood.

Kit leaned over and gave her an awkward hug. "OK, so we need to think about this." She pulled back on to the road. "I'm assuming you still like Ryan?"

"Yes." A whole heap more than was wise.

"And has he given you any indication that he likes you?"

She shrugged. "I wouldn't recognise it even if he did. Plus, he's been in police mode almost every time I've seen him."

"But you went on a date."

"As friends. He was doing me a favour. He only kissed me because he was almost hit by the car."

"Are you sure?"

"Yes. It was a reaction thing, not attraction. He apologised profusely afterwards."

"Ugh." Kit shook her head in disgust. "Maybe he was covering himself, maybe he didn't want you to be uncomfortable."

"Or maybe he's really not interested. I'm messed up, Kit. Why would any guy want me?"

"Don't give me that bullshit," Kit said. "You're one of the nicest people I know. Any guy would be lucky to have you. You just have a couple of intimacy and trust issues you need to work through."

"A couple?" Hannah snorted. "More like a lifetime."

"Yeah, OK," Kit agreed. "So maybe you need to be straight-up honest with him. Tell him you like him, that you want to kiss him, but you can't guarantee you won't freak out."

Hannah grimaced. "Yeah, because that sounds appealing." The idea of having the conversation with Ryan made her chest tight.

"Well, as you said, he's been in police mode when he's been with you. Maybe he considers it a conflict of interest, or a dereliction of duty, or whatever they call it."

"Some kind of abuse of power?"

"That's it."

Ryan would be noble about that kind of thing. "If that's the case, what do I do?"

"You've got the perfect excuse to see him out of work hours," Kit said. "He's living in your cabin so you can drop by, or ask for some private self-defence lessons." She waggled her eyebrows.

Maybe Kit was right. Maybe this was her chance to fix what was broken inside of her. Maybe Ryan was her chance to get a normal life back.

"Take it slow. Talk to him about something other than this weirdo who keeps leaving you gifts." She pulled on to the road to her farmhouse. "Then when you're ready, kiss him."

Kit made it sound simple, only it wasn't. Not for Hannah. But she was going to try.

There was another envelope tied with a red ribbon on the doorstep when Hannah opened the door to go to work the next day. Anger and fear flooded her body in equal portions. "Damn it," she yelled and kicked at the envelope, missing it. He'd followed her all the way to Kit's farm, he'd been watching Hannah yesterday afternoon.

Kit jogged out of the kitchen. "What's wrong?"

Hannah had had enough of being scared all the damn time. The stalker was affecting all of their lives. Kit should already be out milking her cows, instead of here, waiting until Hannah left for work. She picked up the envelope and held it up to Kit. "This is what's wrong."

"Shit. Is that one of the gifts?"

Hannah nodded, ripping open the envelope.

"Shouldn't you call Lincoln? Don't they need to take prints or something?"

She was so mad she didn't care. She tipped the contents out on her palm. Five rings.

Five of her own *personal* rings, from her jewellery box at home.

Her stomach swirled and she fought back the nausea, stumbling to the nearest chair and sinking down.

The note read, *I can take what's yours.*

"That ring looks familiar," Kit said.

"That's because it's mine – they all are." There was nowhere he hadn't been now, nowhere she could hide. He'd invaded her most personal space.

Fury welled up in her as she called Lincoln. "He's been in my house."

It was time to fight back.

The day didn't get any better. Hannah had gone to work after she'd extracted a promise from Kit that she would call every hour and check in. Kit did have farmhands working with her, but there were times when she worked alone as well. Kit had agreed, clearly shaken that whoever it was had come out to the farm and hadn't disturbed any of the dogs.

Work had been flat out for Hannah, with guests arriving all day, barely giving her enough time to make a cup of tea between them. She was thankful for it. It meant she didn't have time to dwell on the fact that the man had been in her house, had been to Kit's. He knew where they all lived now. She wasn't safe anywhere.

Lincoln had dropped by the caravan park to get Hannah's house key. When he'd finished processing Kit's place, he was going to her shed to look for any evidence. He'd been angry – rightfully so – when she'd told him she'd ripped open the envelope, and she'd apologised.

Now, it was five o'clock and she was calling it a day. Her head throbbed, her eyes ached and she was desperately tired. She was supposed to call Lincoln, but first she needed a few minutes of peace. Whistling to Joe, and picking up a tennis ball, she locked up the office and headed towards the beach. A walk along the shore would calm her and it was still warm enough that there would be people surfing or swimming.

The wind was brisk as she cleared the sand dunes and trudged down the path to the shore. Joe raced ahead, sniffing at clumps of dried seaweed and chasing the gulls.

There weren't as many people on the beach as she'd expected. A few surfers in the waves, though the surf wasn't very good, a couple she recognised from the park and a man and his son building sandcastles. Hannah squinted and her heartbeat tripled. Ryan.

With a joyous woof, Joe raced towards them. "Joe!" she yelled as visions of him trampling Felix crossed her mind.

He slowed and came to a stop but didn't come back. At her yell Ryan and Felix both looked up. Ryan lifted a hand in a wave.

This was her chance to talk to Ryan. He was off-duty, but what the hell was she supposed to say? Nerves tickled her skin as she wandered over, giving Joe leave to greet Felix.

Felix giggled in excitement as he gave Joe a big hug. "Hiya, boy."

Ryan's hair was wet, full of salt and sand, and his chest was bare. She clenched her hands into fists to stop from reaching out to touch him. "Hi. I wasn't expecting to find you here."

"Felix wanted to go swimming." He raised his eyebrow. "Should you be here alone?"

"I've got Joe," she said. "And now you." She swallowed. That sounded like she expected him to protect her. "I mean, you're here so I'll be fine." Nope, not much better. She changed the subject. "There's a path down to the beach at the retreat. If you take the other fork in the road it leads to the path and you won't have to drive into town."

"Great. Thanks for telling me."

"Hannah, can I throw the ball for Joe?" Felix asked.

"Sure." She tossed it to him and watched him play with Joe for a moment. Then she remembered the sandcastle. "Sorry, I'm interrupting." She took a step back.

"Not at all. We were about finished anyway." He was quiet for a moment. "Lincoln filled me in on the latest."

Hannah held up a hand. "Please, don't. I don't want to talk about that at the moment. I came down here to get a few minutes of peace before I go and see him."

"We're disturbing you." He nodded to Felix.

"Oh, no. He's fine. Joe could do with the exercise. He's been cooped up with me for the past few days." She hesitated. She could do this. "I was going to walk to the rocks and back. Do you and Felix want to join me?"

He smiled. "Sure." He got to his feet in a fluid movement and brushed the sand from his body. Hannah's mouth went dry. She swallowed, clenching her hands to stop herself from helping him to brush off the sand, and walked down the beach.

"The park looked almost full when we drove past," Ryan said.

She nodded. "I had a huge number of people check in today. It was non-stop."

"Is it always like this?"

"School holidays are, and long weekends. The rest of the time we get a steady business." She spotted a sea eagle and pointed it out to Ryan.

When it flew away he asked, "How's the cabin coming along?"

"Slowly. I haven't had much time over the last couple of days."

"Have you got a name for the place yet?"

"Hideaway Resort." Did it sound trite? Could he even understand what it was like to want to hide away from the world for a time? She glanced back to where Felix and Joe were running all over the sand, chasing each other. "Has Felix settled in?"

"Yeah. He had a great time at the Christmas wind-up on Thursday. Mrs Z wrote down the names and numbers for the kids he made friends with and I'm going to arrange some playdates over the break."

"He's welcome at the holiday park at any time," Hannah said.

"Thanks. I appreciate it." His smile made her heart flutter.

"And I appreciate all the help you've given me."

"All part of the job."

Of course it was. Her joy faded. "I'm sorry I hurt you yesterday."

"So am I." He chuckled. "But it was the right thing to do. I shouldn't have threatened you."

"Threatened me?"

"I said I'd kiss you if you didn't move."

She laughed. "That's hardly a threat. It's more of a reward." Realising what she'd said, Hannah snapped her mouth shut. Aw, hell. He was staring at her, his eyes wide. "Sorry," she muttered, heat flooding her cheeks.

"I, uh, didn't think you were comfortable with men."

She needed to be honest. "You're becoming the exception."

He was silent and she didn't dare look at him.

"Hannah, that's not a good idea. I mean – it's great you're comfortable with me – but I'm working on your case. That can only get messy."

She was sure her face couldn't get any hotter. "You mean if you weren't involved in a police capacity, it would be OK?"

He hesitated.

Nope. She'd read too much into it. "Forget I asked. I'm sorry. I'm messed up. It can't be appealing." They had reached the rocks so she turned back.

Ryan grasped her wrist, stopping her. She tried to push away the fleeting panic as she checked where Joe was.

"Sorry." Ryan let go. "You're not messed up." His gaze was intense. "You've had something awful happen to you that you have to deal with." Slowly, he took hold of her hand again and his thumb rubbed against the back of it. "You're also incredibly attractive. Any guy would be lucky to have you."

The pulse in her wrist throbbed.

He sighed, letting go of her wrist. "I'm not ready for another relationship."

She rubbed the spot where he touched, trying to get her heart rate under control.

"There's too much at stake. I have Felix to consider."

She recognised a rejection when she heard one. At least he was being kind, letting her down gently. Still, it hurt. "Of course. I'm sorry. I put you in an awkward position." She continued walking, not looking back at him.

She was foolish. Just because he was the first guy she was interested in since forever, didn't mean he was going to reciprocate those feelings.

An uncomfortable silence stretched between them and Hannah didn't know how to break it.

She really had no clue of what she was doing.

She shouldn't have bothered to try.

Chapter 10

Hannah had never been so happy to reach the path back to the caravan park. She fought the urge to run as she called Joe to her side. "I'll see you both later." She gave Felix a friendly wave before getting out of there. It was mortifying. She'd practically thrown herself at the man and he wasn't interested in catching.

Of course he wasn't.

Reaching the pavement, she brushed most of the sand off her feet before slipping her shoes back on. She didn't want to still be there when Ryan came up.

"Hannah! Hi!"

She turned at the call, glad for the distraction, and found herself face to face with Justin and his friends, all wet and dishevelled and carrying their surfboards. She recognised Smithy, who had been Justin's roommate when they'd dated.

Her embarrassment faded as anger welled up. She'd had it with men today. It was his fault that she was in this predicament. He'd made her into this pathetic mess. Well she was done with it. She'd given Justin power over her for far too long. "What do you want?" she demanded.

He took a step back, his grin fading. "I, uh, well, we're leaving tomorrow, so I was hoping to catch up before we did."

She shook her head, the disbelief making her almost lightheaded. "Why the hell would I want to catch up with you after what you did?"

His friends glanced at each other, but Justin looked confused. "What did I do?"

Her breath left her and she stared at him. She lowered her voice and hissed, "You raped me."

His eyes widened. "No, I didn't."

She blinked, not quite believing what he was saying. "Yes, you did." She said it slowly, clearly. "I asked you to stop, I said I wasn't ready, I struggled and you held me down until you'd got what you wanted." It hadn't been her fault, no it had all been Justin.

His friends were gaping at him. "That's not how I remember it." His smile was forced.

The rage welled up in Hannah so fast she couldn't control it. She slapped him hard across the face, her palm stinging at the contact. "Go to hell." She strode away as one of his friends said, "What the fuck, Justin?"

She had done it. She had confronted Justin, she hadn't frozen, hadn't run, she had told him the truth. And now his friends knew.

A part of her that had been locked away for so long sprang open, making it easier to breathe. Justin may never go to jail for what he did, but he wasn't going to get away with it scot-free. His friends wouldn't see him in the same light as they had before.

Hannah made it all the way to her car, fighting back the tears of relief, the footpath in front of her a blur. She didn't check what his reaction was, she didn't care. She was done with him, done with men in general.

She slammed the door of the car shut, cocooning herself inside the vehicle before the tears overwhelmed her. Lowering her head to the steering wheel, she sat and sobbed.

Her throat hurt by the time she'd cried herself out. Wiping her face with the bottom of her polo shirt, she then drove to Lincoln's house. She could deal with anything now.

"Rough day?" he asked as he opened the door to her and Joe.

She sniffed. "I look that bad, do I?"

"You've looked better." He glanced both ways down the street before closing the door. "Want a drink?"

"A Coke would be great." She sat at his kitchen table and braced herself for whatever he had to tell her. "So, what's the latest?"

"We got the same prints from the envelope, but there's nothing on file." He handed her a glass of Coke with ice, and took a sip from his beer. "The lock had been jimmied open at your place. I'm going to need you to check if anything else has been taken."

She nodded. The thought that he'd been in her home gave her the heebie-jeebies. She wanted to wash everything in case he'd touched anything.

"The ground is too dry and hard to get any footprints or tyre marks," Lincoln continued, "but I found the same fingerprints there."

"So, it's just one guy."

"Seems that way."

"What do we do now?"

"I bought some surveillance cameras," he said. "He leaves the gifts some time at night, so we'll set them up at the park office, your place, and at Kit's and Fleur's."

She shook her head. "No. If he's watching me, he'll see you do it." She squeezed her eyes shut. She wouldn't cry anymore. "I need this to be over, Lincoln. I'll spend the night at my own place. Give him a chance to come and say what he needs to say to me and we can move on."

Lincoln sat back and crossed his arms. "Don't be dumb."

Hannah scowled. "I'm not. We're making this into more than it is. He's done nothing to threaten me, and I've been with someone pretty much the entire time since it began. Maybe he just wants to talk to me in person." OK, so the argument sounded thin to her ears as well, but she was so over this.

"He killed those chickens."

That made her pause. "Maybe it was an accident, maybe he was mad at seeing me kiss Ryan." Maybe he was like her father and had lost his temper. Hannah's blood ran cold. "OK, you're right. Let's do the cameras."

"I'm glad you agree because I've already set up the ones at Fleur's and Kit's, so we just need to do your office and shed."

She stared at him.

"What? It didn't occur to me that you'd disagree, and you didn't really, so it's done." He placed a hand over hers. "I swore to protect the musketeers."

She was unable to be mad at him. "All right. Shall we go and do it now?"

"You don't have to come with me. I'll drop off your keys wherever you're staying tonight."

"I want to go home, Lincoln."

"No."

"I have to check if he stole anything anyway." She sighed. "And get more clothes. I hate that I've brought the musketeers into this."

"That wasn't your fault," he said. "We'll go to the office first, and then I'll take you out to your place." He stood up. "But first, I've made some spaghetti."

Hannah grinned at the first bit of good news she'd had all day. "Nonna's recipe?"

"Of course."

She sat back. "Bring it on."

An hour later, Lincoln had installed the camera at the office and they arrived at her shed. The big roller door was shut, but the side door was wide open and her outdoor chairs had been tipped over. The shed wasn't much, but it still hurt that it had been left so open.

"You could have shut the door," Hannah complained as she came around the side of the car.

"I did." Lincoln put a hand on her arm. "Stay here while I check it out."

Nerves thrummed over her skin. Had her stalker come back? Was he inside right now, waiting for her? As fear fought with logic, Lincoln walked towards the door. Fear for Lincoln had her calling out, "You can't go in there by yourself."

"I'm a cop, Hannah."

"An off-duty, unarmed cop," she reminded him, pulling out her phone and moving forward with him. "I'm not letting you go in alone." She couldn't live with herself if something happened to him.

He frowned. "Stay behind me, then."

They approached the door and he carefully nudged it wider. There was no one inside, but the place was a shambles. The sheets had been ripped off her bed, photo frames had been smashed and the clothes that had hung on a rack were spread out on the floor. In the kitchenette, doors were open, bits of broken crockery were strewn on the floor and food had been emptied out of its packets.

Her place had been destroyed. She wrapped her arms around herself, taking a step backwards. It was much worse than she'd expected. Surely, Lincoln should have warned her about the mess. All of her things had been gone through. She felt violated. She placed a hand on her stomach to keep the nausea down.

Lincoln swore. "I didn't leave it like this."

Hannah swallowed as anger welled inside her. "You mean he came back?"

"Looks like it unless something else happened today."

She'd not left the office all day. The only place she'd gone was ... "I saw Ryan on the beach. We went for a walk together."

"That could have been it." He sighed. "Justin's still in town, isn't he?"

Red-hot anger swept through her. "That bastard!" she growled.

Lincoln gripped her arm. "What happened?"

She took a breath to calm the anger and told him what happened on the beach.

"Hell. What did he say?"

"Nothing. I didn't let him, but his friends all heard."

"Well, that definitely could be the catalyst, if it is Justin." He sighed. "I'm sorry, Hannah. I'm going to have to process this. You can't stay here and you can't take anything away yet."

Damn it. She was tired of this affecting her life. "Are you going to call Sue in?"

He shook his head. "I'll do it myself. I've had enough

practice at it lately." He grimaced.

She didn't want to leave. Leaving felt like she was letting this arsehole win. "Take my car and drive into town to get what you need. I'll stay out here, make sure no possums explore the mess."

"I'm not leaving you out here alone."

She couldn't explain her need to stay. She'd been constantly running away, hiding, and she didn't want to any longer. She'd stood up to Justin, she'd been rejected by Ryan, and if she could handle that, she could damn well deal with this creep. The anger felt good and she embraced it, but kept her argument logical. "I need to clean up after you're done," she said. "And I want a few minutes to myself."

Lincoln opened his mouth to refuse.

"*Please*, Lincoln. He's not likely to come back again."

He huffed out a breath. "All right. Ryan is just down the road."

She nodded, though she wasn't going to call him unless she was in real danger. Not after their conversation on the beach. She tossed him her car keys, picked up the deck chair that had been knocked over and sat down. Joe was off exploring in the bush, rustling through the undergrowth. "I'll see you when you get back."

"I won't be long," he promised.

She waited until the sound of the car faded and then she closed her eyes with a sigh.

There was a crunch in the bushes and her eyes flew open. It was Joe. She put a hand to her heart and then picked up one of the heavy sticks that Joe had collected and tested its weight.

It wasn't much, but she felt better having a weapon in her hand.

Ryan sat on his verandah staring out at the dusk. Today had not been a stellar day. He'd completely stuffed up his conversation with Hannah. What was worse was his reaction to her admission. The surge of pleasure and need at her words was unexpected and had scared the hell out of him.

It didn't matter that it had been over a year since he'd split up with Paula. He was still gun-shy. Life with Paula had been a constant roller-coaster ride and it had got to the stage where he couldn't enjoy the highs because the lows weren't far away. He wasn't ready to try the ride again.

The thought of Paula made him feel ill – the manipulation, the neediness, the secrets. She had him constantly guessing what she was thinking and when he inevitably got it wrong, she'd let him know in no uncertain terms.

He sipped his beer to rid himself of the bad taste in his mouth.

Paula was a case study in everything that could go wrong in a relationship.

Even after the split she'd appear at events he was at, or drop by his house with the excuse that she wanted to see Felix. The one time he'd accepted an invitation to drinks with a female colleague, it had ended with Paula slapping the woman and being charged with assault. That had been when he'd decided to make a complete break from her and take Felix as far away as possible.

But it was hardly fair to compare Hannah with Paula. She was nothing like his ex.

He shook his head. Perhaps he was foolish to have shut Hannah down like that. They could have casually dated, with no expectations. He liked her and she was kind to Felix. But what if Felix fell in love with her and things didn't work out between them? He'd be devastated. Ryan had let Paula's influence scar them both and they needed more time to heal.

The crunch of tyres on the gravel cut through the silence. Felix had just gone to sleep so he hurried out the front to make sure whoever it was wouldn't wake him.

It was Hannah's four-wheel drive and his heart jumped in excitement until Lincoln climbed down from the driver's side. Ryan frowned. "What's up?"

"I took Hannah back to her place and it's been trashed."

Ryan swore.

"I need to head into town to get my kit and she insisted on staying. I wanted to tell you in case you hear anything."

Ryan didn't like the idea of Hannah being there alone, but he couldn't leave his son alone either. "Felix is sleeping, but I could bundle him up and go and say hello."

Lincoln grinned at him. "Thanks, mate. I appreciate it. I won't be long." He got back into the car and drove off.

Felix was a heavy sleeper, and didn't stir when Ryan picked him up and carried him to the car.

Light reflected off the shed's silver sides, making it shine. Hannah was sitting on a deck chair, staring out at the darkness, looking lost. He wanted to hug her, tell her everything was going to be all right.

As he got out of the car, there was a low growl in the bushes off to his right. He paused. "It's me, Joe."

Joe trotted out and sniffed him, before trotting over to the shed.

Hannah sighed and frowned at him. "Did Lincoln ask you to come over?"

"Yes." He shut the car door.

"He's such a pain."

"He cares about you," Ryan said as he walked on to the concrete slab that was her front porch. "Mind if I take a look inside?"

She waved her hand. "Go ahead."

She was avoiding his gaze, and he couldn't blame her. He was embarrassed by their conversation on the beach as well.

The light inside illuminated the destruction as if a tornado had ripped through. Many of her possessions were scattered over the floor and the kitchen was a complete mess.

He turned back to Hannah. "How are you feeling?" He kept his distance, sitting on the deck chair on the other side of the outdoor table.

"Tired." She sat back down, angling her chair a little away from him. "Sick and tired of all of this."

"I'm sorry. It must be hard for you." What an inane thing to say.

"Of course it is. I've done nothing, *nothing* to deserve this." Her voice rose and her eyes flashed.

He took in a quick breath. She was stunning. Her blonde hair shone in the light like a mane and her green eyes narrowed. For the first time, she looked like a warrior rather than a victim.

He'd think twice before crossing her. "I'm glad you've found your fighting spirit." He kept his words light, hoping to calm her.

She shrugged. "Maybe your class helped after all."

"I hope so." Memories flashed through his mind of what it felt like to have her breasts pushed up against his chest, her body so close to his and the scent of frangipani invading his senses. He blinked. Talk about inappropriate. "We should, uh, make another time to train." Now he sounded like a fool.

"Why not now?" she demanded, getting to her feet. "You're going to stick around until Lincoln comes back. We might as well make good use of the time." Defiance ran off her in waves. She was spectacular.

"The ground's pretty hard."

"So we work on technique – hand holds and such." She was standing straight, but the tiny shake of her hand showed her vulnerability. He couldn't say no.

"All right." He stood and grasped her wrist lightly, wanting her to work on this technique first.

She reacted fast, freeing herself, so the next time he held her tighter. Her concentration was intense. He could almost see her considering the steps, working through them one at a time until she worked free. "Good. Now faster this time." Her skin was soft and smooth, and when it grew red from his hold, he swapped to her other hand.

They went through it a dozen times, with both hands, each time she was faster and more relaxed.

She turned away from him, laughing. "I'm getting the hang of it."

Her laughter was so joyous, and it tugged at something deep inside of him. He wanted to hear more of it. But that wasn't why he was here. He couldn't be distracted.

She still had her back to him and she was unprepared, so he seized her from behind. She froze.

He couldn't let that sway him, had to ignore the softness of her body against him. "Come on, Hannah," he murmured in her ear. "You can get out of this."

She struggled and whimpered. The noise cut through him, but he didn't relax his hold. "Grab my fingers."

She shook her head, her whole body stiff.

He hated the fear radiating off her. "Hannah, there's no need to be afraid. I'm not going to hurt you. You can get out of this. Grab my fingers."

She did it this time, peeling his two little fingers back until they hurt and he let her go.

She spun around and took a couple of steps back, her breath coming fast. He couldn't read the expression on her face. "Are you all right?" He was an arsehole for not letting go, but a real attacker wouldn't.

She hesitated, then nodded.

This was a great way to win her trust. Disgust filled him. "Do you want to try it again?"

She was silent for a moment, staring at him. Had he gone too far? Finally she said, "OK."

He stepped up, wrapping his arms around her. "Remember, if you can't get my fingers there are other things you can do," he said, keeping his voice low, near her ear. "Stamp on my instep, throw your head back and hit mine, do a Calypso, or you can use your butt to hit me in the groin."

She chuckled at the reference to Mai's cat and wiggled her butt backwards as if trying to get a sense of where he was. He was instantly hard. Shit. He loosened his hold as she gripped his fingers and twisted them, spinning on the spot and grasping his shoulders, pretending to bring her knee up into his groin. His hands found her hips and she stilled.

Ryan was unable to step away. Her eyes captured him, gazing at him with an expression he didn't want to interpret. He had to let go now, before he did something foolish, but the message wasn't relaying from his brain to his body. Ever so slowly, Hannah rose to her toes and lightly brushed her lips against his.

The kiss was sweet, sensuous, and all the paths in his brain said more. He wanted more. He was an idiot to believe he wasn't attracted to Hannah. A fool not to want to see where this could go. He deepened the kiss, slowly bringing one hand up her side to cradle the back of her head, as he kept things gentle, focusing on the kiss.

Hannah moaned, the sound sending a shot of lust straight to his groin. He pulled her closer, his hands tight on her butt, and she broke the kiss. "No!" She pushed against his chest.

Alarmed, he let go and she took a couple of steps back. "Shit. Sorry, Hannah." He ran his hand through his hair. "I shouldn't have done that." What kind of creep was he?

"Don't be sorry. Just give me a second." She paced away, shaking her hands as if she was shaking something off.

Ryan was the lowest form of scum. He'd taken advantage of the kiss and pushed her too far. He *knew* what she'd been through and had forgotten the second his hormones had taken control.

Hannah turned back to him, her hands clenched together. "I'm sorry. I shouldn't have kissed you when you said you weren't interested." Her cheeks flushed. "Then I panicked when you kissed me back. I'm not trying to be a tease. It was the way you held me."

He shook his head. She shouldn't be apologising to him. "Hannah …" He wasn't sure what to say. She'd been so honest with him, he had to be truthful in return. "You read me right. I *am* interested in you." He closed his eyes for a second. "And I'm also scared as hell about stuffing up another relationship and how it might affect Felix."

Her eyes widened. "I'm sorry. I'm being completely selfish."

He took her hand. "Paula left me with a lot of baggage and Felix will always be my priority," he said. "But if you're OK with that, we could take it slow? Starting with telling me what I did wrong with that kiss?"

She hesitated and then smiled. "I'd like that." Slowly, she took his hands, putting them on either side of her hips. "This is OK. I can deal with this. But this," she moved his hands around to her back and pulled him closer. "This harder grip hits all my brakes – short-circuits all the pleasure and goes straight to panic." She let go of his hands.

This was foreign territory for him, but he wanted to kiss Hannah again. He placed his hands lightly on her hips. "So this is all right?"

She nodded.

He brushed his lips against hers, enjoying her sweetness, and ran his hands lightly over her back. "What about this?"

She arched into him and closed her eyes. "Really nice."

The trust she was showing hit him right in the gut. Hannah was unlike any other woman he'd ever known. He wanted to experiment with her, find out what she liked. He kissed her again and then trailed kisses down her neck.

Her gasp sent heat straight to his groin and he hardened again. He deepened the kiss, tasting her, and let his hands slowly, gently, travel down her back and over her butt.

She moaned again and he was careful to keep his touch light, not to let his other brain take over. Then he heard a car approaching and saw the flash of light between the trees. He pulled back reluctantly.

Hannah's eyes were full of desire.

He cleared his throat and shut down the part of his brain that told him to ignore the sounds. "Lincoln's almost here." He gestured and she took a step back.

"Damn," she said.

"I couldn't agree more." He moved away from her as Lincoln drove up.

Lincoln was in the police car, which reminded Ryan why he was here. Hannah's place had been trashed.

"Thanks for dropping by," Lincoln said to Ryan.

Ryan shifted his feet. He wasn't sure Lincoln would be thanking him if he'd known what they had been doing. "Are you going to process the place now?"

Lincoln nodded.

It would take a lot of time with only one person. "I can help."

"What about Felix?" Hannah asked.

Ryan nodded to the car. "He's in the backseat fast asleep."

She frowned. "Do you want me to take him back to the cabin? You're not going to want me in the way here," she continued. "Felix can go back to bed and I'll stay at your place to keep an eye on him."

It was a lovely offer. And they would both be safe there. The cabin was only a couple of hundred metres down the road. "If you're OK with that?"

"Yes." She held out her hand for the keys. "I'll check what's on television."

"I'll drive you while Lincoln sets up. Felix is heavier than he looks." Ryan waited until they got into the car before squeezing Hannah's hand.

She turned to him. "Would you prefer Lincoln didn't know we kissed?"

"No. I wasn't sure how you felt."

"I'd like to kiss you again."

"Me too." But this wasn't just about the physical. He wanted to get to know her better. He cleared his throat. "Have you got any plans tomorrow?"

She smiled. "It's pancake day at the park."

"Pancake day?"

"Sunday mornings I make pancakes for whoever wants them at the park. We fire up the barbecues and have a communal gathering so guests can meet each other. You're welcome to come down if you want. I'm usually done by ten and the last guests are arriving by lunch."

She'd been working every day since he'd arrived. "Do you get much time off?"

"It'll settle down during the week without the check-ins and outs. Then Lynette works nine to three and Shirley has a few shifts so I can work out here."

Yet still, it was work. "I'm taking Felix on a picnic tomorrow, maybe to the beach. Would you like to come with us?" He was surprised by how much he wanted her to say yes.

He parked in front of the cabin.

"I don't want to intrude if it's father–son time."

He liked that she considered it. Paula never would have. He wanted to see Hannah and Felix together before things got more serious. If they didn't get along, he would end it before it went too far. "I don't think he'll mind, particularly if you bring Joe."

She laughed. "They have bonded to each other." She smiled at him. "I'd love to go with you, but ask Felix first. I won't be upset if he doesn't want me there."

He unlocked the door. "All right. Let me get him."

He carried Felix into his bedroom, and laid him gently on the bed. Felix snorted and immediately turned on to his side, burying his head into the pillow. Love flooded his body. He was the luckiest guy in the world. Ryan adjusted the sheets so they covered Felix, and brushed a kiss against his cheek. Felix didn't stir.

Hannah stood near the couch with Joe, her gaze a little uncertain. He wanted to kiss her again. Slowly he walked over to her. She stepped forward to meet him halfway.

She wound her hands around his neck and he reminded himself to be gentle as he slid his hands down to her hips and bent his head to kiss her.

He wished he could spend the whole night kissing her, but he had to get back to Lincoln. They had to find whoever was doing this to her so they could stop it and Hannah's life could get back to normal.

He broke the kiss. "Lock the door behind me."

She nodded, her tongue running over her lips. He resisted the urge to pull her close again.

"I'll see you later." He walked out the door.

Lincoln was already at work when Ryan got back. "So, you and Hannah, huh?" were his first words.

Ryan blinked. Lincoln sat back on his heels and looked at him. "You think I didn't notice how close you two were standing when I arrived, or how you took your time driving her back?"

"I, uh …" No real words came out.

Lincoln laughed. "Relax. I know you wouldn't take advantage of her. She's a great girl. I'm surprised you aren't more wary after Paula."

"Hannah's different."

Lincoln nodded. "That she is."

Relieved Lincoln wasn't going to give him the third degree, Ryan put a pair of gloves on and got to work.

Chapter 11

Hannah woke early after not enough sleep. With a sigh she stretched, groaning at the aches in her muscles before heading for the shower. She tried to be quiet, not wanting to wake Lincoln. It had been late by the time Lincoln and Ryan had finished processing her shed and so she'd accepted Lincoln's invitation to crash at his place. She was quite pleased by her progress – she hadn't been scared about staying with him at all. Lincoln had offered her his bed, but she'd refused to make him sleep on his own couch. She kind of regretted the decision now. She needed to be at the park in half an hour to whip up a whole heap of pancake mix for the guests. She stood under the warm spray and stretched out the kinks.

Last night had been a roller coaster. Seeing all her things flung about the shed had been hideous, but it *had* led to the best make-out session of her life. She wanted to celebrate – she felt like a woman again. She felt sexy and aroused and *normal.*

When she finally got out, she almost bumped into Lincoln in the hallway.

"What are you doing up so early?" she asked.

"I could ask you the same question. We didn't get in until late."

"Pancakes," she explained. "Go back to bed and when you get up again, stop by the park and I'll make you some."

"I'll come with you now."

"You don't need to," she protested.

He shook his head as if he couldn't believe she was arguing with him. "Chances are you'll need to call me as soon as you arrive anyway. What's today's gift – six geese-a-laying?"

Her mood deflated. For a second she'd forgotten all about it. "Yeah."

"Give me five to have a shower."

While he was in the bathroom, she called Mai and asked her for a couple of bee stings and two coffees to go.

"What was it this morning?" Mai asked.

"Nothing as yet. I'm at Lincoln's place. He's coming with me to the office."

"Why Lincoln's?"

She explained what had happened to her shed.

"Oh, that sucks. I'll come out and help you tidy up this afternoon."

"Thanks, Mai." She hesitated, her face growing warm. "I, uh, might be going on a picnic with Ryan and Felix this afternoon."

"Woo hoo. Tell me more."

Hannah smiled and looked over her shoulder as Lincoln came out, dressed in his civilian clothing. She hated that she was taking up so much of his time. "I'll tell you later. I've gotta go. I'll drop by in five."

"I'll be waiting."

"Where are you going?" Lincoln asked.

"Ordered us a coffee and treat from Mai's," she said.

Lincoln's face brightened. "Have I told you lately how much I love you, Hannah Banana?"

She smiled. "You're such a sucker for Mai's bee stings."

"Yep," he agreed. "Let's go."

They took two cars and made it into the office without seeing any gifts. Hannah made pancake batter while Lincoln logged in to check the video feed of the cameras he'd installed. "Nothing at Fleur or Kit's place," he called. "I'm checking yours now."

Hannah wandered out, bowl under one arm as she mixed the batter. She peered over his shoulder. The camera had a good view of her whole porch. "Is this live?"

"Yeah. There's nothing there."

"That's good, isn't it? Maybe he's stopped."

"Or maybe he saw me set the cameras."

Disappointed, she checked the time. "Help me carry some things out to the barbecue area?" she asked. Going back into the kitchen, she poured the batter into two jugs and handed Lincoln a box of condiments. She never knew how many people were going to turn up, but this would be enough to get started.

Her footsteps slowed as she reached the barbecues. Frustration welled in her as she took in the damage. The walls had been decorated in eggs and there was a carton of half-dozen eggs sitting on the table with a red ribbon tied around it. She should have known it was too good to be true.

They both swore.

"We need to get this cleaned up fast," Hannah said. "I can't have this affecting my guests."

"Hannah—" Lincoln began.

"No, Lincoln." She was pleased that her voice was calm, despite the turmoil surging around inside her. "I've had enough. Take the carton and do what you have to do with it, but egg stains are a bitch to remove."

"Let me get a couple of photos first."

She dumped the jugs of batter on one of the benches and went to get a bucket of warm, soapy water.

When she arrived back, Lincoln was dusting the surface near the carton. She left him to it as she quickly scrubbed the walls. The egg was almost dry, and the walls of the enclosed area were exposed brick, but she managed to remove it in the end.

"Any card?" she asked when she was done.

He handed her a plastic sleeve.

Things are easy to break. How long until you crack?

It was a taunt. Was he watching her, waiting for her to completely melt down? Was this all a game to him? Did he want her to fall apart? Fear inched its way inside her and she tried to shut it out, but it knew all of her secret hiding places. "If I knew who it was, maybe I could talk some sense into them."

"It's never good to interact with a stalker," Lincoln said. "They thrive on the contact. Let me put this in the car and then

I'll help you cook. People are surfacing."

Sure enough, people were heading to the toilet blocks and beginning to make their way over to the barbecues. She switched on two and as they heated up she greeted her guests.

Then Lincoln returned and they were too busy for the next hour flipping pancakes and chatting to people. Lincoln was a natural at it, always knowing what to say to put people at ease.

When she was close to running out of batter, she said to Lincoln, "You keep an eye on these and I'll make some more." She poured the remaining mix onto the hot plate and then took the empty jugs into the office. Joe got up from where he was lying under a tree and followed her in.

It didn't take her long to mix the ingredients, and as she was stirring there was a knock at the back door. She wandered over to it. Not many people came to the back door and she'd left it open because she was only going to be a second.

She stopped, her heart pounding in her chest. Joe was with her. He'd protect her.

"Hannah, please, can we talk?" Justin asked.

Was he the one doing this to her? Had he sent the note? Well if he was, she wouldn't let him break her. "I have nothing to say to you."

"I've got something to say to you."

"I'm not interested." She moved forward to shut the main door.

He put his hand on the handle and she lunged forward to lock it. He stepped back and held his palms up facing her. "Please, Hannah, I want to apologise."

The words were so unexpected that she paused. "Apologise?"

He nodded. His eyes were shadowed and his shoulders were slumped – he looked thoroughly miserable. "For what I did to you."

Her mouth dropped open.

He glanced behind him. "Can I come in for a minute?"

"No."

His eyes glistened with tears.

She couldn't get sucked in. She didn't owe him any of her time, but part of her was curious about what he wanted to say.

If she went outside, Lincoln would be in view and she'd have room to run. "I'll be out in a minute." She shut the main door and locked it.

She stood there for a moment, still unsure. The last thing she'd ever expected from Justin was an apology. That had to mean he acknowledged that what he did was wrong. A part of her was soothed. It was a validation of her feelings. Slowly, she walked back into the kitchen and poured the batter into the two jugs.

She opened the back door and Justin was leaning against a tree a couple of metres away. He straightened when the door opened. Hannah let Joe out first before following. She stopped about two metres away, holding the jugs. She felt ridiculous. "I'll be back in a minute."

He nodded.

As she neared the barbecue area, she noticed that Ryan and Felix had arrived. A thrill raced through her. Ryan had come. She smiled, her concern about Justin lessening with every step she took. "Good morning."

"Morning, Hannah!" Felix chirped. "Can we have pancakes too?"

"Of course," she said. "I just made up some more batter." She poured some of it onto the barbecue and then put down the jugs.

"How are you today?" Ryan asked quietly, running a hand over her arm.

"Good." She glanced over his shoulder to where Justin was waiting. "Can you do me a favour?"

"Sure."

"Can you help Lincoln with the pancakes, while I talk to Justin?"

He frowned and scanned the people gathered until he spotted Justin. "I'm not sure that's a good idea."

"He says he wants to apologise."

"Apologise?"

"Yeah. I ran into him yesterday after I left you on the beach and I let him have it," she said. "I'd like to hear what he has to say." She shrugged.

Ryan nodded. "All right. I'll keep an eye on you."

Warmth flooded her at his protection. "Thank you." She kissed his cheek.

With a breath to fortify herself, she walked back to where Justin was waiting. When he saw her approaching, he glanced away, as if embarrassed.

Here was the man who had caused her so many sleepless nights, who had disrupted her life for far too long, and he couldn't even look her in the eye. She stopped a couple of metres away from him. "What did you want to say, Justin?"

He shuffled his feet. "I'm so sorry, Hannah."

She didn't say anything.

"I haven't stopped thinking about what you said yesterday." He cleared his throat. "I wanted to deny it, but ... I never saw you again after that night. Maybe on some level I realised what I'd done, because I never got up the courage to track you down. I'd wanted you so badly that I was sure after we'd started you'd enjoy it."

Hannah's mouth dropped open and she stared at him.

He ducked his head. "It was stupid. I let my dick rule my head." He sighed. "I didn't mean to hurt you. I did really like you." He was sincere, looking at her as if asking her to understand.

She clenched her hands as the anger welled up in her. He had no idea what he'd done to her. "Saying sorry doesn't cut it, Justin." She glared at him. "You not only stole my virginity, but you also destroyed my trust in men and you made me fear my own judgement. I haven't been able to be intimate with anyone since! Hell, I haven't even been able to be alone with a man."

His eyes widened. "Fuck, Hannah." He ran a hand through his hair. "I didn't realise. I'm so fucking sorry." He seemed genuinely remorseful.

"How many other women have you ignored?" she asked, refusing to feel sympathy for him. "How many more have you forced yourself on?"

"None! Honest. It was just you."

"Lucky me," she said, her sarcasm dripping.

"If there was anything I could do to take back that day, to make it up to you ..."

"Nothing can change that day." She was right. There was no

going back, there was only going forward. It was time she stopped letting it rule her life, time she forgave herself for not fighting back. And maybe she could make this work for her. "I appreciate you apologising," she said. "The only thing you can do for me is to let the police take your fingerprints."

"What?"

"Someone trashed my place yesterday and has been leaving me gifts."

"And you think it's me." Justin scowled.

"The gifts began the day after you arrived. If you really want to help me, you'll allow yourself to be eliminated from the suspect list."

He hesitated, and then nodded. "All right."

The satisfaction was swift. "I'll get Sergeant Zanetti." She stared at him for a long moment and he met her eyes this time. "Goodbye, Justin." With that she walked back to the barbecue area. Ryan raised an eyebrow in question. She was done with being the victim. She was taking control of her life now, starting with Ryan Kilpatrick.

"Everything all right?" Ryan asked as she reached him.

"Yes." She smiled. "Justin has agreed for the police to take his fingerprints."

Ryan's eyebrows rose. "Really?"

"Yeah, can you or Lincoln take them?"

"I'll do it," Lincoln said, coming over. He handed Ryan the egg flip. "You make pancakes." He grinned and then strode over to Justin.

Hannah almost wished she was a fly on the wall, because Lincoln had a great bad-cop face. She turned to Felix, who had a pancake covered in jam, cream and maple syrup, and was stuffing it in his mouth. "Nice pancake, Felix?"

He nodded, his mouth full.

She smiled. This is what she needed. To be around people, to be normal again. She took over cooking from Ryan and made him a pancake, before chatting to the guests who were waiting for their turn. It was a lovely communal vibe and the conversations were about what people were planning to do that day, and asking for recommendations for where to go. She couldn't fully relax though. If Justin was her stalker, he wouldn't have let his fingerprints be taken. So that meant it could be anyone, even someone who was standing here right now. She had to stay alert.

Around ten o'clock the crowd thinned, and before long there was only Ryan and herself left. Felix was off playing in the playground with a couple of the kids who were staying at the park.

"Did you get a gift today?" Ryan asked as he cleaned one of the barbecues.

"Eggs," she said. "He covered this area in eggs and left a carton on the bench."

Ryan frowned. "That suggests he knows you do pancakes every Sunday."

He was right. Why else target the barbecue area?

"Did Lincoln get any useful information?"

"I don't think so." She glanced towards the office as someone walked over to it. "I'll come back and clean up in a minute."

Calling Joe, she headed back to the office.

By the time the small rush of people had left, Lincoln had returned from taking Justin's prints and Ryan had cleaned up the barbecue area. Both were waiting for her in the kitchen.

"How did it go?" Hannah asked.

"Great. I'll run the prints to Albany this afternoon," Lincoln said. "But this probably means Justin isn't your stalker."

She nodded, but at least now his prints were on file.

"Hannah, you still shouldn't be alone," Lincoln continued. "Can one of the girls spend the day with you?"

Ryan cleared his throat. "I was going to invite her to go on a picnic with Felix and me."

Hannah's heart jumped and she smiled.

"Ah. Well I'm not sure I approve," Lincoln joked.

Hannah chuckled. "Shut up, Slinky."

Lincoln winced.

"I'd love to," Hannah said.

"All right, I'll see you two later." And with that, Lincoln left.

Hannah turned to Ryan. "I won't be long. Shirley should be here soon." She stepped closer, wanting to be near him, and slid her hands over his shoulders. He rested his hands lightly on her hips and then his mouth met hers.

Passion, lust and joy flooded her. Perhaps, the overpowering emotions were simply because it had been so long since she'd felt like this, so long since she'd allowed herself to be attracted to a man, and acted upon the attraction. All she knew was she had all the feels.

The back door banged and she took a shaky step back, breathing heavily.

Lincoln walked in. "Sorry, I forgot my sunglasses." He picked them up from the kitchen table.

Hannah's face heated.

"I'll knock next time," he said.

Ryan grinned. "Good idea."

Lincoln chuckled and left, but Shirley arrived before Hannah could kiss Ryan again. She sighed and focused on work. "Everyone's checked out."

"Thanks." Shirley smiled. She noticed Ryan and said, "How's it going, Senior Constable?"

"Great, Shirley. You and Fairy Floss are looking well."

Fairy Floss had joined Joe on his bed.

"Thank you." Shirley was positively beaming.

"How are things with Mark?" Hannah asked.

"Fabulous," Shirley gushed. "He's the nicest guy, so attentive."

"You should have brought him over for pancakes," she said. "I'd love to meet him."

"We were going to." Shirley's face reddened. "But we got distracted."

Hannah grinned. "Some other time, then." She was pleased her friend had found someone nice.

"Absolutely."

Hannah grabbed her bag and turned to Ryan. "Are you ready to go?"

He nodded.

"See you later, Shirley." Now, it was her turn to spend time with her own nice guy.

Ryan was a little nervous as he followed Hannah's directions to a small grocery store near Mai's bakery. He wanted this day to go well. Felix had been surprisingly unconcerned when he'd mentioned asking Hannah to go on the picnic with them. He'd simply said, "It's good you're making new friends too." Ryan had suppressed a smile. Perhaps Felix had heard the sentiment from the Zanettis.

They walked up and down the aisles, adding what looked good to the basket, with Felix adding his opinions mainly regarding chocolate.

As they stood in line to pay, Felix yelled, "Look, Dad, there's Mum."

Ryan darted his gaze to where Felix was pointing, but he couldn't see anyone who looked like Paula. "Where, mate?"

Felix grasped his hand, his eyes wide. "She went into the bakery."

It was doubtful that Paula was anywhere near Blackbridge considering Karratha was two thousand kilometres to the north, but he didn't discount it. She was known for doing unpredictable things. Unease swirled in his gut. "We'll head there next and check it out."

Hannah glanced at them. "Why don't you two go now, while I pay?"

"No, I'll pay. I invited you." He kept half an eye on the bakery down the street while they waited and then carried the food out to the car. He hadn't seen Paula come out and he wanted to check. They crossed the road and went into On the Way. There were plenty of people inside, but as he scanned the faces, Paula wasn't amongst them. He breathed out a sigh of relief.

Felix wandered through the crowd and then came back to his dad. "She's not here."

"Maybe it was someone who looked like her," Ryan said.

"No, it was her," Felix said with absolute conviction.

Ryan wasn't sure what to say. Perhaps he should ring his ex-wife and check where she was, but knowing Paula, she'd take it as an indication that he wanted to get back together with her and then she *would* turn up unannounced. "We'll keep an eye out for her, champ," he said to Felix. "Do you want to buy something for dessert?"

Felix brightened and turned his attention to all the delicacies in the display cabinets.

"There's so much choice," Ryan murmured to Hannah.

"Yep. Everything tastes good as well."

In the end, they bought a few different options and then got into the car. "Where do you recommend we go for lunch?" Ryan asked.

"Do you want to go swimming afterwards?" Hannah asked.

"Yes," Felix called from the back seat.

"How about Shipwreck Beach?"

"Sounds good." He followed her directions out of town.

Hannah twisted in her seat to look at Felix. "Thanks for letting me tag along."

"That's all right. I wanted to play with Joe."

Ryan winced. "That's not very polite, Felix."

Felix frowned. "Thank you for keeping Dad company while I play with Joe."

Ryan chuckled. It wasn't quite what he'd meant, but it would do. He'd talk to Felix about manners later. Right now, he was pleased he could spend time with both of them.

It was a nice drive out to the beach. This area of the south coast had no end of beautiful places to go, and when they reached Shipwreck Beach he was pleased there weren't too many people there. Hannah picked up her picnic rug and Ryan took the food, and they walked down the wooden staircase to the sand. The view from the carpark was immense, looking out over the vast Southern Ocean. The wind was coming from the land, which meant the ocean was smooth and glistening in the sun. The water looked cool and inviting. As they reached the white sand, Felix and Joe raced across it, Felix's laughter lighting up Ryan's heart.

"I'm glad Joe is such a big hit," Hannah said.

"Me too."

They found a spot on the sand away from the other group of people and Hannah spread out the rug.

"Dad, can I go swimming?"

"Do you want something to eat first?"

Felix shook his head.

"All right. Let me put sun cream on you." He handed Felix his rashie and then slathered him in sun cream. "Don't go out too deep."

"I won't." Felix turned to the dog. "Come on, Joe."

With a deep woof, Joe loped next to Felix as they both ran to the water.

"Is Felix a good swimmer?" Hannah asked.

"Yeah. He's always loved the water. I need to teach him how to identify rips though."

"Good idea. The ocean can get pretty rough."

Ryan handed her a roll and took one for himself.

"Will you teach Felix how to surf?"

Ryan smiled. "I'd like to. I think he'll enjoy it." Keeping one eye on Felix in the water, he asked, "So what do you do in your spare time?"

"At the moment, all I do is work on the cabins," Hannah said. "I'm doing most of the internal work myself – the kitchens, bathrooms, and all of the painting. I'm getting the electrician and plumber out when I need them."

He was impressed. "Must be hard work."

"It was at first, but now that I've learned the skills, it's time-consuming more than anything." She shrugged. "But it keeps the budget down."

It took guts and confidence to do it yourself. Hannah impressed him more each time he spoke with her. "Tell me if you want a hand."

Her smile warmed him. "Thanks. I might do."

"So when that is done, what will you do?"

"In winter I ride vintage motocross."

His eyes widened. "Motocross?" She didn't seem the type.

She nodded. "Pre-seventy-five motorbikes," she said. "Fleur and Kit are a sidecar team and we all ride solos."

"All?"

"All the musketeers," she said. "Kit had a motorbike on the farm and we all learned to ride."

"Neat."

"You could always join us," she said. "I remember you riding a motorbike over at the Zanettis."

He smiled. He'd enjoyed riding around their property. "Maybe. If I ride, then Felix is going to want to."

"There's a juniors' section."

He could imagine Felix tearing around a motocross track, but he wasn't sure he had the money to buy them both a bike yet. "I'll think about it."

"What about you?" Hannah asked. "What do you like to do in your spare time?"

He couldn't remember having the freedom to choose in such a long time. Even after he'd split from Paula, he'd spent every spare moment with Felix so she couldn't claim he was neglecting their child. "Felix and I watch the wrestling together," he said. "And after we're settled I'd like to join a basketball or football team." It was time he got back to living. He didn't have Paula here to follow him around and cause embarrassment when he wanted to do something for himself.

"I'm sure Lincoln will sign you up in no time," Hannah told him. She finished her roll and grabbed the sun cream, putting some over her face and arms.

"Did you bring your bathers?" he asked.

"Yeah, I'm wearing them underneath."

Ryan could well imagine what was underneath her work gear. She had the most luscious curves.

Felix came running up from the water, his body dripping. "I'm hungry," he announced.

Ryan handed him a towel. "Don't drip on the food."

Felix grinned and scooted back a couple of steps while he dried himself, and then flopped onto the picnic rug and snatched a roll.

Joe was lying on the other side of Hannah, panting happily and chewing on a rawhide bone.

"Did you discover the tide pools, Felix?" Hannah asked.

Felix glanced at her. "The what?"

"Over by the rocks there are clear pools where you can

always find crabs and other sea creatures."

His eyes lit up and he got to his feet.

"Not so fast, mate," Ryan said. "Finish your lunch first."

Felix pouted but sat back down. "We can check it out afterwards, can't we, Dad?" There was such a hopeful expression on his face.

"Sure can." He loved his son so much. He was the best thing that had come out of his marriage.

Felix gobbled down his food and then leapt to his feet again. "Come on." He held out a hand to help Ryan up, his mouth still full of food.

Ryan chuckled and let Felix pull him to his feet.

"Can I come?" Hannah asked.

Ryan waited for Felix to answer. He was very conscious that the weekends were largely his time with Felix and he didn't want Felix to be resentful of Hannah – particularly when Ryan was hoping to spend a whole lot more time with her.

"Yeah. You gotta show me where it is." He gripped her hand as well and they walked across the sand to the smooth dark-grey granite boulders that came out of the ocean. Joe trailed along behind them.

At the rocks, Felix let go of both their hands and scrambled towards the first rock pool. He squatted down on the edge and peered into the water.

"What do you see?" Hannah asked, squatting down next to him.

"Not much."

"Well then, you're not using your sea goggles." She looked into the water.

"What are sea goggles?"

"Sea goggles enable you to view the things of the ocean, rather than the things of the land." She took off her sunglasses and handed them to Felix.

Wide-eyed, he put them on.

"Ready?"

He nodded.

"There's a red starfish." She pointed it out. "Then you've got the tiny little crab in the crevice there ..."

Ryan stood back as Hannah pointed out all the things in the

pool. She made it sound exciting, like a whole underwater world, and he smiled. She was good with children, good with Felix.

In Karratha they hadn't done a whole lot as a family. Paula hadn't been the least bit interested in her son, unless it was to use him to get Ryan to do something she wanted to do. And here Hannah was, taking Felix over to the rocks, chatting to him the whole time and listening to what he had to say. She was treating him like a person, not an object. When they were finished in one pool, they went to the next and then the next, Felix's excited chatter loud above the wash of the waves against the rocks.

Ryan was happy to trail after them. He'd never seen Hannah this relaxed, her whole posture free of tension and her short hair blowing in the breeze. She spoke enthusiastically to Felix and was unguarded. This was the Hannah he wanted to see more of.

They reached the end of the rocks and on the way back to their towels, Ryan noticed a guy about their age staring at them. He looked away when Ryan caught his eye. "Do you know that person?"

"That's Dan from the motocross club." She waved and the guy hesitated before waving back.

"Is he a friend of yours?"

"We race in the same class, but he's not keen about being beaten by a woman."

Ryan smiled. "You're that good?"

"Absolutely." She laughed.

"Let's go swimming, Dad." Felix tugged at Ryan's hand.

"More sun cream first," he said. He'd ask Lincoln about Dan later.

"Aw," Felix complained, but stood still while Ryan did the back of his neck and his legs.

"Can you do my back while you're at it?"

Ryan froze. Hannah's back was to him, but at some point she'd stripped off her clothes and was wearing bathers. There was nothing immodest about the aqua one-piece suit, but it showed off her delicious curves and had him longing to touch her, to run his hands over those curves and hear her moan.

She looked over her shoulder at him. "Ryan?"

"Sure." He squirted the cream into his hand and then rubbed it slowly into her back, making sure he was gentle and careful not to startle her. Her skin was smooth and soft.

When he was finished she said, "Do you want me to do you?"

Yes, please. His body hardened as his brain said, *She didn't mean it that way.* He nodded, unable to talk, and stripped off his T-shirt. Her hands were warm and strong, rubbing the cream in firmly. Then as she went lower, her hands slowed.

"Anything the matter?" he asked.

She cleared her throat as he turned. Her cheeks were red, her eyes dark and full of desire.

"Dad, come on!" Felix yelled.

Hannah blinked and grinned. "Last one in is a rotten egg," she yelled and sprinted for the water.

Felix whooped in delight and chased her, and Ryan followed more slowly, trying to figure out what he was going to do about his feelings for the divine Hannah Novak.

Chapter 12

It was late afternoon when they headed back to town. Hannah's eyes drifted shut as warmth and drowsiness filled her. After all of the issues of the past week, this afternoon was the first time she had fully relaxed in ages. She'd had fun playing with Felix and talking to Ryan, had been comfortable with them both. If that wasn't worth celebrating, she didn't know what was. She felt free for the first time in forever.

Ryan dropped her off at the holiday park so she could get her car and then followed her out to her property. She was going to show him the other cabin she was building before heading back to her shed to clean up the mess the intruder had made.

She pulled up in front of the cabin she was currently working on and smiled. This one was smaller than Ryan's, with only one bedroom, suitable for a couple wanting to get away from it all. As Ryan drove up she opened the front door and the scent of wet paint hit her. She frowned. It had been three days since she'd painted, the smell should have dissipated by now. She walked into the living area and her spirits plummeted. Nausea rose in her stomach as she took in the smashed bi-fold doors and the now empty can of paint, the contents of which had been flung about the room and was congealing on the walls, over the brand-new kitchen and on the concrete floor.

Trashed. Again.

156

All of her hard work, cancelled out by a nutter with an issue against her. She squeezed back the tears and wiped away the couple that escaped as she took a few deep breaths. She would not let him win, she would not let him break her.

Ryan walked in and swore.

"Dad, what happened?" Felix asked.

That's what Hannah wanted to know. She stepped forward and dipped a finger into a glob of paint on the floor in front of her. It was still soft. "This happened today," she said. "If it had happened when someone trashed my place, the paint would be dry by now." Could it have been Justin on his way out of town? Had his friends helped him?

Ryan nodded. "I'll call Lincoln and then take you both back to my place."

She didn't want to leave, wanted to help find whoever it was that was interfering with her life, but she didn't want Felix to worry about the destruction. "You don't need to." She held out her hand. "Come on, Felix. Let's leave your dad to do his work here."

Felix frowned. "Can I watch?"

"Not today, mate," Ryan said. "Why don't you show Joe and Hannah your board-game collection?"

"All right." He pouted as he took Hannah's hand.

Her heart went out to him. "I'm sorry, Felix. I hate that this means your dad has to work instead of be with you."

"Why would someone break the glass and tip paint everywhere?" he asked.

"That's what your dad and Lincoln are going to figure out."

"Did you make someone mad?"

"Not that I know of."

"Maybe you didn't know. Dad never knew why Mum was mad half the time."

Hannah was curious about Ryan's ex, but not enough to stoop to asking Felix about her. They drove the short distance to Ryan's cabin and Felix got out a board game for them to play.

It was a couple of hours before Ryan returned with Lincoln.

Hannah was playing Battleship with Felix. "Find anything?"

"We got some good prints from the paint can," Ryan said.

They hadn't got a match so far, so she had no expectations that they would now. She got to her feet. "I'd better clean it up."

"It's done," Ryan told her. "Lincoln and I did it when we finished."

Tears pricked her eyes. She'd been dreading going back in there. "Thank you."

"You need to get the glass in the doors replaced," Lincoln said. "But I've covered it with some ply in the meantime."

She nodded. It would have to wait until the insurance claim came through, because she didn't have the spare money at the moment. "All right, well I'd better clean up the shed, then." If it wasn't one thing it was another. "Thanks for playing with me this afternoon," she said to Felix.

He smiled. "No worries. It was fun."

Hannah walked over to the two men. She gave Lincoln a hug. "Thank you for everything."

"We'll get whoever's doing this, Hannah Banana," he promised.

She hoped so, but she was losing patience. She turned to Ryan. "I'm sorry this ruined your time with Felix," she said. "But thank you for the lovely day." She kissed him quickly, almost chastely, and moved towards the door.

"Hannah, where are you staying tonight?" Lincoln called.

She shrugged. "It's going to take me some time to clean up, so I might as well sleep at the shed."

"By yourself?" He raised his eyebrows.

"Yes, Lincoln," she said, exasperated. "You've got the camera set up and Joe is with me."

"Hannah—"

"No. I'm tired of hiding, tired of being scared."

"Dad, Hannah could stay here," Felix said. "She can share my bed or yours."

Ryan's eyes widened and Hannah smiled at the innocent offer. "Thanks, Felix. If I get scared, I'll come over, but Joe usually shares my bed, so I'll be fine."

"Really? He must take up the whole bed."

"Almost," Hannah agreed. She opened the door. "I'll see you later." Outside, with the door closed behind her, she took a deep breath of the warm evening air. The light was beginning to fade and shadows were growing longer, so she hurried to her car and then drove to her shed. She'd be fine out here. Ryan wasn't far away if anything happened. But maybe she should stay at Fleur or Mai's place tonight, after she was done. The evening quiet wasn't as soothing as it usually was.

Standing at the entrance of her shed, she surveyed the damage. Along with the ripped fabrics and broken frames, there was now fingerprint dust and a trail of ants running to some of the crumbs that hadn't been picked up. Her chest tightened. She needed to search the shed, make sure there was no one hiding, before she could clean.

With Joe by her side, she checked under the bed and in any spaces where a person would fit.

It was clear.

She fought against the tears in her eyes. Where did she even start? Everywhere she looked there was mess. Everywhere were remnants of her life. She shuddered.

These were only things. They could be fixed or replaced.

But some arsehole had violated her sanctuary, had trashed the place where she was building her dream, was trying to make her fail. Someone had made her fearful of being here alone.

Resolve strengthened her. She would tidy up, repair what was broken and move on. She was strong. She walked over to the little kitchenette and got a bin bag out of the cupboard. She'd survived worse.

This wasn't going to break her.

Half an hour later she heard a car approaching. Her heartbeat accelerated as she tied the current bag of rubbish and set it aside. Picking up her phone, she strode to the door. Her shoulders sagged in relief as she recognised Kit's ute and Mai's little red car. She crossed her arms. She'd bet her savings that Lincoln had called them. As the cars pulled up, her friends got out, Fleur riding with Mai.

"Need a hand?" Kit asked.

"You didn't need to come out," Hannah said.

"What are friends for?" Mai was carrying a large white bakery box.

"When we're done we'll have a musketeer meeting." Fleur held up a bottle of wine.

Hannah smiled. It was nice not to be alone. "Sounds good. Thank you." She led them inside.

"Oh my gosh," Mai said.

"This is fucked up," Kit commented.

Fleur put a hand on her arm. "How are you coping?"

"I'm over it," Hannah said, some of the distress dissipating now that her friends were with her. "I want to clean up and move on."

"We can definitely help," Mai said. "Where do you want us to begin?"

She gave them all tasks to do and they chatted while they worked. Fleur was moving books back into the overcrowded bookshelf when she asked, "What's this?"

Hannah frowned. Fleur was holding a small surveillance camera, kind of like the one Lincoln had installed at her front door. Her chest tightened and her skin went cold. "That's not mine."

Fleur carefully put it down as if it was going to bite her.

Hannah forced herself to breathe. "Maybe it's one of Lincoln's." She dialled his number, already suspecting the answer.

"Lincoln, how many cameras did you install at the shed?" she asked when he picked up.

"Just the one by the door. Why?"

She closed her eyes, fighting back the storm in her stomach. "We've found another one." Not only was he destroying her things, he was also spying on her. Her hands shook.

"What?"

"There's a surveillance camera on my bookshelf," she said, proud of how calm she sounded. She wasn't going to give the bastard the satisfaction of seeing her freak out. "I didn't put it there."

Lincoln growled. "I'll be out as soon as I can."

How long had the camera been there? Just since yesterday when her rings had been stolen, or longer than that?

"This is beyond a joke," Kit said. "Lincoln has to find who's doing this." Her eyes flashed.

"He's trying, Kit," Hannah said. "I swear I've single-handedly kept the police force employed for the last week."

"Well, he should have something by now."

Mai smiled at Kit. "I'm upset too."

Kit kicked the sofa and winced.

Hannah examined the video camera. "Do you think it's video or audio as well?"

Fleur shrugged.

This was her best chance of speaking to whoever it was. She crouched down so she was in front of the lens. "Listen to me, you're nothing but a bully. You don't even have the guts to confront me." It felt good to be yelling at him, to finally be able to do something.

"Hannah, is that a good idea?" Kit asked.

Hannah ignored her and continued. "If you've got a problem with me, stop hiding and tell me what it is."

"Hannah!" The disbelief and fear on Mai's face had Hannah regretting what she'd done. She'd challenged her stalker. She put the camera face down. "Come on. Let's finish cleaning this place."

A couple of hours later, Lincoln had been and gone, taking the camera with him, and Hannah's shed was clean. She had gone through everything to make sure there were no other cameras hidden anywhere, but it didn't stop the unease in her shoulders. She sat at her small kitchen table with her friends around her, all drinking wine and eating the quiche that Mai had brought with her. The mood was kind of sombre.

"I need to go Christmas shopping in Albany next week," Kit said. "Anyone want to come with me?"

The new subject was a relief. Hannah had forgotten Christmas was next week. She'd already bought gifts for her friends but wanted to buy something for Lynette and Shirley. "I will."

"Me too," Fleur said.

They looked at Mai. "I've got all my gifts, but I'll come for the ride."

"Are your parents coming to town this year, Kit?" Hannah asked.

"No, they're going to my brother's place. I'm going to sponge off the Zanettis again."

"When is Jamie coming down?" Fleur asked.

"Christmas eve," Kit said.

"Make sure you drag him along to my Boxing Day barbecue," Fleur said. "It's been far too long since he's visited."

"Will do," Kit promised. "What are you guys doing?"

"The usual Christmas Eve at Mum and Dad's," Mai said.

Fleur sipped her wine. "Dad and I are heading to Walpole to my aunt's." She turned to Hannah. "You haven't said if you're coming or not."

Hannah shrugged. She'd be welcome at any of her friends' places, but after all that had been going on, she wasn't sure what she wanted to do. "It's a Sunday, so I'll be cooking pancakes for the park in the morning. I'll probably have a quiet one afterwards and save my energy for your party."

All three of her friends stared at her.

"You can't be alone on Christmas," Kit said.

"I'll hardly be alone. The park is full."

"You know what she means," Mai said.

"Yeah, well I'm not feeling very festive this year." Her mobile rang, and she got up to answer it. "Hello?"

Silence. She checked the screen to make sure it was still connected and then said, "Blackbridge Holiday Park. Hannah speaking."

No response, but there was heavy breathing on the other end.

Was it the stalker? Had he heard her message? Her bravery left her and she hung up, goosebumps breaking out over her skin. Maybe she shouldn't have confronted him.

"Who was that?" Fleur asked.

"No one." She dumped her phone on the table and got Joe some dinner while she was up. She closed the curtains above the sink.

"Mrs Z won't mind if you crash Christmas lunch at their place," Kit said. "It's the more the merrier with her."

"Or you could spend it with Ryan," Mai said with a mischievous smirk. "I hear you two were quite the couple when you came into the bakery today."

"What's this?" Kit asked, staring at Hannah. "Why haven't you told us already?"

Hannah smiled, remembering her lovely day. "Well it's a matter of where to start."

Ryan walked into the police station on Monday morning eager to begin work. Lincoln was already in his office and had dropped in the night before to tell him about the surveillance camera Hannah had found. Ryan was pissed. It was time they caught this son of a bitch.

"Did you get any time off over the weekend?" Ryan asked, placing a takeaway coffee and a small white box in front of his friend.

"A bit." Lincoln took a long sip of his coffee. "Thanks."

"What's the latest?"

"Justin's prints aren't a match for the gifts or the break-in." Lincoln scowled. "I'd hoped it would be him." He sighed. "The camera we found is a fairly common model, but can you check if there have been any recent sales in the area? There aren't too many places around here to buy them."

"Sure." It was good to have something to do, even though the chances were high that the guy had bought it online. "Did you check out Dan?"

"On my list to do today."

Sue walked in. "Morning." She dumped her keys on her desk and switched on her computer. "Hey, Ryan, did your sister find your place all right?"

Ryan frowned at her. "My sister?"

"Yeah. I heard her talking to Erin at the cafe on Saturday. She said she'd lost your address and couldn't get you on the phone. Erin told her where you were staying."

Dread washed over him. There was no way it had been his sister. He hadn't told her he was living back here. "What did she look like?"

"Bleached blonde hair, short, kind of petite with big boobs."

Ryan closed his eyes. "That sounds like my ex-wife." What the hell was she doing here? Ryan didn't like the idea of Paula being anywhere near him and Felix. "Felix thought he saw her yesterday," he said. "I guess he was right." Now, he had to find out where she was staying and make sure she didn't see him with Hannah. He wanted to avoid that kind of chaos.

He froze. If Felix had seen her, chances were good that she'd seen them as well. Perhaps she'd already exacted her revenge. The destruction at Hannah's shed had looked a lot like the aftermath of one of Paula's rages. Could she have thought Hannah's place was his?

He swore. "Lincoln, we need to check those fingerprints from both Hannah's break-ins against Paula's."

Sue frowned. "What happened to Hannah?"

Lincoln filled her in. "We'll need something more than your hunch to get Paula's fingerprints," he said to Ryan.

Ryan shook his head. "They'll be on file," he said. "She was arrested six months ago for assaulting a woman I had drinks with."

Sue gaped at him.

"Could she have seen you with Hannah on the weekend?" Lincoln asked.

He nodded. "Hannah ran into us on the beach on Saturday. We went for a walk together while Felix played with Joe." That was more than enough fuel to light Paula's fire. She wouldn't bother to find out who Hannah was, or what their relationship was, she'd skip straight to the assumption that they were sleeping together. "And she could have easily seen us shopping together yesterday."

"All right. Sue, I need you to call Albany and get them to check the prints against Paula's record," Lincoln said. "If it's a match, we'll find out where she's staying. I also need you to run the prints from yesterday's break-in to Albany. Ryan, you can work on tracing the camera."

Ryan stared at his computer screen while the other two got

to work. He'd travelled as far south as possible to get away from Paula. But it hadn't helped. She'd come to find him. What would she need this time? What excuse would she use? Would he ever be able to escape her completely?

Could she even be responsible for Hannah's gifts? Paula's normal MO was to make a scene, but perhaps she was trying to scare Hannah instead.

He blew out a long breath.

How was he going to tell Felix that his mother was in town?

And how was he going to tell Hannah that it was his fault her house and cabin had been destroyed?

Hannah woke feeling more refreshed than she had in a long time. Her friends had all crashed at her place, after an awesome girls' night of chat and laughter. Mai had got up at an ungodly hour to work and Kit had left before sunrise to milk her cows.

She poked Fleur, who was on the couch. "If you want a lift into town, you'd better get up."

Fleur groaned. "It's my day off."

"Sucks to be you," Hannah said with a laugh. "If you're fast we can swing by Mai's."

That got Fleur moving. They both showered and headed into town, stopping by the bakery for breakfast before continuing to the holiday park. There were no gifts waiting anywhere at the office and Hannah hoped that meant her verbal attack had worked. When Lynette arrived at nine, Fleur walked home and Hannah headed out around the park. Her whole body felt lighter. Perhaps things were finally going to get back to normal.

It was mid-afternoon by the time she was sitting in the office, flicking through the mail. There was a postcard amongst the letters with black swans on it. She flicked it over to see who it was from.

The typed black text almost glared at her.

Today. 3:30pm. Community Park Bridge.

Come alone.

She slowly turned the card back around and counted the

swans on the front. Seven swans a-swimming. Her heart thumped painfully in her chest. Her stalker wanted to meet.

She took in a deep breath, her hands a little shaky. The community park was on the edge of town and right next to the river. The pedestrian bridge led over the river to a walking trail and was surrounded by paperbark trees, which blocked the view of the park.

She checked the time.

Three o'clock.

She called Ryan and it went straight to voicemail.

She tried Lincoln and his harassed voice answered. "What now?"

"Where are you?" she asked.

"There's been a major crash on Mortimer Road. We've had to close it and I've got the whole team here."

They wouldn't be able to help her. "It's not urgent."

Nerves played in her stomach. She couldn't let the opportunity pass – not if she could resolve it. Fleur was at work, but she'd call Mai and Kit. There was just enough time for them to get to the park with her if they were free.

She jumped to her feet and called for Joe, scribbling a "back at four" sign for the door.

She went out the back and locked up, and as she walked around to lock the front door, she found an older man on the porch.

She hesitated, checking the time. She had to speak to him, had to lock the front door. Hopefully he wouldn't need much. "You almost missed me," she called cheerfully. "I've got five minutes if you need a hand." She was at the front step when the man turned.

He was in his sixties, his hair almost all grey and starting to thin. His frame was wide, a little stooped, and as she met his eyes her heart leapt into her throat. She took a step back, hand to her mouth and dread filling her stomach as she stared at those familiar green eyes.

The man gave a small smile. "Hello, Princess. It's been a while."

Chapter 13

Ryan didn't allow himself to dwell on Paula and why she was here – he didn't have time. He spent the morning ringing around to find out whether the surveillance camera had been purchased in the area, and addressing a number of calls that came in.

Mid-morning Sue called from Albany. "Prints from the cabin and Hannah's shed are a match for Paula."

Ryan squeezed his eyes shut as disappointment filled him. It had been pointless to hope it hadn't been Paula. He knew better than that. "All right. I'll call and ask her where she's staying." He hung up and rang Mrs Z to tell her Paula was in town. There was a small chance Paula could track Felix down there and he didn't want Mrs Z involved in any unpleasantness.

When that was done, he braced himself and called Paula, his chest tight.

"Ryan," she gushed. "To what do I owe this pleasure?" She was bright and chirpy, as if she spoke to him regularly.

"Paula, where are you?"

"I'm in Karratha of course. Where else would I be?" Her carefree laugh set his teeth on edge. She lowered her voice to a sultry tone and asked, "Do you miss me?"

He wasn't touching that question. "Felix saw you on the weekend."

"He must have been imagining things. Perhaps he misses

me. It was cruel to take him so far from his mummy."

"So you're not in Blackbridge?" Like always, he gave her another chance to redeem herself.

She didn't take it. "Of course not." She paused and then lowered her voice. "But if you need me, babe, you just call. I can give you what you like."

He grimaced. "Stop playing games, Paula. I know you're in the area."

"Honest I'm not. Felix is trying to turn you against me."

He'd had enough. "He didn't need to, you did a good job of that yourself." He hung up on her gasp of outrage. The tightness in his chest disappeared. He didn't need her, he didn't want her and he'd be damned if he let her hurt either Felix or himself again. He brought up the list of accommodation available in Albany. It was a very long list. Finding Paula was going to take a while.

But nothing about Paula was ever easy.

After Ryan returned from attending a vehicle crash out of town, he managed to find Paula at one of the highest-rated motels in Albany. After a discussion with Lincoln, Ryan called the Albany station to pick her up.

"How are you holding up?" Lincoln perched his hip on the edge of Ryan's desk.

Ryan sighed and ran a hand through his hair. "Like crap," he said. "Hannah's place was trashed because of me."

"That's bullshit. It's Paula's fault and no one else."

He couldn't help feeling responsible. "I want to know what she's got to say for herself."

Lincoln nodded. "You can't be involved in the interview."

"Yeah," he agreed. "She'd go crazy if I was there." She wasn't going to like being arrested. He'd warned the cops going to pick her up.

"All right. I'll wait for Albany to call. Why don't you knock off and go get Felix?"

He did want to see Felix, reassure himself that his son was fine. "You need to take a break too, Lincoln."

"I will after this is sorted."

Ryan wasn't sure which "this" Lincoln was referring to, but

he recognised the stubborn expression on his friend's face. "Call me in if you need a hand. I'll see you tomorrow."

Now, he needed to tell Felix about his mother.

"No." Hannah shook her head, unable to believe her eyes. It couldn't be. It wasn't possible. He was supposed to be in prison. Her heart raced so fast she thought it would drill right out of her chest. She swallowed hard to get some moisture back in her mouth. "Dad?" she whispered.

"I tried to call …" he said. "But I couldn't figure out what to say." He stepped towards her and she stepped back. He grimaced.

She took a great gulp of air and then another one, her head light. She wasn't ready for this, wasn't the least bit prepared. Surely, someone should have contacted her to tell her he was out.

"I'm sorry. I shouldn't have come."

Hannah stood where she was, unable to move as he walked towards her and then past. She couldn't let him leave. At the last moment she reached out, brushed his arm. He stopped.

She swallowed. "Give me a minute."

He nodded and she shifted away, needing space, needing to move. Joe was next to her, alert, keeping an eye on her father, who had sat on the small garden bench outside the office.

She examined her father. He'd aged, but of course he had. He'd been in prison for … eighteen years. He'd been sentenced to twenty years for killing her mother.

One part of her mind was yelling that he was evil, that he'd murdered her mother, that he was a *very bad man*. She recognised the words as those of her grandparents, the ones who had lost a daughter because of him. Hannah was so glad they weren't here, because her grandfather would likely go ballistic.

The other part of her mind echoed his words, *hello, Princess.* They brought back a flood of memories of being loved and cherished, of playing soccer in the backyard with her father and half-brothers, of riding on his shoulders when her legs had been too tired to walk. She had so many good memories and one so very bad one. A lump formed in her throat and she blinked back tears. She hadn't seen him since that night. She had to talk to him. She needed it for her own peace of mind.

But what the hell should she say?

Slowly she walked over. He gave her a tentative smile. "Shall we go for a walk?" she asked.

"I'd like that." He got to his feet and she gestured for him to follow her.

She walked towards the beach. "When did you get out?"

"A couple of weeks ago," Ivan said. "They gave me early parole for good behaviour."

"Where are you staying?"

"Phillip lives in Albany," he said. "I'm staying there until I can sort my life out."

She'd had no idea he lived so close. She hadn't seen either of her half-brothers since her mother had been killed. The boys' mother hadn't liked her, had blamed Hannah and her mother for breaking up their family, and her grandparents hadn't wanted her to have anything to do with her father's side of the family. There was a little pang of jealousy that her father had gone to his sons first. "Have you seen both the boys?"

He nodded. "They visited me regularly while I was in prison."

She stopped walking. "You weren't allowed visitors." That's what her grandparents had always told her.

"Of course I was."

Hannah shook her head, not willing to believe it. "No. What you did was so bad, they wouldn't let anyone visit you." As she said the words aloud they sounded ridiculous. She'd been lied to. Of course she had. There was no way her grandparents would let her visit the man who had murdered their daughter. Still, the betrayal stung. She continued towards the beach.

"Ah," Ivan said. "I suspected your grandparents kept you from me, but I had hoped you would come on your own accord when you were old enough."

The guilt was sharp. She had considered it briefly when she'd been in Perth at university, but it had been too hard. What did she say to a man she hadn't seen in ten years? A man who had destroyed her childhood. It had been easier to believe what she'd been told. "You killed Mum."

"I loved your mother."

"You used to argue all the time." How could that be love?

"We were passionate people. We used to drive each other crazy, but I loved her with all my heart."

"Then why did you stab her?" It was the question she'd wanted to ask for such a long time.

He was silent for a while. Finally he said, "It was an accident."

Hannah closed her eyes. "How could it be an accident? What were you doing with that knife?"

"It doesn't matter now." He sounded so thoroughly defeated.

"Yes, it does," she argued. "I have a right to know. Haven't you ever considered how I felt seeing Mum dead on the floor?"

"What?" He stared at her, his face pale. "You were in bed that night. You didn't see anything."

"I saw it all. I came out of my room to beg you to stop yelling. I saw you holding the knife, Mum bleeding on the floor. You were shouting and I got so scared I hid under the bed."

"That's all you saw?"

Wasn't it enough? "Yes."

"I'm so sorry." He reached out to touch her and she backed away. He held up his hands in apology. "I've regretted my actions every night since."

She didn't want an apology, she wanted an explanation. "So tell me what happened."

He sighed. "It's in the past now."

Hannah stared at him. Did he really think that was good enough? Perhaps for him it was, but she had so many unanswered questions. She barely knew this man, not anymore. He wasn't the loving father she remembered. He was virtually a stranger.

He cleared his throat. "Have you lived here all your life?"

She blinked at the sudden change in topic. "No! If you're not going to answer my questions, you don't get to ask me any." She wasn't ready for this conversation, this general chit-chat about what they'd both been up to for the past twenty years. She couldn't ignore the questions she still had.

Her father stepped back in shock.

Hannah wasn't going to feel guilty. This was all too much on top of everything else that was going on. She needed to think, to feel, to decide what the hell she was going to do about her father being back in her life.

"Give me a couple of days." With that, she walked away.

Hannah had to get away from here. She drove, not sure of her destination, tears streaming down her face. She needed to be alone, away from everyone. She drove on autopilot to her property – the perfect hideaway.

Parking outside her shed, she wiped her tears and got out. She needed fresh air.

Joe followed her as she took the path to the beach, then turned up the track that led to the lookout. It wasn't much more than a cleared area on top of the limestone cliffs, but the view was spectacular. The sea breeze was strong and cold today, with enough bite to make her shiver.

It matched her mood.

Her insides felt as cold and as rough as the dark ocean with its foaming sea. She stood close to the edge, and looked down at the sharp rocks below. The ocean came right up to the cliff at this point and surged like a washing machine. There was one spot below her where there were no rocks, just a deep hole of water. But if you were lucky enough to hit that spot when you fell, you'd soon be swept up by the waves and smashed against them. It was why she needed to fence off the area.

The wind played with her hair and clothes, whipping them around. She embraced the ferocity, opening her arms wide, letting it blow over her, wishing it could blow through her and rid her of all the confusion filling her brain. She took a step forward and the limestone crumbled under her foot, reminding her not to get too close to the edge.

She took a deep breath of the fresh, salty air.

Her father was back.

That one thought kept going around and around in her head like a broken record.

She'd been so unprepared. She should have kept track of where he was, what he was doing, when he was due for parole. But it had never occurred to her that he would get out early.

It had been easier not to think of him at all.

After the trial, her grandparents had never mentioned her father, and the few times Hannah had asked about him they'd been so upset she'd stopped asking. It went into the-things-we-don't-talk-about basket.

She groaned.

Was this what her life had become? Did all her responses come from that one event? She didn't talk about her father because it upset her grandparents, she didn't fight Justin because she was too scared she'd end up dead like her mother, she didn't go to therapy because of the way the therapists had hammered her for answers about her parents' relationship.

When had she become so frightened?

Had she spent her whole life hiding?

Tears ran hot down her face. She sank to the ground, pulling her knees up to her chest. Joe dropped the large stick he'd found at her feet and licked her cheek. She pulled her dog close and hugged him, the sobs racking her body.

"Dad, what's up there? Can we go see?" The shout was unmistakable – Felix.

Hannah pressed her palms to her eyes to stem the tears, but it was too late. "Dad, it's Hannah and Joe!" Felix ran up and then stopped short. "Why are you crying?"

She couldn't answer him. There was a lump in her throat the size of Uluru.

"Dad, something's wrong with Hannah," Felix called.

She didn't look up, didn't want Ryan to see her like this. She buried her head in her knees.

"Felix, why don't you take Joe and go down to the beach?" Ryan said. "Don't go into the water yet, because those waves are rough."

"Is she going to be all right?"

"I'd say so, but I need to talk to her."

"OK. Come on, Joe."

Hannah gave Joe the gesture to go with Felix as Ryan sat next to her.

"Rough day?" he asked.

The tears wouldn't stop. She couldn't speak, it was hard to even breathe. She lifted her head, met his eyes.

"Oh, baby," Ryan crooned and pulled her close to him, his arms warm and comforting. "I've got you."

She believed him. For the first time in a long time she felt truly safe. All of her barriers came crashing down at his gentle words. She wrapped her arms around him and let all of her tears out.

It was some time before she cried herself dry. As she came back to her senses, the awkwardness flooded in. She must seem like a complete basket case. She lifted her head and dried her eyes on her shirt before daring to glance at Ryan. "I'm sorry. I didn't mean to break down like that."

His smile was gentle. "People don't usually mean to break down." Ryan used his thumb to brush her hair back and then cupped her cheek as he kissed her. "That's why it's called that."

His kindness made her ache.

"Want to talk about it?"

She really did. She had to talk to someone and somewhere along the way Ryan had become a person she trusted. "I saw my father today."

His eyebrows rose. "I thought he was in jail."

"So did I. Early parole."

"You didn't know?"

"Not until he showed up at the park."

Ryan swore. "That must have been a shock."

She nodded. "Apparently he tried to call, but didn't know what to say." She shook her head. "He thought turning up unannounced was the better option." She couldn't help the sarcasm in her tone.

He ran a hand up and down her arm in a soothing motion. "How long has it been since you've seen him?"

"Eighteen years." A lifetime. "My grandparents never took me to visit him."

"So, how did it go?"

"Badly." Her chest tightened again. "We spoke a little, but he wouldn't answer my questions about that night."

"How do you feel?"

She shrugged. "Confused, angry."

He got to his feet and offered her a hand. "Come on. Let's take a walk."

A distraction would be good. She let herself be pulled to her feet and they strolled down to the sand, hand in hand. Felix was throwing a smaller stick for Joe and Ryan called to Felix to follow them.

"Tell me about your father," Ryan said. "What was he like when you were a kid?"

The memories were bittersweet. "He was my hero."

"Why?"

"He always had time for me. He'd play with me when he got home from work and he'd help me with school stuff. He called me his little princess. We'd go to the soccer together and I'd help him in the garden. Mum used to say we were two peas in a pod."

"It was just the three of you?"

"My two half-brothers would come for weekends."

"Were they nice?"

"No." He skin grew tight. "Phillip was four years older than me, and Marko was six years older. They used to tease me whenever Dad wasn't around."

"Teasing is normal sibling behaviour."

Hannah shook her head. "No. I've seen the way Lincoln and Jamie tease each other, it was nothing like that. They used to call Mum nasty names and they'd pinch and hit me. I haven't seen them since that night." And hadn't missed them at all.

"It sucks that they were mean." He squeezed her hand. "So, your dad wants to have a relationship with you?"

"Sounds like it." She shrugged. "But, he won't answer my questions. He won't tell me why he had the knife."

"And you want to know?"

Desperately. There had to be a reason, a good reason why he would hurt her mum. "Yeah. No one would ever tell me exactly what happened," she said. "Eventually I stopped asking."

"Have you seen the police file?" Ryan asked.

"You mean of the murder?"

He nodded. "You could put in a request under the *Freedom of Information Act*. Or at least talk to the lawyers involved in the trial."

It had never occurred to her, but she might get some answers. "Thank you. I'll do that."

He kissed her cheek. "You're welcome." They walked on in silence for a bit longer before he asked, "So what will you do about your dad?"

She shrugged. "I don't know."

"Do you want a relationship with him?"

It had been so long, but she had yearned for her father when she was younger. She'd been jealous on Fathers' Day and whenever the school had activities involving parents. Sure, her grandparents had come, but it wasn't the same.

"Do you hate him for killing your mum?"

"I never actually hated him … I was so confused, not sure what to believe. He said it was an accident." There had to be an explanation for what had happened, but did that make it any better? She'd been told how she was supposed to feel for so long, she hadn't ever examined her own emotions.

"We can read what the coroner's report says," Ryan told her.

She sighed. She didn't have to decide right now. "I need answers and I do want to speak with him again, when I've got my head around him being back."

"I can go with you when you do."

She embraced him, taking comfort in his arms lightly around her. "Thank you." Having his support meant more to her than she could express. She brushed a kiss against his lips and they turned back along the beach.

Felix jogged over to her and asked, "Are you OK now, Hannah?"

"Yeah." It felt good to talk to someone about it.

"I'm glad." He gave her a quick hug and then ran off again, calling Joe.

Hannah's heart swelled. "Your son is beautiful."

"He is," Ryan agreed.

Hannah wanted to change the subject. She wanted some normalcy. "So, how was your day?"

Ryan winced and guilt flashed across his face.

She frowned. "What happened?"

He cleared his throat. "I have some news, but you might want to wait until you're feeling better."

It couldn't possibly be worse than what she'd already been through today. "What have you found?"

"We know who broke into your shed and cabin."

She stopped walking, her heart beating fast. "Who?"

Ryan checked where Felix was and then said, "My ex-wife, Paula."

"What?" She'd never met the woman.

"She's in town and found out where I was staying. When I heard about it, I got them to run the prints we found against hers and they matched," Ryan told her. "We don't think she's your stalker though, because the prints are different."

Hannah's eyes widened. The stalker. The meeting. Her heart raced. "Shit. What time is it?"

"Four-thirty."

"I completely forgot about it." She put a hand to her head. "I was meant to meet him an hour ago and then Dad arrived."

"Meet who?"

"The stalker. He sent me a card today, with a time and place."

"What?" Ryan's face went red as he scowled and his whole body tensed. "And you didn't tell us this?"

"You were out at the crash and I discovered the note right before the meeting time."

Ryan reached for his phone. "Where were you going to meet?"

"The community park, by the bridge. Who are you calling?"

"Lincoln, our stalker was going to meet Hannah by the bridge at the community park an hour ago. Can you send someone past?" He paused. "Yeah, I'm pissed too. I'll talk to her about it." He hung up, the anger on his face clear.

Hannah held up a hand. "Don't start with me," she said. "I've had a shit week. It was more important that you were at the crash, and I was taking Joe and Mai with me." Though she hadn't actually got around to calling Mai.

Ryan briefly closed his eyes. "We don't know what this guy

is capable of, Hannah. I don't want you to get hurt."

"I don't want to be hurt. I just want this to end." She took a breath and then remembered what they'd been talking about. "Why would your ex-wife trash my place?"

He grimaced. "It's probably time I told you about my marriage."

Chapter 14

Ryan hated to drop more issues on Hannah after the bombshell she'd just been dealing with, but she needed to know about Paula. There was curiosity on her face and Ryan wasn't entirely sure where to begin. How did you admit you were a complete and utter fool?

He checked to make sure Felix was out of earshot. He wasn't.

"Dad, can I go for a swim yet?" His eyes were pleading.

Damn. He hated to let Felix down. His son didn't care that the ocean was rough and wasn't nice for swimming.

"Why don't you two have a swim?" Hannah said. "I need to freshen up anyway." She ran a hand through her hair. "You can fill me in later."

He hesitated. "You shouldn't be alone. The stalker may be mad that you didn't show up and come looking for you."

She sighed.

"Why don't you stay here and we'll walk you back after we've had a swim?" He saw the refusal on her face. "Then you can come over for dinner," he added. "We'll talk after Felix goes to bed." And that would give him more time to figure out what to say. "Please?"

Reluctantly she nodded. "All right. I'll take Joe for a longer walk. He needs it."

She moved away, and he gently pulled her back to give her a

tender kiss. "Take care."

"Always."

Her smile soothed some of the worry inside him. It had broken his heart to see her so desolate. Sometime in the last week, she'd come to mean a lot to him.

"Da-ad," Felix called.

The whine made him chuckle. "Coming, mate." He stripped off his shirt and then picked up Felix, who shrieked and wriggled as Ryan ran into the ocean and dumped them both under the water. Felix came up spluttering and laughing and Ryan's heart sang. No matter what happened with Paula and with Hannah, he would always have Felix.

They splashed and played, with Ryan throwing Felix into the waves again and again on his demand. Finally, Ryan ran out of puff. "Enough."

"Once more, Dad."

Ryan grinned. "*Once.*"

Felix giggled as Ryan threw him into the waves. They waded out of the water together and dried themselves. Hannah was slowly making her way back along the beach towards them.

"Is Hannah OK now?" Felix asked, his voice quiet.

Surprised, Ryan noticed the concern on his son's face. "She's going to be."

"Is that why you kissed her – to make her feel better?"

Ryan paused. He'd forgotten Felix was there. "That's one of the reasons."

Felix was silent for a moment and then asked, "What are the other reasons?"

What was the right thing to say? "I kissed her because I like her," Ryan told him.

"Is that why you don't kiss Mum anymore?"

Hell. "Yeah. I don't like your mum as much as I used to."

"Are you going to marry Hannah?"

Ryan blinked. Marriage hadn't even entered into his thoughts. That was something *way* in the future, if ever again. "I've got no plans to at the moment." He glanced at his son. "I wouldn't marry anyone unless you liked them too. And anyone I marry has to love you as well."

"What if Hannah doesn't like me?" His voice was quiet.

Ryan crouched down to give Felix his full attention. "I'm pretty sure she already likes you," he said. "But if she doesn't, then she's not the right woman for us." He ignored the twinge in his heart. His priority was Felix – always.

"I like her," Felix said. "And Joe." He was silent for a moment. "Maybe you could ask her if she likes me. That way you'll be sure." His eyes were filled with concern.

"I can do that, if you want," he said. "She did appreciate the hug you gave her."

Felix brightened. "Really? I like your hugs after I'm upset, so I thought she'd like one too."

"She did."

"OK. What are we going to make them for dinner?"

Ryan was more than happy with the change of subject. "Shall we ask her what she likes?"

Hannah had almost reached them and he noticed that she was no longer hugging herself; her arms swung relaxed by her side.

"Hannah, what do you want for dinner?" Felix yelled.

Ryan smiled. He was relieved that Felix liked Hannah, but he needed to take things slowly.

There wasn't only himself to consider.

There was Felix too.

They walked Hannah back to her shed, and Ryan made sure it was empty and there were no surprises before he left to make dinner.

He made Felix have a shower and called Lincoln. "Did you find anyone at the park?"

"No one," Lincoln growled. "He might never have shown up. Have you told Hannah how stupid she was?"

"She realises that. But that's not the worst part – her father's out of jail."

"Shit."

"Yeah, we'll need to interview him." Ryan pushed back his wet hair. "I should have chased up Corrective Services today. Then at least I could have warned her."

"Not your fault, mate. She should have been told he was getting out."

Bureaucracy had failed again. Ryan wasn't surprised.

"By the way," Lincoln continued. "Paula's in custody. They picked her up this afternoon."

"That's great," but he didn't want to hear about it now. "We'll go through it all tomorrow." They said goodbye and he hung up.

When Hannah and Joe arrived at the cabin, Ryan was in the kitchen with Felix, chopping a salad. Felix ran to get the door and Ryan double-checked he had everything ready. He acknowledged the nerves in his stomach. For him to spill his guts about Paula meant that he and Hannah were serious, or at least that he wanted them to be. That was a huge step for him after everything Paula had put him through.

Hannah walked in and his heart beat a little faster. The simple white tank top she wore clung to her breasts and the green skirt accentuated her lovely curves.

"How are you?" he asked.

"Much better, thank you. Have you heard from Lincoln?"

"Let's have dinner first." He flicked his eyes to Felix and she nodded.

"What are we having?"

"Nachos!" Felix called.

"And salad," Ryan added.

"Sounds good."

"Would you like a drink?" he asked. "I've got lemon, lime and bitters."

She beamed at him. "Yes, please."

"Felix, do you want one?"

"Yes, Dad." He was showing Joe his cars, but the dog didn't appear interested.

Ryan poured the drinks and gave Hannah hers, and then finished putting the nachos together. "Are you hungry?" he asked Hannah.

"Yes. Can I do anything to help?"

"No. Felix," he called. "Set the table."

"OK, Dad."

They had an enjoyable dinner, followed by a game of

Hungry Hippos before it was Felix's bedtime.

"Dad, you're still going to read me a story, aren't you?" Felix asked.

"Of course." It was his favourite time of the day.

Felix beamed. "Do you want to hear a story too, Hannah?" He glanced down at his toes and then back at her. "Dad does the best voices."

Ryan's face warmed. He didn't want Hannah to hear the silly voices he used.

Hannah smiled. "I'd love to, if you don't mind."

Felix shook his head and led them into his bedroom. Ryan found the book they were reading, then sat on the bed next to Felix. Felix patted the bed on the other side of himself. "Sit here, Hannah."

Ryan's throat thickened. He loved how inclusive Felix was.

Hannah lifted Felix's teddy bear off the bed as she settled down. "Who's this?"

"That's Barney Bear," Felix said.

"He's very handsome. I bet he gives good hugs."

Felix took the bear from her and cuddled him. "He's the best."

Joe leapt onto the bed and Felix laughed with glee.

"Joe, get down," Hannah commanded.

"He's fine," Felix insisted. "He can sleep with me."

With all of them on the bed it seemed to shrink in size, but Ryan had no problems with the dog on the bed as long as Felix was happy. "If the landlord doesn't mind him there, I don't."

She smiled. "I guess it's fine this once."

Ryan started reading, doing his best not to be self-conscious about Hannah being there. Felix snuggled into Hannah a little as he grew tired. It was sweet, but highlighted how much Ryan needed to be careful about Felix's feelings. He'd never had a good maternal figure in his life.

When he finished the story, he and Hannah returned to the living area. "Would you like a cuppa?" he asked her as the nerves gathered again.

She nodded. "You've done such a good job with Felix. He's so sweet."

"Thank you." It didn't stop him worrying all the time

though.

They made their drinks and carried them outside. The night was dark and moths hovered by the windows of the cabin where the light shone through. The wind whistled through the trees, but the cabin blocked the majority of the breeze so it was pleasant and not too cold.

Ryan took a sip of his coffee.

"What did Lincoln say?" Hannah asked.

Relief swept through him. He could delay talking about Paula. "He didn't see anyone out of the ordinary at the community park." The stalker had been long gone, if he'd even turned up in the first place.

"That's a shame." Hannah glanced at him. "I was really hoping it would end."

"I understand, Hannah, but you should have called us."

"You were busy." She held up a hand to stop his argument. "It doesn't matter now. I won't do it again. Do you want to tell me why your ex broke into my place?"

He would have much preferred to continue talking about the stalker. Ryan sighed. Would she think less of him when he'd explained everything?

"Near as I can tell, Paula saw us on the beach the other day. When she came out here to find me, she must have gone to your shed first and thought we were together. Then she saw us yesterday with Felix and discovered the cabin I was staying in was yours, so she decided to punish you for breaking up her family."

She shifted in her seat. "I thought you were divorced."

"We are. Paula doesn't want to acknowledge it. She didn't take it seriously until I told her I was moving."

She frowned at him, obviously confused.

He needed to tell the whole story. "I met Paula a couple of years after I moved to Karratha." He sipped his drink. "We started dating and it wasn't long before she moved in with me. I didn't actually ask her to, but suddenly she was there all the time and I realised her clothes were in my wardrobe." That should have been his first warning.

"Did you want her there?" Hannah asked.

He thought about it. "I guess so. I liked being in a

relationship and she understood me, she liked all the same things that I liked and we hung out together a lot. It wasn't until later that I discovered she was only pretending to like what I did." He'd been so thirsty for love, so desperately lonely and Paula had been an end to the drought.

Hannah ran a hand along his arm in sympathy.

He closed his eyes, taking the comfort she offered. He opened them again. "Then she got pregnant."

"That must have been a surprise."

He nodded. "It was, but I was excited as well. I wanted to have a family, though Paula wasn't as keen. She talked about getting an abortion, saying she wanted to travel with me first." He should have listened to what she was really saying – she didn't want the baby.

"So what happened?"

"I proposed to her, told her I wanted to have a family with her. She accepted."

"Did you love her?"

"Yeah, I did, but I think I was in love with the idea of having a family more." It had taken him a long time to realise that. "My family was ... unconventional." It was a word Mrs Z had used once and he'd always thought it sounded better than crazy or weird. "Mum and Dad were all about freedom and choice. For them it meant doing whatever they wanted, not considering what was best for us kids. We moved constantly because we were squatters, living on land we didn't own, and didn't have permission to be on. We'd stay until we were discovered and kicked off." He remembered the fights – often physical – when the police or property owner had found them. He remembered not being able to say goodbye to school friends, having to start again at a new school months later when they found somewhere new to settle. "I hated it, the constant upheaval, their disinterest in me, the lack of a proper family."

She squeezed his hand. "It can't have been easy."

He shook his head. "It's one of the reasons I gravitated to the Zanettis. They were a real family and there was structure there. When Lincoln mentioned he wanted to be a cop, it seemed the perfect job for me as well – law and order, two things I'd never had."

"What happened after Felix was born?"

He ran a hand through his hair. He hated thinking about it. "Paula got increasingly irrational during her pregnancy. She complained she was fat, accused me of looking at other women, was convinced I would leave her." He shifted in his seat. "I thought it was pregnancy hormones and she'd be all right after Felix was born."

"It didn't get better?"

"It got worse." He'd been such a fool. "Felix cried a lot during the first six months, he barely slept. When I was at home, Paula wanted nothing to do with him. She would often go out with friends as soon as I walked in the door, and never got up for him during the night."

"That must have been hard." She gave him a sympathetic smile.

"Yeah. I told myself she was tired and scared." It had been easy to lie to himself. "As Felix got older, she organised babysitters for him all the time so we could go out, just the two of us. I tried to get her interested in family activities like camping, but she hated it."

Hannah glanced towards the bedroom. "She didn't bond with Felix?"

"No. She was jealous of the time I would spend with him and jealous whenever I was away from her. She became very possessive of me, sometimes leaving Felix with the neighbour so she could have lunch with me at work." He cringed as he remembered how clingy Paula had been at the police station, how his colleagues used to make fun of him.

"What did you do?"

"I tried to split my time evenly between them, tried to find something we could do together and then finally talked to her about family counselling." He grimaced. "That was the first time she had a complete meltdown. It scared the shit out of Felix and me." And he'd backpedalled all the way back into her good books. "It was around this time, Felix was about four, when Lincoln came to visit." He smiled. "Lincoln's not one to put up with any bullshit."

"No, he's not." Hannah grinned. "What did he say?"

"He told me Paula was manipulating me, that she didn't care

for Felix and that Felix was showing the characteristics of a neglected child." It had woken him right up. "He said I needed to keep a journal, documenting everything Paula was or wasn't doing with Felix, because mothers still more often get custody of children."

"From what you've said, I can't imagine she would have wanted it."

"She tried when I asked for a divorce." It had truly terrified him. There was no way he was going to leave Felix with her. "It was her way of controlling me."

Hannah took a sip of her drink. "Is that when you left her?"

He shook his head. "I wasn't ready to give up yet," he said. "But I took Lincoln's advice and kept a journal locked in my desk at the station so she couldn't find it. In my heart I knew it wasn't going to work, but I didn't want to accept it."

"What happened?"

"Over the next couple of years I made Felix my priority. I invited Paula to do everything we did, but she rarely accepted. She would manipulate Felix, tell him he was selfish for not letting us have mummy and daddy time, attempt to play us against each other." He sighed. "If Felix and I went away together, she'd sometimes call, threatening to harm herself and force us to come home early." He'd been so easy to manipulate. He could never take the risk that she was lying, didn't want the guilt he'd be left with if he'd ignored her threats and came home to find she'd delivered on them. "It was when Felix made a comment about being worthless that I realised I was doing him more harm than good by staying with Paula. I asked for a divorce and told her I was taking Felix with me."

"She didn't take it well," Hannah guessed.

He grimaced, remembering. "No. She destroyed most of the living room." He sighed. "Then she sobbed and told me she would kill herself if I left. That she would die without Felix."

"That's awful! Did you believe her?"

"Not this time. I did write it down though. In the end it was my journal documenting three years of her manipulations that had the courts deciding to grant me full custody of Felix."

"I'm glad."

"Me too."

Hannah put her empty mug on the table. "So although you're divorced, she still thinks she has a claim on you?"

He nodded. "We split up over a year ago, but she would constantly drop by the station, or home, or pick Felix up from school. I didn't trust her with Felix and it was one of the reasons I moved down here." He didn't think she would ever wilfully hurt Felix, but he wasn't a hundred per cent certain.

"And now she's followed you to Blackbridge."

He sipped his coffee. "She told the Albany police she missed us and wanted to get back together. She's convinced I've made a mistake."

"What do you think?" She was watching him closely.

"I'm sure she believes what she says, but I won't ever let Felix live with her again." He'd wasted enough of his life on Paula.

She took his hand, ran her palm over it. "What's going to happen to her now?"

"She'll go to court and be charged with her offences."

Hannah bit her lip. "How will that affect Felix?"

He blinked. She was an incredible woman to consider his son. "He's worried she'll take him away, so it might be a relief for him."

"For both of you," Hannah said. "If she goes to jail it won't be for long, will it?"

He shrugged. "I don't know."

"It seems so wrong for her to go away for something as petty as jealousy."

The anger was swift and surprising. "She needs help and maybe this way she'll get it. I did everything I could to help her when we were together." It had been exhausting, and still he'd failed.

"I'm sorry, Ryan. Sorry you had to go through that, and sorry Felix doesn't have a loving mother. How could anyone not love your son?"

Her words were a balm to his soul. He remembered Felix's question. "So you like Felix?"

"Of course. He's wonderful."

Ryan cleared his throat. "Maybe you could tell him some time. He's a little worried no one will like him."

"I will," she promised. "Perhaps we can do something together. I bet he'd love to help Kit milk her cows or feed the calves."

"He would," Ryan agreed, pleased she'd suggested it. With Hannah he was sure the offer was genuine.

She stared into the darkness and then sighed. "It's getting late. I should go."

He didn't want her to. He liked being with her. "Where are you staying tonight?"

"I thought I'd go back to the shed."

He shook his head. "That's not a great option." Her stalker was still out there.

"It's too late to disturb my friends," Hannah said.

"Why don't you stay here?" The words were out before he considered them. Though he'd love to spend the night with Hannah in his bed, it wasn't what he meant. "I can sleep with Felix."

Hannah's eyes were wide, but he couldn't quite tell what she was thinking.

Was it too soon?

Had he made a mistake?

Ryan's expression was so earnest it touched something deep inside of Hannah. The idea of staying the night at his cabin was appealing and that made it a little scary. They were moving fast, but considering her lack of relationships over the past five years, anything would seem fast.

Though perhaps he wasn't implying more than she had a safe place to stay.

She wanted to take things further with Ryan. His kisses and the way he touched her made her desperate to experience what she'd been missing out on.

She had to be honest with him. If they were going to have any kind of relationship – and she did want them to – she had to communicate her fears so he didn't think she was playing games with him. Especially after what he'd been through with his ex. "I'd like to sleep with you," she said. "But I don't know if I'm capable."

The mood shifted and his eyes darkened. "We're all capable of sleeping." He grinned.

She made a face. "You know what I mean."

He stood and gently pulled her to her feet. "Yeah, but if you want we can just go to sleep. It's been a stressful day." He pressed a kiss against her forehead.

She closed her eyes, enjoying the touch of his lips against her skin. The day *had* been exhausting and she wanted to forget about everything that had happened. She wanted to pretend, just for a while, that there was only the two of them and she was a healthy, sexual woman without any issues. "Can we try?"

He nodded. "If you're comfortable." He brushed her fringe out of her face. "Tell me what you need."

Emboldened by his patience and his concern for her, she pulled him inside, pausing at the entrance to his bedroom. She slipped her hands around his waist and brushed her lips against his. He tasted like coffee and he opened for her, teasing her tongue with his own. Her whole body woke up as warm tingles flooded through it. "I'd like to touch you," she admitted.

He smiled, slow and sweet as he wandered into the bedroom and switched on the bedside lamp. He moved back to her, kissed her and whispered, "I'm all yours."

Nerves coalesced in her stomach. She didn't know what to do.

"I'll tell you if there's something I don't like." He smiled with encouragement.

She could do this. She was an adult for goodness sake. Stepping forward, she ran her palms firmly over his chest to hide the slight shake in them. She pressed her lips against his, running a hand through the back of his hair, then she pulled him closer as he gently rested his hands on her hips.

That he'd remembered what she'd said the other day filled her with more confidence and aroused her further. She slipped her hands under his T-shirt and ran them against his firm muscles. He whispered, "Yes."

His eyes were open and filled with enjoyment. Power rushed through her. She was pleasuring him. She shoved his T-shirt further up and he helped her by stripping it off.

He was a gorgeous example of man, all lightly defined muscle, tanned from the summer's sun. Heat pooled between her legs. She touched his nipples and then bent to kiss them, to taste them.

He trembled and brought his hands up to caress her breasts. It was so unbelievably good. Her nipples puckered and she pressed into his hands. She wanted more. She shed her top and he took a step back to shut the door.

The click of the door closing was like a trap snapping shut and she stepped away from him, away from the closed door, wrapping her arms around herself as her heart raced.

He held up his hands. "It's OK. I don't want Felix waking and walking in on us."

He was right. Of course he was, but her body wasn't listening to her head. Joe wasn't even in the room with them.

Ryan walked away from the door and sat on the bed, taking off his shoes. She inched closer to the entrance, trying not to panic. It was fine, she was safe, this was Ryan.

He shuffled on to the bed, sitting so his back rested against the headboard and his legs were crossed at the ankles in front of him. His posture was relaxed, casual and pretty darn sexy. She glanced to the closed door. She had clear access to the exit.

"Did you ever play the game hot or cold as a kid?"

The question had her focusing back on Ryan. She frowned. "What?"

"It's the game where you hide something and others have to find it. And you say hot or cold depending on whether they're getting closer to or further away from the object."

She nodded, still confused.

He beckoned her forward, the motion so sexy that she took a couple of steps towards him. "We could play it now," he said. "Except the object is your desire." He paused. "The door closed makes it ice cold, right?" His voice was low, cautious, but kind.

"Yes." She wanted to go back to when Ryan was touching her and her body was hot and alive.

He held out a hand and after a split second of hesitation she took it. His thumbs made a slow, circular motion on the back of her hand that sent lovely ripples through her body.

"You tell me when I'm getting warmer." He tugged her

closer and kissed her palm. "You say cold and I stop."

His slow, gentle kisses up her arm were clouding her mind. She smiled, thrilled that he hadn't given up on her, thrilled that he was trying to make this work. "So my desire is like a kids' game?"

"Not at all, but it might help, might make it kind of fun."

She liked the idea and she trusted that he would do what he promised. The enormity of that trust flooded her mind. He wouldn't hurt her. She wasn't afraid. She toed off her sandals. "Can I be on this side – closest to the door?" It would help, she was sure.

"Of course." He shuffled over and she carefully climbed on to the bed next to him.

Ryan cupped her cheek. "You only need to say the word," he whispered, before kissing her.

She let herself relax into the kiss. His hand gently trailed down her bare side. "Hot or cold?"

"Warm," she said. She turned away from the door, concentrating on the sensations his hands were causing in her body.

His hand drifted to her stomach. "What about now?"

"Warmer."

He brushed her nipple with his thumb and her groin throbbed. She wanted more. "Hot."

His smile was slow and full of pleasure as he moved down the bed and replaced his thumb with his mouth.

Holy shit. Hannah's back arched as his tongue teased her nipple, wanting, needing … She moaned. "More." His breath was warm against the fabric of her bra. She didn't want any barricade against their skin. She reached around and unclasped her bra, pulling it off.

Then his mouth was on her breast and it was sheer pleasure. No man had touched her in this way and it was a revelation. She closed her eyes and let herself feel.

Ryan shifted and tasted her other breast and it felt just as good. Every nerve in her body was singing in celebration.

He brought his mouth back to hers and she kissed him, pouring all of her passion into the kiss.

"Lie down, Hannah," he murmured as he kissed her neck.

She shuffled down in the bed, more than happy to do as he suggested. Her groin throbbed and she was hot, so hot.

He kissed her again. "You're so beautiful. I want to kiss every part of your body."

"All right." She wanted whatever he wanted to give her.

He chuckled and moved on top of her, his arms either side of her body and his weight over her legs.

She froze. "Cold!" She squeezed her eyes shut, her heart pounding in her chest, praying he would move, that he would listen to what she said.

"Shit, I'm sorry." Quickly, he moved off her and stood up.

Relief rushed through her as she sat up, shifting away. Then misery poured through the valleys the relief had left. "I'm sorry, so sorry." He must think she was such a tease. She wrapped her arms around her middle, unable to look at him.

"Open your eyes, Hannah." He ran a hand down her side and she flinched instinctively. He sighed. "Talk to me."

Reluctantly she opened her eyes.

"Was it my weight on top of you?"

She nodded.

"OK, can I sit on the bed? We could maybe try again and figure out what works for you."

She stared at him. How could he still be interested? He didn't seem mad at all. Instead he was concerned. She didn't want him to feel bad. It was she who had the problem, and she still wanted him. "All right."

Slowly, he lay on the bed beside her. He took hold of her hand, kissing her knuckles. "Do you want to scoot down next to me?"

She did. She really wanted to conquer this. She slid back down the bed and he placed his arm across her, turning her head so he could kiss her again.

The kisses relaxed her and she breathed in his scent. He pressed himself closer to her side. "Is this OK?"

"Yes." She ran her hand down his back, enjoying the smoothness of his skin.

"How about this?" He draped one leg over her legs.

"Yes."

"So it's my full body on top of you that doesn't work?"

"I think so."

He smiled. "I can work with that. Can I keep going?"

She squeezed his hand. "If you really want to. This must suck for you."

"Not at all. I'm enjoying myself, and I'm hoping you are too." He tilted his head to the side in question.

"Yes."

"Good. Now, where was I?" He kissed her softly and then began a slow journey down her body, spending time with each breast until her whole body was hot and relaxed and needy. His hand slid up her skirt and brushed her core, and it felt so hot she was amazed she didn't burn him. "Hot."

"I'll say." Ryan grinned at her. He brushed up against her underpants, once, twice and she pressed herself against his hand.

"Can I take off your skirt?"

She nodded, unable to speak. She lifted her hips to reach the zip and Ryan slipped his hands under her butt, pressing her groin to his mouth.

"Yes." She fumbled with the zip, struggling to make her hands work. His tongue licked her through the fabric and she moaned, her body shuddering. She was going to combust. She had to get her clothes off, had to remove the barricade. With trembling hands, she slid down the zip and pushed down her skirt.

Ryan lifted his head and helped her drag away the skirt. She was lying there in only her underwear and she wanted them off as well. She pushed at them, and Ryan stilled her hands.

"There's no rush," he said, sliding his hands along her mound, making her groan. Slowly he ran a finger under the fabric, touching her most intimate place. "Hot or cold?"

"Hot. *Very* hot."

His smile was pure smoulder.

"Please, Ryan."

"As you wish." He peeled down her underpants and she kicked them off, and then his mouth was on her. His tongue teased and tasted and her body shuddered. She'd never felt anything like it, never dreamed it could be like this. His finger nudged her entrance and then he stopped. "Hot or cold?"

"Hot." She wanted to feel him everywhere. As his finger caressed her inside, and his tongue kissed her outside, the intense pressure built up inside her. She was helpless to stop it, she didn't want to stop it.

And then all thought ceased and she cried out as she came.

Chapter 15

Hannah felt *amazing* – there was no other word to describe this incredible relief and joy and satisfaction swirling around inside her. She stared at the ceiling, not quite believing it. Ryan had worked with her past, her triggers, and she'd had the best orgasm of her life. Tears welled up. She wasn't broken.

Ryan lay down next to her and pulled her close. "Are you all right?"

She nodded, hugging him. "Thank you."

"My absolute pleasure." He licked his lips.

Hannah blushed, her senses slowly returning to her.

He shuffled, adjusting himself, and then pressed kisses against her arm.

Guilt stabbed her. He hadn't come, he wasn't even completely naked. "I'm sorry." She sat up. "You must be aching."

He smiled that slow, sweet smile. "We're taking this as slow as you need us to," he said. "I can wait."

The evidence of his arousal strained against the fabric of his jeans. She ran a tentative hand down his stomach and over his erection. It twitched and she snatched her hand back as fear swept through her. "Cold." She remembered having her legs forced wide, that thing pressing against her. "*Shit!*" Misery pooled in her stomach. Ryan wasn't Justin, Ryan wasn't going to force her to do anything.

"Hey, it's all right," Ryan said. "I'm guessing the last time you felt one of those, it wasn't in the best circumstances."

She nodded.

"So, we'll make new circumstances when you're ready." He kissed her cheek.

God, he was so understanding and it made her feel worse, like the most selfish person in the world. "That's hardly fair to you."

"I've loved every minute of tonight," Ryan said. "I loved you relaxing and letting go." His hand caressed her breasts and her nipples puckered. He smiled. "Besides, I realised halfway through that I don't have any condoms."

Damn. She hadn't considered condoms. She was so inexperienced. It was lucky he wasn't. "Thank you for … everything." Her chest was tight, puffed up to twice the size, trying to contain all the emotion swirling around inside of her.

"You're welcome." He stood up. "Why don't you have a shower? I'll make us a couple of drinks and we'll watch some TV before we go to bed."

Even now, he wasn't pushing to join her and he must have a serious case of blue balls. Her feelings for him intensified, and she pulled on the reins. She couldn't let them run away. Ryan was a seriously great guy, he was kind, considerate and so unbelievably patient. She liked him so very much, but they'd only known each other a week. It would be foolish to get carried away. Particularly when he'd admitted he wanted to take things slow, that he was worried about Felix. "All right."

He left the room and she instantly missed his presence.

"Dad, what are you doing in my bed?" Felix's voice right next to his ear woke Ryan the next morning.

He groaned. "Hannah's sleeping in my bed."

"And probably Joe," Felix said, delighted.

"Probably." After they'd watched television the night before, he'd decided it would be best if he slept with his son.

He didn't mind. Sure, he wanted her with a desire that made him hurt, but if he rushed her now, he might lose her and he didn't want that. Last night had been an experience unlike anything he'd had before. He'd wanted to show Hannah how good intimacy could be and he'd celebrated every moan and sigh he'd received from her. He hadn't felt so good about himself in a long time.

Felix yawned.

"Scoot over, you hog." Ryan pushed Felix to the other side of the mattress.

Felix giggled. "You're almost falling out of bed."

"I know." He stretched and sat up. Felix was not a restful sleeper, and Ryan had been pushed and kicked most of the night. "What do you want for breakfast?"

"Eggs and soldiers."

Ryan raised his eyebrows.

"Please," he added.

"All right." He checked the time. "Why don't you get dressed and I'll make breakfast?"

"Sure, Dad."

Ryan pulled on his jeans and walked into the kitchen, switching on the kettle. His bedroom door was closed and the shower was running. Figuring Hannah wouldn't be long, he put enough eggs on to boil for the three of them and made a couple of coffees. It was six o'clock and they both had to be at work at seven.

Her phone rang in his bedroom and when it stopped, his started.

Ryan braced himself. "Lincoln."

"Do you know where Hannah is?"

"Yeah, she's here. Why?"

Lincoln paused. "She's at your place?"

Ryan grinned, debating whether to lead his friend on. "She stayed in my bed and I bunked with Felix."

"Oh. Right. Well tell her not to go to the office."

"Why not?"

"Our friend has broken in and covered the whole area with milk."

"Milk?"

"It's day eight – eight maids a-milking."

Ryan closed his eyes. "This person really likes his twelve days of Christmas. He must have been pissed about her missing their appointment."

"The note says, *Lying, selfish whore.*"

"Did you catch him on camera?"

"Yeah, but it's not clear. He smashed that first. We've got a body build, but that's all."

Ryan swore.

"I'm going to arrange it so Hannah's not alone for the next couple of days," Lincoln said. "She's going Christmas shopping with the girls tomorrow so she'll be in Albany all day."

"That's great." Hannah came out of the bedroom, her hair damp and her cheeks flushed pink. He wanted to wrap his arms around her and tell her he cared. But those words were too scary, too much, he'd only just met her. Worry flooded him and he focused on the phone call. "Do you want to speak to her?"

"Tell her it'll take us a couple of hours to investigate."

"Will do. I'll be there as soon as I drop Felix off." He hung up.

"Who was that?"

"Lincoln."

She sighed. "What now?"

"You can't go to your office this morning."

"Why not?"

"Because your stalker broke in and spread milk around the whole area."

"Shit!" She grimaced. "Eight maids a-milking. How badly damaged is everything?"

"Lincoln didn't say. How do you remember the song so well?" Ryan asked. "I barely remember the first couple of lines."

"I checked when the gifts first started," she said. "Plus, Mum used to sing it and made Dad and I both gifts for the twelve days before Christmas."

Ryan's instincts went on red alert and almost immediately Hannah made the same connection.

Her eyes widened. "Oh, shit."

Felix came out. "Morning, Hannah!" He ran over to Joe, who was standing by the door to be let out. "Hiya, boy." He rubbed Joe's fur and then opened the door.

Hannah was standing there, her face pale. He wanted to

reassure her. "It might be a coincidence." Though he highly doubted it.

"Is breakfast ready yet?" Felix asked.

Ryan moved on autopilot, putting bread into the toaster. "Almost." He handed Hannah her coffee and poured Felix an orange juice.

"Dad, can I play with Jacob today?"

Ryan's mind switched gears instantly. "I'll have to call Lynette and Mrs Z and ask."

"Thanks."

"I need to go," Hannah finally said. "I need to ask Dad if he's doing this."

He shook his head. "No. He'll just deny it." And if he had anything to do with it, Ryan didn't want her anywhere near him. "We'll go and question him. Where is he staying?"

She huffed out a breath. "At his son Phillip's place. It's somewhere in Albany."

"Do you have any contact details?"

"No. He was going to call me."

Ryan made a note. "He won't be hard to find. There'll be something on his parole file." He buttered the toast and cut it into strips for Felix, before placing it and the egg cup in front of him.

Hannah grabbed her keys from the bench. "I need to go and assess the damage."

"Hannah, you're not going to be allowed in." He stepped in front of her to stop her from leaving.

She glared at him. "So what am I meant to do – sit and twiddle my thumbs while this bastard tries to ruin my life?" Her anger was clear and he was pleased. It was far better than her being scared.

"Dad, is everything OK?"

Hannah grimaced.

Ryan turned to Felix. "Yeah, mate. Someone has been doing mean things to Hannah and she's upset."

"Like the cabin?"

"Yeah." He hadn't mentioned yet that it was Paula, or that she was in town. Hadn't decided what he should tell Felix. "We're getting closer," he said to Hannah. "Maybe your dad can shed some light."

She sighed and sat at the table. "Sorry, Felix. I didn't mean to yell."

"It's all right. I yell sometimes when I'm upset." Felix hesitated then hugged her. "You can yell if it makes you feel better."

"Thanks," Hannah said, "but I'm not sure it does. I don't like yelling at my friends."

Felix glanced at Ryan, his expression uncertain and then asked, "Am I your friend?"

"Of course – if you'd like to be," Hannah said. "I like you, you're nice."

He beamed. "OK."

The joy on Felix's face warmed Ryan and worried him too. If Ryan stuffed up things with Hannah, Felix would be affected as well.

He turned his attention to the issue of Hannah's father. "It can't be your father. His fingerprints would be on file and we had no matches." But still, the coincidence was too strong for him to ignore. Maybe he was paying someone to do it – but why? He put a boiled egg in front of Hannah. "Why don't you eat something before you go?"

"Thanks."

"I want you to still keep Joe close." There were only a few days left until Christmas. Would the gifts stop if they still hadn't caught him by then?

"I always do."

After she had eaten and calmed down, he walked her to her car. She insisted on going to the park to check the damage for herself. "Call me if you need anything." He wanted to be there for her, wanted to be the one she called when she needed someone, and that surprised him. Hadn't he learned anything from Paula? He shouldn't be so needy.

She smiled. "I will."

He wasn't quite ready for her to go. "Maybe we could do dinner again this week." If she was with him he wouldn't need to worry about her safety.

"I'd like that." She kissed him and drove off.

Ryan lifted a hand in a wave and then rubbed his chest. She

stirred up all of his emotions; the desire to protect, the urge to nurture, plus he lusted after her too. He wanted to spend more time with her, wanted to watch her with Felix, make sure they were fine together. The way he ached as she drove away wasn't a sensation he was comfortable with, but still he wanted more.

Was he going to make a fool of himself again?

Hannah set up the gazebo and a table outside the office, while Lincoln and then later Ryan investigated. There wasn't much to find. The front door had been smashed and several litres of milk had been tipped all over her desk, over the tourist brochures and computer. In the hot summer heat, it was already beginning to smell. She didn't know whether the paperwork and computer would be salvageable.

Lynette arrived as Ryan and Lincoln were packing up.

"What the hell has happened now?" Lynette asked.

"Break-in," Hannah said. "I'll clean it up if you do the bathrooms around the site." She scribbled a note to stick on the front verandah, directing people to the back door again.

"Are you all right?" Lynette asked, her expression sympathetic.

She clenched her hands to stop them from shaking. "No, but I'll deal." There was too much going on in her life right now. She wanted to find this bastard so she could concentrate on whatever it was that was happening between Ryan and her. She wanted time to dwell on last night, wanted to savour being in a relationship with someone.

"We'll ask the guests if they heard or saw anything," Ryan told her.

"Thanks." She gave him a quick kiss before heading inside to clean.

Whoever it was, they had been thorough. Although luckily, the collection of files that were kept on the desk had protected most of the computer from being damaged. The carpet was soaked and everything had an off-milk smell that would be a bitch to get out. But as the saying went, there was no use crying over spilt milk.

By midday, she had the majority of the mess cleaned up and had a dozen incense sticks burning – courtesy of Shirley – to mask the stench. When the computer booted up without an issue, she breathed a sigh of relief.

She spent her afternoon on the phone to the insurance company and catching up on paperwork.

She'd had little time to work on her retreat in the past couple of days and she still had to assess how much the damage Paula had done was going to set her back. The insurance assessor hadn't been yet and she didn't want to do further work on it in case someone else broke in. There was no way the cabin would be completed by the end of the year. She sighed.

The money from Ryan's rent had to go towards the hard fixtures – being up at the lookout had reminded her how crumbly the limestone was, and fencing it off was a priority. At least she could borrow the fencing gear from Kit.

Who was she kidding? The whole idea was doomed to fail. She shouldn't have given in to her grandparents. She'd been caught up in their positivity. She had nowhere near the money she needed to complete her vision.

Disgusted with her negativity, she cursed the stalker again. He was messing with her head. She *would* make her retreat work. Just as she would find out who was stalking her.

Could it be her father causing all the damage? She hadn't allowed herself to think about it, hadn't wanted to. But he could have hired someone to leave the gifts – he'd have the necessary contacts after all his time in jail. And he had been upset that she hadn't visited him.

The message today had simply read, *Lying, selfish whore.* She hadn't lied to her father, though maybe he thought her selfish for not greeting him more enthusiastically. Was he simply toying with her?

Lynette came through the back door. "How are you holding up?"

Hannah lifted her head. "I'm coping."

"Are you going to call your grandparents about the damage?"

She swiftly shook her head. "There's no need," she assured her. "The insurance is going to cover it."

"It's not just the damage to the building," Lynette argued. "Shouldn't you tell them that some arsehole is targeting you?"

"No. I don't want them to worry. And anyway, there's nothing they can do about it."

"They'd want to know."

They would, and they'd pack up and drive back to Western Australia from wherever they currently were. She *really* didn't need them here while she was figuring out what to do about her father. They wouldn't understand at all. "It's better if they don't."

Lynette opened her mouth and Hannah interrupted. "Please don't push it."

"I'm worried about you too." Lynette squeezed her hand. "This is plain creepy."

"There isn't anyone in Blackbridge who has a problem with me, is there?"

"Not that I know of." And Lynette knew most of the gossip.

"If you hear of anything tell me."

"Will do. Lincoln put a picture of the guy who broke in here on their Twitter feed. People will be keeping an eye out for him."

Hannah opened the social media site. The picture was dark and grainy, not much more than an outline of baggy clothes and a hoodie covering the face. It could have been male or female and was no one she recognised. She glanced at Lynette. "Are you finished for the day?"

She nodded. "I'm going to take the boys down to the beach."

"Felix has been asking to play with Jacob," Hannah told her.

"He's coming around tomorrow afternoon and then he's sleeping over on Friday." Lynette shuddered. "I might be regretting agreeing to that come Saturday morning."

Hannah chuckled. "You love your boys."

Lynette nodded and then smiled slyly at her. "You kissed Ryan before he left," she said. "Perhaps you and Ryan can arrange a sleepover of your own."

Hannah's face flushed. "Ah …"

Lynette laughed. "Something to think about. I'll catch you later." She headed out the back door, passing Fleur as she arrived. The timing couldn't be coincidental.

"This totally sucks." Fleur gave Hannah a hug.

"Yeah. Did Lincoln call you?"

"No. Ryan was at the hospital."

Her mouth went dry. "Is he all right?"

"Yes. Felix somehow managed to run into a barbed wire fence and needed a couple of stitches."

"Oh, the poor thing," Hannah said.

"He was pretty chuffed with himself after he'd got over the tears," Fleur said. "He thinks stitches are manly."

Hannah laughed. "How was Ryan?"

"A bit pale when he first ran into the ED, but he coped well."

"Good." Ryan was a fantastic father and the way he cared for Felix made Hannah like him all the more.

"Why didn't you call me?" Fleur demanded.

"You were at work," Hannah said. "And there was nothing you could do."

Fleur nodded. "So fill me in on the latest."

Hannah put a "closed" sign on the back door, before going into the kitchen. "You're going to want to take a seat."

"That bad?"

"You be the judge." Hannah smiled and proceeded to tell her friend about Paula and her father.

"Bloody hell," Fleur said. "Your father's out of jail and you didn't ring me?" She stood with her hands on her hips, her eyebrows raised.

Guilt stung Hannah. Fleur had always been there for her, had always been the person she shared things with, but yesterday it had been Ryan instead. She shrugged, as if it was no big deal. "I was upset, not thinking straight, and then I ran into Ryan and he invited me to dinner."

Fleur's anger faded and she grinned. "OK, I completely understand. So how are you now?"

"I honestly don't know what to feel." The hopelessness of the situation scuttled back into the forefront of her mind. "Ryan said they were going to question Dad because of the twelve-days-of-Christmas connection. That won't go down well I'm sure." Being on a suspect list only weeks after getting out of jail couldn't be good. "I hope it won't cause problems with his parole."

"It's not your problem," Fleur told her. "You didn't ask for this, and if it is him, then he deserves to be questioned."

"You're right."

"Of course I am. Now tell me about dinner with Ryan."

Hannah's face heated.

Fleur chuckled with glee. "It was more than dinner, wasn't it?"

She nodded.

"Awesome! How was it?"

She didn't want to go into detail, didn't want to express all the emotions in words. She wanted to treasure them, keep them to herself a little longer. "Amazing."

"He was, you know, careful?" Fleur was concerned.

Hannah smiled at the memory. "Yeah. Completely careful."

"That's good. I didn't want to have to ask Kit to bring her rifle over."

Hannah laughed. "Don't go all Neanderthal on me. It was good. We didn't have sex, but he understands I need to take it slowly."

"He's a keeper right there," Fleur declared. "How about we give the other musketeers a call and do dinner at my place? You can all sleep over and we can get an early start on our shopping trip."

She didn't want to be alone tonight. "Yeah, let's do that."

Chapter 16

Ryan was tired even before he walked into the police station by mid-morning. None of the park residents had seen anything, though one had heard glass smashing sometime during the night. The smell of off milk lingered in his nose and he wanted a shower. He greeted Adam as he turned on his computer.

"Did you find anything?" Adam asked.

"There was a bit of blood on some glass," Ryan said. "We might get something from it." But it had to be sent to Perth to be analysed and it could be weeks before they got the results.

"How's Hannah?"

"Angry, but coping." He was impressed with how well she was dealing with it. The Hannah he'd first met would have crumbled and hidden, but she'd changed over the last few days, grown stronger, become a fighter. He was glad. "Did you find an address for her father?"

"Yeah. His son's place is in Torbay, just this side of Albany. Are we going to pay him a visit?"

Ryan nodded. It was the best lead they'd had so far. "Get your things. We'll go now."

Lincoln walked in and dumped his gear on the table. "This is getting beyond a joke."

"Yeah. We're going to question Hannah's father."

"Great. When you get back I'll head into Albany with Sue and question Paula."

Ryan had forgotten about Paula in all that had happened. He didn't envy his friend.

"We'll swap notes this afternoon," Lincoln said.

"Yeah." He headed out the door with Adam right behind him.

It took about half an hour to reach Phillip Novak's place in Torbay. He lived on the top of a hill in a two-storey wooden house surrounded by garden and bush. The nearest neighbour was a kilometre down the road. "How big are the blocks out here?" Ryan asked.

"I reckon about five acres," Adam said. "Maybe more. We can check when we get back to the station."

Ryan pulled up in front of the house and they both got out. Two boys were playing in the garden, and when they saw the police car they ran inside, calling their mother.

Ryan was curious about Hannah's father. Would Hannah resemble him? Would he show compassion to Hannah's situation? Or was he the stalker?

He walked up to the front entrance and knocked. A woman about his age opened the door, with two young boys behind her. "Mrs Novak?" Ryan asked.

She nodded.

"I'm Senior Constable Kilpatrick and this is Constable Marshall. We'd like to speak with Ivan Novak if he's at home."

"What is this about? He checked in with his parole officer yesterday."

"It's an unrelated matter," Ryan said. "We'd like to speak to him about his daughter."

"Hannah?" The voice was accented and clear as an older man stepped into the hallway. He was stocky but stooped with greying hair, and when Ryan looked him in the eyes he jolted at how alike Hannah's they were.

"Yes, sir. Could we have a few minutes of your time?"

He nodded and the woman at the door gestured them in.

The house was light and airy and they were led into a lounge room that had large windows framing the view down the hill towards the ocean. Ivan sat on the maroon sofa chair and motioned for them to sit. Adam took out his notepad.

"Is Hannah all right? Is she hurt?" Ivan asked.

"She's fine," Ryan told him. "Someone has been damaging her property over the past week."

"And you think it's me." The statement was flat.

Ryan ignored the comment. "The acts of vandalism have all been themed around the twelve days of Christmas and Hannah mentioned today that the song held particular significance for you and your wife."

Pain crossed Ivan's face. "It was my wife's idea. We used to get little presents for each other in the lead-up to Christmas." He hesitated, but didn't say any more.

"Is there anything you want to add?" Ryan prompted.

"Have all the gifts been vandalism?" Ivan asked.

Adam checked his notebook. "The first two weren't."

"Do you know who gave her those gifts?" Ryan questioned.

After a long pause, Ivan shook his head. He might not know, but Ryan could see that he had his suspicions.

Anger stirred in Ryan, but he kept it under control. Ex-prisoners often didn't trust the police. He had to show Ivan that he was there for Hannah. "Who else knows about your Christmas tradition?"

"Hannah's grandparents, I guess." He pursed his lips. "I might have mentioned it to my boys when they were kids." He shrugged. "I don't know many people anymore. You lose contact when you're in jail."

"Are either of your sons here?"

Ivan shook his head. "Phillip's at work and Marko isn't coming down from Perth until tomorrow."

"Where does Phillip work?" Adam asked.

Ivan frowned. "Now wait a minute. You're not suggesting either of my boys had something to do with this, are you?"

Ryan kept his expression pleasant, although it was exactly where his thoughts had headed. "Not at all. I need to cover all the bases. After I establish their alibis I can continue with other lines of investigation. You want me to be thorough for Hannah, don't you?"

He nodded.

"What time does Phillip normally get home from work?"

"About half past five." Ivan called Phillip's wife into the room. "Where does Phillip work?"

"At a doctor's surgery in Albany." She gave the name.

Adam took a note.

"In the last week, has he been out at night at all?" Ryan asked.

"He had a work Christmas party last Wednesday night," she said. "But aside from that he's been here to spend time with his father."

Wednesday he'd gone on the date with Hannah.

"He never went out again after he got home?" Adam asked.

"Only to take the kids to the beach with me," Ivan said.

It didn't fit. All of the gifts had been left at night. Still, he'd check Phillip's alibi for Wednesday. "Are you a deep sleeper, Mrs Novak?" Ryan asked.

She frowned at him. "No. I suffer from insomnia, so some nights I don't sleep at all."

That was a little too convenient. Could they all be in it together? "Have you ever met Hannah?"

"No. I didn't know Phillip had a half-sister until Ivan came here."

Adam took the image they'd got from the surveillance camera and showed it to Ivan. "Do you recognise this person?"

Ivan's eyes widened for a split second before he shook his head. "No. Who is it?"

"It's the person who broke into the holiday park last night," Ryan said.

Adam showed the picture to Phillip's wife.

"It's kind of blurry." She squinted at it and then glanced at Ivan. "No, I don't think so."

Ryan didn't believe her. "Are you sure?"

She straightened. "Yes."

He got to his feet. "Thank you for your help."

Ivan stood. "Hannah's not in any danger, is she? These things are just pranks, right?"

"I can't say for sure," Ryan told him.

Real worry flashed in Ivan's eyes. "Then you'd better be protecting her," he demanded. "I couldn't bear for anything to happen to my princess."

The man seemed genuinely upset, but still Ryan suspected that Ivan wasn't telling him something.

"We're doing our best with the information we have." Ryan waited for him to offer more insight.

Ivan said nothing.

As they drove back to Blackbridge, Adam said, "He knew something about those gifts."

"Yeah."

"That's got to mean it's one of the brothers, right?"

"Maybe it's all of them." But why? Hannah had mentioned she hadn't got along with her brothers, so perhaps that antagonism had resumed now that Ivan was out of jail. "Can you call the surgery and confirm Phillip was at the Christmas party? Find out what time it started and what time he left."

Adam got out his mobile. "No reception. I'll have to do it when we get back to the station."

Ryan nodded. If it wasn't Hannah's half-brother then they were back to square one.

With nothing.

Hannah woke early and lay in Fleur's guest bedroom. What nasty gift had been left overnight? Part of her didn't want to know, wanted to pretend it would all go away, and wanted to head off for the day trip to Albany without checking. But she'd promised herself there would be no more hiding.

She got out of bed, noting that Mai had already left for work, and tiptoed into the kitchen. Kit was still asleep on the sofa bed. She turned on the coffee machine and then checked Fleur's front porch. There was nothing there. She texted Ryan.

Good morning! ☺ Anything on the cameras?

It didn't take long for the response to come back.

Nothing.

The response didn't comfort her. Pouring her coffee, she

then made her way to the backyard, letting Joe out to sniff and do his morning business. She rang Ryan. "Is that a good thing?" she asked when he answered.

"Maybe." His voice warmed her, reminded her of what they'd shared two nights ago. "The stalker might have caught wind that we questioned your dad and be worried he'll be caught."

"Or he might have left something somewhere else," she said. "I should stop by the park before I go to Albany."

"Lincoln's already on it," Ryan said. "He was heading there after he spoke with me this morning. If he finds anything, we'll sort it out. You only need to worry about enjoying your day."

Hannah smiled. Their concern was nice. "I'll worry about what you might find anyway."

"All right. I'll call you later," he said. "Stay with your friends and take care of yourself."

There was that unsaid warning again not to be alone. "Thanks." She hung up. Joe was getting reacquainted with all of Fleur's fruit trees. She should take him for a walk before they went out. She didn't want him getting bored and digging up Fleur's backyard while they were gone.

"There you are," Kit called.

Hannah waved at her friends on the back porch and walked towards them.

"Mai rang to say she'll be another hour," Fleur said. "We thought we'd head to the beach. Kit wants a surf and I could do with a run."

"Sounds good." At least the beach did. The run sounded like torture. She whistled for Joe and followed her friends inside.

When they arrived back from the beach, Mai was pulling up. She got out carrying a white box that smelled like freshly baked goods. Hannah inhaled deeply. "That smells divine."

"Tastes it as well," Mai said with a grin. "Let's get it inside before it gets cold."

The breakfast consisted of warm chocolate croissants, brioche and Vietnamese breakfast cakes. Hannah loved the international flavours that influenced Mai's cooking. After eating more than she should have, Hannah drove them to Albany.

"So where do you want to go?" Hannah asked as she drove into town.

"Can we swing by the hospital first?" Fleur asked. "I need to drop off Dad's crutches."

"Sure." She made her way to the hospital and pulled up at the entrance. As they waited for Fleur to come back, a guy hobbled out, one leg in plaster, struggling a bit on crutches. Unease crept across Hannah's shoulders. It was Smithy, one of Justin's friends. What was he still doing in the area? He caught one of his crutches in the crack on the pavement and with a yell he fell to the ground.

Hannah jumped out. "Are you all right?"

Smithy's eyes widened. "Hannah. What are you doing here?"

"I could ask you the same question." She helped him to his feet. "Didn't you go back to Perth with Justin?"

"Nah. I'm having Christmas with my aunt and uncle." He leaned on her, his hand brushing her breast and she almost dropped him. "That's why we brought two cars down."

As soon as he got his balance she took two steps away, distancing herself, not liking the crawl of her skin.

"I'm, uh, glad you're all right." He cleared his throat. "I want you to know that if I'd known what Justin had done, I would have helped – I would have stopped him." He was clearly uncomfortable.

"Thank you." It soothed her that Justin's friends knew the truth, that they wouldn't look at him in the same way anymore. She nodded to the plaster on his leg. "What happened?"

"Broke my leg yesterday when I fell off my cousin's motorbike."

"Ouch." She looked around. "Is someone picking you up?"

"Yeah. My cousin's gone to get the car." As he spoke a black sedan pulled up behind Hannah's four-wheel drive. "There he is."

"I hope you heal fast," she said. "Have a merry Christmas."

"Thanks for your help." He moved over to the car.

Hannah climbed into her four-wheel drive, her skin tight. She glanced in the rear-view mirror to confirm that Smithy got into the sedan. She disliked the suspicion in her gut. Could he be her stalker? He'd arrived at the same time as the gifts had started and if he'd broken his leg yesterday it would account for why she'd not received any gift today. She had to tell Ryan.

"Who was that?" Mai asked.

"One of Justin's friends."

Fleur got back into the car. "I'm done. Shall we get shopping?"

"Let me call Ryan first." She quickly dialled his number and told him about Smithy. When she hung up she smiled. "OK, what do you need to buy?"

"I haven't got anything," Kit grumbled. "My family are so hard to buy for."

"Shall we start on York Street?" Fleur suggested. "See if that sparks some ideas."

Hannah managed to find a parking spot and as they climbed out, Kit asked Hannah, "Who are you buying for?"

"Lynette and Shirley," she said. "And I'd like to get something for Felix and Ryan."

"What about your dad?" Mai asked.

Hannah stopped walking. She'd forgotten about him. She'd never bought anything for her father, had no idea what he would want. "I don't know." She wasn't sure what to do about the whole situation.

"You can always buy him a bottle of wine," Kit said. "Don't sweat it."

Hannah nodded and followed her friends into the first shop.

They stopped for a late lunch at a popular cafe and the boot of Hannah's car was filled with bags. Kit had been a buying machine, purchasing presents not only for her family and the Zanettis, but also for herself. Hannah had picked up a couple of small gifts for Ryan and Felix, as well as some things for her workmates, and had been talked into buying a gorgeous red dress with matching underwear by her friends. They were right. She needed something pretty to cheer her up and she would have a new dress to wear when she went out to dinner with

Ryan.

Hannah's phone rang. "Hello."

"Hannah, it's your father."

Hannah closed her eyes. She didn't want to deal with him now. Not when she was relaxed and having fun.

"Hi, Dad."

Her friends all stopped talking.

"I'm sorry with how things went at the holiday park. I should have warned you I was getting out early." He sounded tired and she couldn't help feeling sorry for him.

"I need answers too, Dad," she said.

He sighed. "It's hard for me to talk about." He cleared his throat. "I had a visit from the police yesterday. They told me you've been getting nasty gifts."

Her chest tightened. Was he responsible? "Yes, I have."

"I'm sorry. I hope they stop soon."

Hannah frowned. That was a weird sentiment. Shouldn't he hope they caught whoever was doing it? Before she could ask, he said, "What are you doing for Christmas?"

"Christmas?"

"Yes, it's on Sunday."

"I'll be working at the park." What was she supposed to say? Was he going to ask her to have Christmas with him? Her pulse fluttered in anxiety. She wasn't ready for that. They'd barely spoken, she didn't know this man.

"With your grandparents?" There was an edge to his words.

"No. They're away."

"So you'll be by yourself?"

She didn't want to admit that. Not when so many things were happening that she couldn't explain. "I'll be working," she repeated. "We do a pancake breakfast every Sunday morning."

"And after that?"

"I'll play it by ear depending on what happens at the park."

He sighed. "I would love you to have Christmas with me and your brothers."

It was a huge step. She hadn't got used to her father being out of jail yet. "I haven't seen Marko and Phillip in years," she said. "I'm not sure I'd be welcome."

"Of course you're welcome. You're their sister."

As if being related by blood had anything to do with whether you liked someone. "They never liked me."

"Of course they did." There was an edge to his tone.

Hannah didn't bother to correct him. He had always been a bit dense when it came to his sons, always wanted to believe the best of them.

"Where are you having Christmas?"

"Phillip's. He lives with his wife and two kids in Torbay. They'd both love you to be there." He paused. "Please, Princess."

Goosebumps sprang to her skin at the endearment. She had been his princess, had thought herself invincible when he was around, had believed she was special. Memories of those lovely times with him flooded her mind and for a moment she longed for those days again.

But the idea of seeing her half-brothers didn't thrill her.

When she didn't speak he added, "It'll be like old times – unwrapping presents, eating fritule, crostoli and turkey."

She hadn't had fritule since she was a kid. She'd forgotten how her mother had made traditional Croatian food at her father's request. Was it possible to begin a relationship with these people again? Did she want to?

"Princess?"

She didn't know what to do. She still didn't know the truth of that night, she had no clue why he'd killed her mother. She blocked the longing in her heart. "I'll think about it."

"It'll be a wonderful opportunity to reconnect with your brothers. I hope you'll come."

She wouldn't feel guilty about this. She didn't owe her brothers anything. "I'll let you know." She hung up, let out a shuddery breath.

"What did he want?" Fleur asked.

"To invite me to Christmas at Phillip's place."

Kit frowned. "Ugh. You said no, right?"

"I said I'd think about it."

Mai covered her hand. "That's really brave of you."

"Or really stupid," Kit added.

Hannah glared at her. "Thanks." Kit didn't understand that part of her wanted to ignore the past and have her father again, but she had listened to the warning in her head.

"Where does he live?" Fleur asked.

"Torbay."

"That's pretty isolated," Kit said.

"What's he going to do?" Hannah demanded, hating her defensiveness, even as she spoke. "Hit me over the head and bury me?" Her voice grew louder and people looked over.

Kit opened her mouth to retort and Mai covered her hand. Kit let out a hiss. "Sorry," she said. "I'm worried. You don't know this man and you *are* being stalked."

She sighed. She hated being mad at her friends. "I'm sorry too." Kit was just echoing her own concerns. "That's why I said I'd consider it. I'm sure my brothers have matured past the torturing-their-little-sister stage, but I still need my dad to explain what happened that night." She'd lost both of her parents in one horrific moment and she was never going to get her mother back – but perhaps there was a way to regain her father. He claimed it had been an accident. "Let's finish lunch. I might have some more Christmas shopping to do."

It was mid-afternoon by the time they got back to Fleur's place. They were all laden with purchases and Hannah helped her friends carry their bags to their respective cars. Aside from the phone call from her father, it had been a fantastic day. The musketeers hadn't spent a whole day together in a long time and she'd needed their company, their teasing and good nature, their friendship.

Hannah went to the back door to let Joe in. He wasn't waiting there, so she whistled.

Nothing.

"Joe!" she called.

Still nothing. She frowned and trotted down the back steps. A whimper from around the side caught her attention. Her breath hitched and she ran towards the sound. Joe was lying down, his body shaking and his mouth frothing.

Her stomach lurched. "Help!" Hannah yelled as she fell to her knees next to him, placing a hand on his hot skin. She had to get him to the vet.

Footsteps pounded and then her friends appeared.

"Fuck!" Kit said. "I'll call the vet. You guys get him into the car."

Hannah nodded, her heart racing. She couldn't lose him. "Stay with me, Joe." Her voice cracked and she swallowed hard. She had to keep it together.

"I've got a rug," Fleur said. "It'll make it easier to carry him."

"I'll open the gate and the car," Mai said.

Hannah was so relieved her friends knew what to do without her asking. She noticed a black plastic tray containing the remains of a half-eaten sausage on it. Blue pellets that looked suspiciously like snail bait were sprinkled around it.

He'd been poisoned.

Rage welled up in her – this bastard had hurt her dog. That was the last straw. He could mess with her as much as he wanted to, but Joe was off limits. As soon as Joe was all right, she was going to hunt this person down. Fleur came back and between the two of them, they managed to roll Joe onto the rug. Then they each took two corners and lifted.

He weighed a ton, but fear gave her strength. She followed Fleur out of the side gate to her car.

"Mai, pick up that sausage," Hannah called on her way past. Mai swore.

"Oscar's expecting you," Kit said, hurrying over.

Hannah nodded. "I'm going to need all of you to help me lift him into the car."

Between them, they managed to get him into the back. "I'll sit with him," Fleur said. "You drive."

Hannah jumped in the front seat while Kit and Mai jumped in the back. She sped through the streets to the vet, Joe's raspy breathing the only sound in the car. When she pulled up, the local vet hurried out with a trolley.

"What happened?" Oscar asked.

"Poison," Hannah said.

Mai handed him the sausage.

The vet winced.

Inside, Oscar ordered Hannah's friends to stay in the waiting room and took Joe and Hannah out the back. "How long ago did he eat it?"

"I don't know. We just got back from Albany. We've been out since ten."

"The good news is he's a big dog. He can handle a bigger dose of poison than smaller dogs." He hurried around getting what he needed while Hannah stood near Joe's head, stroking him. Drool was collecting on the trolley and Joe was shaking. Her eyes welled with tears as fear lodged in her throat. "Stay with me, Joe. You're going to be all right." Her voice broke. She refused to contemplate that he wouldn't make it through this. She needed Joe. He was her guard, her companion, her friend.

"We need to take him into the operating theatre," Oscar said. "We're going to pump his stomach."

She stood back as Oscar gave Joe an injection of something. One of the vet nurses came over. "Hannah, you need to wait outside."

She didn't want to leave him. "How long will it take?"

"We have to put him under a general anaesthetic, so it'll be a couple of hours before you can see him." The nurse led Hannah out into the waiting room.

Her friends all stood. "How is he?" Fleur asked.

"They're going to pump his stomach." Hannah sat on one of the hard plastic seats. Fear swirled around her like a cyclone. She'd had Joe since he was a puppy. He'd been her constant companion for years now. She'd be lost without him.

Her friends surrounded her, Fleur with her arm around her shoulders, Mai with her arm around her waist and Kit crouched in front of her, holding her hand. Their silent support gave her strength. She settled in to wait.

Chapter 17

"Your ex-wife is a piece of work," Lincoln said as he came into the station on Wednesday afternoon.

Ryan looked up from what he was working on and grimaced. They hadn't had a chance to discuss the interview with Paula the day before. "What did she do?"

"After a lot of drama, she admitted to the two offences. She posted bail, but the conditions are for her to stay away from Hannah and her property."

"Bail conditions won't stop her," Ryan said. He'd warn Hannah and keep an eye out for Paula.

"Yeah, I got that feeling too. They also asked her about the gifts, but she swore she didn't know anything about them."

"Did they believe her?"

"Her fingerprints don't match the gifts, but she could have hired someone."

Lincoln's mobile rang. He answered and then swore. "When?" he demanded. "Where's Hannah?"

Ryan leapt to his feet, his pulse racing. "What?" he demanded.

Lincoln raised a hand for him to wait. "All right. Tell her I'm thinking of her and we'll investigate as soon as we can." He hung up. "Joe's been poisoned."

It took a second for Ryan to process that it was Joe not Hannah and relief swept through him before he swore. Hannah was going to be devastated. "How is he?"

"At the vet's. He might not make it."

He squeezed his hand into a fist. "I need to see her."

Lincoln nodded. "We'll both go. Fleur said they have evidence."

Not long later Ryan strode into the veterinary surgery. Hannah was staring at the ground, her friends gathered around her. She didn't move even as he approached her. His heart hurt.

Ryan crouched down, rested a hand on her hip. "I'm so sorry, Hannah."

Her eyes were red from crying. "We need to find this bastard, Ryan."

"We will. I promise." He had no idea how he was going to keep his promise. He kissed her hand and pulled her into his arms to hug her. She shuddered and he stroked her back, his stomach in knots. There was nothing he could do to stop her pain.

When he let her go, Kit said, "I'll show you what we found." The receptionist directed them to a back room. Kit whirled around to face them as soon as the receptionist left. "Lincoln, this has gone on long enough. Why haven't you caught him?"

Kit stood with her hands on her hips, anger in her every pore. Ryan frowned. Did she think they were doing nothing?

"We're trying." Lincoln ran a hand through his hair, his frustration clear. "We have a couple of new leads."

Phillip's alibi had proven solid, but they had Smithy to investigate and they hadn't been able to confirm whether Marko was still in Perth. "We're waiting on lab results as well," Ryan told her.

"Can't you put a rush on them?"

"There's one lab in the state and testing blood from a break-in has a low priority," he said. "There's nothing we can do about it."

Kit swore.

Ryan glanced back to the treatment-room door. "What are Joe's chances?"

She sighed. "They're pumping his stomach now. We're staying with Hannah."

Ryan wanted to be the one to stay, to be with her, and the

depth of his longing surprised him. It was a foolish desire – he had Felix to look after and she didn't need him if she was surrounded by her friends. "Call me if you need anything." He wrote his mobile number on the back of his card.

"Will do."

They needed to catch this bastard. He'd escalated to poisoning Hannah's dog, who was always with her, who could protect her. What was he planning next?

On his way out, he gave Hannah another hug. "I'm here for you," he murmured.

She nodded, sniffing. He hurt seeing Hannah so upset.

As he and Lincoln walked out to the car he asked, "Do you think your mum will have Felix for an extra couple of hours?"

"Probably. Why?"

"I want to go over everything again. Check if we missed anything." And he'd track down Marko Novak and get Smithy's alibi confirmed.

"I'm sure she will, then. Let's get some food on the way back to the station."

They had to find something. The stalker had escalated alarmingly and abandoned the twelve-days-of-Christmas theme. They were running out of time.

It seemed like an eternity before the vet came out. Hannah had bitten all of her nails down to the quick and her eyes burned.

"I've done all I can. Now we have to wait and see," Oscar said.

Hannah stared at him, her skin cold. "What do you mean?"

"There's no antidote to snail bait, but we've emptied his stomach and given him activated charcoal to soak up anything that remains. He's either going to pull through, or he's not." The man's expression was apologetic. "I'm sorry, Hannah. I can't be any more specific than that."

Hannah closed her eyes, her chest heavy, the urge to scream and rage strong. She couldn't lose Joe. She took a deep breath to make sure she wasn't going to explode before answering. "So what now?"

"You can take him home tonight, but he needs to be monitored. If he gets worse you have my number."

She followed him into a treatment room, and Joe was pushed in on the trolley. He was awake and his tail gave a tiny wag. Her pulse leapt.

"He's going to need another half an hour to recover from the sedation," Oscar said. "Then he'll be fine to leave."

Hannah nodded. Joe was so still, so sick.

"You can both stay at my house," Fleur said. "It's closer."

"Thanks." She didn't want to be far from the vet.

"I'll drop around in the morning on my way to work and check on him," Oscar said.

Her eyes filled with tears. Joe's eyes were wide as they stared at her, as if asking what he'd done wrong. A lump formed in her throat. "It's going to be all right," she whispered. "You're strong, Joe. You're going to pull through. Fight for me."

Mai and Kit put their hands on her shoulder.

Hannah burst into tears and they surrounded her.

Joe roused himself enough to walk out of the vet, but it took them all to lift him into the car. They got him settled in Fleur's guest room and Hannah dragged the mattress from the spare bed onto the floor so she could lie down next to him.

It was the longest night that Hannah could remember. She stayed next to Joe as her friends took turns being with her, their presence a constant support. Joe's breathing steadily improved as the night wore on, but Hannah wasn't willing to be optimistic. She kept herself curled up against him, her arm around him, and murmured comforting words that he didn't understand.

It was around seven in the morning when Oscar arrived carrying a tray full of coffees from Mai's bakery. "How's my patient?"

"Alive." Hannah let him in and took one of the coffees he offered. She stretched out the aches in her body, keeping her eyes firmly on the vet, watching for any sign that Joe wasn't going to make it.

"He's looking good," Oscar said after he'd examined him. "He'll need to rest for a couple of days, and it might be good if he comes back to the clinic so we can monitor him today, just in case."

Hannah let out the breath she hadn't been aware she'd been holding. "Of course." Fleur and Kit rubbed her back and she took a sip from the coffee, her hand shaking slightly. "Are you sure he's OK?"

Oscar smiled at her. "Yeah, I'm sure. Why don't you girls get some proper sleep? I'll take Joe now and call if anything changes."

She hesitated. What if Joe thought she was abandoning him?

"He'll be in good hands with Oscar." Kit put her arm around her.

Of course he would. He'd be safer than with her. Hannah nodded, and helped Joe up before walking him out to Oscar's small car.

"I'd better get back to the farm." Kit yawned.

Hannah felt a stab of guilt. Kit had stayed all night and now had a full day of work ahead of her. "Thank you." She kissed her friend's cheek.

"Anytime," Kit said. "Though next time we do an all-nighter I'd prefer it with booze and dancing." She flashed a tired smile.

"I'll come out and help you after Lynette arrives," Hannah promised.

Kit shook her head. "No need. I gave Paul a call last night and he's taking care of the milking this morning."

Hannah was relieved that one of Kit's farmhands was helping. She checked the time. She should already be at the park. It wouldn't be fair to call Lynette or Shirley at such short notice. Especially not after what had been going on lately.

Shit.

She scrubbed her eyes. She had to check for gifts. "I'd better get going too."

"Where are you going?" Fleur asked.

"To work," she said.

Both of her friends frowned at her.

"I'll be fine." If the stalker dared show his face she'd beat the crap out of him for what he'd done to Joe.

"You barely slept last night," Kit said.

"Neither did you, and you're going to work."

"I'm crawling into bed for a couple of hours first," Kit admitted. "Paul will have everything sorted."

"I'll take a nap when Lynette arrives," Hannah promised. "But I need to check on things."

"You mean check if that bastard has left any more gifts," Fleur said. "I'll come with you."

Annoyance welled in her. "I can check for damage on my own." She sighed, trying to push back her irritation and fatigue. "Besides, Lincoln's probably down there already."

Fleur nodded in acknowledgement. "I'll come with you in case he's not."

"No," she argued, turning Fleur around so she faced her door. "You need to sleep."

"You shouldn't be by yourself, especially when Joe's not with you," Fleur said, a stubborn tilt to her chin.

"She's right," Kit agreed.

"Let the bastard just try something today," Hannah snarled. "It'll be the last thing he ever does." The rage was so hot and fierce inside her, and both Fleur and Kit stared at her as if her head had started spinning around.

"Geez, Hannah Banana," Kit said. "You're terrifying when you're angry."

Hannah burst into a nervous laugh. "I'll be fine, I promise. I appreciate your concern, but I want you both to get some sleep. I'm worried about you."

"We're worried about *you*," Fleur said.

"I know, but right now it would make me feel a whole lot better if you were tucked up safe in your bed and getting some shut eye. I'll call Lincoln and ask him to meet me at the park."

"Promise?" Kit asked, holding out her hand in the musketeers' solemn-promise handshake.

"Promise," Hannah replied, taking her hand. "Now go get some sleep."

"Take care of yourself," Fleur said as she finally headed into her room.

Hannah forced a smile. "You too."

She rubbed her hands over her face, to wipe away the

fatigue. She waved with more enthusiasm than she felt and drove to work.

Who was she kidding? She was so exhausted, she probably shouldn't be driving, but there was little traffic on the road. She parked and took in a deep breath. There were a couple of people wandering around, but it was mostly silent except for a few cockatoos calling to each other in the still morning air. She got out of the car, holding the door open for Joe, before she remembered he wasn't with her. Feeling a little vulnerable, she called Lincoln like she'd promised as she walked around the back of the office.

"What's new, Hannah?" Lincoln asked as he answered.

"Nothing. I promised the girls I'd call and tell you I'm at the holiday park."

"By yourself?"

"Yeah." She stopped as she reached the back door. It was partially open. She frowned at it, her tired brain trying to compute what it meant. It was too early for Lynette or Shirley to be in.

"Hannah, you know—"

"Have you been by the park this morning?" she interrupted as she took a couple of steps back, her heart pounding hard in her chest. She was alone. There was no one with her.

"Not yet. Some idiot decided to crash his car into my neighbour's fence. Why?"

"The office is open." Shit, she should have listened to Fleur and Kit.

"Don't go in," he ordered. "I'll send someone around. Go back to your car." He hung up.

Hannah backed away from the door, all her bravado gone as her brain played out all of the possible ways the stalker could hurt her.

She had to get away.

Had to run.

The door swung open.

"Hannah, what are you doing hanging out here?"

She stiffened as the familiarity of the voice hit her. Her mouth dropped open. "Granddad? What are you doing here?"

"Surprise!" Her nanna pushed past her granddad, her arms

wide open and smothered her within them. "As if we'd let you be alone at Christmas."

Hannah automatically returned her nanna's embrace as her heart rate slowed and her brain flooded with relief. "When did you get here?"

"Last night," her granddad said. "We thought you'd be here an hour ago. Are you slacking off without us here?" he joked.

She shook her head, still trying to process what was going on.

"Where's Joe?" her nanna asked.

The question got her brain moving again. "At the vet." She walked into the office, wanting to be inside instead of out in the open.

"Is he all right?" Her Nanna's concern was obvious.

How much should she tell them? She didn't want to worry them, but in a town this size it wouldn't be long until they heard anyway. "He is now." She could fill in the details later.

"No wonder you were late," her granddad said. "I won't dock you any pay this time." He laughed.

She smiled as she looked around the office, to check if there was anything out of place, if any gifts had been left. It was clear.

"Hannah?" her nanna asked.

They were both looking at her as if they were waiting for something. "Sorry. What did you say?"

"What happened to the door?" her granddad said.

She debated how much to tell them. "It broke."

"Are you all right?" her nanna asked.

"Just tired," she said. "I didn't sleep much last night, worrying about Joe."

"Oh, you poor thing. Let me make you a cup of coffee." Her nanna hustled into the kitchen.

Hannah tried to focus. "Are you staying long?"

"We'll play it by ear," her granddad said. "We still want to head up to the Northern Territory and north Queensland, but we're in no rush."

There was a noise at the back door and Hannah whirled around as Ryan strode in, his hand on the gun on his belt. He glanced between Hannah and her grandfather. "Is everything all right?" His hand relaxed at his side.

She'd almost forgotten she'd called. She longed to hug him, but he was here on official business.

"It's a bit early for a visit from the police," her granddad said.

"I called Lincoln when I noticed the back door open, Granddad," Hannah told him. "We've had a couple of break-ins over the last few months."

"The storeroom again?" he asked.

Hannah nodded.

Ryan held out his hand. "I'm Senior Constable Ryan Kilpatrick."

Hannah winced. "Sorry, I should have introduced you. This is my grandfather—"

"Stan Walter." He shook Ryan's hand.

Her nanna came out of the kitchen with a mug of coffee, which she handed to Hannah. "I'm Maureen," she said. "You're new to town, but your name's familiar."

"I lived here for a couple of years when I was a teenager," Ryan said. "I've just moved back."

Her nanna nodded. "I remember now. You were friends with Lincoln Zanetti."

"Still am," Ryan said, his tone friendly.

Hannah wasn't quite sure what to say. Should she mention she was dating Ryan? Her brain wasn't working fast enough this morning, but she didn't want her grandparents asking more questions about the break-in. "I'm sure you've got a whole lot to do today," she said to Ryan.

He raised an eyebrow at her in question.

Her face flushed.

"Find any evidence of who has been breaking in?" Stan asked before she accompanied Ryan to the door.

"Some prints," Ryan said. "But right now, we're focused on who's been stalking Hannah."

"What do you mean?"

Hannah winced at the concern in her grandfather's voice.

Ryan frowned at her.

She closed her eyes, too tired after her night with Joe. "I hadn't got to that bit yet."

"Hannah is being targeted by a stalker," Ryan said. "She's

been left something nasty each day since last Tuesday.”

Her granddad gestured to a chair. “You’d better sit and tell me the details, since Hannah neglected to mention anything.” There was a harshness to his tone that Hannah didn’t recognise.

Perhaps she could gloss over it so her grandparents wouldn’t worry.

“Both the office and Hannah’s shed have been broken into, she’s been left dead animals on the doorstep and yesterday Joe was deliberately poisoned.”

OK, so no sugar-coating it. She glared at Ryan. Didn’t he understand how fragile her grandparents were?

Her nanna sank onto a chair and her granddad frowned. “Who’s doing it?”

“We have a couple of leads,” he said. “With Joe at the vet, I wouldn’t recommend Hannah goes anywhere alone for the next couple of days.”

“You think he might hurt her.” It was a statement, not a question, but Ryan nodded.

“The gifts have been erratic, sometimes threatening, sometimes more like pranks. While I’m here I’ll take a look around and check if he left anything today.”

Her nanna gasped.

Ryan turned to her. “What is it?”

“There was a note on the door when we came in,” she said. “I didn’t think anything of it.”

Dread pooled in Hannah’s stomach.

Ryan got to his feet. “Can you show me?”

She fished something out of the rubbish bin. Ryan used a couple of pens to smooth out the crumpled piece of paper. It simply read, *You’re next.*

Hannah frowned. “Next?”

Ryan’s expression was sombre. “He’s referring to what happened to Joe.”

She took a couple of steps back, her hand to her stomach as she thought of Joe lying close to death in the vet hospital. If they hadn’t arrived home when they had, Joe would have died.

Her whole body went cold.

He meant to kill her too.

She turned to her grandparents. “You should leave. If this

person is targeting my loved ones, then you're in danger too. He just has to find out you're here and then …" She didn't want to think what could happen. She couldn't lose any more people she loved.

"We're not leaving you," her granddad growled, getting to his feet. "We'll protect you this time."

She squeezed her eyes shut at the pain. He was thinking of her mother. They didn't know about her father being out of jail. That was not going to go down well.

"So far he hasn't approached Hannah directly, but that might change now that Joe isn't around," Ryan said. "We don't even know if it is a male, it could be a female."

"You don't know much, do you?" her granddad snarled.

"Granddad!" Hannah said. "They're doing everything they can."

"I won't let anyone hurt you. I've already lost one daughter."

Hannah willed Ryan not to say anything about Ivan. The back door rattled open and Hannah looked up. It was too early for Lynette, but maybe it was Lincoln.

She wasn't that lucky.

Nausea stormed into her stomach as she saw her father. "Hannah, I need to talk to you." Ivan didn't glance at the others in the room, he had his eyes on Hannah.

"You!" The shout from her granddad made Hannah jump and she stepped back to put a hand on his arm, her stomach clenching. He shrugged her off as he lunged for the cricket bat.

Ryan placed himself between the two men.

Ivan paled. "I'm sorry. I didn't realise you were back."

"What the hell are you doing out of prison?" her granddad said. He turned to Ryan. "Arrest that man. He's a murderer, he's escaped from jail!"

"Ivan got early parole," Ryan said calmly. "We've already interviewed him in regards to this case. Why don't you put the bat down, Mr Walter?"

Hannah's throat tightened at the fury on her grandfather's face as he held the cricket bat like a baseball bat. He didn't lower it. "Granddad, put it down." She stepped over and tugged it away from him. Her nanna was pale, standing there, staring at Ivan, and there were tears in her eyes. She looked older than she had in years. "Sit down, Nan." She pulled a chair over and her grandmother sat, her eyes never leaving Ivan.

"I'll come back later," Ivan said to her.

"No you bloody well won't!" her granddad yelled. "You're not welcome here. You step one foot on my property again and I'll call the police for trespass!"

"I have a right to see my daughter." Anger tinged Ivan's tone.

"No, you don't. You gave up that right when you murdered her mother."

Hannah put her hand on her granddad's arm. "Granddad, calm down."

"Calm down?" He turned to her. "You can't mean to tell me you want him here? He killed your mother." The grief of almost twenty years was still there on his face, in his voice.

Nausea swelled in her stomach. The look of betrayal on her granddad's face stung. What was she supposed to say? They had taken her in and raised her when she'd had no one left. She loved them, but Ivan was her father. She had loved him once too.

"It might be best if you left," Ryan said quietly to Ivan.

He hesitated a moment and Hannah gave him a small nod. "I'll call you." He walked out.

"You're not going to speak to him, are you?" her granddad demanded.

Hannah did not need this confrontation right now. Not when she was so exhausted. She longed to curl herself into a ball and pretend this hadn't happened, but that was the old Hannah. The new Hannah was stronger.

Still, that didn't mean she wanted Ryan to see her family fall apart. He had enough dysfunction in his life. He didn't need hers as well. "Why don't you take a look around the park?" she said, the plea clear in her tone.

There was compassion in Ryan's eyes and she wanted him to hold her, wanted to go with him so she didn't have to deal with this. Finally he nodded. "I'll drop back in when I'm done."

When the door shut behind Ryan, her nanna asked, "How long has he been out?"

"A couple of weeks." Hannah would stick to the facts. "I

didn't know until he dropped by on Monday. It was a shock."

"Did he threaten you?" her granddad asked.

"No. He wants to get to know me."

"Like that's ever going to happen."

Hannah couldn't meet his gaze, couldn't see the pain on his face.

"Do you want to see him?" her nanna asked, her voice quiet.

"Of course she doesn't want to see him," her granddad said. "He killed her mother."

"He's also her father," her nanna said. She was waiting for Hannah's response.

Hannah shrugged, miserable. Her grandparents had been the one constant support for her whole life. She hated to upset them. "I loved him once," she said. "I remember what it was like when he and Mum were happy."

Her granddad snorted. "How can there be happiness in an abusive relationship?"

"It wasn't abusive," Hannah argued. "Sure they used to fight, but they loved each other."

"He stabbed her."

She couldn't deny it. She'd seen him with the knife. Not that she'd ever told anyone that. "I'll make sure he doesn't come here anymore."

"You'll make sure you never go near him again," her granddad growled.

Guilt stabbed her at the pain in her granddad's eyes. "He's my father."

"And we raised you," he argued. "If you continue to see him, you're not welcome here."

Hannah gasped. "Granddad!"

He stared at her. "He murdered your mother."

She glanced at her nanna, whose eyes were wide in surprise.

Nothing she could say would make this right. She couldn't decide anything while there was so much anger in the room, and while she was so tired. She needed time to think.

Her grandmother nodded towards the door and mouthed, *I'll talk to him.*

Hannah took a step back. She wasn't going to make any promises she couldn't keep. "We can discuss this later. I'm going to get some sleep. Lynette will be in at nine." Not waiting for a response, she walked out.

What the hell was she going to do now?

Chapter 18

Ryan made a quick, thorough tour of the holiday park, but couldn't see anything out of place. He was more concerned about the threat that had been made against Hannah's life. They had to find this guy *now*. As he walked back towards the office Hannah came out of the door, pressing her fingers to her eyes. He hurt for her. First Joe had been poisoned and now this confrontation. He'd wanted to drag her away and tell her everything was going to be all right, but he couldn't lie to her. He jogged over, intercepting her on the way to her car.

"How are you holding up?" he called.

She stopped, waited for him, tears glistening in her eyes. "It's been a hellish week." She hugged herself in a protective gesture.

"It sure has." He wrapped his arms around her, pulling her against him. She stiffened only for a second before relaxing and clinging to him, sobs racking her body. He rubbed her back, wishing he could take away all of her pain.

When she stepped back, he let go and asked, "How did your grandparents take Ivan?"

Her laugh was harsh. "Granddad gave me an ultimatum – Dad or them."

He grimaced. She didn't need this extra grief right now. "I'm sorry."

She sniffed. "Yeah, so am I." She squeezed her eyes shut. "I'm so damned tired, I can't think straight at the moment."

"You need to get some sleep." And she shouldn't be alone. "Can you go to Fleur's?"

Hannah checked the time. "She'll be asleep already. I don't want to wake her. I'll call Mai though. She's at work."

"Why don't you call her now?" He wasn't going to let her leave until he knew where she was going to be.

Hannah got out her phone and after a short conversation she hung up. "Yeah, Mai said I can crash at her place."

"Good. Do you want me to drive you over there?"

She shook her head. "I'm OK to drive."

He wasn't convinced, but he recognised the stubborn expression on her face. "Don't go anywhere alone today, Hannah. Promise me." Today's threat had completely escalated matters. He wanted to keep her by his side, where she'd be safe, but it wasn't possible.

Her eyes were tired. "I promise. I'll spend the day with Mai and stay at her place tonight as well."

He hated the defeated expression on her face. "Call me if you need anything." He embraced her again, wanting to give her his support. "I'll follow you to Mai's."

She nodded.

He drove the short distance to the bakery, keeping watch for anyone following them. His hands clenched the steering wheel as she trudged into the building. She was hurting so much and he couldn't find the guy responsible for some of that pain. Frustration coursed through him as he watched the place for a few minutes, unable to summon the will to leave. Finally, when he was sure she wasn't coming out again, he headed for the station.

Lincoln was in his office, talking on the phone, when Ryan arrived. He indicated he would be out in a second so Ryan sat at his desk and put the latest evidence – the screwed-up note – in front of him, staring at it as if it could give him answers. This time it wasn't typed, it was printed in capital letters, the letters sharp and the paper indented as if the person who'd written it had pressed down hard. If only they could find a suspect to match the writing to.

He pulled Hannah's file in front of him and flicked through it in frustration. They'd gone through everything last night and found nothing new. Smithy's alibi had checked out, so their best lead was Hannah's older brother, Marko, with whom they still hadn't been able to make contact. The office he worked at had been at their end-of-year Christmas party yesterday. He'd try again today and find a photo of Marko to circulate as a person of interest. It might be a false alarm, but he wasn't willing to bet Hannah's life on it.

Lincoln came out of his office. "Did someone break into the caravan park?"

Ryan shook his head. "Hannah's grandparents are back in town. They wanted to surprise her."

"Probably more of a surprise than she wants right now," Lincoln said. "At least they can keep an eye on her."

"It gets worse," Ryan said. "While I was there, Ivan arrived."

Lincoln swore. "That couldn't have been pretty."

Ryan told him about the ultimatum.

"Christ. She doesn't need that shit right now."

Ryan nodded in agreement. "And then there's this." He pointed to the note. "It was stuck on the front door of the office this morning. Hannah's grandmother had thought it was rubbish."

Lincoln scowled. "Where's Hannah now?"

"She went to Mai's," Ryan said. He'd drop by when he finished work to check on her.

"We've got next to nothing. How can we have next to nothing after a week?" Lincoln was disgusted.

Ryan was trying to stay positive. "I want a photo of Marko Novak," he said. "It's the best lead we've got so far."

"Will Ivan or Phillip give us one?"

Ryan shook his head. "We can ask."

"Sue, call Ivan Novak and ask if you can get a photo of his son Marko," Lincoln said. "If that doesn't work, check if he's on social media."

"Will do."

Ryan flicked over the rest of the suspects. Justin and his friends were no longer under suspicion.

Sue hung up the phone and let out a deep breath. "It's a no on the photo from Ivan. He was pretty darn mad that I asked him."

So much for doing anything for Hannah.

"Check the internet, then," Lincoln ordered.

Sue nodded.

Before Ryan could get back to his file, a flood of calls came in, and he and Sue were directed to attend a domestic in town. He hated putting aside Hannah's case, but he had other responsibilities as well. She should be safe as long as she stayed with Mai.

As he left the station he couldn't shake the sensation that they were rapidly running out of time.

It was one o'clock before Hannah woke up. Her head pounded and her brain was still fuzzy. She stretched out the kinks in her back and groaned.

"Are you finally awake?" Mai asked.

Hannah sat up. Mai was sitting at the kitchen table, her laptop in front of her.

"What time did you get back?" She hadn't heard a thing.

"Just after ten," Mai said. "I've had my siesta." She got up to put the kettle on. "How are you feeling?"

"Like I could sleep for another few hours." But she didn't want to. She wanted to check how Joe was and work out what to do about her grandparents and her father.

Calypso jumped up on the couch and pushed his head into Hannah's hand to be scratched, so Hannah picked him up and carried him over to the kitchen table. "How are you?"

"Fine. I'm used to small amounts of sleep." Mai poured them both coffees.

Hannah hated disrupting her friends' lives. "What are you working on?"

"My business plan. I'm putting together the costs to expand into the shop next door when I buy the place." Mai held out a shaky hand.

"That's fantastic." Hannah knew how nerve-racking it was.

Her grandparents had loaned her money to build the cabins and the responsibility of paying it back sat heavily on her shoulders. Would they demand its return if Hannah continued to see her father?

The idea left her cold.

Calypso butted her hand to remind her she'd stopped stroking him. She smiled as she brushed over his soft fur.

Mai placed a mug in front of Hannah and she put Calypso down on the floor. "Thanks."

"So, what are you going to do for the rest of the day?" Mai asked.

She wanted to do something normal, but she hated that her grandparents weren't talking to her. "I need to talk to Granddad, but first, I need to call Oscar." She dialled the vet. A short conversation later she was reassured that Joe was resting comfortably and had even eaten a little bit of food.

"He's doing well?" Mai asked.

Hannah nodded. "I can pick him up this afternoon." She blinked back the tears of relief. Oscar was pleased with his progress. "Now, I need to talk to Granddad."

"He'll come around," Mai told her. "He loves you, he's just upset at the moment."

Hannah hoped she was right, but she'd give him a couple more hours to calm down.

Mai placed some Vietnamese spring rolls on the table in front of Hannah. "I made these for lunch."

"Thanks."

"When we're finished eating, I'll take you through your new website," Mai said. "Then you can update it yourself."

"That would be great." It would keep her busy for a short while.

She needed the distraction.

A few hours later, Hannah pushed away her laptop. "I've had enough," she declared. "If I look at the computer for much longer I'm going to go cross-eyed."

Mai grinned. "I know what you mean. Did you get much

done?"

"Yeah, once you showed me how to use it, it wasn't difficult. I just need photos and prices to finish it off." And she wouldn't get photos until she'd done some more work on the site. She checked the time. "I should visit my grandparents before I pick up Joe."

"All right. Let me pack up."

"No, you don't have to come with me," Hannah protested.

"Yes, I do," Mai said. "I promised Lincoln I wouldn't let you go anywhere alone." She shut her laptop with a smile. "Besides, it gives me a good excuse to put this aside."

Hannah hated the guilt that had found a home in her stomach. She was nothing but a nuisance, a bother to her friends. She didn't protest further though. She'd promised Ryan as well.

As they drove up to the caravan park, Felix was playing with Jacob on the lawn.

"Check out that woman," Mai said with a laugh. "She looks like she's going out to dinner."

Hannah disliked the blonde woman on sight. She oozed glamour and had a body like a model on the cover of a swimsuit magazine. Why she was carefully picking her way across the lawn to avoid her four-inch high heels from digging into the soil was a mystery, but she was heading straight towards the boys. Maybe she was going to tell them off for being noisy.

Mai pulled into the car park as Felix noticed the woman. He took a couple of steps back from her, obviously afraid, and the blonde grabbed his arm, pulling him towards a car parked on the street. Jacob yelled and gripped Felix's hand, tugging him back, but the woman was too strong.

Hannah's heart raced. "Mai, find Lynette." She jumped out of the car and ran over. "Hey!" she yelled. The woman ignored her, but Felix's face lit up in relief. "What the hell are you doing? Let Felix go."

"I'm taking my son—" The woman's smile froze on her face. "You," she snarled, dropping Felix's hand. Felix scurried away and stood next to Jacob.

Hannah's mouth dropped open.

This beautiful woman was Ryan's ex.

She wasn't supposed to be anywhere near Felix. Hannah put herself between Felix and Paula. "You must be Paula." Anger simmered in her belly. This was the woman who had trashed her shed and her cabin. There was no way she was letting her take Felix anywhere.

"You've done enough to break up our family, you slut." Paula lifted a hand to slap Hannah, but Hannah deflected it, anger bubbling in her stomach. She couldn't let it go, not with Felix here to witness it.

Hannah raised her eyebrows and continued to smile. "You won't endear yourself to Felix by hitting me."

Paula didn't as much as glance at him, but snatched her hand back. "You can't stop me taking my son."

"Sure I can," Hannah said. She turned to Felix. "Who are you supposed to be with today?"

Felix's eyes were wide. "Mrs Z dropped me off to play with Jacob. Dad's picking me up after work."

That's what she thought. "So, you didn't know your mum would be here?"

He shook his head.

"I rang Ryan. He obviously didn't tell Felix or Felix forgot," Paula said. The anger slid off her face and she became very earnest, and almost sweet.

Hannah didn't buy it. "I'll call Ryan and check."

"There's no need. I don't have time to wait." She tried to reach around Hannah to get to Felix. "Come here."

Hannah shifted and put her arm around Felix. He leaned into her. "You'll wait, or you'll go without Felix." Hannah slid her phone out of her pocket.

"Bitch!"

Paula swung her arm, this time connecting. Hannah's face stung, but she pushed Felix away to protect him as Paula yelled, "You'll pay for what you did!"

Ryan strode across the lawn, his chest tight. After Lynette's call, he'd rushed out of the police station, bringing Adam with him. The crack as Paula slapped Hannah split the air and anger rushed him like a criminal on speed. How dare she hit Hannah!

"Dad!" Felix ran over.

Ryan stopped and embraced him, giving himself a moment to control the anger that was snarling to be released. Hannah could take care of herself. "Are you all right, mate?"

"Mum wanted me to go with her, but you told me I should always check with you."

"That's right," Ryan told him. He hated to think what Paula's game was. Why would she want to take Felix with her? What the hell was she doing here anyway? "Why don't you go with Hannah while I talk to your mum?"

Felix nodded. But before Ryan said anything else, Paula screeched, "She's not taking my son anywhere!"

Ryan winced.

"Jacob, Felix, let's go inside," Lynette called.

Felix glanced up at him and he nodded. "I'll come in when I'm done here," he promised.

He waited until Felix and Jacob were out of earshot before he turned to Hannah. Her cheek was red from Paula's hand and her eyes were angry, but she smiled at him. "I was going to see my grandparents, but I'll come back later."

"I'll call you," he murmured, resisting the urge to brush his fingers over her cheek. She and Mai walked towards the carpark and Ryan turned his attention to Paula. "What are you doing here?"

"I was looking for somewhere to stay and saw Felix playing on the lawn."

There was no way Paula would ever stay in a holiday park. It was beneath her. "Try again."

"What do you mean?" Now that Hannah was gone, she was all sweetness and guile.

"You've got a place in Albany. Your bail conditions don't allow you to stay elsewhere."

"I wanted to see you." She looked down, acting coy, with a hint of a tear in her eye. That move used to get him every time. He'd been such a sucker.

He crossed his arms. "You have my mobile number. If you wanted to see me, you could have called."

"I wasn't sure you would answer."

She was lying. "Why are you in Blackbridge, Paula?"

"I missed you. You left Karratha and all I could think was what a fool I'd been."

He hated that Adam was there listening to this. "Paula, I've told you before, we are never getting back together. I don't love you, I don't even like you anymore."

"It's because you've found someone else, isn't it?" Paula asked, the innocence being replaced by venom. "That slut is trying to steal my husband away." She gestured angrily towards the car park where Mai and Hannah were getting into Mai's car.

He took a step back. There was no way he was going to tell Paula how he felt about Hannah. It far exceeded what he'd ever felt for Paula, even in their earliest days together.

The realisation was like a bell ringing in his head. He wanted Hannah in his life. He wouldn't let Paula scare Hannah away. "Hannah's been the victim of some nasty pranks. The police have concern for her safety and it's my job to make sure she's safe."

Paula frowned. "It didn't look like that. You went on a picnic together."

"We did. She was appreciative of the police help and offered to show us around. It was a friendly, small-town thing to do."

"She took her time putting sun cream on your back. She wants you."

Ryan kept his expression blank. Paula had followed them when they'd gone on the picnic, she hadn't just seen them in town. He hadn't noticed her at all.

Adam had his notepad out and was documenting the information.

"Paula, you shouldn't even be at the holiday park. Your bail conditions prevent you from going near Hannah."

"I didn't know she worked here," Paula said. "I was searching for my baby. I want to talk to Felix, but that bitch wouldn't let me."

"I didn't say Hannah worked here."

Caught in her lie, Paula didn't say anything.

Ryan continued. "As far as I'm concerned, she did exactly the right thing. You were taking Felix without consent."

The tears formed in Paula's eyes, but before she could speak,

Ryan said, "What do you want to say to Felix?"

She hesitated a second. "I wanted to wish him a merry Christmas."

"Do you have any presents for him?" She looked surprised and Ryan shook his head. Of course she didn't. She never remembered to buy Felix anything. "I'll ask him if he wants to see you. You have to stay in Albany until your court hearing, so if you want to visit Felix, call me and we'll arrange a time." He hated the thought of her seeing his son, but she was Felix's mother.

Ryan walked around to the back door of the office. Lynette, her three boys and Felix were sitting in the kitchen having a drink.

"Everything all right?" she asked.

Ryan nodded. "Felix, your mum wants to wish you a merry Christmas."

"Do I have to go?"

"Not if you don't want to."

Felix hesitated. "Will you come with me, Dad?"

"Of course." He held out a hand and Felix took it. Together they walked across the lawn to where Paula and Adam were waiting.

Paula leaned over Felix. "I've missed you, baby. Can we have Christmas together? You'd like to have Christmas with your mum, wouldn't you?"

"No." She was still trying to manipulate them. She didn't care about Felix, didn't want to be with them. "Felix is with me this Christmas and we already have plans."

The relief on Felix's face was obvious.

"Your dad's being a meany," Paula said. "If you tell him you want me there, I'm sure he'll change his mind."

Ryan had had enough. "Have you said everything you want to say, Paula?" he asked. "Felix has somewhere he needs to be."

Perhaps his steely tone, or his glare, finally cut through the bullshit she was spouting.

"Merry Christmas, baby." Tears welled in her eyes again. "I miss you." She squeezed Felix tight and he winced.

When she was done, Felix stepped back next to Ryan and Ryan put a hand on his shoulder in support. "Wait here, Paula."

He was going to have to take her into custody for breaching her bail conditions and she really wasn't going to like it, but first he wanted to get Felix out of the way. He left her with Adam, took Felix's hand and walked to the office.

When they were out of sight of Paula, Ryan stopped and crouched down next to Felix. "How's it going, mate?"

He shrugged, looking at his feet.

"I'm glad you didn't go with her," Ryan said. "Then I wouldn't have known where you were."

"She said you asked her to pick me up," Felix said. "But Hannah wouldn't let her take me." His eyes were wide. "She was so brave standing up to Mum."

"Mate, if I ever ask your mum to pick you up, I'll tell Lynette or Mrs Z, or whoever you're with, OK?"

Felix nodded. "That's what I thought."

Ryan pulled his son in for a hug, wanting to erase the sadness from his face. They went inside and Felix wandered over to Jacob, while Ryan pulled Lynette aside. "Thanks for calling me."

"No problems. She's really Felix's mum?"

"Yeah." He ran a hand through his hair and forced a smile. He thought he'd left all the drama behind when he'd left Karratha. "I need to arrest her because she's breached her bail conditions. Can you keep Felix in here for a little longer? I don't want him to see it."

Lynette's eyes widened. "Sure."

He said goodbye to Felix and Lynette's sons and then headed back to Adam. Paula was nowhere in sight. "Has she gone?"

"Yep. She got in a hire car and tore off down the street."

The tension in his shoulders relaxed. He didn't have to deal with her. "All right. Can you report she broke her bail conditions? Albany can pick her up. I don't like the way she's talking about Hannah. Hannah's got enough to deal with at the moment without adding my ex to it." He was past making excuses for Paula. She'd had enough second chances from him to last her a lifetime. There was no way he was going to let her hurt Hannah.

"Will do."

With a sigh, he headed back to work.

On Friday when Hannah woke she felt more human. She'd gone to bed early and slept solidly, secure in the knowledge that Joe was next to her and he was going to be fine. In fact, he looked quite content with Calypso curled up next to him.

She fed both animals and then went downstairs to the bakery where Mai had been at work for hours already.

"I made doughnuts today," Mai said as she walked in, gesturing to where they were resting. "The oil's heated so throw a couple in."

Hannah did as she asked, greeting the other baker, Penny, and admiring how Mai had multiple things happening at all times. The kitchen was always surprisingly clean considering how much flour was used every day.

"How's Joe?" Mai asked.

"He's doing well," Hannah said. "I'll take him for a short walk later." She drained the doughnuts and then rolled them in the sugar-and-cinnamon mix on the bench. "Do you want one?" she asked Mai.

"No, I'm good." Mai was icing some vanilla slice as she spoke. "What are you doing today?"

Hannah shrugged. "I might head out to the cabin and do some work out there. I've still got to fix some of the paintwork from Paula's tantrum." The only problem was she didn't feel like it, didn't want to do much, in fact.

Plus, she still had to figure out what to do about her granddad and father and hadn't had a chance to speak with either of them. Her phone rang.

"Princess, can we meet today?" her father said.

She took a deep breath. This is what she wanted, a chance to clear the air and figure out what to do about him. "All right. Where and when?"

"How about we meet at the park by the river?" he said. "About nine o'clock?"

She checked the time. It gave her an hour. "Sure."

Taking the doughnuts she'd cooked and the coffee Mai

handed her, Hannah sat in the seating area of the bakery. Did she want a relationship with her father? She couldn't decide until she'd had her questions about that night answered. Only her father could tell her that.

But would he be honest?

Would seeing her father mean she lost her grandparents? Was she only ever going to have one or the other?

Her chest squeezed.

She'd missed her father dreadfully, had been sure there was an explanation for what had happened, but no one would talk to her about him.

Mai took a seat next to her, carrying a coffee and a croissant. She groaned as she sat. "Some days it feels good to get off my feet."

Hannah smiled. "I don't know how you get up so early every day."

"I love that time of the morning," she said. "After so many years living with all my siblings, it's a blessing to be alone." She sipped her coffee. "Any news from Lincoln this morning?"

Hannah shook her head. "I haven't called yet." She wanted a couple of minutes of peace before she discovered what else had gone wrong in her life.

"Want me to?"

It would be better to get it over and done with. "No, I will." She dialled Ryan's number. They'd spoken briefly the night before after the Paula incident, but she hadn't seen him. He'd been concerned about Felix and wanted to spend the evening with him. When he answered she asked, "How's Felix today?"

"He's doing really well." Ryan's voice instantly soothed her, made her smile. "You're his hero for standing up to Paula. He wants to know when you're coming over next."

So did Hannah. She wanted to spend some time with both Ryan and Felix away from all the craziness. "I'm glad I got there when I did."

"Me too." His tone was grim. "I don't know what Paula was playing at." He changed the subject. "How are you holding up? How's Joe?"

She smiled at the concern. "Joe's good."

"And you?"

"I'm … OK," she said. "Did you find any new gifts today?"

"No," Ryan said.

"Is that good news?"

"I'm not sure. Did Mai find anything at her place?"

"I don't think so." She turned to Mai and asked her the question.

Mai shook her head. "No."

"Nothing," she told Ryan.

"I still don't want you to go anywhere by yourself," he said. "Just because we haven't found anything today, doesn't mean the person has given up."

"I'm meeting my father down by the river this morning," she told him. "But there'll be a lot of people there."

"What time?"

"Nine."

"Can someone go with you?"

She hesitated. "Hang on a second." She put her hand over the phone and asked Mai if she could accompany her. "I can help out here afterwards," she added.

"Sure."

Hannah smiled and told Ryan.

"Great." He paused. "Do you want to have dinner with me tonight? Full disclosure, Felix will be at Jacob's place at a sleepover."

Her pulse leapt in anticipation. Something normal after all that had been happening. "I'd love to."

"Where do you want to go?"

Hannah hesitated, remembering the last night they'd spent together. Her cheeks flushed. She wanted to spend time with Ryan and not have to worry about who was watching or who might interrupt. She wanted to be with him. "We could do dinner at your place again."

"Are you sure?" His concern was clear.

"Yes. I could bring a salad."

"Don't bring anything but yourself," he said. "I'll be home by six."

She embraced the tingles on her skin. "I'll see you then." She hung up. She was going to be alone with Ryan. She smiled. She was ready.

Noticing the time, she said, "We'd better get going."

"Of course. Let me take this off." Mai stood and put her apron out the back, calling out to Penny that she would be back in an hour.

Hannah placed her rubbish in the bin, fetched Joe from upstairs and then together they walked down to the river.

She couldn't see her father when she arrived. There were a couple of families with small children playing in the playground, so she wandered to a bench seat not far away to wait.

"Do you want me to wait with you?" Mai asked.

"Yeah, that would be good." Now that she was out here in the open, she felt vulnerable. Joe was definitely slower today, not as perky as normal. She scanned the area, alert. There were a couple of seagulls hovering around, hoping to get a scrap of food, and a lone kayaker paddling down the river. He could be her stalker and she wouldn't know it.

Her father got out of a blue Hyundai and scanned the area. "There he is." She waved to get his attention. He acknowledged her and moved towards her. She was determined to get some answers from him this morning – they couldn't begin a relationship until the truth was out. A police car drove slowly down the street with Ryan and Adam inside. Hannah smiled. They didn't park but continued to cruise along the road.

"I'll wait here," Mai said.

"Thanks." Nerves swirled in her stomach as Hannah stood, smoothing down her T-shirt and taking a calming breath before she walked to him with Joe by her side. "Hi, Dad." It didn't feel right to hug him, so she just smiled.

"Can we walk along the river?" he asked. "Since I got out of jail, I feel like everyone is watching me. I like to keep moving, enjoy the ability to be out in the fresh air and not surrounded by a fence."

On this side of the river there weren't a lot of shrubs to hide in. She should be safe, Joe was with her and Mai had her back. "Sure."

They were silent as they made their way across the grass to

the river and then Ivan said, "I'm sorry about yesterday."

So was she. "It wasn't your fault. I wasn't expecting them home for Christmas." She still wished they'd stayed away.

"I'm sorry for causing you more grief." His tone was pained.

"It's all right."

Ivan shook his head. "No, it's not. I've done nothing but cause you pain and still I'm adding to it." His voice broke on the last words and he took a moment to compose himself.

Touched by his concern, she placed a hand on his arm. "Granddad will come around," she said. "We'll work out an arrangement."

"Not just your grandfather." He stopped and covered her hand with his, his face stricken.

This was the opening she was waiting for. "You're right. We need to talk about what happened with Mum."

He shook his head. "Not that."

Frustration welled up in her. "Yes that, Dad. It's the elephant in the room, can't you see that?"

"It can wait—"

"No, it can't. I have a right to know what happened, I *need* to know what happened for my own peace of mind. So many of my decisions have been made based on what happened that night."

His eyes widened. "You don't understand."

"No, I don't, but I want to. I want you to tell me how you could have killed Mum."

His mouth moved, but no words came out and his hands fluttered by his side.

"This is important, Dad." She wasn't going to back down this time.

"I can't talk about it."

Hannah closed her eyes and the hurt swept through her. "Then I can't talk to you. Don't call me again until you're ready to explain."

With that she walked away, her heart breaking all over again.

Chapter 19

Mai met Hannah halfway across the lawn. "How did it go?"

Hannah kept walking, needing to move. "Badly."

"Why?"

"He won't tell me what happened the night Mum died." Her chest was so tight it was hard to breathe.

She strode up the street and Mai put a hand on her arm to stop her. "I'm sorry it went badly." She squeezed Hannah's hand in support and some of the aggravation melted away.

"Me too." She sighed. "Have you got some dough that needs beating up?" If she didn't do something physical she was going to explode.

Mai smiled. "I'm sure I can find you something."

"Good." Hannah followed her friend into the back of the bakery.

By the time Mai finished for the day, Hannah had worked out her tension. They headed to the beautician's and had a half-day of pampering – waxing, massage, pedicure and manicure. It was absolutely what Hannah needed after the stress of the last two weeks.

Now, however, some of the nerves were seeping back into her as she got ready for her date with Ryan.

"What are you going to wear?" Mai asked.

Hannah fed Joe. "Is the red dress too much?"

"No, it's perfect. It's flirty without being overtly sexy."

Flirty was good. "All right." She went into the bathroom and stepped under the spray.

Tonight was going to be just her and Ryan. Perhaps she should have suggested they go out to dinner instead, to keep the pressure off both of them. But she did want to be alone with him, she wanted to explore what they had together, and explore her sexuality. Ryan had proven he was patient and they could avoid the things that had freaked her out last time.

She also wanted to pleasure him. She wanted to make him feel as amazing as he'd made her feel.

There was one issue – she didn't know how to make the first move. Should she come out and say it? "Ryan, I want to have sex with you."

She cringed. That wasn't going to work.

Hannah took her time drying her hair, rubbing moisturiser into her legs and then put on the underwear set she'd bought. The rich red of the lace and satin gave her confidence. She slipped on the summer dress, which showed a hint of cleavage and settled on her curves in a flattering way. Mai was right, it was flirty without being overtly sexual.

Checking the time again, she quickly applied some makeup and then headed back into Mai's living room.

Mai was sitting on the couch reading a book. "You look gorgeous. You're going to knock Ryan's socks off."

Hannah slid on some flat, black sandals and picked up her bag, checking she had put the condoms inside. "I hope so."

"The man's tongue will be on the floor when he sees you," Mai assured her. "Are you ready to go?"

With a breath to calm her nerves, she nodded and then called Joe. Her concern wasn't for her own safety, but for his health, which signalled a whole change of being. If Joe hadn't been ill, she could have left him with Mai and gone to Ryan's by herself. She really did trust him. A thrill raced through her and she grinned.

"Do you want a lift?" Mai asked.

Hannah shook her head. "It'll be easier to take my car."

"I'll walk you down," Mai said.

She had the best friends. They had been so understanding over the past couple of weeks, making sure she wasn't alone. She hugged Mai and then winced as Joe gingerly jumped into the car. He still wasn't one hundred per cent.

The evening was warm, the sun slowly heading for the horizon, and the cicadas were chirping noisily in the trees. She inhaled the eucalyptus scent as she drove out to her retreat. For the first time in a week, she pushed all that was happening to the back of her mind. Tonight was all for her, and she wasn't going to think about stalkers or ex-wives.

Ryan's car was outside when the cabin came into view. Hannah tapped on the front door and he called, "Come in." With a smile, she walked in. The delicious aromas of roasted tomato, garlic and fresh bread floated through the air. She followed her nose into the kitchen, where Ryan was stirring something on the stove.

He'd changed out of his police uniform and was wearing a pair of black cargo shorts and a blue muscle shirt. It was casual, and she suddenly felt completely overdressed.

His eyes widened and he grinned at her. "Welcome. You look sensational."

Heat warmed her cheeks at his appreciative gaze. "Thank you. Something smells good."

"Tomato-and-basil pasta with garlic bread," he said. "A Zanetti recipe."

"Yum."

Joe made himself comfortable on the rug by the sofa and Ryan walked over to her. She smiled as she moved forward to meet him halfway and brush a kiss against his lips. It was natural, so normal, as if her coming home to Ryan cooking was something they'd done many times before. He gently slipped a hand around her waist, kissing her again, deeper this time.

His kisses were warm, gentle and drugging. His hand on her waist was a comfort, not a concern. He pulled back and cleared his throat. "I'd better check dinner."

Lightness flooded her. She was sensual and in control. "Can I help with anything?"

"No. Why don't you get yourself a drink?" he said as he stirred a pan.

As she went to the fridge Ryan asked, "What did your dad say to you?"

Her mood plummeted from pleasant to annoyed. "I don't want to talk about it, not tonight."

"All right," Ryan said easily. "Joe looks as though he's recovered."

"Yeah. He has to take it easy for the next couple of days though."

"Great." He dished up the pasta, threw the garlic bread into a bowl and carried everything over to the table. "Do you mind if I have a beer?"

"Not at all." And wasn't that a wonderful truth? She wasn't scared – she had come so far in the last two weeks. She sat down with her glass of lemon, lime and bitters. "To new beginnings."

He clinked his bottle against her glass. "Absolutely." He took a sip of his beer. "How was your day?"

"Excluding the conversation with my dad, it was really nice. Mai and I had a massage, manicure and pedicure."

"That's great. You deserve to be pampered."

Hannah smiled. It had helped to push everything aside and focus on herself and what she wanted.

"Have you spoken with your grandparents?"

She closed her eyes as her mood went south again. "Not yet. I'll call them tomorrow." She didn't want to think about that mess at the moment, she needed a nicer topic of conversation. "What are you doing for Christmas?"

"Mrs Z invited us around. Jamie arrives tomorrow and Kit's coming over, so it should be fun. What about you?"

She shrugged. "I'm not sure anymore. Dad invited me to Phillip's, but that won't work. I'll do the pancakes at the park at least."

Ryan frowned. "I'm sure Mrs Z won't mind an extra person if you want to come."

He was right and the idea of spending Christmas with Ryan,

Felix and her friends was a hell of a lot more appealing than dealing with her father and grandparents. Christmas had definitely lost its sparkle this year. "Thanks. I'll think about it."

He covered her hand with his. "I can guarantee Felix will like you there."

"What about his dad?"

Ryan smiled, picked up her hand and kissed the back of it. "His dad definitely wants you there." The intensity in his eyes captured her. This attraction had happened so fast, so out of the blue, especially with everything else that was going on. For the first time since her assault, she trusted her emotions, trusted Ryan. "That's nice to know."

They finished their meal and Ryan got to his feet. "Would you like more?"

"No, thank you." She carried her plate to the kitchen and ran the water to do the dishes.

"Leave those," Ryan said.

She smiled at him. "I'd like to help. You cooked, it's only fair." And it would give her time to figure out how to tell him what she really wanted.

"All right." He grabbed a tea towel. "I'll dry."

They worked in companionable silence until the dishes were done.

"Shall we sit outside for a while?" Ryan asked. "It's a nice night." He was right next to her, so close she felt his body heat and she liked his nearness.

She washed her hands, drying them slowly on a tea towel. Was she brave enough to ask for what she really wanted? She brushed a hand along his arm. "We could play hot or cold." Heat rose to her cheeks.

He glanced at her, and then that sweet smile curved his lips. "We could."

Feeling braver, she stepped forward and pressed her lips against his. He tasted like tomatoes. She wrapped her arms around his shoulders, deepening the kiss as the intensity rose. He slid his hand over her breast, cupping it, and her whole body went hot. His touch was so damn good. She wanted his hands all over her body, directly on her skin. She broke the kiss, feeling empowered by his heavy breathing, and clasped his hand, leading him into his bedroom.

"Is Joe likely to bother us?" Ryan asked as they went through the door.

Hannah hesitated. She had no idea.

"Door open or closed?"

Her pulse spiked in fear and she pushed through it. She could do this, she *had* already done this. "Closed." The last thing she needed was her dog ruining the mood. She shut the door and Ryan moved over to the bed, giving her the space she needed. Slowly she closed the distance, her eyes on Ryan's. The desire was clear in them. He wanted her as much as she wanted him.

She ran her hands over his chest, felt the strength of his muscles beneath her palms. He was so strong and yet so gentle, such a wonderful contrast. She slipped her hands under his top, and he murmured his approval as he ran his hands over the back of her dress. Hannah wanted his hands on her, but they were both wearing too many clothes. With a confidence she hadn't known she possessed, she reached behind her, unzipped the dress and allowed it to slide from her body, so that she was standing in her new red underwear.

"Jesus, Hannah, you're beautiful." Ryan's eyes roved her body and he clenched his hands into fists. He met her eyes. "There's nothing I want more than to take you into my arms and show you how much I want you, but I don't want to scare you. You need to talk to me, tell me what you like."

She revelled in his concern. She stepped towards him, ran her hands underneath his shirt again. "Take it off."

He ripped his shirt off, throwing it on the ground, and reached for her, but then he hesitated and pulled back his hand. His restraint was admirable and made her feel safe, in charge.

Hannah ran her hands up his chest, loving the hardness of his muscles not far under his skin, tracing his nipples with her thumbs. His breath was shaky, but he stood there, not moving. She wanted to taste him and cautiously licked first one nipple, drawing it into her mouth, and then the other.

He hissed and she glanced up, concerned she was doing something wrong, but his head was back and his eyes were closed. "Is that all right?"

He nodded.

She touched his cheek and he opened his eyes. "You need to tell me if I do anything you don't like."

"That's not going to be a problem," he said, his voice strained, then smiled at her.

Reassured, she continued her exploration of his body, sucking his nipples and brushing kisses all along his chest and neck. He groaned when she nibbled just below his earlobe.

Her body filled with desire and she wanted his hands on her. "Ryan." She waited until he was looking at her. "Touch me."

With a muttered prayer of thanks, he pulled her close, kissing her with a passion she had never known. His hands seemed to be everywhere and she loved the way they slid over her body, managing to be gentle at the same time as they were insistent.

He pressed kisses down her neck, towards her chest and then his mouth found her nipple. Heat flooded her body and she arched towards him.

"Hannah," he murmured in question as his hand found the clasp of her bra.

She nodded and in a moment he was peeling it off her. Then his mouth was on her skin and her whole body shook. "Bed." He turned them both and pushed her so the back of her legs hit the bed and she fell backwards onto it. In the dim light of dusk, Ryan was in shadow and the memory of that other night stabbed through her brain.

Fear gripped her chest. "No!" Frantically she scrambled back, off the other side of the bed and Ryan froze.

She cringed, hating the instinctual fear, hating that it still held so much power over her when all she wanted was to enjoy this man and his body. "Sorry," she gasped, hand to her chest, trying to slow her heartbeat and push the awful image of Justin out of her head. She didn't need to be afraid, that night was in the past, this was Ryan.

Ryan slowly sat on the edge of the bed as if not to spook her. "It's all right."

She reached over to switch on the bedside lamp and the extra light banished the nightmare. Ryan's eyes were filled with concern.

"The dark," she tried to explain. "Your shadow."

He nodded and she gazed at him, replacing her flashback with what was actually in front of her – his beautiful hazel eyes, his strong, muscled chest, the bulge in his black cargo shorts. Her gaze locked on his groin. Part of her wanted to touch him there, to see him and make new memories to replace those that caused her so much fear. She sat back on the bed, shuffling so she was closer to him.

"Do you want to stop?" Ryan asked.

She shook her head. "No. Can you be patient with me?"

"As patient as you need." He brushed her cheek with his thumb.

His words and his touch sent butterflies fluttering in her chest. She leaned forward and kissed him, keeping it gentle, and the desire began to stir in her body again. She ran a hand down his chest, hesitating as she reached the waistline of his shorts. The last time she'd touched it, it had thrown up all her brakes.

"You don't have to if you don't want." His voice seemed louder in the night and she realised she was staring at his groin. Heat rushed her cheeks as she glanced at him. He was waiting for her response. She had to be completely honest with him.

"I'd like to, but I'm worried it will freak me out again."

"How about you put your hand on top of mine?" he said. "I'll show you what I like."

She nodded and he shifted so he was sitting with his back against the headboard and his legs in front of him. He held out his hand and she placed hers over it, then he touched himself through his shorts. Slowly he rubbed himself, his eyes closing. He'd been so careful with her, had made her feel so amazing, and she wanted to be the one who made him moan. She slipped her hand under his, touching the heat of his hard erection. He trembled as she ran her fingers along his length. "Show me what to do."

His eyes popped open and he gently wrapped his hand around hers, demonstrating what he liked. The stiff fabric of his shorts made it difficult to feel him. Annoyed, she unbuttoned his shorts and slid down the zip.

His hands stopped her. "Are you sure?"

She nodded. "Take them off."

In an instant, he'd lifted his butt and pushed his shorts down his legs.

Hannah stared. Cautiously, she touched him again and slid her finger under the elastic of his briefs.

Ryan's quick intake of breath had her stopping.

"Hot," he said.

She smiled, and emboldened, she ran her hand over him again, squeezing gently, and his whole body jerked. His eyes were closed and his hands were clenched. "More?" she asked.

He nodded. "Please."

This time she slipped her hand underneath the fabric. He was warm, hard and kind of silky, and she explored the texture with her fingers.

"Hannah." His tone was tense. "Can I take them off?"

Was it uncomfortable for him? She shifted down the bed so she was kneeling by his side. "Let me." Slowly, she slid her hands under the elastic and dragged off his underpants. It was an impressive sight, hard and erect and pointing towards his chest to where he was watching her, the desire in his face clear. A heady wave of power washed over her. She was in charge.

She ran a hand lightly up his leg towards his groin. "Hot or cold?"

His lips twitched. "Warm."

She moved closer towards his penis.

"Warmer."

She gripped him and squeezed, running her hand up and down his length.

"Hot. Oh, geez, Hannah stop."

Alarmed, she snatched her hand away. "Did I hurt you?"

He shook his head, reaching over and hauling her across the bed so she was straddling him. "No." His kiss was passionate, a little rough. "It's been a while. Let me touch you."

He already was. His erection pushed hard against her mound, nestling between her legs as she straddled him. The heat was incredible and she grew wet. She nodded and his hands roamed over her body, touching and teasing.

Hannah's head fell back as he sucked her nipples, his hands everywhere at once. Her skin was on fire and her groin was pulsing, almost painfully. She wanted to take off her underwear, wanted to demand he touch her down there.

As if he heard her thoughts, his thumb rubbed her clitoris and she shook with need. "More."

He flipped them so she was on her back and he was next to her, slowly sliding off her knickers. She wriggled to hurry him along. "Faster."

He stripped them off and then his mouth met her heat.

She groaned as pleasure filled her. Her whole body was so hot, like it was going to explode. He slipped a finger inside her and her body jerked, but it wasn't enough. She wanted more. "Condom," she gasped.

He froze.

Need was pulsing inside her. "Please. I need more." She wriggled away from him.

"In the bedside drawer."

She grinned and pulled one out. When she turned back he was lying on the bed. She hesitated.

"You should be on top." He took her hand. "You'll be in control that way."

She swallowed the lump in her throat at his thoughtfulness even through the passion. She slowly straddled him, the sensation of skin against skin divine.

He kissed her, and the desire flooded her again as his hand squeezed her butt. She moaned. She wanted him inside her.

He took the condom from her, rolled it on and then tugged her forward so she was lying on his chest. He kissed her slowly, his hands running over her body, finding her sweet spot again.

"Take as long as you need," he murmured. He nibbled her neck, caressed her breast and her nerves disappeared. This was right, he was right and all she wanted was him inside her. She took hold of him and shifted so he was where she needed him.

The first bit of pressure had her tensing and he kissed her again, his hands making languorous motions along her skin, relaxing her. She kissed him back and slowly pressed into him. They moaned together as he filled her.

This. This is what it was meant to be like.

Ryan shifted slightly to suck her breast and the sensation rocked her core. She wanted more.

His thumb found her clitoris and she moved against him,

needing to experience everything. Wonderful, glorious sensations built inside of her, all competing with which was the best. Her breath came in short gasps and she moved faster and faster, a slave to the pleasure, and then suddenly she exploded with Ryan right along with her.

"Wow," Hannah breathed as her brain slowly came back online.

"I'll say." Ryan stared at her for a moment before kissing her softly. "How are you feeling?"

So many emotions swirled inside of her, she wasn't sure which one to voice aloud. "Fantastic," she finally said. She didn't want to move, she wanted to bask in the sensation of being pleasured. She'd just had sex. Lovely, wonderful, delicious sex. She wanted to jump up and down in joy, pop a champagne bottle and toast her newfound freedom. She closed her eyes to savour the moment for a little longer and then climbed off and collapsed on the bed next to him.

Ryan shifted, cleaned up and then pulled her against him so her head rested against his chest.

She snuggled in, inhaling his scent as another emotion took hold. Gratitude. He had freed her from her fear and she finally understood how good sex could be. Tears welled up inside her and a lump lodged in her throat. How had she got so lucky? Ryan was better in real life than he'd ever been in her fantasies. He was so kind and patient and damn sexy. She loved him.

She squeezed her eyes closed as panic washed through her.

Was that the good sex talking? Was she so overwhelmed that she was confusing pleasure with love?

Ryan ran a lazy hand down her side and kissed her hair. The rush of love came again.

She didn't dare look at him, not until she got the tears blurring her vision under control. Her body shook with the effort and Ryan tilted her head so he could see her. She squeezed her eyes shut.

"Hey, what's wrong?"

She shook her head. "Nothing," she whispered. Everything was so damn right, but she couldn't voice that.

"Then why are you crying? Did I hurt you?"

"No!" She swallowed hard. "It's dumb."

"You could never be dumb." Ryan squeezed her hand.

"I, uh, never knew it could be like that," she finally said. She took a deep breath. "I feel free."

He smiled and kissed her. "You're an amazing woman, Hannah. Thank you for trusting me." He ran a hand gently along her cheek.

"Thank you for, you know …" She glanced down at his penis.

He laughed. "You're more than welcome."

His laugh was so joyous it broke through her tears. She wiped her eyes and was suddenly self-conscious. What did one do after great sex?

She ran a hand along his chest, loving that she could.

"Will you stay the night?" Ryan asked, his voice loud in the silence.

Her face warmed. "OK."

"Good." He absently ran his hand along her side. "I promised I'd take Felix to the beach tomorrow morning. Do you want to come with us?"

She did. A lot. "Sure, if Felix doesn't mind."

"He won't. He likes you and Joe, almost as much as I like you."

She wasn't sure what he meant by that.

"And that's a lot," he continued and kissed her.

Her chest tingled. It might not be love, but she could hardly expect it after so short a time. She was happy with him liking her a lot.

They could take it from there.

<h1 style="text-align:center">Chapter 20</h1>

Hannah woke in the morning when the phone rang. It wasn't hers, and as she tried to move she found she was wedged between two bodies: Ryan and Joe. She chuckled. Before they'd gone to sleep the previous night, she'd checked on her dog and left the door open so she could hear him during the night. He'd obviously decided to join them.

Ryan slid out of bed, giving her space to move, and padded naked into the kitchen to answer the phone. He had a delicious body, maybe there would be time to explore it some more before they left. She sat up as Ryan's tone changed. Was something wrong with Felix? Suddenly concerned, she got to her feet as Ryan came in, his expression unreadable.

"What happened?"

"We know who your stalker is," he said.

Her heart leapt. "Who?"

"Your brother Marko. He's Shirley's new boyfriend. She saw his picture on the Twitter feed and called it in. He's gone to the shop to get some milk and we want to be there when he gets back."

She sank back on to the bed, her legs weak with relief. But why would Marko do this to her? She hadn't seen him in almost two decades – it made no sense. And poor Shirley, she'd been so excited about her new man. Had Marko been using her?

"I have to call Lynette and ask if she can have Felix for a bit longer."

"She can't," Hannah said. "She's going on a cruise with the family today." Lynette had been looking forward to it all week. "But I'll pick him up. We can go to the beach."

He smiled. "Thanks, but I don't want you alone until we catch Marko."

"Then I'll call Kit and ask if we can come out and visit her calves," she said. "Or if she's busy, I'll treat him to something at Mai's bakery."

"All right, that would be great." Ryan was already pulling on his uniform. He did look damn good in it.

She dressed hurriedly and calling to Joe, they walked out of the cabin together. She climbed into her car. "I'll have a quick shower at my shed and then pick Felix up," she said. "Do you want to tell Lynette I'm on my way?"

"Will do." He kissed her again and Hannah was reluctant to leave, but they both had places they needed to be. "I'll call you when Marko's in custody."

"Thanks." She wanted to sing and dance, her whole body lighter than it had felt in weeks. It was almost over. Another hour and Marko would be caught and she could get back to her normal life. She could focus on her cabins and her relationship with Ryan and Felix.

The sun was already strong, the bright light reflecting off her shed as she drove up. After Marko was behind bars they could take Felix to the beach and then get an ice cream in town.

She grinned. Things were finally going right.

Hannah filled up Joe's water bowl, fed him breakfast and then she showered. Ten minutes later she was back at her car, holding the door open for Joe to jump inside. As she shut the passenger door there was a crunch behind her.

She whirled around and froze, her heart pounding in her chest. A large man with brown hair and thick-set muscles was walking towards her. He didn't look a lot like the boy she remembered, but it couldn't be anyone else.

And he didn't look happy.

She lunged for the front door handle, managed to get it open a crack before Marko slammed it shut and pushed her away from the car. "Not so fast."

Stumbling, she managed to catch herself before she crashed into the table.

His smile was malicious. "It's been a while, Hannah."

"Marko," she gasped, backing away from him, then she took one slow, calming breath. She wouldn't let her fear take over. "Aren't you supposed to be getting milk?"

He laughed. "I knew the bitch would see the photo sooner or later. Still, she served her purpose telling me everything about you."

Hannah winced. Shirley was going to be devastated to discover she'd been used.

Joe barked wildly, scratching at the window of the car. Her front window was open a crack, but it wasn't enough for him to get out.

Marko glanced over. "That damn dog of yours doesn't know when to die."

Anger shoved the fear out of the way. "You poisoned him."

"I sure did. You never went anywhere without him. Kind of hard to get close to you."

"What the hell do you want, Marko?" Hannah demanded. "I haven't seen you in almost twenty years."

He chuckled, a low, unpleasant sound. "What I've always wanted. You and your whore mother out of our lives." He slid a switch blade out of his pocket and flicked it open. "One down, one to go."

Terror clutched her lungs. She was alone and Marko stood between her and both the shed and the car.

There was no point screaming, no one around to hear her, not now that Ryan had headed to town to catch the man in front of her.

Ryan.

He'd know something was wrong when she didn't pick up Felix. Lynette was sure to call him, because she had to be in Albany for her cruise. So she needed to delay, try to talk her way out of this. "I don't understand why you hate me so much." She kept moving backwards and he followed, only a couple of metres away, the blade glistening in the sun.

Marko kept his eyes on her, his face hardened into a sneer of hate. "You destroyed my family," he said. "Dad was perfectly happy until your skanky mother seduced him away. He left us for you." His voice shook a little as he spoke.

He was hung up about something that had happened twenty-seven years ago. It was crazy. Fear raced along her skin. "I had nothing to do with that." She kept her voice calm. "I wasn't even born."

"He loved you more than he loved us – you got to be with him all the time and we only got weekends." His whine had every nerve in Hannah's body on high alert.

"That was almost twenty years ago," she said. "Mothers always got custody."

"If it wasn't for you, my parents wouldn't have split," Marko snarled. "But that wasn't enough, you had to send him to jail. Well your plan didn't work, I visited him every week," he said. "Kept our relationship strong."

If she couldn't keep him distracted long enough for Ryan to return, her best chance for help was the beach, where someone might be fishing or surfing.

"That's good. I'm glad." If she agreed with him, maybe he wouldn't be so upset.

"He used to ask about you, ask if we'd seen you." He sneered. "You didn't love him like we did. You never visited. That hurt him."

"I didn't know he was allowed visitors."

"You're such a dumb bitch." His contempt was clear. He continued towards her, the knife held low in his hand. "I thought he'd forgotten about you," Marko said. "But the first thing he said when he was free was he wanted to find you. Find the stupid little fat princess who never bothered to visit him, who hadn't cared to call, who had destroyed our family – he wanted to see *you*." His voice was full of disgust and outrage. "I thought I'd talked him out of it, but then Phillip told me he'd been sending you gifts." He was shaking. "Phillip made him stop, and I knew I had to get rid of you."

It was her father sending her the gifts? Her hand went to her throat. No, he couldn't have been responsible for them all.

Her phone vibrated in her pocket and she jumped as the clear notes of her ringtone broke the morning air. Her hand went to her pocket and Marko yelled, "Don't even think about it!"

She lifted her hand away. It had to be Lynette or Ryan. She needed to stall a little bit longer. "Marko, you don't need to do anything. I don't want to see him," she assured him, hoping he would believe her.

He frowned. "Why not?"

"He killed my mother."

"You ungrateful bitch." His face went a dark shade of red. "Turning on him when he did nothing wrong. I'm going to make you scream before I kill you."

Hannah's blood turned to ice and her pulse raced. "Marko, you don't want to become a killer. They'll throw you into prison."

He laughed. "They say the first one's the hardest, so you should be a piece of cake."

Hannah glanced around for a weapon of some sort and his words sank in. She whipped her head back to stare at him. "What?"

His grin was malicious. "Your mother bled so much I could have painted a mural."

She lost her breath as if he'd punched her. "What?" He hadn't been there. Surely, someone would have told her if he'd seen what had happened.

He chuckled. "I killed your mother." There was glee in his eyes and Hannah wanted to be sick.

She shook her head, not wanting to believe it. "Dad did. I saw him with a knife in his hand, standing over Mum."

"He took it from me." He suddenly looked sad. "Dad wasn't supposed to be there. He had a Christmas party, but he came back early, before I could clean up. I was going to make it look like a robbery gone wrong."

Horror stormed in her stomach. "You were fourteen."

"I would have done it sooner if I'd had the opportunity. I figured with her out of the picture, Dad would come back to us."

Her brain whirled. It didn't make sense. "Why didn't Dad say something?"

"I said it was an accident. He didn't want me to go to jail, and he helped me clean up, put me to bed before calling the ambulance."

She stood there, shaking her head, not quite able to process what he was saying. Marko lunged and she scrambled back, the knife grazing her arm. Pain shot through her as she turned and ran.

Marko roared and she was two steps along the path when she realised she was heading up to the lookout.

Shit. She'd be trapped.

Her phone rang again and she dug it out, pressed answer on Ryan's call. "Help! I'm at the lookout. Marko's here!" She shoved it back in her pocket, hoping he'd heard. At the top, she spotted the stick Joe had found the last time they were there. She swept it up and whirled around, swinging it at Marko. He dodged her attack, keeping his distance, grinning. "This place is perfect. I can make it look like an accident."

She jolted. He was right. If he pushed her off the cliff her chances of survival were slim.

"The cops won't believe it's an accident," she said. "You threatened me in your notes and they can tie you to those gifts with your fingerprints." The cut on her arm was bleeding and she held it against her clothes, hoping it would stop.

"The most they can pin me to is a couple of pranks I was playing on my kid sister." His smile was slimy.

He couldn't be so delusional. "You poisoned my dog! You sent a note to say I was next."

He held up his hands in a gesture of surrender. "There's no evidence," he said sweetly.

His reasoning was weak. "I'm meant to be in town now," Hannah said. "They'll question why I came here instead."

"Bitches are flighty," he said. "You changed your mind."

She wasn't going to die, not when she'd just started living again. She'd met an amazing man, who had an equally wonderful son, and she wanted to be with them.

She glanced behind her as she backed closer to the edge. Should she jump? If she was lucky she'd hit the right place and maybe swim under the swell past the rocks. The waves smashed against the cliff, the spray almost reaching her.

No, she had a better chance fighting Marko.

Determination settled over her like a cloak. She assessed

Marko. He was bigger and stronger than her and he had a knife. He wasn't afraid to kill. But he had weak spots – eyes, throat and groin.

She was at the edge of the cliff and the ground here was loose. It was time. She brought the stick up to her shoulder like a baseball player on the pitch.

Marko laughed. "What are you going to do with that?"

She didn't answer, just swung it wildly, hoping to move him back. He dodged left, giving her a slim gap between himself and the path back down.

In the distance a police siren was getting louder. Marko glanced over his shoulder and Hannah lunged, swinging the stick as hard as she could. It hit him in the head and cracked in two. Marko stumbled back and roared, the knife flying out of his hand.

Hannah ran, half a stick in her hand as she dashed past him. The path was right in front of her, she'd made it.

Marko seized her shirt, but she pulled free, stumbling. He charged towards her and the force of his blow knocked her down. Pain speared through her as she hit the ground. She gasped for breath and rolled over the sharp rocks. He towered above her, his body blocking out the sun.

Groin.

Hannah kicked him squarely between the legs. Rage crossed his face and he bellowed as he bent in half.

She scrambled to her feet, too late to stop Marko from scooping up the knife he'd dropped. She ran, but she wasn't fast enough.

This time he grabbed her and pulled her close so she was chest to chest with him, the sharp blade of the knife pressing into her stomach.

"You bitch," Marko snarled. He backhanded Hannah and the sting made her eyes water, made it hard for her to see. She lashed out, trying to gouge his eyes as he brought the knife up under her chin.

Hannah's pulse pounded in her head as the knife dug sharply against her throat.

"Your mother was much quieter than you," Marko commented.

She swallowed, fighting back the fear. All she had now were words. "Do you think Dad will visit you in jail if you kill me?"

He hesitated.

"Hannah!"

They both turned as Ryan appeared at the top of the lookout, his hand going to his gun. Relief filled her. He was here.

"Fuck." Marko hauled her back towards him, one arm firmly around her waist and the other holding the knife pressed against her side. She struggled until the knife pricked her and pain speared through her. He could still kill her, she needed to be focused.

"Stay back, or I'll slit her open." Marko backed them towards the cliff edge.

Ryan's eyes flicked to Hannah's. "Are you all right?"

"Yes." Her voice was shaky and she swallowed. She was going to survive.

Lincoln ran up the path behind Ryan and drew his gun.

Ryan focused on Marko. "How are you going, Marko?" His voice was so relaxed, so friendly, as if Marko wasn't holding a knife pressed against her side. Maybe Ryan hadn't seen it.

Marko grunted.

"Looks like you're upset about something," Ryan continued. "Why don't you tell me about it?"

The knife dug further into her side and she winced, squeezing her eyes closed for a second. Lincoln moved around Ryan as Ryan moved slowly forward.

"Stay there!" Marko yelled. He swore. "This isn't what was supposed to happen."

His breath was hot against Hannah's ear and the smell made her want to gag. She had to get away from him.

"Why do you want to hurt Hannah?" Ryan asked.

"Because she ruins it all. She always has."

"How does she ruin it?"

As Ryan continued to talk to Marko, Marko's hold relaxed slightly. The knife wasn't digging into her anymore. His focus wasn't on her, it was on Ryan. Ryan was distracting him.

"She keeps taking Dad away from me." He sounded like a petulant child.

"Taking your dad away, huh. That's rough."

Marko nodded.

Ryan glanced at her for a second and then back to Marko. He was trying to tell her something, but what? She let out a breath. She had to trust him. Had to figure it out.

"What did you and your dad used to do together?" Ryan asked. He'd relaxed his stance as if he was talking to a friend, but Lincoln still had his gun drawn, pointing at Marko.

"We'd play soccer and go fishing."

"I take my boy fishing when I can," Ryan said. "It's great fun. Though he always wants to bring his teddy bear Calypso along."

Calypso? Hannah's eyes flew to Ryan's. The move. His nod was infinitesimal.

Hannah let her body get heavy, dropping down into a dead weight. Pain shot up her knee as she landed on a rock and she gritted her teeth. She had to keep moving.

A shot rang out and Marko grunted.

She scrambled forward, but Marko gripped her hair and yanked her to her feet. Pain radiated through Hannah's scalp as they stumbled together, closer to the edge of the cliff.

She had to get free, they were too close.

"Marko, the edge!" she cried.

She was too late. The unstable edge crumbled away under their weight. Marko fell, yanking her over with him.

Chapter 21

Hannah screamed as Marko let go of her hair and they both fell through the air. She windmilled her arms, her heart in her throat.

She hit the water, the force jarring through her body, and pain seared up her leg.

Broken.

She opened her mouth to scream and water flooded in. Coughing, choking, she flailed, fighting the pull of the water, trying to surface. Her lungs burned and the salt stung her eyes. Something hit her. Marko was next to her, battling the waves as well.

She had to get air.

Struggling, she kicked with her good leg and used her arms to fight to the surface. She managed a short gasp of air before a wave hit her in the face, filling her mouth with water and slamming her against the rocks.

Pain radiated through her back as she hit it hard and she screamed in agony as the swell twisted her broken leg. Her vision blurred and she fought the urge to close her eyes. If she passed out, she was dead.

Suddenly Marko was in front of her, blood running down his face, his lips pinched in a grimace. She braced herself for the attack, but another wave hit, pushing them apart. She was a rag doll, unable to do anything but be a slave to the pull of the ocean. She hissed as her uninjured side slammed against the rocks.

She had to get out of the water.

The receding wave pulled her away from the rocks and she swam with it as best as she could to get away from the shore. If she got beyond the break, she had a chance.

Where was Marko? On the other side of the pool, his hand was the only thing above the water in supplication.

Another wave hit.

"Hannah!"

Was that Ryan? As she was dragged under, she lifted her hand, hoping he would see her. Her lungs burned as she fought for the surface, but the pull was so strong. Her head broke free and she gulped the air. Strong hands seized her and she opened her eyes, struggling.

Ryan.

The relief overwhelmed her and this time she couldn't resist the drag of the darkness.

Don't let her be dead.

Lungs burning, Ryan pulled Hannah close to him. Her eyes fluttered open briefly and then closed.

She was alive.

The relief was overpowering. "I've got you, Hannah."

At that moment a wave picked them both up and pushed them towards the jagged edge of the rocks. He held Hannah tightly against himself and angled his body so his feet hit the rock, pushing them away. He had to get them out of the water, but there was no way they were going to get out here. The rocks were too unforgiving and Hannah was unconscious. He felt for her pulse and found it, slow and faint.

"There's Marko!" Lincoln yelled. He was standing on the rocks back from where the waves were breaking and gesturing wildly.

Ryan braced for an attack. Marko surfaced face down about ten metres away. A wave picked him up and smashed him against the rock. Marko didn't move.

"Ryan, swim across to the shore," Lincoln yelled.

Ryan grunted. Easier said than done.

His clothes and Hannah's body were weighing him down, and the waves were relentless. He swallowed a mouthful of water and coughed, battling to keep them both above the waves.

He swam as best as he could with one arm around Hannah, trying to keep her head above water, but they both went under far too many times.

"Hannah, come on," he called, hoping to wake her.

His arms and legs burned with the effort of swimming, and he was at the mercy of the push and pull of the waves.

And still Hannah didn't stir.

She couldn't be dead. He didn't want to lose her. He wanted her in his life.

He loved her.

The realisation gave him a needed boost of strength, and finally the rocks gave way to sand and Lincoln waded out to them. Ryan's feet found the bottom, but his legs were weak. He panted as Lincoln took Hannah from him, lifting her into his arms. She groaned in pain, but the noise was music to his ears.

She was alive.

She was far too pale, her arms had nasty scratches on them that were bleeding and her leg was at a funny angle. "She's broken her leg."

Lincoln swore. "Can you brace it until we get her to shore?"

Ryan's arms were like rubber, but he placed his hands under her leg and held it as steady as he could. The ambulance sirens were getting louder.

They carried Hannah up the beach, away from the waves, and laid her on the ground. She was still breathing. Some of his fear receded as Ryan checked for further injuries while Lincoln ran to meet the ambulance.

Hannah had a nasty bruise on her forehead, a cut on her arm and the broken leg. "Hannah, wake up." He gently stroked her wet hair out of her face. Her eyelids fluttered and then the paramedics were there, pushing him out of the way.

He stepped back, relief coursing through him.

Lincoln put a blanket around his shoulders and pulled him aside. "Are you all right?"

"Yes." His eyes didn't leave Hannah. "We need to get Marko out of the water."

"Sea rescue are on their way," Lincoln told him. "You go with Hannah. I'll manage things now. Sue's here and there's backup from Albany on the way."

Ryan nodded.

"I'll let Mum know what's happened," Lincoln continued.

Felix. He'd called Mrs Z to pick Felix up from Mai's bakery and then forgotten all about him. What kind of father was he? "I should call Felix."

"You need to be checked over too. I'll tell Mum you'll call later."

Felix would want to see him and he couldn't yet. There were going to be questions about what had happened.

The paramedics put a neck brace on Hannah and lifted her onto the stretcher before carrying her up the beach. Ryan trailed along after them. "Is she going to be all right?"

The woman glanced at him. "She's stable, but we need to get her to hospital to check if there's any internal bleeding." She scanned him. "How are you?"

He shivered. "I'm fine, but I'm coming with you." There was no way he was letting Hannah out of his sight.

She nodded. "I'll check you over in the ambulance."

Within minutes they were on the way, sirens blaring.

Chapter 22

Hannah woke, her eyes stinging from the bright lights, her whole body sore.

"You're awake."

She focused on the nurse who had spoken.

"Can you tell me your name?"

Where was she? Hannah opened her mouth to speak and found it dry. She swallowed and answered, "Hannah Novak." She took in her surroundings. Her leg was in plaster and she was in hospital – but why?

She answered the nurse's questions as her vital signs were checked.

"What happened?" she asked.

"You're in the recovery ward," the nurse said. "The doctor will be in soon to tell you more." And with that she left.

Hannah frowned as her brain fought through the cobwebs.

Marko had tried to kill her.

Her heart raced. She remembered hitting the water, the agonising pain as her leg broke and struggling to keep afloat. Ryan had been in the water with her, she was almost certain of it. Was he all right?

And what had happened to Marko? Was he dead? Or was he somewhere in the hospital with her?

She shifted, wincing as she moved into a seated position, ready in case Marko walked through the curtains.

She braced herself as the curtains moved and the doctor walked in.

"Hannah, how are you feeling?"

"Is Ryan all right?"

The doctor frowned. "The officer who came in with you?"

"Maybe." She couldn't remember. "Ryan Kilpatrick."

The doctor smiled. "He's fine. We checked him over, but he only had a few cuts and bruises and was discharged."

The relief was comforting, but where was he?

The doctor flicked through her chart. "Are you in much pain?"

"Yes."

"I'll prescribe some pain medication." She smiled. "You're very lucky to be alive. You've broken your left tibia, have a concussion and have a number of cuts and bruises, but no internal bleeding. We'll move you to a room shortly and then you have some police officers wanting to talk to you if you're feeling up to it."

Ryan. Her heart swelled. "Of course." She needed to see he was all right.

The doctor left and about ten minutes later she was moved to another room. A policewoman and man came in – she didn't recognise either of them. "Where's Ryan?"

"Senior Constable Kilpatrick is helping us with inquiries," the woman said. "I'm Sergeant Flinders and this is Senior Constable Travis. We'd like to ask you a few questions."

"But Ryan *is* OK?" she asked.

"Yes," Sergeant Flinders said. "Can you tell us what happened?"

She blinked at the no-nonsense expression on the woman's face. They didn't care how she was. But she wasn't saying anything until they gave her something first. "Is Marko dead?"

Flinders nodded.

Hannah let out a deep breath. He couldn't hurt her anymore. He couldn't hurt anyone she loved. "What do you want to know?"

An hour or so later Hannah had had enough. Exhaustion hovered over her like a cloud, fogging her brain. She'd told her story several times and answered the same questions over and over again. She wasn't sure Flinders would ever be satisfied.

The nurse came into the room, took one look at Hannah and frowned at the officers. "Hannah needs rest."

The sergeant stood up. "We have what we need. We'll type up a statement for you to sign."

Hannah nodded, relieved it was over. As the police left, the nurse said, "You've got a lot of visitors waiting. Are you feeling up to it?"

She was desperately tired, but she needed to see for herself that Ryan was well. "Yes."

A few minutes later her grandparents entered the room, followed by Kit and Mai.

Her nanna gasped and hurried over. "Are you all right? They wouldn't tell us what happened." She kissed Hannah's forehead.

Hannah frowned. "Lincoln didn't tell you?"

"He didn't get a chance," Kit said. "He told us there'd been an incident and you were in hospital."

She closed her eyes. Damn. They were going to want to hear the story and she didn't have enough energy to tell it. Not today.

"We took Joe to the vet," Mai told her. "He was a little dehydrated, but he's going to be OK."

Joe. Guilt swept through her. She had forgotten all about him. "Thank you."

"What happened?" her granddad demanded. "No one's told us a damned thing."

Hannah sighed. There wasn't going to be any rest until she'd explained everything again. "What do you know?"

"The first we knew anything was wrong was when Lynette dropped Felix off at the bakery," Mai said. "Then Mrs Z called to say she was on her way to pick him up. Ryan had told her they had a lead on your stalker."

"Lincoln called me," Kit took up the story, "and said you'd been injured but were OK. He asked me to get Joe from your place."

"She took him to the vet and then we all came here," Mai finished. "Fleur will be here as soon as her shift is over."

So they knew nothing about Marko. Hannah wasn't sure where to start.

She wanted to sleep for a couple of hours. A glance at the

clock told her it was only mid-afternoon. Somehow, she was going to have to tell her grandparents the truth about their daughter's death and she didn't have the strength to deal with the fallout right now.

What she really wanted was to have Ryan there, to have his arms around her, maybe even go to his place and curl up on his bed and sleep. But that wasn't going to happen. Where was he?

At that moment, her father walked into the room, his eyes red as if he'd been crying.

Her granddad took an outraged breath as he stood. "Get the hell out of here!"

Hannah groaned. She didn't need this animosity now. She put a hand on his arm. "Granddad, he needs to hear what I have to say." Her voice wasn't as loud as she would have liked it to be.

How much did her father know?

"I won't have him anywhere near me and mine."

Her patience snapped. "Fine!" she said. "Leave, then. The door's over there."

Her granddad's eyes widened and he stared at her in shock.

Hannah refused to feel guilty. "I've been through hell today and I'm only going to tell my story one more time."

Mai and Kit immediately stood next to her, ready to support her. She squeezed both of their hands.

"Stan," her grandmother said. "Now's not the time."

He scowled but gave a sharp nod.

"I'll get some more seats." Mai left the room.

Her father had aged ten years overnight.

"You know about Marko?" Hannah asked as Mai came back in with a couple of chairs.

He nodded, tears glistening in his eyes. "But, no one will tell me what happened."

"Sit down," Hannah said. "Marko was my stalker."

Her grandparents gasped. "Like father like son," her granddad growled.

"No, Granddad." She reached out a hand in entreaty. "*Marko* killed Mum."

Her father's eyes widened.

"He admitted it to me," Hannah said.

"What?" Her nanna's voice was shaky. "He was a child."

"A child who hated Mum and me for taking Dad away from him." Her mother had been killed because of a childish jealousy.

Her father was silent. She waited for him to say something.

"This is ridiculous. The police found his fingerprints on the knife," her granddad said, pointing at Ivan.

"I thought it was an accident," Ivan finally said. "He said he'd slipped, he hadn't meant to do it, he was so upset." The words were soft.

"You came home too early from the Christmas party," Hannah said. "He was going to make it look like a break-in."

Ivan shook his head, as if not believing it.

"He was jealous of both of us," she told him.

"He was a boy, *my* boy. I couldn't let him go to jail."

"He thought you'd forgotten about me while you were in prison. He was so mad that you still wanted to see me even though I hadn't visited you. He wanted me out of the picture as well."

Ivan shook his head in denial.

"He killed Mum, poisoned Joe, and he died trying to kill me today." Her voice was flat.

Mai squeezed her hand and Kit growled.

"What happened?" her grandmother asked.

She closed her eyes and the fear rushed in. She opened them. "He came to my place," she said. "He had a knife and told me he didn't want me around, told me about killing Mum and how he was going to kill me." Her throat tightened as she continued to explain what had happened. "Ryan saved me." Her throat was dry and her eyes hurt. She wanted to curl up into a ball and sleep.

Her nanna got up and gave Hannah a fierce hug, squeezing her so tightly that Hannah winced. Ivan lowered his head into his hands and sobbed.

Hannah's heart broke for him. He'd done what he'd thought was right, had tried to protect his family, as misguided as he was. "I'm sorry, Dad."

She glanced at her granddad and even he was at a loss for words.

"No." Ivan sat up. "I'm so sorry, Princess. So sorry."

Her smile was sad. "Me too." So much pain had been caused by Marko. But now that the truth was out, perhaps they could move on. Perhaps they could start again.

Perhaps they could be a family.

After being checked out in the emergency department at the hospital, Ryan was given the all clear. "How's Hannah?" he asked the nurse who was giving him the paperwork.

"She's in surgery to have her leg set," the nurse said.

One of the Albany police officers who'd been waiting for him said, "We'll call for an update later. We need to get your statement."

He didn't want to leave Hannah, but there was paperwork to be filled out and questions that needed to be answered. "Of course."

He closed his eyes when he got into the back of the police car and saw Hannah fall off the cliff, helpless to stop it. His chest squeezed. She was alive, she was going to be all right – he refused to believe anything else.

He couldn't keep dwelling on that moment. What he needed to do was check on Felix. He needed to hear his son's voice and reassure himself that he was fine. He dug his mobile phone out of his pocket. It was dead. Of course it was. It had gone swimming with him. "Can I borrow a phone?" he asked.

One of the cops handed him a phone and he called Mrs Z.

"Ryan, is everything all right?" Her concern was clear.

"Yeah, it's a long story. Can I talk to Felix?"

"I'll put him on for you," Mrs Z said.

A moment later Felix's voice asked, "Is everything OK, Dad?"

"It is now," Ryan told him, relaxing at his voice. "I'm sorry Hannah and I couldn't pick you up from Jacob's place."

"It's all right. Mai let me have anything I wanted at the bakery."

"That's great." Ryan smiled.

"When are you going to be back?"

Ryan was torn. He wanted to visit Hannah before he left.

"As soon as I can."

"All right."

The disappointment was clear in Felix's voice, but he couldn't tell him what had happened.

Mrs Z came back on the phone. "You're both welcome to stay the night at our place," she said. "Jamie just arrived and Lincoln should be here later as long as whatever's happened won't keep you for longer. It is Christmas tomorrow."

Ryan had forgotten. "Thanks. Can I tell you later?"

"Absolutely."

He hung up as he walked into the station.

"This way."

Ryan followed the senior constable into the interview room.

By the time he'd finished answering questions, his patience was wearing thin. Lincoln came into the room and gave him a plastic bag of clothes.

"How's Hannah?" Ryan asked.

"She's out of surgery and recovering well," Lincoln assured him. "They're questioning her now. How did it go here?"

The relief swept through him. Hannah was OK. "Fine. It was all standard procedure."

"Good. I'm heading over to the hospital. Do you want to come?"

He did, but Felix's concern played heavily on his heart. He needed to see his son as much as he needed to see Hannah.

He closed his eyes.

He didn't want a life without them both in it. He loved Hannah. Today had shown him that. Part of him had died when she'd fallen off the cliff.

"Ryan?"

Hannah was going to be busy with her family and friends around her for the next few hours and the things he needed to say weren't for an audience.

"Are you finished here?" Lincoln asked.

"I need to talk to Felix. Can I drop you at the hospital and take your car?"

"Sure. I'll get a lift with Kit out to the farm."

"Thanks." He took the keys Lincoln handed him.

Life was too short to hesitate. He knew what he wanted.

But he needed to make sure Felix was on board too.

Ryan hadn't come.

After the nurses had finally shooed everyone out of her room, telling them Hannah needed to rest, Ryan still hadn't been to visit her. Even Lincoln had dropped in before everyone had left and told her Ryan was with Felix.

Of course he was. It made sense for him to make sure Felix was safe.

But it hurt that he hadn't at least dropped by before he'd gone.

There was the clatter of the dinner cart in the hallway outside, as dinner was being served to patients. She wanted to sleep, but the painkillers were wearing off. She embraced the pain though. It meant she was alive.

She closed her eyes, the exhaustion of the day catching up with her. The truth had finally come out. Her grandparents had been shocked and they needed time to process it, but as they had left, her grandmother had embraced Ivan and expressed her sorrow for his loss. Perhaps in time the hurt would heal and Ivan would be welcomed back into the family.

Hannah wanted that. Now that she knew the truth, she wanted to get to know her father. His misplaced loyalty for his son had caused her grief, but she wanted him back in her life. So much of their lives had been needlessly wasted. She didn't want to waste a minute more.

Which was why she wanted to tell Ryan that she loved him, even if he didn't feel the same way. She was done with hiding. But surely, he would have come if he had truly cared.

And that hurt more than any of the physical pain she'd endured today. She'd thought their relationship had shifted last night, had become deeper, more important, but perhaps it had just been sex to him.

Her skin tightened.

"Is she sleeping, Dad?" Felix's loud whisper cut through her self-pity.

Her eyes flashed open and both Ryan and Felix were standing at the end of her bed. Felix was holding a bunch of home-grown flowers, and Ryan was looking so damned good, so alive, she wanted to throw her arms around him and hug him.

Ryan smiled at her. "How are you?"

Her heart warmed. "I'm fine."

"These are for you." Felix thrust the flowers at her. "I picked them from Nonna's garden."

"Thank you." She sniffed the strong rose fragrance.

Felix was staring at her cast, which was above the covers. "Did you break your leg?"

Hannah nodded. "And got a few bumps and bruises."

"I'm sorry the bad man hurt you," Felix said.

"Me too." She kept her attention on the boy, more than aware of Ryan standing close by, not saying anything. "But I'll be home tomorrow. I just won't be particularly agile for a while." She wasn't going to be able to do any work on her retreat for at least a couple of months, but she wasn't going to worry about that now.

"Dad said he won't be able to hurt you anymore."

Hannah glanced at Ryan, who gave a small shake of his head. He hadn't told Felix all of the details. "That's right," she said. "I'm sorry we didn't get to spend the day together."

"Me too," Felix said. "We would have had fun." He picked at the sheet covering her. "I wanted to bring Joe to visit, but Dad said he wouldn't be allowed in the hospital. So, we left him at the farm with Lincoln."

Hannah frowned. "Isn't he at the vet's?"

Felix glanced at Ryan.

"Lincoln picked him up when he went back to Blackbridge," Ryan said. "Your grandparents agreed to come to the Zanettis' tomorrow for Christmas." He cleared his throat. "We were hoping you would come too."

Hannah's heart swelled in her chest.

"You will come, won't you?" Felix beamed hopefully at her.

"Felix, why don't you ask the nurse for a vase and some

water for those flowers?" Ryan said.

Felix grinned. "Right. Sorry, I forgot." He took the flowers from Hannah and hurried out of the room.

Suddenly alone with Ryan, Hannah didn't know what to say.

He came closer, sat in the chair next to her bed, and took her hand in his. "Today ..." He shook his head. "I've never been so scared in my entire life. Seeing Marko with that knife at your throat. And when you fell off the cliff ..." His eyes filled with pain.

Hannah ran her hand over his shoulder. "It's all right. I survived."

Ryan gently pulled her into his arms. "I was helpless to stop it."

Hannah savoured the feel of him. "No, you weren't. You distracted him, enabled me to get out of his hold." Her scalp still hurt from where Marko had pulled it. "Then you dragged me out of the ocean when I was sure I was going to drown."

He squeezed her tightly and she winced.

"Sorry." He let go of her. "I thought you were dead," he said. "I didn't think you'd survive the fall." He took a deep breath, his eyes wide. "I thought you'd died before I had a chance to tell you I love you."

Hannah stared at him. The drugs she was on shouldn't make her hallucinate. "What?"

"We haven't known each other for long, but I want you in my life." His eyes were wide and honest. "I love you."

Hannah's heart jumped.

He held her hand. "Have Christmas with us. I know this has all happened so quickly, but today showed me that life isn't guaranteed. I don't want to waste any time."

Was this real? She shifted and pain shot through her. Yep, she was awake. She tugged him closer, placing both hands on his shoulders. "I agree. We shouldn't waste any time." She smiled. "I love you and I love Felix. I want you to know that."

"I do." Ryan kissed her.

His lips and his taste were so right. They brought comfort and desire at the same time. "I'd love to have Christmas with you and Felix."

"Woo hoo!" Felix yelled from outside the door.

Hannah laughed as Ryan called, "You can come back inside now."

Felix ran to the bed and threw his arms around both of them. "This is the best Christmas present ever. I love you, Hannah."

Lightness blazed through Hannah. "I love you too, Felix."

Felix was right. There was no better Christmas present.

She was loved by two very special men.

Her fear hadn't beaten her.

Epilogue

Ryan and Felix picked Hannah up from the hospital at nine o'clock on Christmas morning. Felix raced into her room, a red Santa hat on his head.

"Merry Christmas, Hannah!" He flung his arms around her.

She pressed him close, wincing a little at the pain. Then Ryan walked in. He too was wearing a Santa hat and it looked good on him. Instantly, she forgot about the pain. "Merry Christmas to you both." She kissed Ryan.

"Ew." Felix groaned.

Hannah laughed.

"Are you ready to go?" Ryan asked.

She nodded and he moved the wheelchair closer to the bed. Felix grabbed her bag of clothes and together they left the hospital.

They drove out to the Zanetti farm and as she got out of the car with Ryan's help, Joe raced around the side of the house, his tail wagging a mile a minute. She tapped her lap and Joe rested his front paws on it. Hannah grinned and hugged him, relief filling her that he was fine. He didn't seem any worse for wear after the adventures of the last few days.

Ryan helped her up the stairs and then wheeled her inside. The living room was full of people: the Zanettis, her grandparents, Kit, Fleur and Mai as well as Fleur's father. She frowned. What was everyone doing here?

"She's here," her nanna called.

Suddenly, Hannah was surrounded by people wanting to hug her and wish her merry Christmas.

"Geez, I don't come down for a couple of months and you get into all sorts of trouble," Jamie said and gave her a hug. "I'm glad you're all right."

She squeezed him back. He was a younger, prettier version of Lincoln and they'd been friends for a long time. "Thanks. It's good to see you."

When the greetings were done, Felix said, "Now that Hannah's here, can we *please* do the presents?"

Hannah sucked in a breath. "You didn't need to wait for me." Poor Felix must be itching to open his gifts.

"Yeah, we did," Felix grasped her hand. "You've got to come out the back." He pushed her towards the door.

"Hold up, champ," Ryan said. "I'll push her."

Felix let go of the wheelchair and bounced up and down on the spot, beckoning to them both. "Come on."

Something weird was going on.

Not sure what was in store for her, Hannah let Ryan push her through the house and out the back door. The backyard was full of supplies: wooden posts, rolls of wire and planks of wood.

"Merry Christmas," Ryan murmured in her ear.

She frowned. "What?"

"It's for the retreat," he said. "We've got enough supplies to fence off that damned lookout, make the walking trails and the path down to the beach."

Tears sprang to her eyes. It was too much. She hadn't dared think about her retreat and what her injury would mean to it. It had been too hard. And here her friends were, putting together everything she needed.

"We're all going to pitch in over the next week to get it done," Fleur said. "And since you're indisposed, you can tell us what to do."

"Thank you." She sniffed back the tears.

"Your dad wants to help too," her granddad said. "We should have it done in a jiffy."

Hannah stared at him and he shrugged a little self-consciously. "Many hands and all that."

Perhaps her grandparents and father would work things out. Her heart swelled as she looked at all her family and friends and their excited faces. They had done this for her.

Ryan crouched down and wrapped his arm around her shoulder with Felix perched on his knee. Surrounded by their love she smiled. Her life was hers again.

She had nothing to fear.

Thank you for reading!

I hope you enjoyed the book. It would be super awesome if you could leave a review wherever you bought it, because I love to hear what you thought of the story (yes, even if you didn't like it!)

ACKNOWLEDGEMENTS

Nothing to Fear is the first romantic suspense I've written and it required some work to get the right balance between romance and suspense. I want to thank my critique group for all of their feedback and also my beta readers, Jill, Jane and Susy for reading the whole book and giving me wonderful suggestions.

This is the first book I've written which is completely set in Australia, in an area that's about four hour's drive from where I live. Though Blackbridge is a made-up town, it's based on towns in the Great Southern region and I was fortunate enough to visit the area while writing the book. I must thank my aunt, Libby Corson for playing chauffeur/tour guide on my trip and introducing me to a number of people who helped me with my research for the whole series.

Also the biggest thank you to Matt Hartfield, a sergeant in the WA Police who answered my million questions about what life as a small town cop was like. He enabled me to write about Ryan and Lincoln with more realism – and any mistakes are my own, or for the good of the story.

I also need to thank Lana Pecherczyk for the gorgeous cover, as well as my editor Alexandra Nahlous and my proof-reader Teena Raffa-Mulligan.

Finally I really want to thank you, the reader, for picking up the book. Your reviews, emails and messages cheer me up when I'm having a bad writing day.

Nothing to Gain

A Blackbridge Novel #2

Mai's story is coming in 2018